Building a Pack is Ruff – Part 1

The Pack Pets Omegaverse

Galadreal Simmons

Coffee After Dark

<u>*Dedication:*</u>

To all people who feel out of place, out of the loop, or just left
behind while the world moves on
I see you...

Unless you're hiding in the bushes or behind the couch, I never
check there.

<u>**Music that inspired this story and these characters:**</u>

Dirty Little Secret – The All-American Rejects
Chop Suey – System of Down
Scar Tissue – Red Hot Chili Peppers
Hallelujah – Rufus Wainwright
Famous Last Words – My Chemical Romance
I Hate Everything About You – Three Days Grace
Adam's Song – Blink 182
A Long December – Counting Crows
Wake Me Up When September Ends – Green Day
Undone (The Sweater Song) – Weezer
Dance, Dance – Fall Out Boy
Numb – Linkin Park
Heart Shaped Box – Nirvana
Jumper (1998) – Third Eye Blind
Sweet Child O' Mine – Guns N' Roses
Lose Yourself – Eminem
Fake It – Seether
Val Kilmer – Bowling for Soup
What Makes You Beautiful – One Direction

Contents

Author's Note:

What do you mean by Omegaverse?

Omegaverse, often known as ABO, is an alternate reality where humans share some characteristics of wolves. In this one, we have fated mates and attraction based heavily on scent. Thus most people's scents will be compared to common items, our current female lead smells like thin mint cookies. You get the idea.

There are three known designations, Betas are like you and me, but with a better sense of smell, they make up 75% of the population.

Alphas make up 20%; they are predominantly male. Alphas often form familial packs of three to five other individuals, which may or may not include a beta or an omega. In addition to an average larger body size over betas or omegas, alphas are generally known to be stronger and more aggressive. Male alphas also come equipped with a knot for sexual purposes, specifically to tie the alpha and omega together and help increase the chances of procreation. Female betas can—with practice and patience—take a knot, but it's not something they're built to do.

Last are the omegas, approximately 5% of the population, which are predominantly female. Generally described as petite or waifish they lack the physical strength of alphas or even betas. Omegas are natural caregivers and peacekeepers, helping to balance their more aggressive counterparts, and are physically built to accommodate a knot during sex. They are incredibly tactile, craving touch and companionship. They go into heat approximately every six months which is their only fertile time. Heat requires medication, special toys, or the assistance of multiple alphas for each heat.

Due to their limited number and lack of physical strength, omegas are regulated in the sense that they are considered a protected group, a rarity that is often targeted for assault, kidnapping, human trafficking, etc. Thus laws that have been made to protect omegas often also restrict their freedoms and require that they live with a guardian or in an omega-specific complex for their safety. To make it harder for omegas to avoid these laws certain items, such as de-scenting products and heat suppressants, require the approval of a non-omega head of household to purchase. This does not always work out as intended, as it makes omegas without these products available easier to identify and therefore, take advantage of.

Simmons, or you can email me at galadreal.simmons.author@hotmail.com

<u>*Foreward:*</u>

This story takes place about 5-6 months after epilogue 2 in book 1, The Purrfect Pack, about 2.5 years from the main storyline. It is March, just in time for spring break.

(Candice is 6 months pregnant)

This book is much darker than my first one. I wanted to warn you in advance. There are recurring character cameos, but these main characters talked to me a lot differently. They have seen some shit.

Chapter 1

Kelly

I don't know the name of the faceless man moving on top of me, but he feels so good. His arms wrapped around me, his weight pressing down on me. His delicious scent, spicy and sweet—I can't quite place it—but I need to kiss him. I need to have him on my tongue as well as inside of me. I wrap my arms around his back, pulling him tight. His face is buried in my neck, licking along my pulse point, and his breath sends shivers down my spine.

Burying my hands in his long hair, I can't tell the color in this light, just that it's dark and thick. I need to kiss him though—if I can just do that, then nothing else matters. I tug against his scalp, and his teeth scraping over my skin makes me cry out, almost overwhelmed with the sensation. He eases back, finally letting me see him, letting me put a face to the man pumping into me.

His head turns towards me and a high-pitched ringing fills the room...

Ugh!!! My alarm clock!

Burrowing under the covers, I try to hang on to the dream, I was so darned close. Close to orgasm, yeah, but also close to seeing his face. It's the third night this week I've had this dream, and while I don't believe in any sort of mystical mumbo jumbo, I'm starting to get super frustrated...and horny. Like really dang horny.

But I've got to get up, or I'm going to be late...It's Saturday, and I made a promise to my bosses. I mean, they're already bonded, so it's just a formality. Still, I agreed to be part of the mating ceremony.

And, hey, free cake!

So, I drag myself out of bed, and plod down the hall to the shower. It's too bright out, and I stumble into the wall, trying to get my eyes to adjust. It doesn't help any that Rufus keeps dancing around my legs trying to get attention. He still thinks he's a puppy, but that was several years and about a hundred pounds ago.

I finally manage to get into the bathroom—accidentally closing my hand in the door while trying to keep him out—and turn on the shower. I want a super-hot shower...and some time alone. What I get is a lukewarm shower and my little brother, Tucker, banging on the door and yelling at me to hurry up. So,

I take the fastest shower in human history, get out, get a towel wrapped around me, realize I missed a big blob of conditioner in my hair and have to get back in the now freezing water to rinse it out. Then, of course, I forgot a change of clothes, so I put my pajamas back on, wrap my hair in a towel, and bolt back to my room to avoid seeing Tuck.

Seriously, all those people who talk about how long girls spend in the bathroom have clearly never had to deal with a teenage boy. I don't even want to think about why he spends so much time in there. Can't he just stay in his room for that like a normal person? I can't wait to graduate college and move out into a place of my own—or at least a place that has more bathrooms.

I'm almost to my room when Rufus comes scrambling back up the stairs and knocks into me again, spinning me out and slamming me into the wall, toe first—and it hurts so much when you whack your toe on something. It's a tiny area, but UGH! "Gosh darn it, Rufus! Go see if Momma has breakfast or somethin', I gotta finish gettin' ready." I shoo him away from my door and slide in before he can wiggle in behind me, hobbling as quickly as I can with my poor toe.

"Kelly, you used up all the hot water!" The loud, slightly-strangled voice of Tuck filters through the upstairs hallway, and I snort laughter as I flop back onto my bed. I know I just need to get into a pair of jeans and a T-shirt to head over to Candice's. She said she'll have my dress waiting, and Jacks can help with my hair and makeup. I never would've pegged him as knowing how to do women's hair, but the way he dotes on Candice, I can see it.

It's barely spring right now, but it's warm enough today that it should be fine for me to wear shorts. I shaved last night, because I knew today was going to be crazy, and it seems a shame to waste the effort. Smiling, I pull on a pair of cut-offs and a T-shirt that I got from some college event or other. I can't believe I finally get to graduate in a few months. I mean, it's not an advanced degree or any-thing—just a bachelor's in kinesiology—but I just want to get out of school and get on with my life. I'm so tired of hearing the jokes about it being a B.S. degree. Ugh! I am *so* over that snark.

Grabbing a pair of socks, I head downstairs to see Rufus trailing Mom around the kitchen. He's staring longingly as she plates up a tall stack of pancakes from the griddle before turning around and giving me the stink eye. "Kelly, you need to get Rufus out of the kitchen since you're the one who sent him down here—unless you want him to eat all your pancakes." I grab him by the collar and gently pull him towards the back door.

"Come on boy, you wanna play outside for a bit while I finish gettin' ready?" His tail thumps against Mom, and the table, and the doorframe as I lead him outside and then let him loose. He goes tearing off across the lawn chasing after a bird, and I step back inside, heading over to the sink to wash my hands. "Need any help?" I ask Mom over my shoulder.

She tugs my ponytail and I bend over for her to kiss the top of my head. "No thanks, Honey, but I appreciate you getting Rufus out of here while we eat. You know your father and brother always feed him at the table, and you don't have time to help me hide any bodies this morning." She chuckles at her own joke. Mom's a beta like me, and a pacifist, but she sure does threaten familial destruction sometimes.

I snag a pancake with my fingers, slather it in butter, and roll it into a tube before shoving half of it in my mouth at once. "Really, Kelly, can't you at least pretend to be a lady today?" She hands me a napkin, and offers me another pancake when I choke down the rest of the one I'm holding. I grin at her before heading into the entryway to put on my socks and shoes.

One of the few things my mom will get super angry about is shoes. When we come home, they have to go into the shoe rack by the front door, then socks off—so we don't slide and get hurt—and into the laundry room off the kitchen. I don't know why that one thing stuck in her craw, but that's her one inflexible rule, so we all just go with it.

"Sorry. If you don't need me, I'm gonna head on over to Candice's so I can start gettin' ready. I'll see y'all later this evenin', after I help Stephanie clean up the community center, yeah?" Mom comes out of the kitchen with another pancake for me already rolled up. "OK, Honey, just be careful. Tell Candice and the boys congratulations again. We'll see you in a few hours," she calls over her shoulder, heading back into the kitchen before she finishes talking.

My dad opens the front door, walking in just as I reach for it to leave. "Where you goin' this early, Sprout?"

"Sorry, Daddy, I gotta go, Candice's mating ceremony, remember?" He just chuckles and ruffles my hair, like I'm not twenty-two and about to be the first college graduate in our family.

"Ok, be safe Sprout, and text me when you get there." I nod a quick affirmative and head out the door towards my car. It's in my name, but it used to be Candice's.

When Xan gave her that old Mustang he re-built, she sold me hers for really cheap. I mean, Gabe gave me a bonus to pay for it, so it was sort of a gift anyway. But still, I carry the insurance on it and it gets me to college and back so I'm not complaining. Besides, Xan lets me bring it in for free for any work it needs done as a job perk. Candice has turned him into a big ol' softie. All of them really, not that they were ever bad to work for before, but now it's like having four overprotective big brothers.

Chapter 2

Kelly

It takes less than ten minutes for me to get to Pack Asher's house, and even though it's super early, and he's getting married today, Xan is outside working on the new room addition. He's been rushing through it, so it can be ready in the next three months for when the twins are born. I've never seen him this excited, but I'm so happy for all of them. Heck, Jacks has already picked out three different variations of wallpaper, and their office is stuffed full of baby blankets, clothes, and furniture—just waiting to be assembled.

Candice said it's almost as bad as when he went nest shopping for her, but she smiles every time she talks about it; I don't think she really minds. I wave to Xan as I get out of the car and walk towards the front door, but it opens before I can knock. Jacks is standing there, curling iron in one hand and dress in the other. "Oh, Thank fuck you're here. Sorry, Candice didn't want to get out of bed, and I know she needs her sleep because she's pregnant, but I need to get started if I'm gonna get everybody ready!" He continues talking without taking a breath, and I want to ask if he's ok.

He shakes himself a bit and takes a harder look at me. "Shit, I thought you were Stephanie. That's ok! I can start with you just as easy. Lemme go grab the other dress." He turns around and walks away, leaving the door open for me to enter. With nothing else to occupy me, I follow him inside and up the stairs to Candice's room.

"She's been sleeping in the nest a lot lately," Jacks answers my unspoken question. "The obstetrician says that wherever's most comfortable, we should just let her do it." He sighs loudly, pulling a second dress out of the closet. It looks identical to the first one he had, but maybe he knows something I don't. "Twins don't really run in any of our families, but she can't exactly ask her side. Still, we're worried about how much she sleeps right now."

I reach out and pat his arm gently, offering reassurance where I can. Jacks used to be very wary around non-pack members. I didn't talk to him much, because he never left the house, but he's doing *so* much better since he met Candice. Heck, all the guys are. I love Gabe and Xan like family, but they have been *so* much more chill for the last couple of years. It's been awesome at work.

Jacks hands me the dress and I step into the bathroom to put it on. It fits perfectly, and I had completely forgotten that they were tailored for each of us. Thank goodness he knows what's going on; I'm super scatterbrained right now. I step out so he can zip up the back for me, and afterwards he sets me in front of a mirror and starts curling my hair. I don't really go to the salon; Mom has always just trimmed it for me at home. This is kind of a fun new experience.

Once he finishes curling and twisting part of it up with a bunch of bobby pins, he moves on to my makeup. Everything's in a deep purple and gray color, and I was worried it could look strange on my skin tone, but he really seems to know what he's doing. By the time Xan leads Stephanie up the stairs, Jacks is finishing up a smokey cat eye with pale shimmery lids.

Stephanie steps into the bathroom to put on her own dress, and when she comes out, Jacks hands me a small cardboard canister and sends me back to the bathroom to put it on. I open the box to find a fake rabbit makeup puff. Not knowing what to expect, I smack it against my hand to see what comes out—glitter. *So* much silver body glitter. I try to wipe my hands off on my own arms and shoulders, before dragging the puff over them to smooth everything out...I feel so sparkly right now. Leaving the bathroom, I'm super self-conscious of how shimmery my skin is.

When the door opens Candice is sitting on her bed, and she bursts into tears when she sees me. Worrying about what I did to upset her, I start to stammer, "Sorry, Candice, I can go wash it off if you want. I...What's wrong?

"You just look so pretty!" Candice sobs, as Xan takes my hand and leads me towards the door and down the stairs.

"Sorry about that. Pregnancy hormones have made her a little emotional lately. She cries every time we watch a movie."

"Well, then why are y'all making her watch sad movies?" I huff, genuinely surprised at him. I never thought any of the guys would do anything to upset their omega.

"Well, they're her choices. She's been hogging the remote every night for the last two months. I know so much more about anime than I ever wanted to." He laughs, but there's still a lot of strain in his eyes. The whole pack's worried about her, but Xan's the one who usually fixes problems, so I think the fact that he can't help is really throwing him for a loop.

"You ok? You know I'm here, even if you just feel like venting." We don't hug—it would just be freaky—so I just pat him on the shoulder. That at least earns me a halfhearted smile.

"Thanks kiddo, I appreciate it...I would totally ruffle your hair right now, but I think Jacks would kill me." At least his smile's more genuine this time. Unsure how to change the subject or what to do to fix the awkwardness, I'm saved by the doorbell. Xan lets out a relieved sigh and practically runs to answer it.

Sal's here too, and she beelines straight for me to give me a hug. "You look beautiful, Kelly." But her smile doesn't really reach her eyes. She *is* a wonderful and amazing woman. That's why she's the best man...er...woman...person? We dated for a couple of months, but it just didn't work out, and it wasn't either of our faults. She is so sweet and loving, and hot—holy crud is she hot—but we just don't have anything in common except our love of cars and dogs. Sadly, that does *not* a relationship make.

Ok, so totally my fault. But I may have also freaked out when she brought me lunch at school a couple of times, people started calling me an alpha chaser and being butt-heads, and I shouldn't have listened. Because I know they're full of crap, but confidence has never been my strong suit. And when people make fun of you for something, it can sometimes be too easy to let that something go. But she really is a wonderful person, and I wish our feelings lined up better. I hope she finds someone soon; she deserves to be happy.

"Thanks, you're not so bad yourself." And I mean it, she looks amazing in a tux. I don't know if I've ever met anyone who doesn't look good in a tux really, but she's totally rocking it. Luckily, I'm saved from embarrassing myself when Stephanie comes down the stairs, holding onto Candice's hand, and I watch as all of Sal's attention is suddenly on Steph. I'm adult enough to admit that there's a little stab of jealousy there, but I'm also super happy for Sal.

"Stephanie...wow, you look...amazing." Sal has to swallow a few times to keep talking, and Stephanie's cheeks turn an even darker pink under Jack's skillfully applied makeup. Candice looks back and forth between the two of them as they reach the bottom of the steps, and her smile turns into a wide grin as she hurries over to Xan and me.

"Oh, I'm so glad you two are here, I need some help in the nest getting my dress on." She's yanking hard on Xan's arm while stealing glances back at our friends.

"If I gotta go, kiddo, so do you," he says, grabbing my hand before he's dragged towards the nest.

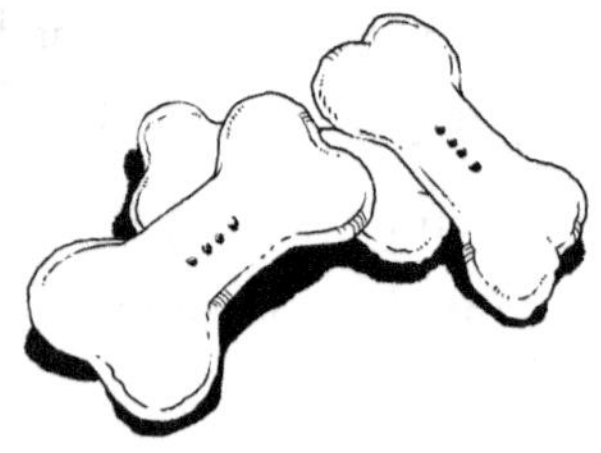

Pack Asher rented out the community center for the ceremony and reception. I'm not sure who they got to decorate it, but it looks amazing. There are flowers and garlands everywhere, and a beautiful archway covered in gauzy netting with fairy lights. I don't see myself ever getting married, but if I do, I want to recreate some of this. It's gonna be even more beautiful during the reception just as the sun's starting to go down.

Sighing wistfully, I wonder again about the lack of romance in my life. It's not that I don't want to be swept up off my feet. I just...I haven't met anybody yet that really calls to me. Someone that I can see myself getting old with. It's not that I'm against dating or anything, but with school and work, I don't really have time. *Also* no one's really asked me. I mean, Sal and I went out a few times, but that's really been it since my high school boyfriend broke up with me just before graduation.

I don't even know if what I want *is* romance, so much as just...someone to talk to, companionship, camaraderie maybe?

Stephanie and I arrived at the community center early. She's Candice's Maid of Honor and needs to make sure all the decorations are set up properly and the food's running on schedule. I just came along to help because otherwise I'd be sitting at the pack's house like a lump on a frog watching everybody else run around in a tizzy. At least here I can be an extra set of hands if Stephanie needs it.

I think Sal wanted to offer, but Jacks took one look at her hair and dragged her upstairs to "make you look fabulous!" At first, I thought he was embracing his metrosexual side, but Candice says he just really likes doing hair, and regularly styles hers. If it makes him happy, who am I to judge? Also, he did an wonderful job on mine.

Stephanie runs around in a whirlwind of activity, cell phone in hand, confirming catering, adjusting flowers, fluffing curtains and netting. She's like a one-woman organizing army. Eventually she gets tired of me following her around and hands me a broom. "I'm super sorry, Kelly. Can you just go check the front entryway? It was really windy last night, and I just want to make sure there aren't any sticks or leaves before I put down the rug." It seems an odd request, but I want to be useful, and I know she's stressed since guests should start arriving in the next thirty minutes.

Something must be stuck, because when I try to push open the front door it just jiggles and makes a clacking noise. I check for locks around the base and up the center, but can't see anything. I can't quite reach the top, but I don't see anything up there that looks like a lock. Leaning heavily against the bar I heave as hard as I can while wearing heels, and the door suddenly springs open halfway. There's a loud thump and a groan, and I tumble out onto the sidewalk, hitting the concrete hard, pain flaring up both my knees. Looking down, I hope I haven't messed up my dress.

Well, shoot!

My knees are bleeding.

"Are you ok?" I don't recognize that voice; it's deep and makes me shiver in a not unpleasant way. Looking up I see Brice and Joseph from Pack McKinley, as well as a guy I don't know standing behind Brice. He has dark hair and eyes, and he's taller than Brice, but I can't tell much more than that from my spot on the ground.

I've got to get up before I ruin my dress!

Standing up from the ground in heels is super hard, and I fall over two more times before a pair of big hands wrap around my waist and lift me to my feet. They stay around me as I regain my footing and stop wobbling like a baby horse. Even after they let go, they don't pull away. "Come on, Honey, let's get you cleaned up, ok?" That unfamiliar voice is a deep rumble that sends more shivers down my spine.

Who the heck's callin' me honey?

"Sorry about that. Thank you." I raise my head from my wobbly and scraped knees up into the face of the dark-haired stranger. He's younger than I thought, a few inches taller than Xan, but shorter than the rest of the guys or Joseph. His long black hair's pulled into a ponytail, and oh, he has tiny silver hoops though the sides of his bottom lip, and gauges in his ears. He's also big, has broad shoulders, and looks like he belongs in a heavy metal band. I can almost picture him with a guitar.

His black jeans and sneakers are faded, but it's paired with a nice black dress shirt with the sleeves rolled up, and what look like black leather cuffs around both wrists. His outstretched arms each have a rectangular tattoo, almost like a colorful card down the inside that disappear under the cuffs, and I want to get a closer look.

I take a deep breath, wincing again at the sting in my knees and get hit with the strong scent of vanilla and cinnamon. He smells like a snickerdoodle. And the sudden thought of this big intimidating alpha smelling like my favorite cookies sends me into a fit of giggles. He jerks away from me like he's been burned.

Joseph and Brice exchange a look before Brice reaches towards me. "Kelly Girl, are you ok? Did you hit your head?" He starts feeling along the back of my neck and up my scalp before I can answer, and a low rumbling growl erupts from the stranger, surprising us both. Brice looks from me to the stranger and back again before pulling his hand away.

"Oh, sorry, Kelly, this is my baby cousin, Teddy. He was here in town visiting, and Candice said he could come to the ceremony. Teddy, this is Kelly, she works over at Gabe's Garage and goes to the community college outside town."

The stranger, Teddy, ducks his head and rumbles out a quiet, "Ma'am."

"Oh, you can just call me Kelly, it feels weird being called ma'am. It's nice to meet you." Stretching my hand out I wait for his in return to shake, but he just stares down at it until I pull back, not sure what sort of faux pas I made.

"Sorry," he rumbles as he stretches his own hand out just as I start pulling back, and we both just kind of hang there in limbo, not quite touching, but not sure how to proceed until another voice breaks the tension.

"Nice to see y'all too...now if somebody could help me up, I'd appreciate it." I spin around to see who's behind me, and Joseph's brother, Sam, is sitting on the ground, holding his nose with blood dripping down his chin and onto his white dress shirt.

Crud.

"Yeah, it seems someone pushed on the door, right as I pulled...and well...I seem to be bleeding here. So, if somebody can help me up, I need to go treat this shirt before it stains." I would laugh at the absurdity if I didn't feel so bad about this. Reaching out to help him, I hear that low rumbling growl again, and pull up short, my head snapping around to see Joseph standing next to me. He was probably coming to help Sam too.

Unfortunately, the rapid movement just makes me dizzy and, well, at least I know gravity's still working. I start to go down when those big hands wrap around me again, and I'm lifted completely off the ground, and cradled against a hard cookie scented chest. Joseph walks over and pulls Sam off the ground and away from the point of impact, as Brice holds the door open for all of us.

We're barely inside the building when Stephanie comes down the hall, and I realize I lost my broom. *Oh, there it is, leaning against the wall.* Stephanie stops short at the sight of me in the arms of the big dark alpha, her mouth opens and closes a few times, and then Brice walks around us and her gaze snaps to him. "Stephanie, oh my god girl, you look so pretty. Did Jacks do your makeup?" Stephanie blushes again, and I don't think she gets nearly enough compliments.

Then she catches sight of my legs. "Oh, Kelly, your knees. Let's get you to the bathroom and get cleaned up. I can go get my first aid kit out of the car if we need to, ok?"

I tilt my head up to Teddy. "Thank you for your help, but I can walk." He rumbles at me again, but gently lowers my feet to the floor, his hands staying on me until he's sure I'm stable, for real this time. Stephanie takes my hand and we head back towards the main office and the women's restroom, but when I turn my head and look back, he's still watching me.

Chapter 3

The sweet little beta follows her friend around the corner. With no idea what the fuck came over me, I turn back to Brice to apologize for growling at him, but he's just grinning up at me. Brice is what omegas are supposed to look like, tiny, cute, kind of sweet. He calls me his baby cousin, but I was bigger than him by the time I was thirteen. Then again, I was supposed to be an alpha, everybody thought so. Hell of a shock all around, really.

"Kelly's really pretty, huh?" Brice sidles up to me, still smiling like the cat that ate the canary. I hate talking, hate my voice. It's too deep and I always sound like I'm growling. Though, to the best of my memory, today's the first time I've actually growled, and I didn't even mean to. He's right though, she is pretty, with big brown eyes and long honey brown hair. Her little silver glasses even match her dress, she's fucking adorable, and so tiny.

With her hair twisted up, and that dress, she looks like she should be floating around somebody's garden, sprinkling some kind of magic sparkles on flowers and shit. Fuck, she even smells like flowers. Not that heavy cloying sweetness that *omegas* normally have, but light, like some kind of lilac, barely there. The kind of subtle that makes you want to bury your nose in her hair and breathe deep, trying to find more.

Where the fuck did that thought even come from?

What the actual fuck am I thinking about?

"You should go talk to her when she gets back, and totally make sure you get a dance during the reception!" Brice is practically wiggling as we stare off towards the hallway she disappeared down. I turn around to keep my feet from following after her, but also to check on Sam. The guy's cool, not part of Brice's pack, but he *is* Joseph's brother. We're about the same size, which is awesome, since I didn't bring any formal clothes for this trip, I was able to borrow some of his nice stuff, and fuck but it smells good too.

I don't know Pack Asher, but with how everybody else is dressed, I'm guessing showing up in my normal all black T-shirts and ripped jeans would not be appreciated. Not that I blame them. It'd be fucking rude anyway. I totally would've gone out and gotten some nice stuff myself if I had to, but this was just easier. I was exhausted when I got here yesterday. Must be fucking jetlag, I can't have slept more than a few hours last night, and then all this today. No wonder my mind's going nuts.

But Brice asked me my size and called Sam to bring over a spare dress shirt. Then I had to rush getting ready, because as soon as I smelled this fucking thing, I needed to go take matters into my own hands, or risk making a fool out of myself for the entire reception. Is that a lead pipe in your pocket or are you just happy to see me? Fucking omega hormones.

Still, I take one last long look at that hallway after Kelly before turning and following Brice and his family into the main seating area. He kisses Joseph, a quick peck on the lips, and then pushes him gently towards the back. Joseph's a groomsman for Pack Asher, he works with them at the fire department. I feel out of place here, everybody knows each other, and here's the giant lumbering omega. Male omegas are rare enough, but I definitely got my alpha dad's genetics.

That's why I've been stuck at that stupid omega center for the last few years. I mean, I can go to college there, but only for omega approved degrees. We had a plan, and this was not fucking it. Me and Steve and Garret, we were supposed to be alphas together, start a pack together. *Fuck*. Especially Vee.

Rubbing my hand down the back of my head, careful not to fuck up my ponytail, I follow Brice up to the chairs in the front. The rest of his and Joseph's pack aren't in the actual ceremony, so it's us minus Joseph hanging out waiting. Brice helped out with the decorations. Candice didn't ask him to, but he loves doing floral arrangements and other crafty shit, he even made her a new necklace and earrings for the ceremony. He told me about it on the way over. I'll admit to being curious why he didn't tell me about this beforehand. We've been planning my visit for months now, why wouldn't he tell me he already had plans this weekend, and to a bonding ceremony no less. These are supposed to be for close family and friends, not some random omega you've never met. I just feel awkward being here.

The rest of the chairs slowly fill up, and I now know why Brice wanted to get here early, every time I hear someone compliment the decorations he wiggles a little bit. I'm happy he's happy, but this is all kinds of overwhelming. It doesn't take long before the chairs are mostly full. The woman who led Kelly away—Brice said her name was Stephanie—pops her head out of a room that says 'Office', looking around, before ducking back in, and shortly thereafter a group of four guys in tuxes head out. Then a taller woman in a tux—huh, a female alpha. She's pretty. Joseph comes last, running his hand along Brice's shoulder when he passes him in the aisle.

I guess we're about to start.

I look up at what can only be Pack Asher, waiting at the front of the crowd. The pack leader's probably the guy in front, big fellow, built like a bear, not as tall as the one he's standing beside though. Heck, even I'd feel short next to him, but he's still hot. Next are two guys who look like total opposites, one really put together, his long blond hair pulled back like mine in a low ponytail, and the other one with a mohawk, tattoos up his neck, a septum ring, and a couple of eyebrow rings. Dude looks like he should be on a British punk band album cover.

Oh, they're holding hands, that's sweet.

Though, looking at the punk one, it seems to be more to keep him in place than anything else. He looks like he's about to vibrate off the fucking platform. Seems like this Candice is a lucky omega. I've seen too many packs at the center that only get an omega for a status symbol, they don't really care other than to have one to show off.

I'm drawn from my ruminations when the music starts, and I see Stephanie walking down the aisle holding a bouquet. She's followed shortly by Kelly, who has bright neon pink Band-Aids across both knees. She's blushing furiously and staring at the floor. As she gets closer, I see her inhale, and her eyes snap up to mine, the bright blush from earlier expands until she's practically glowing.

I try to smile my encouragement, but the movement feels out of place on my lips. She returns it anyway, her shoulders relaxing a fraction and settling back. The music changes to Hallelujah, from the first Shrek movie, and a tiny omega in a silver and purple mating gown steps out. I like that they went nontraditional, but I'm not sure which one of the grooms is supposed to be the ogre. Probably the first one, he looks growly.

Once she reaches the dais, she steps up to stand across from her alphas. The punk one's now wiggling in place and Brice turns to glare at me when I try to cover my laughter with a cough. Looking over at Kelly, she's still smiling at me, and I feel my own face start to get hot in return.

The ceremony was really nice, as they said their vows, each alpha bent down and kissed their bonding mark. When she said her vows, she kissed each one on the neck as well, but I only saw a mark on the growly one. Then I notice that while she kisses the others, she trails her hand down the chest of the tall one. She also runs her hands down matching spots on the hips of surfer dude and punk. I think this might be a kinky omega, and I'm all for it.

Once the ceremony's over and the reception starts, I follow Brice over to meet up with Joseph and Sam. They're talking to the growly groom, who I hear them say is Gabe. Looking around, I don't see Kelly, but I see the other grooms. They're gathered around the bride, the tall one and the punk each have a plate of food, offering her tiny bites. The shortest one, the surfer, is staring at me.

It's actually kind of creepy since he's being so blatant about it, and I'm relieved when a small hand lands on my arm. Then delighted that the other end of that hand's attached to Kelly. She still looks beautiful, but she keeps blushing and looking down at her knees. "They didn't have anything in the first aid kit that was skin toned."

She stares at the floor, and I brush her slightly mussed hair back from her forehead. "Trust me beautiful, nobody was looking at your knees."

She blushes harder when she looks up at me, but then surprise crosses her face. "Oh, you haven't met Candice yet, have you? Let me introduce you." She's pulling on my hand and I let her drag me along, because I'm not entirely sure I could tell her no—to anything.

Which is how I end up in front of one tiny curvy omega and three possessive alphas. The surfer stands in front of the group, his look challenging. Which quickly morphs to confusion when I get close enough that he can smell me. They're all staring at me now, and the omega, Candice, looks up...confusion slowly morphing to surprise as Kelly speaks. "Candice, I wanted you to meet Brice's cousin, Teddy." She's holding my hand now, I'm not sure if it's for my benefit or hers. Maybe just a reflex. But I like it.

"Oh my god! Teddy, I haven't seen you in years. You got so big!" All the alphas relax at once, their heads swivel back and forth between us. Then I see it, the girl who used to live next to Brice, she was actually at his bonding, though I barely remember that. It's been at least ten years since I've seen her.

"Holy fuck, I didn't know this was your bonding. Well, ok, I mean, Brice told me your name, but I didn't connect the dots.

He just said that Joseph worked with your mates at the fire station." She laughs and steps closer and the surfer alpha gives her a little more room. Her eyes widen as she smells me.

"Oh Teddy, I thought you'd be all packed up now with Garret and Steven, what happened?" But she can smell what happened, and the sad look in her eyes almost undoes me, So I just shrug and try to smile—it doesn't really work.

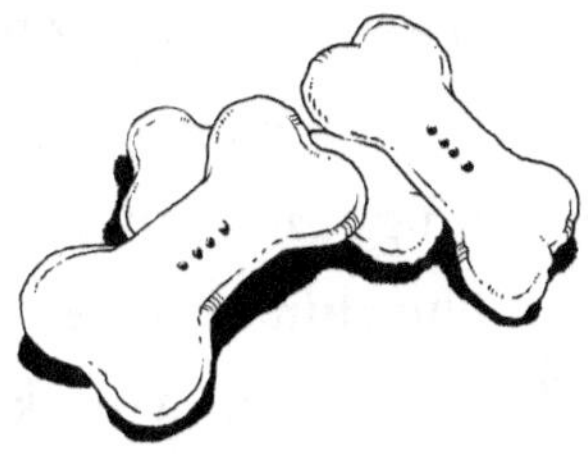

Kelly

Teddy stiffens beside me, his shoulders hunch like he's trying to make himself smaller. I'm not sure what's wrong, or who Garret and Steven are, but I kinda want to kick their butts when the look of sadness crosses Teddy's face. Rubbing my hand up and down his arm, I lean into him. I don't know him well enough to really offer any advice, but hugs help everybody feel better...most of the time.

His face brightens as he looks down at me, and I try to offer an encouraging smile. He replies to Candice, but his eyes don't leave me. "Yeah, that *was* the plan...but as it turns out they want a female omega for the pack, and that's not me. Clearly." He chuckles, but it sounds sad, and I hug him tighter, despite how confused I now am by his statement.

"I'm so sorry Teddy, I know…Well, you and Steven were close, even back then. I thought…" Candice trails off. Jacks looks back and forth between the two of them, rubbing his hand up and down her back in long soothing strokes.

Teddy seems to shake himself, drawing up to his full height again. "It's ok. That's life, right? But, enough with my issues. I'm so happy you found a pack, and really, congratulations." He's smiling again, but it looks forced, and I take his hand again, pulling him away.

"I'm gonna take Teddy to go get a drink. Candice, let me know if you need anything, ok? And congratulations again, you look beautiful! Jacks, you did great!" I pull Teddy away, not sure if he wants a drink or not, but knowing he needs to get away from whatever's making him so sad. Also, I'm curious to know what was wrong with his pack members wanting a female omega. Most omegas are female. Oh, maybe Teddy isn't into girls. I guess that could be a problem, and I suddenly feel like an idiot for flirting so much with him earlier.

Not that I need an alpha, I don't, but he's just so sweet, and his big rumbly voice gives me the shivers, and darn-it, he smells so good.

I lead him over to the reception area we set up and sit next to him. "Do you want me to leave you alone, or go get Brice?"

I ask, not really wanting to do either. But I do want him to be comfortable, even if that means not being near him.

"No, please, Kelly. I...I don't really want to be alone right now, if that's ok." He's staring down at his own lap. But his hand shakes slightly in mine, and his deep rumbly voice quavers. I pet his hand, not sure what else to do. I don't understand how to soothe alphas. I know omegas are supposed to come by it naturally, but I've always been a beta. So I just do what my parents do for me when I feel bad—I rub his arm, stroking the back of his hand, and leaning against him, murmuring a soft nonsense song.

Chapter 4

Sam

Kelly's quiet susurrations against Teddy's arm are like a drum beating against my chest. His spiced vanilla scent is confused. He's happy that she's close—not that I blame him, I feel like a dirty old man for looking at her—but something else, something devastating. The little beta seems to be the only thing holding him together at this point.

Leaning against the wall by the door, I'm alone—I want to go over, offer comfort—but I'm not sure I'd be welcome. He already growled at Brice and Joseph for getting close to her outside, and I want to stay on his good side. Hell, I'd love to be on both their good sides.

Fuck man, you sound like some sort of sick old perv.

Fuckin' stop.

Thirty-four isn't that old.

There's what, an eleven year age gap?

Fuck, I am an old pervert.

She's just so damned sweet and...perfect.

Yeah, and you've been bringing your car into the shop for how many years now?

Kelly never noticed you once.

She's not interested man, just let it go.

Fuck! She didn't even notice earlier when she busted your nose.

To be fair, her knees were bleeding.

I straighten up, pushing off the wall and heading towards Joseph and Brice. He, at least, should know why Teddy's so upset. They've moved on from Gabe and Brice looks like he's trying to figure out how to give Candice a hug without upsetting anyone. I smile, knowing Brice is super touchy feely, even for an omega, and Candice is, well...not. From what Xan says she was really touch starved when they first met, but even now only likes to be touched by her pack.

Can't say I blame her much for that. Then again, I'm not an omega, and it's not unusual for an alpha to be standoffish. I'm not standoffish, I just don't know where I fit in. When I was little, I always assumed I'd be in Joseph's pack. But as I got older it became obvious that wasn't going to work, and I guess it just fell by the wayside for me. I realized later that I was just following him and his friends around, never bothering to make any of my own, and now I don't know how.

Fuck me, but most of the alphas my age are already packed up. This isn't a huge town to start with, but when you grow up in an area and know everybody...Well you learn pretty damned quick if you can stand someone for more than five minutes, let alone live together. Maybe I'm too picky. Maybe I'm just not supposed to be with anyone.

I look over at Brice again and let out a loud bark of laughter. Candice has backed away, trying to avoid the awkward hug, and Jacks is puffed up like a fuckin' rooster with that damned hair of his strutting and circling his little hen, keeping all outsiders away. All eyes swing my way and I blush at the look of annoyance on Joseph's face. He's a good alpha and brother. But he worries a lot about being embarrassed, and I think having a loner alpha brother is an automatic embarrassment sometimes. At least it distracts Brice enough for Candice to escape though, so I'll count it as a win.

Giving up on being any help that way, I decide to meander over to Kelly and Teddy. I guess I'll see if I can help without Brice. Sitting down on Kelly's other side, opposite the big omega, I stretch my arm behind her, lightly touching his shoulder. Their combined cookies and lilac scent invades my head and I bite back a groan.

He looks up at me but doesn't growl like he did at Brice and Joseph earlier, so he must really be feeling bad. That or he just doesn't see me as any sort of threat considering I'm older *and* pack-less.

"You ok, man? You're lookin kinda down there. I just wanted to check on you."

Kelly leans into me whispering conspiratorially, "You didn't tell me that he knew Candice when he was little, I felt like a dork when I introduced 'em. But yeah, I'm not sure, something about a pack he was supposed to be a part of...But they wanted a female omega...I'm not sure exactly. Maybe he doesn't like girls." Her voice is quiet, but not *that* quiet and it's enough to finally bring a smile to Teddy's face.

He strokes his hand down her hair. "I like girls well enough, Little Pixie, but omegas aren't known to share, and I couldn't sit around waiting to get kicked to the curb when they found one they wanted." Kelly's gaze swings back and forth between us, her brows scrunched together. "Are you sure? Candice doesn't have a problem with Jacks and Xan being together even without her."

Teddy snorts. "Yeah, but Xan and Jacks are both alphas."

Kelly's eyebrows scrunch even lower, and her eyes turn from me to Teddy and back. She leans in, ready to whisper something else and I see her eyes widen as realization hits. She leans in closer, taking a deep breath against my chest. "Ok...wait a second...Sam, you smell kind of like cedar trees and sawdust. But...But Teddy smells like my favorite cookies. Alphas don't generally smell like desserts, do they?"

Her face drops into her hands, and her voice is muffled. "Oh my gosh, Teddy, I'm *so* sorry. I feel so clueless here. But..." Her head pops up, looking accusingly at him. "But you don't look like an omega. I mean…Brice…and…and you….” Teddy's smile gets bigger the more flustered she gets, and I want to take them both home. They are so fucking cute together.

Finally taking pity on her, Teddy leans over. “No, Little Pixie, I don't smell like an alpha because I'm not one. I'm just kind of a freak.” He smiles, but it's not a *happy* smile. “I was supposed to be an alpha, I had a pack lined up, I was *with* one of them, but they wanted a family. It was kind of a non-negotiable point they had…We had. Then, surprise, not an alpha.” He points to his own chest, and Kelly leans against him, wrapping her arms around one of his.

“I just mean…you're so big…” She looks him up and down. “And heavy metal. I love your hair by the way. You gotta tell me what kind of conditioner you use, 'cause I can never get mine to smooth down like that.”

Teddy wraps the arm she isn't hugging around her. Pulling her against his chest in a tight hug, his hand spans the width of her entire back. “Thanks Kelly, and I use Mane and Tail, it's technically horse shampoo, but it works wonders.” She smiles up at him, and he pulls her tighter against his chest, curling his whole body around hers.

Starting to feel like a third wheel here, I stand up to leave and her tiny hand snaps out and grabs my sleeve. Her voice still muffled against Teddy's chest. “Nope, you need a hug too, you look sad. Stay here for a minute.” Teddy chuckles into her hair, then stands up himself, unwrapping his arm from around her, he pulls me into a hug, with Kelly sandwiched between us.

Ok, this is nice, I could get used to this.

Her lilac scent is subtle, and only adds to his spiced vanilla, wrapping me a warm blanket of comfort.

I could get used to this so fucking easily.

Apparently, I'm not the only one, since when I try to pull back Teddy hangs on tight. I feel wiggling against my chest and Kelly's head pops out under my arm. "Sorry...Couldn't breathe in there." She smiles up at me and cuddles in harder. "Sorry, I know this is super forward, you two just feel so good...I didn't know I needed a hug this much. But it's so darned relaxing...On second thought, if you don't want me to fall asleep right now, you might wanna let me out."

Her eyes are heavy-lidded when she looks up at me, and I try again to let Teddy go. That look on her face—those soft bedroom eyes—doesn't just look sleepy, and soon she is gonna be able to feel what she does to me, what they both do to me, if I don't step away.

I pull back, breaking Teddy's hold on my shirt, and he looks hurt, his big body curling protectively back around Kelly, his sad eyes staring into mine. I want to explain, I need him to know that I pulled away because I don't want to make them uncomfortable.

As his eyes lower, he stops, and they flip back up to mine. Suddenly he's grinning and I don't try to hold back my apologetic smile in return. At least she didn't figure out what happened, and judging by where he has her pressed off-center to his torso, he understands completely, and he doesn't hold it against me.

Maybe later?

Damn, I wish.

Brushing his hand down her hair one final time, Teddy stands to his full height. I've never seen an omega this big before, and I can understand all the confusion. He would be big for a beta, about average for an alpha. But he's downright gargantuan for an omega.

Wouldn't have to worry about him breaking then, would I?
Fuck!

I have got to get my mind out of the gutter. This is neither the time, nor the place, and it's going to be really fucking awkward if Joseph or Brice come over. Scanning the room, I want to make sure no one's noticed our impromptu beta sandwich...and no...yeah...here come Joseph and Brice and boy do they look pissed.

Teddy

"**W**hat the hell do you think you're doing to Brice's cousin!" Joseph whisper shouts at Sam, as Brice tries to pull Kelly and me away. "You cannot fucking take advantage of a vulnerable omega and...a fucking beta...seriously Sam?" His voice is getting louder, losing any attempts at discretion.

I look up from where Brice is practically hanging onto my arm and several people around the room are staring at us. My own low growl rumbles forth at the attention, as well as his overt announcement of my designation. Kelly clings tighter to my other arm, and I pull away from Brice to hold her. I'm not sure if my anger is more from how Joseph is embarrassing Sam or Kelly at this point but fuck him. And fuck Brice if he supports this shit.

I'm not a fucking child anymore and if he refers to Kelly as a "fucking beta" again, I may be forced to take a chunk out of my cousin's mate. Brice is fretting beside me, wringing his hands, his gaze swinging between his brother-in-law and me.

Sam is staring at the floor, taking the dressing down that Joseph's giving him. Just from what I've seen since I arrived, he seems to hold his brother in high regard, but I'm about to topple that fucking pedestal. I tilt Kelly's face up to look at me. "Just a second, Pixie, I need to go deal with some shit." She lets out a tiny gasp and her eyes go wide as I pull away, and step closer to Joseph, blatantly invading his personal space.

I wasn't raised to be an omega, and these people need to get their heads wrapped around the fact that I'm not going to fall in line just because some asshole alpha starts barking. Joseph finally realizes I'm standing practically on his heels and steps forward, trying to put space between us, but he's been in Sam's face, so he can't go forward without knocking his brother over.

Reaching around, I pull Sam closer to my side. Not raising my voice, and not rushing through what I'm about to say. I need him—and by extension Brice—to understand that this is important. "Joseph, I understand you may feel some responsibility about me because of Brice, but if you ever yell at Sam again, or refer to Kelly as a 'fucking beta', I really will beat the living shit out of you." I'm sure my voice is flat and emotionless because I am doing my damndest not to scream at this asshole.

I raise my voice to address the people that had to witness this spectacle. "Candice, Rooster guy, and other *intense* looking alphas: Sorry about the interruption. Candice, you're awesome, and I am super happy you found yourself such an amazing pack. Keep in touch from now on, yeah?"

Candice and the surfer stare at the one I called Rooster and burst into peals of laughter, while he looks back and forth between the two of them, confused at the name. The tallest one is watching, his hand over his mouth, his face red, trying not to join in. Even the grumbly pack leader's lips twitch a bit, but he still shoots a glare in my direction.

I keep a hold on Sam and walk towards the door. Kelly, unsure of what to do, stands there for a second, looking between us and Candice. Unable to stop the giggles, Candice flaps her hand at Kelly, who quickly follows us, catching up just before we exit the room and start down the hallway. My steps peter out once I push through the door to the outside though. Clearly, I hadn't thought far ahead, I was just so angry.

"I don't suppose either of you know of a hotel nearby? I was supposed to be here on a week-long visit for Spring Break, but I really don't want to deal with *that* level of awkward for so long." Releasing my grip on Sam's hand, I try to run my fingers through my hair. When I get snagged on the elastic, I end up just trying to yank it out and breaking it in the process.

Shit.

Kelly looks thoughtful for a few minutes before Sam speaks up. "Yeah, um...Oak Flats isn't exactly known for being a bustling metropolis. There's a hotel out by the interstate, but they're pretty overpriced for the shit you get. I can't promise a continental breakfast, but you're welcome to stay in one of my spare rooms."

My eyebrows must be near my hairline, because he chuckles before he goes on. "Yes, I said rooms. When I was house shopping, my biggest requirement was a good shop building on the property for work. This place was nearly condemned, and I pretty much lived in the shop for the first year while I was doing renovations. But there are six bedrooms. Two are completely renovated, the rest...need some work. Oh, and sort of man cave...thing...in the basement now that it's livable again."

He rubs his hand over his face, looking embarrassed. "I don't know, I was thinking about selling it at some point. It's too much space for just me. But it's home for now, so you're welcome to come over, for as long as you want or need to. I'm usually working, so I won't bother you or anything. You can just have some time to hang." He stares down at the ground, and my mind goes back to what Joseph said inside.

Reaching out, I touch his chin, his beard is short and scratchy on my hand, and I try not to let my mind wander on how it would feel scraping along my neck. "Ok, first off, nobody says *Hang* anymore. *Hang out*, yes, but I'm pretty sure that just saying *Hang* died before 2010. Secondly, I appreciate it, and I'm sure as hell not opposed to hanging-out." I make air quotes, which earns me a laugh from Kelly.

I almost forgot my pixie was here.

I haven't known her long enough to think of her as mine.

"Can I come with you?" She looks up between the two of us hopefully. "It's just...my parents aren't expecting me home for at least a few more hours, so if I go home now there are gonna be tons of questions, and Mom'll be mad at me for leaving Stephanie to do all the cleaning. So, I was thinking I could text her to call me when she's ready to put everything away, and until then I don't have anything to do...or anywhere to get out of this dress and into my regular clothes."

My mind skips like a record when she mentions getting out of her dress, and for the first time in my life I almost let out an omega whine. I don't miss the flash in Sam's eyes either, but if she notices where either of our minds went, she doesn't give any indication.

Thankfully he recovers quickly. "It's not that far to my place, if you want to you can just follow me, and call me if you get lost. Can I see your phone?"

Kelly hands Sam her cell, and his own back pocket rings shortly afterwards, so he now has her number as well. She looks up at me after he hands her phone back. "So, who do you want to ride with?" Somehow, I feel like that's a loaded question.

I look from Kelly's small car to Sam's truck, and smile at her. "Sorry, Pixie, I'm not actually sure I'll fit in yours. Meet you there, yeah?" Her laughter rings out, high and clear, and she smiles and nods. "Yeah, that's a good point, you'd probably bonk your head, or at least make the muffler drag off if we go over any potholes. See you there in a few." She gets in her car, and I watch her put on her seatbelt and pull out of her spot before we've even had a chance to get belted in.

Chapter 5

Teddy

Once we're on the road again, Sam starts apologizing. "I'm sorry, I didn't mean to make things awkward back there, especially between you and Brice. Honestly, I don't even know why I did it, you just looked like you could both use a hug, and I..." He tapers off and I'm intensely interested in how this sentence ends. Somehow, it seems important to me.

Kelly stays close behind, and we arrive in about ten minutes. It's a good thing I did ride with Sam. He lives in a big house down a dirt road, and I fear Kelly's right about losing her muffler if I tried to ride with her.

As we pull up in the yard, I notice there's no real driveway, just a dirt and gravel lot out front, but I can see the shop building back and to the right of the house. "Sam's Shelves and Cabinets" is spray-painted across the front over the double doors.

Kelly bounces out of her car, holding a padded hanger with a long T-shirt and a pair of sneakers tied over her shoulder, clearly ready to get changed. However, she quickly scrambles back inside when a loud barking breaks out and some sort of big red dog comes barreling around the side of the shop. Sam gets out and the dog makes a beeline for him. It slams into his legs and Sam smacks into the side of the truck with a loud "oof". Probably best it didn't get to my pixie first, pretty sure she'd be on the ground now, and she's already had one tumble today.

I turn back towards her car to check on her, but she's not inside anymore. She's squatted in her dress, on the ground, patting her thighs and whistling. The big dog stops trying to jump up on Sam and wiggles over in her direction, doing a full body wag.

"Well, aren't you just a big ole slobber muffin!" she says, wrapping her hands around its head and scratching behind the ears. The dog lets out a garbled huff and flops to the ground, nearly dragging her down as it rolls around onto its back. Its saggy upper lip is flopped over its snout, and its eyes look huge, staring intently at Kelly, pleading for belly rubs, which she seems to happily oblige.

I quickly turn back to Sam, because squatting down in that dress is not doing a damned thing to keep it decent. It scoots farther up her thigh with every move she makes. I'm not sure if I should go lift her up or thank the dog myself. But things are going to get awfully embarrassing if that thing rides up much higher. Sam seems to have the same problem, as he's staring intently at the shop, ears bright red and rubbing the back of his head.

"Yeah, that's Jake, he's supposed to be a guard dog. Um, clearly, he never got the memo. But if you wanna bring your change of clothes in, I can show you two around and get you situated. Teddy, you can see if you feel up to staying here." His head turns slightly towards me while he's talking, but we're both pointedly not looking at Kelly by now.

In retrospect that was probably a bad idea, as I hear her let out a little squeak, and spin around to see her sprawled against her car, her skirt hitched all the way up on one side. Jake is leaning against her, trying his damnedest for more pets and she is flailing under the big dog's weight. Her hands press tight against the driver side door, trying to keep from getting knocked to the ground.

Sam lets out a loud curse and stalks over, clapping his hands and gently chiding the dog, "Oh my god, yes, attention from someone new. You're so starved for affection...." His voice trails off as the dog moves and he takes in the full sight of Kelly and her little blue panties. A low growl rumbles out of him. "Ahh, shit, Sugar, are you ok? I'm sorry about that big lug. He just wants attention, I didn't mean to let him maul you."

Kelly just laughs, her cheeks turning pink as she tugs down her dress. "No, it's my fault. I shouldn't have gotten down there with him. Sorry about that, and you know, flashing you." She's staring at her feet in the pretty silver heels, now covered in dust. "I really would appreciate a place to get cleaned up and changed. I don't want to ruin the dress Candice got me."

Sam takes her hand and makes sure she's steady, before opening her car and getting her clothes back out. "Not a problem, each bedroom has its own attached bath, and there's an extra one downstairs. Let me show you two inside. Kelly can use the primary, and then Teddy can use the finished spare room shower to get cleaned up in. I'm sure I've got an extra T-shirt you can use till we go get your stuff from Joseph's. If you want?" He looks back at me, uncertainty flickering in his eyes.

"Truth? This whole thing has been a bit of a shit-show and getting cleaned up and into something comfortable that doesn't smell like a room full of strangers sounds wonderful right now." I offer him a lopsided smile. I really do appreciate him offering to let me stay, but I'm also wondering if I can keep from making a fool of myself in a house saturated with his scent.

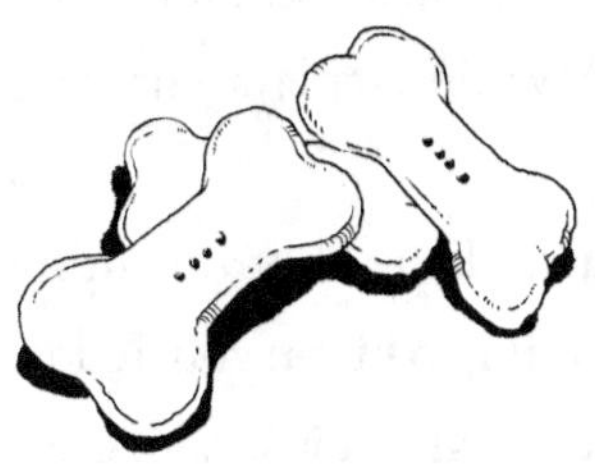

Sam

This is a terrible idea.

What the fuck was I thinking?

I can't have him in my house for a week.

Shouldn't have her here at all.

Both of them are going to think I'm some kind of raging pervert!

I lead Kelly and Teddy into the house, carrying her everyday clothes so that her hands are free to ward off Jake. I pull a towel from the linen closet in the front hall and deposit her and her stuff in the front bathroom. I don't know if she'll want a full scrub-down to remove the dog slobber and body glitter, but I want to offer all the same. The house is two stories, almost a plantation style from the outside with big pillars and a wrap-around porch on both levels. It really was a steal, but it's taking *so* much work.

"Are you more comfortable on top or bottom?" I ask Teddy as I head towards the stairs. When I don't get an answer, I turn back and he's staring at me, his mouth hanging open and the tips of his ears red. My mind replays what I just said, and I groan.

Fuck me.

I point to the stairs. "Top or bottom, upstairs or down. Fuck, I promise, I'm not trying to hit on you Teddy." I drop my face in my hands, mortified by what I just said, even if I didn't mean it that way. Goddammit these two are driving me out of my mind, and it's been less than ten minutes with them in my house. I'm not sure how I'm gonna be able to handle this for another six days. At least it'll just be him, and not both of them.

Strong hands wrap around my lower jaw, raising my face up, and Teddy's there, a small smirk on his full lips. "Well, to be honest, I'm kind of a switch, so I can go either way." He pulls me towards him, and I don't feel like resisting. His kiss is hard, his lips slanting over mine, sucking and nipping at my mouth. I groan into him and he tilts my head down to get a better angle before swiping his tongue across my bottom lip once and pulling away.

"But maybe bottom in this case, not sure I want to deal with an unfamiliar set of stairs in the middle of the night, just to be safe." He's still holding my face, his eyes capturing mine, searching. *Holy fucking shit on a cracker*. I stand there, not knowing how to reply. I want to pull him back to kiss him again. Drag him to one of the bedrooms and peel off these fucking clothes so we can explore this further. But Kelly's here, and I don't know how long she's going to be cleaning up and getting changed.

Clearing my throat a few times before I can speak. "Ok, well, there are two bedrooms downstairs, plus an office and a nesting suite. The other four bedrooms—including the master, which is mine—are upstairs. I can go get you a change of clothes. The first room on the right should be completely ready for you, but if you prefer a different one, I can try to get it fixed up...It won't look pretty, but I want you to be comfortable." I'm kind of proud of how *not* choked my voice comes out, but I also really need to adjust my cock because I'm hard as fuck right now, and it is going to be painfully obvious as soon as I step far enough back that he can see my slacks.

Teddy smirks a bit. "Hmm, maybe I should have picked top then." He turns and stalks off down the hall, opening the first door on the right. I need to get myself under control and get cleaned up. Plodding up the stairs and into the master bedroom, I unbutton my shirt and toss it into the hamper along with my slacks. I don't have time to take care of my aching cock at the moment. Even if I did, I do believe it would only be a stop gap considering the delicious smelling omega and beta in my fucking house right now. Fuck, why did I think this was a good idea?

Because he needed help.

Ok, fair point, but do you really think you're going to be able to keep your hands to yourself if he does that again?

Yeah, I didn't think so either.

Teddy's not like any omega I've met before. Fuck, he gives off more dominance than most alphas I know. That thought sends an image racing through my mind—him pinning Kelly to the wall downstairs, hiking up that short little dress of hers, and pulling aside those tiny blue panties she was flashing at us earlier. While I'm glad she didn't seem overly embarrassed, I've never been so fucking jealous of a dog in my life. I would happily fall at her feet too if that was the reaction.

I head into my bathroom and splash my face with cold water. I wish I had time for more, but that would be rude, and I still need to get something for Teddy to wear. Drying my face, I head to the closet, pulling out a ratty T-shirt and a pair of work jeans. I have several solid button ups I wear when I work out in the shop to save me from flying woodchips, but it can get fucking hot out there too, especially in the summer. Always better to dress in layers so you can take shit off if you need to.

I snag a black jersey and a pair of basketball shorts out of a drawer. I don't play basketball, but they can be comfortable to lounge around in.

Heading back downstairs, I knock on the door that Teddy went into earlier, but there's no answer. I crack it open and hear the shower going in the bathroom. Forcing myself not to look and see if he left the door open, I toss the change of clothes on the bed and leave before I can give into temptation.

Walking back into the front room, I hear humming in the kitchen and turn that way. Kelly's in there, her butt sticking out as she leans far into the fridge. Those cutoffs she has on hug her ass beautifully, her long lean legs tilting her hips from side to side as she hums a tune I can't catch. She straightens up and lets out a tiny scream, almost dropping the armload of sandwich stuff she's holding.

"Crud, I'm *so* sorry! I wanted to do something nice for y'all cause you're letting us stay here for a bit so I don't get into trouble. I already texted Steph, but she says Brice is gonna help her with the decorations since he brought the flowers. If you'll just let me stay for a couple of hours, I'll get outta your hair." Her smile is sheepish, and she still has quite a bit of glitter smeared up her neck, but she pulled her hair down from earlier and it curls in ringlets down her back. She's wearing a scrunchie on her wrist.

Not sure how I can tell her I want her, both of them, to stay for a lot longer than a few hours.

"I appreciate it, really. But Teddy's in the shower, if you need more time to clean up, feel free to do so. I can make us up some food if you tell me what you like." I step forward, helping her spread out the sandwich stuff on the counter and taking a look at her choices. I admit I do the bachelor thing most of the time, it's just not worth putting in a lot of effort for myself. Usually if I want something hot, I just hit the diner down the road. Most of what I eat are sandwiches, so I keep a variety of fixin's on hand, including the lunchmeat she found in the fridge. Seems like she only found the bread I left out on the counter, whole wheat. Maybe I should ask if she wants something else from the pantry.

She smiles up at me, and I take a step back so I don't close the distance between us. She still has traces of Teddy's snickerdoodle mixed with her touch of lilac and I have to grip the countertops behind me to keep myself from leaning down and running my nose along her glittering neck and getting a solid hit of her scent. She swallows a few times before speaking again. "Sorry, Momma keeps trying to teach me how to cook, but the most I can do is a sandwich, a grilled sandwich, or a decent burger...Do you have a grill? Daddy's been trying to teach me how to do pancakes...but that'd probably be kind of heavy for lunch." I know I look skeptical when she huffs. "I've only set myself on fire, like, three times, ok. And my eyebrows grew back just fine." I have to hide my smile at her adorable look of outrage.

"Sorry, Sugar, I don't actually have a grill at the moment. I don't cook much for myself, so I never bothered gettin' one. Maybe if Teddy is gonna be staying for a bit we can get one so you can come over and not set yourself on fire?" Her tiny self-depreciating smile makes my chest ache, and I watch as her fingers twist together before she starts to stammer.

"Sorry, I just...I'm kind of accident prone. It's not on purpose. But like you saw today." She points down at the bright pink bandages on her knees.

How did I forget about that? Oh yeah, I was busy trying to stop my own nosebleed. I reach up and unconsciously rub the bridge of my nose and her face falls, she looks mortified. "Oh...I am so, *so* sorry about that. I never even asked if you were ok. Are you ok? That was totally my fault, I couldn't get that stupid door open, and then it did, and I just fell over, and it hit you. I should have asked sooner..."

She's rambling, but fuck, her blush is adorable, and I reach out to touch her chin, tipping it up so she'll look at me. Her continued apology tapers off as our eyes meet. "I'm ok, Sugar. It was a hell of a shock at the time, but I've had my nose broken more than a few times, this was nothin'." Her smile is sweet as she tentatively reaches towards my face, her fingers tracing the bridge of my nose, there's no real pressure as she feels along the ridge that's been busted at least a half dozen times. Her hands feel so good on me, and I wish I was free to explore her as well, but she's a guest. I reluctantly step back when I hear the door to Teddy's room open down the hall, feeling a small twinge as her hand drops back to her side.

"So, I might have stuff for burgers, or I can run down to the store if you've got your heart set on 'em. Otherwise, a sandwich sounds mighty fine to me. It's still pretty early, so we could do quick sandwiches now, and then maybe burgers for dinner if you are gonna be here that long?"

Please be here that long.

Chapter 6

Buckling the leather cuffs back on my wrists, I walk back into the kitchen. I'm not sure what I missed, but the pheromones coming out of here could knock me over from the living room. Even though Kelly's a beta, her scent calls to me like nothing before, and she smells both nervous and turned on.

Sam smells embarrassed, and I worry I read the whole situation wrong. I shouldn't have kissed him earlier. He tasted so fucking good though, I just couldn't help it. Fucking omega hormones. I thought he wanted me too. He seems like he's attracted to me, and I was walking around half fucking hard all day wearing a shirt that was saturated in his scent.

Running my hands over my face, I wonder if I've made a complete ass out of myself. If I ought to just try to change my plane ticket home and camp out at my parents' house alone for the next week or cut the whole vacay short and head back to the omega center. It's gonna be a boring break alone, but shit. I can't stay with Brice and his pack, I want to stay here...Hell, I don't feel like I ever want to leave.

But I'm not about to stay some place I'm not wanted. Learned my lesson on that one the hard way with Vee and Garret. Fuck, I haven't even seen them since my designation came in. Their dad found out and refused to let me near them. That's not something I want to think about right now though. I miss *him* so fucking much sometimes.

Tiny arms wrap around my middle and the subtle scent of lilac teases my nose as Kelly burrows her face into my chest. She's bigger than most omegas, still tiny by comparison, but she's countered by the larger sturdier weight that's suddenly at my back. Fuck, being between the two of them feels so good. I can't even remember the last time I got a solid hug. Not one of those obligatory hugs that your family has to give you when you haven't seen them in forever, but an actual hug. It feels so right with these two.

I lean my head back against Sam's shoulder, hoping he doesn't pull away, and stroke my hand down Kelly's hair. I want to tell them how good they feel, but I'm worried about scaring them away with my freaky omega bullshit. I'm not sure if that's what this is, but fuck, I don't want it to end. Kelly's face tilts up to mine, "You feel really good. Sorry, I don't mean to keep invadin' your personal space. This just feels..." Her words taper off, and I tilt her chin up so she can't hide away.

"Right?" I hope that was how she was going to finish her sentence.

Please, fuck, let that have been it.

Her eyes widen, but she just nods before she buries her face in my chest again, and I let out a breath I didn't realize I was holding. One of Sam's arms loosens from my waist, and I dread that he's going to pull away. Instead, it comes around my jaw, pulling my face to his, and returning the kiss I gave him earlier. The angle is awkward, but it's still so fucking good.

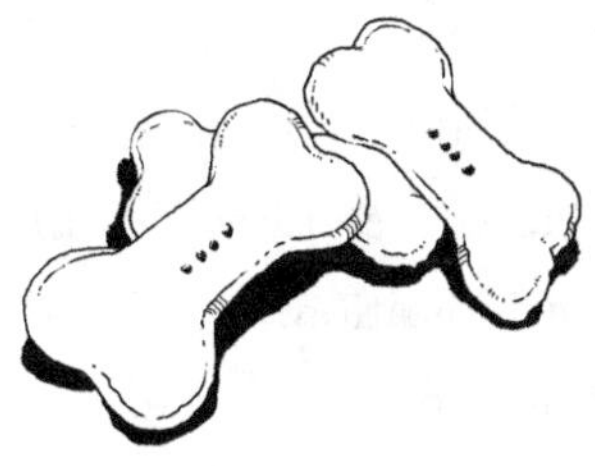

Kelly

Today has been so danged weird. I mean, I was super happy to get to be in Candice's bonding ceremony. Never got my free cake though, bummer. But then things got so tense, and now...well...now something is poking me in the stomach.

I'm not completely naive, I mean, I know the general me-chanics, and I've had a couple of beta boyfriends in high-school, but only really Sal since I started college. Teddy is bigger than any of the betas I was with, and it's kind of a shock. I guess he could just be reacting to Sam behind him, but his arms pressing me tight against his front make it feel like he wants me. Maybe he wants us both?

I know alphas and omegas are often in poly relationships, it's just never something I thought about for myself. Growing up, the plan was always college, and if I happened to meet a sweet beta guy there that I hit it off with, then great. This...this is not the plan, but it feels so right, like I'm supposed to be here.

I press my face against Teddy's chest and breathe in his snickerdoodle scent, I can barely catch Sam's cedar and sawdust because my nose is pretty smooshed right now, but the low rumble I feel moving through Teddy and into me makes me feel like my bones are melting. Heck, everything's melting, if what's going on in my shorts is any indication.

I shouldn't be doing this, I just met Teddy, and while I've met Sam repeatedly over the years, he never gave any sign that he thought of me as...well, at all really. Maybe it's just how close I am to Teddy now, I'm getting purring fallout or something.

Rubbing my cheek against Teddy's chest, his arms tighten and his hips flex against me. He lets out a low moan as he grinds that hard length into my stomach. Should I stop him? I don't want to, but this is moving really fast, and I just met him today. Betas don't pack up often, our sense of smell isn't good enough for there to be that instant attraction, but I'm drawn to both of them.

What am I saying? Sam has always been hot, I mean, he's older. But not like my parent's age or anything. Ew. Just old enough that a few of the dark hairs in his beard have started to turn silver. Pretty sure he could pass for younger if he shaved it off. Heck, he'd still be hot though. Should I stop? I know I shouldn't be wrapping my hands farther around Teddy to run them up Sam's chest behind him.

I shouldn't be touching either of them.

I don't even know Teddy's last name.

They look so good together.

Is it hot in here?

Pushing away from Teddy and Sam, the arms that are around my back and stroking my shoulder let me go reluctantly. Teddy breaks their kiss and they both turn to look at me. Teddy's eyes are glassy, and his cookie scent is strong enough that it's nearly overwhelming, even taking a couple steps back. His erection is obvious in those basketball shorts Sam loaned him. I worry that he's uncomfortable, but I need to take a couple minutes to breathe, because this has never happened before, and I just...I need time.

Stepping farther away, I try to clear my mind, I need fresh air. I can still feel how wet I am, just trying to walk away. I'll have to step outside to get away from Teddy's scent, just to clear my head before I do something I can't take back. Teddy lets out a low omega whine when I turn away and I feel mean, but I need to get out, I need to think for a second.

The whine cuts off and a low growly murmur takes its place, Sam's alpha is trying to comfort the distressed omega pressed against him. I spin back around, wanting to explain that I just need a minute to think, and Sam's hard glare meets my eyes. Teddy has turned around and curled against Sam's chest, his big body shaking as he holds the alpha in a death grip.

Sugarsnaps!

Trying to explain, I don't want to sound like I'm making excuses. Would Teddy let me hug him? I just wanted a few minutes to clear my head, this is all new to me. "I just...gimme a minute, ok? I'm sorry, but I've never felt like this...with anybody...and you two..." I trail off, not sure how to finish this sentence without admitting how scared I am of what might happen.

"I'm sorry, my body is pullin' me one way, my mind is pullin' me the other. I just need a few minutes to think. Teddy, you are so handsome, and all I wanna do right now is touch you. I've never felt that way about anyone. I don't mind hugs, but there's never been anyone that my hands actually ached to touch, like I thought if I didn't, I might cry. It's a little scary. Not you, you're not scary...I'm sayin' the wrong thing here, I just can't get the words out right."

This is embarrassing, and before I can stop it a frustrated tear slips free. Two big sets of arms are around me before I'm able to even wipe it away. "I'm sorry I pushed you, Pixie. Please don't cry." Teddy's own eyes are red when I look up to meet them.

"Neither one of y'all pushed. My body's just really confused right now. I never saw myself gettin' involved with an omega or an alpha, let alone both at the same time. But it's just so easy with you, it feels strange not to be close to you, not to touch you. And it's freakin' me out, 'cause I've only dated a coupla guys before and they were both betas. I mean, and Sal, but it was just the two of us, and things never went farther than holding hands or kissing. I'm not a virgin, I...well...prom. But it just kinda hurt and I didn't see much point....and I'm messing this all up."

A matched set of rumbly growls starts up on either side of my body, and I don't hate it, then Sam's cuts off suddenly. "Wait, you mean Sal from the garage, the alpha who was best man today?" I can't stop the blush that spreads up my cheeks.

But I want to growl myself when Teddy opens his mouth. "Oh, yeah, no, she's very pretty, I can see why you'd..." The rest of his sentence is cut off by Sam's snarl, as he's glaring at the front door like he might need to go hunt down Sal.

I sniff, wiping away another escaped tear. "Yeah, she *is* pretty, and super sweet. We just didn't have much of anything in common. She seemed pretty smitten with Stephanie today though, and I'd totally ship 'em. They'd be adorable together." Teddy laughs at me, and I'm glad to see him smile again, but Sam's just staring between the two of us.

"What do ya mean, ship?"

Teddy snorts laughter at that, finally defusing some of the tension, before wrapping me in his arms. He picks me up—much to my surprise—and carries me into the living room before sitting on the couch, holding me in his lap.

"Sorry, Pixie. I guess it's an alpha and omega thing. Sam's scent calls to me. To the point that I was already distracted before we got to the ceremony. Now being in his space, it's taking a lot of willpower not to just drag him into the bed and bite him. From what I remember of alpha training, it's probably the same with him. We seem to be very scent compatible. I feel like he's mine. But, you...I feel like you're mine too. Which is a bit of a surprise."

Teddy's arms squeeze me tighter before one hand reaches up to turn my face towards Sam. "It doesn't hurt that he's stupidly hot, either, does it?" He chuckles against my hair and lets my jaw go so I can face him again.

"But I'm sorry that my hormones cause the freaky mood swings. When you turned away a minute ago my crazy omega shit read it as rejection, and it felt like everything was falling apart. I don't want you to feel bad, ever. But especially not if you don't want to be with me...us. It's completely up to you, Pixie."

"But I'm not an alpha, or another omega, how could I be yours?" *Yup, I'm still stuck on that.* Other than the basics of sex ed in school, I have *no* idea about alpha or omega relationships. At the same time, my body feels like it wants to melt into Teddy as his rumbly purr starts up again. He's back to poking me in the butt with his erection, and part of me is trying really hard to ignore it.

The other part is deep in thought when Sam settles next to us on the couch a few minutes later. One of his big hands starts rubbing down my back while the other strokes Teddy's hair. Sam isn't that much bigger than my omega, but he seems more dominant with him than me.

My omega, wait...what?

I practically melt into a puddle in Teddy's lap with their dual purrs and stroking hands. My eyes close and I just breathe in—there's a sudden startling thought. Their scents remind me of home. It's not the same as my beta family's subtle scents, but reminds me of Mom baking in the kitchen, especially around the holidays. Teddy's spicy vanilla and cinnamon makes me feel warm and cozy and calm.

While Sam's sawdust and cedar make me think of Daddy's workshop. He built me a hope chest when I was twelve. He isn't very good at it, there are a few gaps in the boards, and it's a little lopsided, but he tried, and while I never used it for keeping mating stuff, I love how my grandma's patchwork quilt always smells like cedar when I take it out in the fall.

His cedar scent also makes me think of holidays. Tromping through the woods with my dad and brother, trying to find just the right tree for Christmas. Sometimes it was pine, but one year the perfect tree Daddy insisted we needed was a cedar that was almost fifteen feet tall. So, he climbed the tree and chopped off just the top seven feet, and we dragged it home. I still see it sometimes, in the winter when I go for walks behind the house. It's taller now, but the top never grew back in the same.

Of course, Tuck and I both had to promise not to tell Mom that he was climbing trees in the ice and snow carrying a saw. Otherwise, I think he would have come back and gotten it without us later. Mom loved it, and Dad was extra proud that year. Sam's smell reminds me of that tree, and I have to fight my body not to lean back across both their laps and just curl up for a nap. Today was kind of stressful, but I shouldn't be this tired.

Sam's hand pauses on my shoulder. "I got the sandwiches, if you two are still hungry?" It drags my attention over to the coffee table, and sure enough there are three plates of sandwiches, a bag of wavy chips with some sour cream and onion dip. I'm about to apologize again for not knowing what each person wanted and just making a variety of stuff I like, but Teddy scoots me around so he can reach down for two plates. He passes one to me before taking a huge bite out of the other one without even checking what's inside.

His arm wraps back around my waist, holding me against him as he eats with one hand. Sam looks back and forth between the two of us before getting his own plate and digging in, offering up the chips after Teddy finishes.

We sit in relative silence, a few mumbles of appreciation, but otherwise just being close. Once the plates are empty, Sam picks up the dishes and heads to the kitchen, while I'm still perched across Teddy's lap, and it's starting to get really uncomfortable. He's comfortable—other than me being poked in the butt—but I don't know what to do now. I should probably message Steph and make sure everything's ok and then head home. Now I feel like whining myself, because I really don't want to. Finally dislodging myself, I make the excuse of needing the bathroom and Teddy reluctantly lets me go.

Chapter 7

Sam

After putting up lunch supplies, I let Jake back in. I left him outside to give Teddy and Kelly some space while they got cleaned up and ate. But this is Jake's house as much as mine, and despite my talk of him being a guard dog, he really is just a big floppy cuddle fiend. He bounds into the house, nearly knocking me over in his search for Kelly and more attention before stalling out, and wagging himself in circles around Teddy.

Teddy reaches down and rubs his hand over the top of Jake's head, flopping his ears around, and Jake immediately drops to the ground, groaning loudly and demanding belly rubs.

I wonder if that would work for me with either one of them?

That thought, of course, flashes my mind back to Kelly earlier in my driveway squatting down in the short dress to pet him, and I have to reach down to adjust myself again. I feel like a fucking letch.

Kelly comes back from the bathroom, and I grab the bottles of water and soda I pulled out of the fridge, just in case either one of them needs a drink. The alpha part of me wants to take care of both of them, make sure they're fed and comfortable, and keep them here. I'm amazed that Teddy agreed to stay earlier, and my mind is circling, wondering how I can ask him to stay longer than the next week, like, maybe forever.

Kelly walks over to him and kneels on the floor next to Jake, rubbing her hands in big strokes down his stomach. His tail is thumping both the coffee table and the couch, and he wiggles from side to side enjoying all the attention. I watch Teddy watching Kelly, the man looks as jealous as I feel right now. The major difference is he does something about it, bringing his hand down and touching Kelly's head as it's bent over Jake. Rubbing his fingers down her hair and through the curls spiraling down her back. Her head tilts up and their eyes meet, her mouth drops open in a little moan as he twists his hand, looping the hair around it, and tugging lightly.

These jeans are not going to do a fucking thing to hide my erection.

Fuck.

I carry the drinks in, sitting them on the coffee table and looking down at Kelly, her eyes are slightly glassy as she continues to stare up at the omega.

Fuck, I want him to be my *omega...*my *omega and* my *beta in* my *house.*

A low possessive growl rumbles through my chest, and Teddy smirks at me before releasing Kelly's hair and offering his hand to help her stand up. "This is what I was talking about earlier, Kelly. I want you, I want Sam too, and I'm pretty sure the feeling's mutual." He looks at me for confirmation and I'm sure I'm doing an admirable impersonation of a bobble head.

"As far as my inner omega is concerned, you two are already mine. Now, I really want to kiss you, maybe more. But there's no pressure, I'm here for at least a week. Do you think you might want to see where this goes?" Kelly's cheeks are bright red as she looks between the two of us, and I can practically hear the wheels turning in her mind.

She addresses Teddy, as he seems to have taken charge. "Is that...normal? I mean, I don't want to get in the way of you and your alpha? I don't know...um...how everything would work?"

Teddy lets out a low chuckle, capturing her chin and tipping her face towards his. "Oh, Pixie, I can think of at least five different ways that this would work with the three of us together, another seven if we're only together two at a time, but to be fair, I've only had this afternoon to come up with it, so if you give me a little time, I'm sure I can figure out a few more."

She's intent on his face, searching for the truth behind what he just said, if he actually wants her, if an alpha and an omega can share a beta. It's rare, I'll admit, but I've never wanted anyone like I do these two. I've never seen myself forming any sort of a pack after what happened with Joseph; I always just thought it would be me and Jake. Now that the possibility for more has presented itself, I want it. I want it so damned much.

Teddy

I don't want to push, I don't want to scare Kelly away, but I need her to make a decision, because I'm all in. Sam seems to be too, if the look of hunger in his eyes is any indication. It's odd because while I've met and been rejected by a ton of packs, I never actually cared before. There's something about Sam that feels completely mine, and now that I found him, he's going to have to pry me off with a fuckin' crowbar if he wants to get rid of me.

"This doesn't need to go any farther right now, Pixie, I just need to know if you want this...want us...before I get any more attached. Ok? Omegas tend to fall hard and fast when they find their pack, I want you both to be mine." I watch Kelly's throat bob a couple of times as she tries to get her bearings, her mind spinning back on anything she knows about alphas and omegas.

It's not much if I'm remembering correctly what they teach in biology. We all went to the same classes, but then alphas went to a separate class and omegas or suspected omegas went in a different group, and the betas were released early. It's no wonder she's confused, but as long as she's ok with trying, a pack of three sounds just about perfect right now.

"I think...as long as it's ok with Sam"—she nods towards him—"that I'd like to try. I mean, I have a lot to learn. I don't know much of anything about alphas or omegas, but I know you two feel right...You make me feel like I'm home."

I cut off anything else she's about to say, scooping her up into my arms, and kissing her until her mouth opens under mine. She lets out a low needy moan, and I pull away enough to see Sam has moved in behind her. His hands come down and lift her thighs, wrapping them around my hips as we sandwich the little beta between our two big bodies.

My hands come up to cup her face, memorizing her, my thumb tracing the line of her jaw, her eyebrow. When it skates over her mouth her tongue flicks out and I bite my lip to stifle the omega whine that's trying to escape. "Do we need to stop, Pixie? The choice is up to you. I'll be happy to drag Sam upstairs by myself if this is moving too fast for you." Kelly shakes her head, which I think means to keep going, but I need actual consent here. "Words, Pixie. Stop or keep going?"

"Going, please Teddy. Keep going." Her hushed whisper is barely a breath across my face. But Sam hears it too, if his rumbly groan is any indication. His hands slide from her thighs to my hips, pulling me tighter against the two of them. I'm already hard as a fucking rock with her grinding against me, whimpering every time she rolls her hips against my length.

I look over her shoulder, meeting Sam's eyes. This is his house, and I'm the omega, but if he wants me to be in charge, I can. He nods and my hands drop to wrap around Kelly's shoulder and under her ass so he can step away. She cuddles against me as the cooler air hits her back. Sam runs his hand down her hair and across my fingers before turning and leading us up the stairs.

It takes a bit of balance, but Kelly isn't heavy enough to cause me problems walking up stairs while carrying her. We follow Sam into what I can only assume is the master bedroom. It's huge, with a large captain's bed in the center, and neatly stacked bookshelves lining the rest of the wall. There's an old brick fireplace recessed into the opposite end of the room with closed doors on either side. Large windows cover the wall across from the entry, looking out over the small back garden and trees behind the house. I can't see his workshop from this point, but I bet if I walked over near the fireplace, I'd see it setting off to the side.

The floor is wood, but mostly covered by large rugs. Runners on both sides of the bed, and another large one at the end. I'm mildly ashamed that I know what runners are, but home decorating is a mandatory class if you want to go to college at the omega center. So is cooking and sewing, but I still burned every damned thing I tried to make in the kitchen. I can make some pretty awesome patches for my jacket now, so I guess that's a win.

Sam's standing beside the bed, hand rubbing the back of his neck like he's not sure what to do next, and I chuckle a little at his discomfort. He's older than I am, but I wonder how much experience he has being a lone alpha. The poor guy looks a little lost.

Kelly wiggles in my grip, grinding against my erection and I don't try to suppress the whine that slips out, causing her to freeze and stutter out an apology. I rub my nose up the side of her neck, taking in as much of her scent as I can get. A shudder runs through my frame. She smells like mine, so does Sam. I want to pull her against me, see if I can get her to grind harder. I nip at the tender skin of her neck, and her arms tighten around me, her body twitching. Sam is watching us now, and I wonder where the dominant alpha from downstairs went. The one who helped me cage her between us.

"Kelly girl, I need you to look at me, ok?" She pulls back, her eyes are shuttered and her face flushed. "Kelly, do you want this, do you want Sam and me? Completely? Are we moving too fast for you?" Consent is key, I'm not sure how many times that's been drilled in at the omega center. I mean, I always knew it was important, but it never really clicked with *how* important. Kelly's head bobs up and down loosely, and the dark chuckle I hear from Sam snaps my own spine straight.

There's the alpha I want.

I can be dominant, despite being an omega, and I always was with Vee. He wasn't submissive unless it was just the two of us. He was never super dominant with anyone, but he always deferred to me. That was before my designation came in. Would he be more dominant now? What does his alpha bark sound like? And why do I care when I'll never see him again?

Kelly's stuttered reply yanks me out of my downward spiral. Her breath warm against my neck. "Yes, Teddy. I want you both. I'm just nervous. This is all new territory for me." Her eyes are huge as they meet mine, big and brown and so deep I could drown in them. Bringing one hand up to rub the back of her neck, I comb my fingers through her hair, using it as an excuse to trace down her spine and back under her ass to keep her against me. Her tiny moan turns into a helpless giggle and I note that she's ticklish for later.

My eyes meet Sam's over her shoulder, nodding slightly, silently asking him to step back in, and relieved when he takes the hint. His hands come around Kelly's front, unbuttoning her shorts, and then sliding up her stomach as she shudders against me. Her arms loosen and she leans into Sam, one hand reaching up to wrap around the back of his neck as well. His low growl sends a shiver up my spine, and my hips jerk against Kelly where she still has us pinned together with her legs.

Sam takes the opening she gives, his hands tracing up under her shirt, cupping her through her bra. I can see his fingers moving under the thin material in front of me, caressing her stiff nipples through the fabric. One hand disappears, sliding behind her, and then the whole thing comes loose and drops to the floor.

Kelly lets out a loud giggle. "Sorry, it's strapless, I had to wear it for that dress." Sam rumbles his appreciation for full access against the side of her throat and her laughter turns into a high moan as he cups her breasts again with no fabric between their skin. Fuck, but I want to taste her. See if she tastes as light and sweet as she smells.

Now that Sam is supporting her as well, my hand slides around her thigh, up her waist, and pushes up her shirt so I can bend forward and taste her skin. She's so soft, and smooth as silk under my lips as I lave her right peak with my tongue, causing her to jerk and moan. Sam pulls gently at the left, as he nips his teeth against the exposed column of her throat. Soon she's a writhing mess between us, whimpering in need and rolling her hips against me. Sam's eyes flash up to mine, and I realize he's wearing entirely too much clothing. Hell, we all are.

"Do you want to see your sexy alpha without a shirt, Little Pixie?" I practically purr against her chest. And she lets out a whimper at the touch of my teeth against her tender flesh. Her head tilts up, meeting Sam's eyes, nodding to him.

Sam growls and steps back. Pulling free of her hold, he strips his shirt off in one quick move and my mouth goes dry. His torn and faded jeans sit low on his hips, showing off most of his v-cut, and hugging the thick outline of his erection. His abs make me feel more than a little self-conscious about my own thicker shape. I guess working for the fire department he has to stay in shape—and what a fucking shape it is.

I drag my eyes away to take in Kelly's reaction, and her head is tilted back as she stares. Her tongue coming out to wet her lips makes me think I'm not the only one who wants to lick the alpha pop in front of us. Part of me is tempted to set her down so we can do just that, see how long it takes the two of us together to bring Sam to his knees, literally.

This train of thought isn't hindered any when he pops the button on those already low jeans and slides them off, his cock springing free and thumping against his stomach. His knot already swelling slightly at the base.

I let out a needy little whine as Kelly wiggles against me. Sam lets out a small laugh, both hands coming down to cover himself. "I'm feelin' a little underdressed over here bein' the only one naked." The tips of his ears are red, and I finally release my arms, letting Kelly squirm free. All her earlier hesitation seems gone as she takes in Sam, standing in front of us. She lifts her own shirt over her head, leaving only those tiny little shorts trying to slide down her hips with the button undone.

Sam growls low and deep, stepping up to our beta, and cupping her chin. Dragging her lips to his, he claims her mouth, devouring her moans as he lowers his hands to wrap around her waist. He shoves against her shorts until they drag her blue panties with them to the floor. Not breaking the kiss, he wraps his hands under her ass, lifting her and wrapping her legs around his waist. She seems completely lost in him, nipping at his bottom lip before nuzzling her face against his scruffy jaw, and down his neck.

Chapter 8
Teddy

Sam's eyes are glued to me now, and I'm super self-conscious. I'm not in bad shape, but I'm thicker than he is. My omega side trying to keep me softer. Even without the extra layers of padding, I don't have his body shape. My gym buddy, Sarah, at the omega center, pulls up the extra thicc meme every time she sees me shirtless in the gym, and we laugh about how hard it is for omegas to get really good muscle definition. Neither of us are even overweight, but I know that it's a way of coping for her too.

If he is my alpha, then he can accept me the way I am. I swallow the lump in my throat and strip off my borrowed shirt, keeping my eyes on the floor as I shuck the basketball shorts I'm wearing before I finally raise my eyes to see them both watching me.

Kelly's cheeks are a deeper pink as she stares unblinking at me over her shoulder. Her lips parted, and I watch in fascination again as her tongue darts out to moisten them. Her eyes flick down briefly to my cuffs, but she doesn't say anything about my leaving them on. Sam meets my eyes, a low possessive growl building in his chest as he lets her slide down before stepping up to me. He takes my face in his hands before kissing me hard and swallowing my whimper of surprise.

I feel smaller hands run down my skin as Kelly circles behind me, wrapping her arms around my waist and pressing her chest against my spine, her fingers trace down my stomach and Sam jerks against me, pulling away when her knuckles graze against his abs. Apparently, he's ticklish too.

He's still holding me, his hands cupping my cheeks. He leans in, rubbing his face against me, scent marking me before leaning down to kiss a trail of fire along my jaw and neck. My body stretches towards him, and Kelly follows the movement, her face pressed against my back. I hear her inhale, breathing in our combined scents as her body softens against mine. Before shuddering and tensing slightly.

"Guys, I'm sorry, but I have a totally unsexy thing we need to talk about." Her voice is muffled against my skin, but I manage to turn in her arms, my own coming around her shoulders. My fingers slide through her hair, wrapping it close against her scalp and tipping her head back so she has to meet our eyes.

Sam's chin rests on my shoulder, his chest against my back, purr melting my tense muscles.

Kelly looks up at me, biting against her lower lip. I watch her throat as she swallows a few times before her tongue flicks out, soothing over the abused flesh. "I'm...um...my...I was having a bad reaction to my last birth control." Sam's snarl draws her eyes to him. "I was taking it to help regulate my periods, they were kind of crazy. But they were causing other problems. So...I'm not on any right now. It's been a few months...and, since I don't...um...I'm not in a...Shoot!"

She swallows again, her eyes squeezing shut before everything comes out in a rush. "I don't know if you have any condoms, but I can't have unprotected sex because I'm not on birth control. And I really want to, but *I* don't want kids!" She takes a big breath and opens her eyes; she looks shocked when Sam chuckles beside my ear.

His deep purr rumbles back to life, his voice now soft and soothing in my ear as he reaches around my body, cupping her jaw, almost like he did mine earlier. "Thank you for telling us, Sugar, and I'm sure we can work somethin' out. I'm not exactly lookin' to start a family right now, especially since I just found the two of you."

He chuckles and his finger boops the end of her nose. "Looks like we'll have to be satisfied just tasting you today, huh?" I don't bother holding back my groan, and Kelly lets out a little squeak when my erection jerks against her stomach.

Sam turns his head, his teeth grazing my neck, and I melt against him. His fingertips take her chin, tilting her face down and I release her hair as he pulls me back against him, his other hand circling around and gripping my cock hard. I shudder in his arms and Kelly's tongue comes out again, another torturous slow swipe of wetting her lips.

"Do you wanna taste our omega first, Sugar? Before it's his turn." He strokes me slowly, his thumb coming up to spread the moisture leaking from my tip. Kelly's eyes seem to swallow her whole face as she watches his hand. I let out a whine of need as he squeezes me harder.

Fuck it feels good to have someone else's hands on me. I've been alone for so fucking long.

My head drops back, resting against his shoulder as his hand continues to pump, my eyes squeeze shut of their own accord, letting the sensations roll through me. I almost miss the soft shuffle against the rug as Kelly kneels in front of me. Sam's hand stops stroking me, but he still holds firm, angling me down. My eyes snap open when I feel Kelly's tongue against my overheated member, a tiny tentative lick followed by a moan then a more confident lick.

Her smaller hands come up to hold me as her lips wrap around the crown, her tongue rolls against the underside of my overheated flesh, and she moans again. The vibration sends shivers up my spine. My knees try to unhinge, and I have to lean heavily against Sam.

He releases my shaft, one hand going around my waist, the other tangling in my hair as he turns my head enough to kiss me hard. Between their mouths I'm nearly undone, and soon I have to pull away from Sam, panting into his neck as he grinds his own arousal against my ass. He rolls his hips against me, and a needy omega whine escapes, unbidden, from my throat. I can feel slick dripping down the back of my thighs, and I have a brief flash of embarrassment before Sam's purr ripples into a possessive snarl.

Fuck, I could die happy right here.

"Do you want this, Omega?" Each word is punctuated by a thrust, and yes, I want it. I want it so fucking much. My hips jerk involuntarily and Kelly coughs and sputters, pulling away.

Sam and I both freeze. *Shit.* "Sorry, Pixie, are you ok?" I feel like an ass.

She squints up at me, her eyes watering, but gives me a lop-sided grin. "Sorry, you're not exactly small, and I'm learning as I go. Also, you taste really good. Sorry if I was being overly aggressive." I laugh a bit, not sure how to tell her I enjoyed her aggression very much. I offer her my hand up, and her bottom lip comes out in a little pout before she takes it, letting me pull her back to standing.

"I don't know, Teddy. I think it's only fair if you repay the favor after that little slip-up." Sam is whispering in my ear, but Kelly can obviously hear him, judging by the flush slowly creeping up her chest and neck. His hands are tight on my hips, as he holds himself against me, his teeth scraping over my pulse.

Kelly watches us, fascination and desire clear on her face. "Go crawl up on the bed, Pixie, get comfortable." She smiles up at me before scampering away, the sway of her hips drawing both our gazes. Sam grumbles when she tries to crawl up on the tall bed and slips twice. Finally, she flops her upper torso across the mattress, holding onto the blanket and scrambling up.

"Remind me to build her some stairs for the bed," Sam mumbles against my back. I didn't even realize it was taller than normal, but I guess when you can build your own furniture you can make it whatever size you want. His arms disappear and I walk towards the bed. Kelly has crawled up the mattress and is trying to pull down blankets, struggling against the heavy duvet and piles of pillows. She finally lowers it enough that she can wiggle down under the blankets.

I can't stop my guffaw as her feet finally disappear and a lump moves around under the covers, her head finally popping back out a few seconds later. It makes me think of an old Bugs Bunny cartoon where he dives into his rabbit hole before springing back out again. Except this bunny is sexy as fuck.

Ok, technically crossdressing Bugs was sometimes hot too, but this is not the time for those sorts of mental gymnastics.

"What the hell is she doin'?" Sam wonders aloud behind me.

"You told me to get comfortable, I need blankets for that." Kelly stares over at us with a look that says we're asking obvious questions.

There's that dark chuckle again from Sam as he circles the bed and looks down at her. She seems to be cozy, but that wasn't really what we were going for. "It's not time to sleep yet, Kelly Girl." He flips the blankets off with one hand, and she does look comfortable, her arms and thighs wrapped around a pillow.

I want to be that pillow.

She ducks her head, that adorable blush back in her cheeks. "Sorry, yeah, that makes sense. I just...It's been a strange day ok, and your mattress is really snuggly and I spaced. Sorry." Her eyes flip up to Sam, but he's just smiling at her.

"Well, I'll be glad to have you curled up in here later, but for now, how about we get Teddy over here to lick your sweet little cunt, while I take care of him, hmm?" Her whole body shudders and I don't think it's from the cold in the room.

Chapter 9

Kelly

*H**oly green guacamole, that's intense.*

My eyes flick back and forth between Sam and Teddy. I understand how this works, I do. I'm not an idiot. But why would anybody want to lick me down there? I mean, ok, I totally understand why you would want to go down on someone you care about.

The look on Teddy's face makes me wish I could purr, but he's an omega, he tastes good. He has the snickerdoodle flavor going on, but I'm a beta, I don't really smell like anything. I don't think I taste like anything fancy at least. The one time I tasted myself, just to check, it was just kind of salty. I don't really see the appeal, but Teddy's eyes are full of heat as he raises his leg onto the bed.

He didn't have to struggle to get up here.

I'm not even short, but this bed is stupidly tall.

My brain is getting sidetracked again.

I stretch my body out as Teddy crawls towards me, finally letting go of the pillow I curled around for snuggles. *I am such an idiot.* He grabs my ankle and pulls it gently to him, causing me to roll onto my back. Leaving a trail of kisses up my leg, he hovers over me. Nipping lightly at my hip, he causes another full body shiver before continuing up my stomach.

It feels amazing when he captures my lips, his big body settling between my thighs. "Sorry, Pixie, I just wanted to make sure I got in some more kisses on these lips before I move on to the others." He smiles the sweetest smile before leaning in.

The sweet smile was a lie!

Teddy devours my gasp, his tongue taking my shock as an invitation and diving in to lick me. He brings his big hands up, holding me in place as he plunders my mouth, and I can't stop my hips from wiggling and squirming underneath him.

What his tongue is doing to me seems to have a direct line of sparks to between my legs. He groans into my mouth as I writhe and thrash. He smells so good right now, and the room is filled with a combination of his and Sam's scents.

I need more. I need some sort of pressure or I might just melt on the bed here, but he just keeps kissing me. Stroking that tight feeling inside me until I need a release. I've been kissed before, but never like this. Kissing never made me squirm, not sure if I'm trying to escape or get closer.

A loud growl beside us makes my head snap in that direction, and Teddy keeps kissing and nipping down my jaw and throat, his big body dragging down mine. A trail of friction against my skin, but not where I need it.

"Fuck, you two look so damned good together." Sam's words grind out, almost unintelligible from his growl. His hand comes down on Teddy's neck, twisting around his hair, and pulling his head back. "You're not the only one who wants a taste, Omega." Teddy lets out a high whine, his eyes rolling back as his hips grind against my leg. His body seeking friction automatically.

"Please, Alpha." Teddy's voice is higher, his pelvis rolling against me. "Please, I need..." His pleas are cut off, Sam comes down and claims his mouth hard, his body hovering over mine as Teddy jerks and twists his hips. I can't see much from this angle, and I wonder if they'd notice if I wiggled around to get a better look.

At the first shift of my body Sam pulls back, Teddy's eyes are glassy and unfocused. And my leg feels kind of slippery and wet. "Please, Alpha. I need you. Both of you." Teddy's voice is a breathy whisper, as Sam pulls him up—leading him by the hair—onto his knees, before pushing his head down towards my core. Teddy doesn't waste any time, his tongue coming out to flick over my clit as his hands spread my thighs wider. Sam's other hand comes down on my stomach, holding me in place while Teddy devours me.

I nearly jackknife off the bed as his tongue slides over my sensitive nub, before moving down to dip inside me. Sam's hand is the only thing keeping me from vibrating off the bed. He holds Teddy in place for a few moments, before releasing his hair, but then he's on me. His mouth devours mine, and it's just as good as Teddy's. Though not in the same way.

His cedar scent invades my nose, still sweet and spicy, but also muskier and the way he holds me down while he plunders my mouth is more dominant. Taking my moans and whimpers, devouring me as his hand slides up from my stomach to tease and flick my hard nipples. Then cupping and squeezing my breasts until they ache.

I cry out against Sam's lips as Teddy's fingers find my entrance, teasing inside before taking up a steady rhythm. My skin feels too tight, and I'm overwhelmed by sensation, everything spinning and flying apart. I shudder and twist against the pressure, the tight cord running through my body finally snapping. I feel like I'll shatter from the recoil, only held together by their hands and mouths against me.

Sam's hands turn gentle, soft strokes and caresses against my sensitive breasts, as he pulls back and looks down at me. "Such a good girl, coming so hard like that for our omega." Something inside me sits up and takes notice at being called a good girl, and I have a brief moment of self-reflection before he continues.

"Now, do you want to help me out with Teddy, reward him for making you feel so good?" Sam reaches down and strokes Teddy's hair. His head is resting on my leg, nuzzling against my inner thigh, his tongue running over the tender skin there. The eyes that meet mine are glazed and hooded.

I look back to Sam, unsure exactly what to say, how to react. Yes, I want to help Teddy feel good, but I don't know what to do. Sex is out, and honestly, I'm super sensitive down there right now, so I say the only thing I can think of, "Yes, Alpha. What should I do?" It probably sounds stupid to him that I don't know, but when he beams down at me, I guess that was the right answer.

"Can you do what you were doing to him earlier, Sugar? Take him in your mouth again? Don't worry, I'll try to keep his hips still, ok?" They already made me feel so good, I want to make them feel good too, so I just nod and roll up into a sitting position. Sam's eyes track my movement, and he licks his lips before taking my chin between his finger and thumb.

"I get to taste you next time, Sugar. See how sweet you really are. But hopefully we can also figure out the contraceptive situation soon for all three of us." He leans down and gives me a quick peck on the lips, then crawls up onto the bed behind the smaller man and runs his hands over Teddy's still elevated hips.

Sam twists his hand into Teddy's hair again, the other hand on his shoulder. He pulls the omega back, and Teddy lifts and bends, his back arching, his breath coming in heavy pants. I crawl towards him, he's already covered in pre-come and slick, and I kneel in front of him, wrapping my hands around his hard length and licking him like a lollipop. A snickerdoodle-flavored lollipop. His whole body shudders and he lets out a long omega whine. Sam meets my eyes over his shoulder. "I know I asked you to help, little beta, but patience, please." He smiles down at me, and I back off.

I can hear soft murmurs as he whispers something in Teddy's ear, but I only catch the response. "Yes, Alpha. Please. I need it. It hurts." Sam's eyebrows draw down and he looks concerned, running his hands over Teddy. Petting his hair and back and arms before pushing him forward again. "Now be good for me, sweet boy, bend forward and kiss our pretty beta."

Teddy reaches for me, and I kneel in front of him as he pulls me close, claiming my mouth in a desperate kiss, moaning into me with whatever Sam is doing behind him. I stroke his face and shoulders, capturing his noises and gently nipping at his lips.

He groans louder and pulls me tight against him, almost crushing the air out of my lungs in his need. His whole body twitching and shaking. Sam groans loudly behind him, and I peer over his shoulder to see him buried all the way to the knot inside Teddy.

Teddy twitches and moans against me as Sam gently pulls him upright again. "You ready my sweet girl?" I don't bother answering, lowering my face back to Teddy and pretending he's a lollipop again. He tastes so good, and my head bobs up and down, sucking him almost to the back of my throat.

I don't want to go too far in case he thrusts again. Still, Sam seems to have things in hand, because while Teddy is twitching and whimpering, he doesn't thrust into me again. His breathing is coming in ragged pants, sawing in and out of his lungs. Pleading words fall from his lips, but I don't know who he's talking to. I can't make anything out other than, "please, please, please."

Teddy's hands come down, wrapping in my hair, pulling it back from my face and I look up at him as he tries to pull me away. "Please, Kelly, I'm...Oh, fuck, Kelly. Please, I'm about to come, please. I need..." I know I want to make him feel as good as possible so I suck harder, taking him as far back as I can without gagging.

His hips twitch backwards, and I can see Sam's fingers tighten on his hip hard enough to dimple. Sam growls against his throat and Teddy jolts, his hips jerking backwards until Sam is flush against his back. Less than a second later he spills in my mouth. And while I enjoy how he tastes, the texture is unexpected. I pull away, trying to swallow, but some of it escapes anyway, it's too thick to get down easily. I really need a glass of water right now.

But it's more than worth it to see the blissed out look in both their eyes as I lean back. Sam has both arms wrapped around our omega's chest, his purr a deep rumble I can feel even from my vantage point, as he rubs his jaw against Teddy's head. Teddy looks completely euphoric, a small smile on his face as he turns and tries to nuzzle into Sam. I kinda want in on the snuggle action, so I move closer again, and as soon as I'm within arms' reach Teddy pulls me against him, both of their arms holding me close.

I could totally get used to this, they feel so good, so...mine.
I wonder if they'll let me stay the night.
Mom is gonna flip.

With that sobering thought, all my muscles tighten. *Way to bring down the mood, Kelly.* Both my guys respond to my body tensing as well, Teddy's eyes coming back into focus as he looks down at me. "Shit, Pixie, I am so, *so* sorry, I tried to move you, you just felt so good—and with Sam...I tried to warn you—"

Sam looks almost as panicked and I don't want to cause either one of them to worry, so I try to rush and explain. "No, it's...it's not you...It's me." Teddy sniffs loudly, his head dropping as I try to rush on. "God that sounded messed up. I mean, I was wondering if you would be ok letting me stay here and cuddle tonight." Sam looks relieved and Teddy's smile could light up a room. "Then I realized I'll have to explain this to my parents, and they are probably gonna freak." I shrug after that last bit, because I realize it doesn't matter.

I don't want to hurt my parents. I love them, and they're some of my favorite people. When I told them I was going to date Sal, they were fine with it. They said they didn't care if it was a man or a woman, as long as they treated me right and we were happy, that was all that matters.

This'll be fine. After snuggles, I'll go ahead and call them. Then if Teddy and Sam are ok with it, I can go grab a change of clothes and pajamas and can come back to make burgers for dinner and have a big cuddle pile in this big cozy bed. Everything will be fine.

Chapter 10

Sam

*T*hings are not fine!

I wake up to the most amazing snuggles. I don't even remember falling asleep. I feel a tug and then Teddy jerks in my arms. Kelly's sitting up in front of him, and he's looking up at her. Both of their eyes are sleepy and dazed, slowly waking up to the sound of Jake barking downstairs. Soon the brain fog clears enough that I'm swinging my leg over the side of the bed to go let him out for a bathroom break. I don't register that he sounds actually aggressive until I hear yelling and someone pounding on my front door.

Kelly scrambles to put her clothes back on while I pull on my jeans from earlier, I don't even know where the hell my underwear went, and I just hope like hell I don't zip up anything important trying to get downstairs. Kelly's rushing out the door while Teddy's still trying to find the basketball shorts I loaned him earlier, and I'm torn between helping my omega and chasing after my beta. I don't think Jake would cause any problems, but he does love to jump, and I don't want him to get overly excited and knock her down again. Regardless, the choice is out of my hands when Teddy waves me after her, looking annoyed.

I hurry down the steps, noticing that Jake finally stopped barking, but the knocking and yelling are getting louder. To my surprise and relief, Jake is standing sideways between Kelly and the door, a low aggressive snarl ripping from his chest.

His side is against her, pressing her away from the door as he watches it like he is going to shred whoever tries to come through. I joke that he's not much of a guard dog, but maybe it just needs to be the right person. He looks at me when I get to the bottom of the stairs, his tail wags a few times before he turns his watchful glare back to the door.

"Police, open up!" More banging on my front door, and I don't know what the fuck is going on. I run my hand down Jake's back, over Kelly's fingers where she's holding him, and head to the door.

"I'm opening the door, hold on." I prefer to give a warning, just in case. I don't know why the hell they're here, but with all the noise they were making, they must think they have a good reason. I undo the deadbolt and door lock and stick my head out. I don't want to open it all the way due to how Jake is acting, but I also don't want to leave them waiting while I put him away.

Two police officers are standing on my porch, both alphas. One I know, Paul Miller. We were in the same graduating class in high school. Nice enough guy, we were never friends, but he has a pleasant oak-y scent that makes me think of whiskey barrels. He's one of the few people in this town I could have seen forming a pack with, if I hadn't been so busy chasing Joseph around.

I don't know his partner, he seems a bit younger, but I don't recognize him, which is strange. In this town everybody knows everybody. So, it's just something I wonder briefly about, more so when he unclips the taser on his belt. His astringent fake lemon smell automatically makes me think of furniture polish.

Miller tosses him a bit of a glare before turning to me. "Hey, Sam. Sorry for the craziness, but we need to talk to you for a minute. Can we come inside?"

I look back at Jake, who's still staring intently at the door before I answer. "Yeah, officers…just…you freaked Jake out, lemme get him put away before I let you in, ok. He's usually really friendly, but all the yellin' and hammerin' on the door seem to have made him a bit possessive."

I don't mention that it might be the fact that he's guarding Kelly that put him in a protective mood, but they'll probably figure that out soon enough. I close the door and turn around, but Kelly already has a hand on Jake's collar. His tail wags happily, a big doggy grin on his face as he follows her towards the bathroom she used earlier.

Jake stops for a minute, turning slightly to watch Teddy come down the stairs. Then turns back and trots happily after Kelly when she snaps her fingers and points to the bathroom door. I sure as hell didn't teach him that, or at least, he never learned it when I tried taking him to obedience classes. I hear her telling him what a good dog he is and see her reach through the door, to give him an ear scratch before she asks him to be a good boy and closes the door. Teddy waits for her at the bottom of the stairs, and they're standing there holding hands when I get the front door open again, both officers walk into my home. Miller is polite, nodding at me, and nodding at Teddy and Kelly before taking a seat on the couch. I'm sure he's curious about Teddy, like I said, everyone knows everyone else in town.

The new guy though, his head swivels around trying to take in everything at once. His name tag says Ross, and I don't really care for officer Ross, right outta the gate. He's being an ass, as he marches over to Kelly and gets into her personal space, trying to scent her. "Ma'am, are you here against your will? We were called out on suspicion of an abducted omega." Officer Ross is showing no concern for her personal boundaries, and I'm sure if she was an omega she would be freaking the fuck out right now.

I turn my hard glare at Miller. "Can you do something about your partner there before I have to kick him out of my goddamned house? You're welcome to stay, and we'll be happy to answer any questions you have, but this is ridiculous." I don't mention that Teddy looks ready to flip his shit now that Kelly is backed up behind him, trying to get away from the overly aggressive officer asshole.

"Ross! Get'cher ass over here and sit down now, you're acting like a rabid dog, and I don't doubt that Miss Kelly—*who is a beta*—will be happy to get the chief involved if you keep it up. Hell, Sam here works at the fire station. This is a check-in, not a fuckin' arrest."

Officer Ross looks between Teddy, Kelly, and Miller, confusion clear on his face. "I hate to contradict you, Paul...er...Miller, but she doesn't smell much like a beta. You sure?"

The low rumbling growl that rips from Teddy seems to surprise everyone, as Kelly's arms slip around his chest from behind. Officer Ross steps back, his hand going back to his belt, and then Jake is slamming against the bathroom door, barking like crazy again.

Fuck my life.

"Alright, you've seen inside my house, let's all step outside before Jake destroys it now. Thanks." Miller stands up, shaking his head as Ross backs towards the door. Teddy turns around, picking Kelly up and carrying her after us.

As we all exit the house, I hear her call out, "It's ok, Jake, my good boy, we'll be right back, just calm down." The frantic thuds against the door quiet but I hear a low howl as we all step outside.

"Now that you've come and disrupted the peace, what the hell's going on, Paul?" I glare at the police officers. I don't have a problem with them normally, but his partner is just pissing me off. I'm not a pleasant person when I wake up anyway, but this shit takes the cake.

"Sorry about that, Sam." Miller glares at his partner again. "Joseph called the station earlier. Brice is frantic, he hasn't seen his cousin since Pack Asher's ceremony earlier today, and he said that they left the community center with you. I don't know if this is some kinda family argument or something, but we had to come out and check. Is anybody else in the house other than you three?"

Kelly is still in Teddy's arms when I look over. She's stroking his face and hair, whispering quietly to him as he stands there, visibly shaking. I turn back to Miller, rubbing my hand down my face. "No, it's just us three. Kelly you already know, and this is Teddy, Brice's cousin, and my omega." Miller looks a bit startled, and Ross's mouth flops open as he gapes at Teddy.

I want to kick the little fuck right off my goddamned porch for making my omega uncomfortable. Instead, I try to explain. "We met earlier today, he had to borrow a shirt to go to the bonding ceremony, since he didn't have any dress clothes when he came to visit. He was uncomfortable and upset and Kelly and I were trying to talk to him and help him calm down. Joseph came over and made a big scene, and Teddy publicly claimed both of us before dragging me out. Kelly followed us. He didn't want to go back to their pack house, so I told him he could stay here for as long as he wanted. We came home, had lunch, and talked about relationship stuff. As soon as the court house opens up on Monday I'm going down to file the necessary paperwork to officially become a pack. Is there anything else?"

This last bit is going to be news to both Kelly and Teddy. While I don't want to rush either one of them, as far as I'm concerned, they're both already mine. Plus, I want to make sure that shit like this fucking circus happening on my front porch doesn't happen again. Miller is nodding to himself, as Ross continues to stare at Teddy like he can't believe what he's seeing.

Fuck man, take a picture, it'll last longer.

A low snarl rips from my chest, startling everyone. Apparently, my inner alpha doesn't like the idea of some random asshole taking a picture of his pack.

Fair enough.

Miller looks deep in thought for a few minutes before turning to Teddy and Kelly. "Miss Kelly, can you please step over here alone?" She strokes Teddy's jaw again and he sets her down gently so she can join us. Unfortunately, that means as soon as she gets close, Ross opens his mouth again. "See sir, she sure doesn't smell like a beta." Kelly comes to stand next to me, reaching out to take my hand, and my chest swells with happiness that she's claiming me back.

Miller openly glares at his partner now. "Of course not, when packs are close...physically, their scents often transfer from one to another. Especially with betas, who don't have much to start with. No offense ma'am." He nods to Kelly at the last bit before turning and walking over to Teddy. He talks to him quietly, confirming my story, and asking if Teddy feels safe, if he needs assistance, and assuring him that they are there to help if he needs anything. I want to growl at having other alphas so close to my unbonded mate, but I understand the legal requirements involved. And honestly, I would appreciate it if an omega was being held against their wishes. But as it is, I'm just frustrated.

Miller talks to Teddy quietly for a few minutes before he comes back over to Kelly and me. "I'm really sorry about all this, Sam. The situation sounds...complicated. Still, I'm happy for you, and you Miss Kelly." He nods again to Kelly. "We'll file the report as a false claim and if Joseph calls again, we'll talk to him. I appreciate your patience." He nods to me one last time before snagging Ross's arm—the idiot is still staring at Teddy, gaping like a fish—and leads him back to their patrol car.

Kelly slips free from my hand and goes back to Teddy, rubbing her face against his chest and wrapping her arms around his waist. I give one final wave to the patrol car before leading my pack back inside.

I immediately go to let Jake out. He hangs his head, looking sheepish and doing his full body wag up to Kelly, circling around her before leaning heavily against her with a huff. I look into the bathroom and see he shredded the shower curtain and chewed up the toilet paper. I can't really blame him, since he was trapped in the bathroom and upset. I just hope this doesn't result in a trip to the vet to have his stomach pumped...again. Damned dog will eat anything that gets near his mouth.

Chapter 11

Settling into the couch next to Kelly, I give in and turn my phone back on. I shut it off when I walked out of the community center earlier. Which ok, my bad that Brice called the fucking cops. I mean, I wouldn't have heard the—I look down at the screen—twenty-five missed calls.

That just seems excessive.

And fifty-two text messages, does Brice have no free time...wait...shit...some of them are from Mom.

Well fuck, why did he have to call them.

I do a quick run-through, Brice starts out as angry, demanding I come back, then asking me to return, then asking if I'm ok. Then Mom, he must have called her when I didn't answer...Fuck my life.

I guess I appreciate being loved, but fuck, I'm hardly helpless.

Brice can go fuck himself, I call Mom back first. She answers on the first ring, crying into the phone. I hear my dads in the background growling and one of them's yelling at me that it's about damned time. I can't tell which one, probably Murph, I don't really care. Fuck, they're supposed to be on vacation right now.

"Calm down, Mom, I'm fine. I didn't mean to worry you guys." I start, since she seems to be having trouble getting words out. I hear more grumbles and then someone must hit speaker phone because everybody's louder.

Suddenly Murph is on the phone. I don't know which one is my biological dad, but he's the pack lead for my family, just another indication that shit has gotten bad if he feels the need to step in. "Son, I love you. Now what the *fuck* were you thinking leaving with a strange alpha!" he yells down the line, and Sam growls at the aggression in his tone.

Even with it not on speaker on our end, he's loud enough that the whole room can hear it. I try to stay calm, because yelling back will just incite more anger, and what I am about to say is already gonna piss the old man off. "Yeah, I need to talk to Mom, not you, so give her back the phone."

There's a brief pause, no one on the other end even breathes before he's roaring into my ear. "You do not make demands of me, young man! Your mother is inconsolable, do you know how worried she's been? We get a call from Brice hours ago that you left a bonding ceremony—that we are just now hearing about—with an unknown alpha and a young beta. Then you refuse to answer his calls or text. We don't know if you turned off your phone, if you're hurt, if you're dead in a ditch somewhere. I was trying to find a way to get home so we could come look for you. You know this cruise was supposed to be an anniversary present for your mother, and now the whole thing is ruined. What do you have to say for yourself?"

Kelly curls around my arm, her whole body shaking. Sam's behind me on the couch. I go ahead and hit speaker because I don't want to risk my eardrums if Murph decides to yell again. "Oh, I'm so sorry if the"—I check the clock on my phone—"five hours I was out of contact was enough to ruin a fucking three week long trip. I'm sorry Brice didn't tell you that I left with his pack leader's brother, Sam, who is my chosen alpha, and our beta, Kelly."

I hear a sharp intake of breath—pretty sure it's Mom—on the other end, but I continue on, my words dripping with sarcasm. "I'm sorry that his public embarrassment of my new pack is a fucking inconvenience for your vacation. Especially since you weren't even home during my only break this year and pawned me off on my cousin, who I haven't seen in years. That is *so* fucking inconsiderate of me. Now, put Mom back on the fucking phone, or I am hanging up, and she can call me when you all get home."

There's a brief pause and a beep before Mom comes back, the rest of the voices all faded to background noise, so I'm guessing she took us off speakerphone. She sniffs loudly in my ear a couple of times. "Oh sweety, I'm so happy for you. Are they nice? How many alphas did you get, are they hot? How about the beta, is he sweet?" Kelly giggles into my arm, and since I'm still on speaker mom hears it.

"Oh, is that him, he sounds kind of...delicate. But that's ok. Hello to my Teddy's new pack, it's nice to meet you! I'm his mom, Jessica. You already heard from my Murphy, but Jared and Noah are here too! Say hi!" We hear mumbles in the background of my dads all giving some form of greeting.

"Ok Mom, well, you heard Kelly earlier, she's our beta, and this is my alpha, Sam." Sam grumbles out his own hello behind me. "So far, it's just the three of us, but yes, they're both hot. I really am sorry that I made you worry. Joseph just started yelling at him for talking to me earlier, and I kind of lost my cool. I didn't mean to mess up your vacation. I miss you guys."

"Aww, Teddy. No, you didn't mess anything up, Honey." I hear a loud snort behind her followed by a slap and Murphy grumbling. "As I was saying, I am so happy for you. And Kelly, hmmm, does this mean I can expect grand-babies soon?" Kelly lets out a croaking sound beside me and starts coughing, causing Jake to wander over and lay his head in her lap, his big brown eyes staring longingly up at her.

"No, Mom, probably not anytime soon. Everything's still pretty new, you know. We're taking things one step at a time, but Sam says he's going to file the official paperwork at the courthouse on Monday. I was going to try to contact the omega center and see about transferring to online classes, so I'll be here once everything's official. I didn't want to bother you on your vacation, so I was going to wait to tell you until you got back. Sorry again."

Jake lets out a low growl and turns towards the door, backing his ass up against Kelly, and a few seconds later someone starts pounding on the door, again. I hear Joseph yelling on the other side but can't make out all the words.

"Mom, I love you, but I'm going to let you get back to enjoying time with your mates. It sounds like Joseph and maybe Brice just showed up here, and I need to—"

Mom cuts me off. "Now just a minute. Let Murph talk to them. I can't believe this; I'm going to have a strong word with Brice's mother that she lets him pull pranks like this." The mental image of my Aunt Sandra chiding her thirty-six-year-old son runs through my mind and I snort out a laugh.

"No, Mom, it's ok. I love you, but this *is* Sam's brother. I think he needs to deal with it, and I'm here if he needs me."

My mom makes a little 'aww' noise before telling me she loves me, and that she'll call once they get home, and I better not be having too much fun to answer.

The pounding on the door starts up again as my dads grumble in the background and I hang up the phone. Joseph's voice is clearer now. "Get the fuck out here you asshole. You've got a lot of goddamned nerve lying to the fucking cops! Do you know what kind of trouble you could get into, man?" This seems to be the breaking point for Sam as he yanks open the front door.

Jake lunges but Kelly grabs his collar, getting dragged off the couch as he tries to get to Sam's side. She makes a loud squeak of protest and Jake turns around looking abashed. He presses his nose against her face, making sure she's ok. She pats his head and calls him a good slobber monster as I help her stand back up. Jake goes back to growling at the door but stays protectively beside her as I walk over to confront Joseph with Sam. Brice is standing at the foot of the steps, fists clenched at his sides. He looks...guilty?

"Hey, Brice. Yeah, I was on the phone with my mom...what the fuck man? You knew they were on vacation. You worried her for nothing. You told them I left with a strange alpha? Seriously, you know Sam."

Brice looks up at me, his chin jutting out. "You weren't replying to messages, you weren't answering calls, what was I supposed to do?"

"Well, not lie to my parents for one, not send my mom into a panic. That would be a good start. Maybe wait for me to cool down and message you back, or come get my shit from your place? I don't know. Regardless, she's pissed now, and she's going to talk to Aunt Sandy." Brice's face drops as he goes pale at the mention of his own mom.

Yeah bitch, see how that feels.

Fuck, I'm being catty.

What the hell, I'm never catty.

Fucking omega hormones. It's probably all the crazy shit today and stress.

Brice's spine snaps straight. "Well, that won't be a problem, you don't need to come get your stuff. It's in the truck. I think it would be best if you cut your trip short and went and stayed at your parents' house for the rest of the school break."

This little bitch.

Before I can verbally shit-slap my cousin, Sam steps in. He and Joseph have been silently glaring at each other the entire time Brice and I were talking. Sam slips his arm around my shoulders. "Thank ya, Brice. We sure do appreciate you bringing his stuff over, since it saves us a trip. And it should be enough to tide him over until we can get back to the omega center to collect the rest of his things." If possible, Brice goes even paler and Joseph's head snaps towards us.

I see Kelly slip out the door, still holding onto Jake's collar, as the big dog glares at Joseph—who sees her and lets out a loud snarl. "What the fuck, Sam? Kelly too? Are you just fucking collecting all the goddamned strays now? Shit, man, she's barely fucking legal. Do her parents even know?" Kelly swallows audibly and tears quickly build in her eyes. Jake snaps his jaws at Joseph, licking his teeth like he wants to take a chunk out of the guy for making Kelly cry. I can't say I blame him.

Sam turns to his brother, his own snarl rumbling out of his chest. "What we do is her decision, always. As for if her parents know, that's between Kelly and them and doesn't have shit to do with you, so keep your fucking nose out of it. Now, I suggest you leave Teddy's stuff here, take your omega, and get the fuck away from my house before *I* call the fucking cops for harassment."

Brice is watching the two alphas, his head swinging back and forth at the conversation, fingers twisted together. He lets out a loud omega whine, and Joseph goes soft as he steps off the porch to join him. "I'm sorry, Honey, but if Teddy wants to stay, we can't make him leave Sam's house. We don't have to like it, but it's his choice"—he turns towards me—"even if it *is* the wrong one."

Sam moves between us. "That's fucking *it*, man, what the hell? Do you want me to be alone forever? Fuck, I thought if anything you would be relieved that I finally found my pack. That I would finally leave you the hell alone with yours. God knows you've been trying to get rid of me for ten goddamned years. What the fuck?"

Joseph steps back up, almost nose to nose with Sam. "Yes, I wanted you to find your own pack, but I wanted you to find someone your own fucking age. First you follow me around for years, like you're going to join my pack that's almost all eight years older than you, now you're fucking robbing the goddamned cradle with an omega and beta that are what, fifteen years younger? What the fuck man? This is sick." All the color drains from Sam's face, leaving him pale and sickly looking, and I know that Joseph's words hit on his own insecurities.

I can't change how he feels about himself, but I'll be damned if I let this be an issue. Stepping up behind his back, I wrap my arms around Sam and stare down at Joseph. "Nine years isn't that much of a jump for me." I swing my glare to Brice. "I'm kind of surprised that Brice is taking your side on this since two of his dads are older. His mom always did have a thing for silver foxes." My eyes flick back to Joseph, waiting for his reaction to my next bomb. "What's the age gap there, Brice? John's...what, twenty-two years older than your mom. If nine years makes your mate so sick, I'd hate to hear how he feels about your dads."

I enjoy Brice turning green more than I should. But I want this done now, it's getting too hot out here, and all this stress is making me queasy. I want to get Kelly back inside and back to bed for snuggles soon.

Fuck, I'm sweating like crazy.

Sam's still pale; I wonder how long that lunch meat was in his fridge.

Kelly seems ok, though.

Joseph grabs Brice's hand, practically dragging him back towards the truck. I'm relieved when he sets my suitcases on the ground instead of throwing them. Brice climbs into the passenger side, but his eyes follow me as they back up and turn around, leaving in a big plume of dust. I see Jake leap off the porch, stopping in the yard to strut back and forth barking at their retreating vehicle, while Kelly's arms wrap around both of us.

Chapter 12

Kelly

I probably should call Mom; I don't want her or Dad to worry. I should have been home an hour ago, but I checked my phone earlier, and there weren't any missed calls. Maybe they expected the reception to last longer. Regardless, I need to call them. I mean, I could go home and tell them what's going on, but I don't want to leave Sam alone. He looks kinda broken right now.

Squeezing my arms tighter around my guys, I hear a loud thump as Jake hops back up on the porch. He leans heavily against my legs, making me glad that Teddy and Sam are here to keep me from falling over again under his weight.

Maybe I can call them tonight, and then head home tomorrow, and take the guys to meet them. They both seem pretty sure about having me in their pack. I really need to have Mom and Dad meet them before we file that paperwork on Monday, anyway. Of course, that depends on how this conversation goes.

Pulling away from where I'm hanging on to Teddy and Sam. "I should probably call my parents too, let them know I'm staying with some friends, so they don't worry. Would you guys be ok meeting them tomorrow...before we go any farther?"

Sam swallows a few times, looking like he might be sick, but Teddy squeezes my arm. "Sure thing, Pixie, go let them know that everything's good. And if you need to go home tonight, we can at least follow you in the truck to make sure you're ok. We can meet them tomorrow regardless so that they know you're getting involved with decent guys."

That's the problem of course. I'm worried that they'll be upset that I'm involved with *guys*, plural, more than one. But I square my shoulders and march out into the yard to make the call. I'll probably be pacing back and forth, and there's less stuff out here for me to trip over. Or at least there would be if Jake wasn't prancing along beside me giving me big puppy eyes for attention. Out of the corner of my eye I see Sam come over and pick up Teddy's luggage, taking it inside before coming back to stand on the porch with our omega.

I call my mom's cell. My dad rarely answers his, he hates talking to people, but after four rings he picks hers up. "Hey, Sprout, everything go ok at the ceremony? Your mom was just about to call you after she gets back inside. She went out to the garden to get some basil for the spaghetti tonight. Are you having dinner over at Candice's or with Stephanie? I know Sal was there, she sure is a sweet girl."

Ugh, I don't need Dad in my love life!

Also, why did he only mention girls?

"Um, Dad, you do know I like men and women, right? I mean, Sal is great, she's an amazing woman, but we didn't have much in common. Also, I kind of think that she has a thing for Stephanie now, so...neither one is really a possibility."

My dad just chuckles. "Well, Sprout, I want you to be happy. I worry about you being lonely, especially since you're almost done with college, and you don't exactly meet a lot of people other than at work."

My stomach does a barrel roll, and I swallow to keep the nausea down. I really wanted to talk to Mom about this before Dad. But here goes. "Well, Daddy, it's actually kinda funny that you mention that. Um, I met a pack today."

Dead silence on the other end, Dad isn't even breathing for a long count. "Ok, Sprout, I need you to come home now, ok? I'm glad you made some new friends, but Mom's expecting you for dinner, we'll see you by seven alright?" Dad hangs up the phone without waiting for a reply and I look down at my screen. Shit, it's already six-fourty-eight...there is no way in heck I can get home by seven.

I turn back to the porch, Sam and Teddy are both watching me. "I...I need to go home, my parents are expecting me for dinner in about twelve minutes, and I'm already gonna be late. I'm sorry. Are you...are you coming with me?" I look hopefully at Teddy. I don't want to face this alone, but I also feel bad dragging them into my family's drama especially after having to deal with their own.

Sam takes a deep breath, his shoulders straightening. "Of course, Sugar, we won't leave you hanging." He turns to Teddy. "Are you comfortable in my clothes, or do you need to change real quick?" Teddy looks back at me, silently asking my opinion.

"You look fine the way you are...better than fine, but I don't have time to show you just how much." He blushes and ducks his head—he has an adorable blush.

"Alright, same driving arrangement as before, or do you wanna ride with us this time, Sugar?" Sam leans in the front door, grabbing his keys from the hook. I bite my lip, this should be a no-brainer that I ride with them, but I think my parents will take it better if I show up in my own car. The guys get in Sam's truck and Sam tells Jake to keep watch before we pull away.

The drive over takes about eighteen minutes, so I'm almost over ten minutes late when I get there. To be fair there was no way to make it on time, and I'm pretty sure Dad knew that when he said it. Still, he and Mom both look upset when I walk in the door. Mom might be upset, though, because I don't immediately take off my shoes—she's staring down at them...and all the dust they picked up in Sam's yard. *Yikes!*

It's ok, take a couple deep breaths, these are your parents.

They love you, and they will accept that you are inexplicably falling in love with two guys at once.

Yeah, I didn't think so either. Crud.

Dad's scowl deepens as the front door opens behind me, and I feel Sam and Teddy at my back. "Mom, Daddy, you've probably seen Sam in town before, but he's the alpha of the pack I was telling you about, and this is Teddy, he's new in town."

There, that went over well, I can make introductions. Go me!

My dad's scowl is now snapping between my alpha and omega, but he manages to grind out a greeting nonetheless. "Hello, boys, it's nice to meet the...people our Kelly's getting herself involved in. Sam, I'm happy that you've found a pack. I hadn't heard the good news until Kelly told me...just now. And Teddy, is it? Well, young man, it's nice to meet you. Did you leave your omega at home with the rest of your pack, or...?"

Teddy leans into Sam, and honestly as much confusion as there has been today about him, I can't blame him for his exhausted sigh. He's still taller than my dad, who's about average for a beta.

I reach my hand back, taking theirs together, and Teddy stands a little taller. "Actually, Sir, I *am* the omega. This is my pack—Sam, Kelly, and me." He says it with confidence, but his fingers shake in mine.

Mom looks surprised, but Dad's scowl grows even more. "Um, Son, last time I checked most omegas are girls. I mean there's Brice, but he's like the exception to the rule."

Sam and Teddy both twitch at the mention of his cousin. But Teddy's voice stays strong as he replies. "Yes Sir, I know. Brice is my cousin. I was actually here visiting him, and I met Kelly at the community center today. She smells like mine, so does Sam. They're my pack now."

My dad snaps, "Now you wait just a minute boy, you can't come into my house and just take my daughter saying she's yours. Did she agree to this?" His gaze flicks to me while Mom stands still and quiet behind him. Tuck walks out of the kitchen, probably trying to find out what's going on with all the raised voices, and Rufus bounds in after him, sliding on the rug and wiggling his way over to me. He slides between me and Dad, sniffing at my legs and whining up at me when he smells Jake.

Now I need to make the dog feel better.

Crap.

One thing at a time.

"Dad, I want to be in a pack with Teddy and Sam, I really care about them. Being with them feels right. I don't know how to explain it better." Dad continues to scowl but Mom steps forward.

"Oh, Kelly, honey, we're not saying you can't join a pack...we just want you to take it slow. Get to know the guys better, make sure they have the proper intentions." I hear Sam and Teddy both growl behind me at what she's insinuating.

"Mom, what the heck? If I was that rude, I would be in so much trouble, are you kidding me right now?"

The look she turns to me switches from placating to glacial in a fraction of a second. "Really now, Honey, you don't know these men. They may be perfectly fine gentlemen. But you just met...Teddy, was it? You just met him today. I know he says he's

Brice's cousin, but we don't really know their family either. I just want you to take some time to think about this. Betas don't join packs, and it's a bit strange that they just met you today and suddenly they need you to join? I don't want you to get taken advantage of, Kelly. And I don't want you to feel pressured into something you're not ready for."

I can understand where she's coming from, I had some of these same ideas go through my head earlier. But I can feel the answers, I know how good it feels just to be near my guys. I don't know how to explain that to either of my parents in a way they'll listen.

<h1 style="text-align:center">Chapter 13</h1>

Sam

These are Kelly's parents. They're betas and they don't understand, but I'm getting tired of their angry stares and how frantic Kelly smells trying to get them to listen. Teddy's scent has taken on a burnt edge, and he's leaning heavily against me sweating like crazy. I need to get him home—get both of them home, and back into my space.

Our home, our space.

Much better.

Maybe he caught a bug or something today being around so many people. It might just be stress, I haven't been around a lot of omegas, so I'm desperately trying to draw on what I learned in school. That was a long-damned time ago.

I wish I had a decent nest set up for him, it's just an empty shell of a room right now. I never bothered doing anything with it since it wasn't something I thought I would ever need. Shit. Still, I think I have the stuff to make him some soup, or I can stop and get some cans of chicken soup. I hate the thought of feeding him something canned, but it might work better as a short-term solution. My hand rubs up and down his back, as a low growl rumbles through him. I can't say I blame him, I'm not happy with the situation myself, but until Kelly gives some indication that she wants my help, I don't want to get in her way.

Also, this is her family, and we're already causing enough strife. After what happened earlier with Joseph and Brice, I don't want to cause her the same kind of issues. Should I offer to leave? I don't want to leave without her, and I don't think Teddy would handle it well if the whine coming from him right now is any indication.

Dammit!

"Kelly, Teddy and I can leave if you want. We don't want to cause any problems between you and your family. I think we've all had enough of that today." Even offering makes me want to scream, but I don't know what else to do. I deal with betas all the time, but this is pack business, and I don't really care what her parents want, but if she does...

Fuck!

Kelly turns her big brown eyes back to Teddy and me. "Don't you want me to come with you?"

Before I can answer, Teddy strides across the room and gathers her up, he's pale and sweating profusely. He looks like he's about to collapse, but he pulls her into his arms and a rumbly purr comes out. "Of course we want you to come home with us, Pixie. But you saw what happened earlier with both my family and Sam's. We don't want you to have to go through anything like that. If it makes it easier on you, we'll leave." Kelly wraps her arms around him, sinking against his purring chest. Her father's scowl deepens, when I step in to put my hand on Teddy's back, keeping him stable.

"Stay, please." It's a quiet whisper against his chest, and I don't think her parents heard. Her mother watches intently, she hasn't said much, but she seems to be taking in every detail. She reaches out and touches her husband's shoulder, pulling him from the room.

Kelly's eyes are closed as she holds Teddy. She doesn't seem to have noticed they left. The younger boy who came in earlier just looks at us before nodding. "Sup?"

Teddy smiles over Kelly's head and nods back. "Not much. Sup with you?"

The kid grins and leans against a wall. "So, you're Kelly's pack huh? Be warned, she uses all the hot water...and she can't cook for anything. So hopefully one of you is better, otherwise you're gonna starve."

Kelly's face turns bright red where it's pressed against Teddy's chest. His purr turns into a low growl, wiping the smirk off the kid's face. Kelly's voice comes out muffled. "So help me Tuck, you better hope I leave tonight, otherwise I'm gonna noogie you so hard your hair falls out."

Teddy snorts with laughter and the grin pops back out on the kids face. "Yeah, Sis, I hope you get to leave tonight too. They seem pretty protective, so I don't see a problem with it. Later gator!" The kid waves at Kelly's back and bolts around the stairs. Well, at least we won one member of her family over.

The longer I stand there, the more awkward I feel. Sometime later, I hear the kid's voice calling from the kitchen. "Let Kelly's pack help her get some of her stuff together, I'm hungry! I just wanna eat dinner!" Well, he's kind of a rude little shit, but I appreciate him being on our side. Less than a minute later Kelly's parents come back in the room, her father still shooting us angry looks. Her mom at least seems less upset.

"I'm sorry, boys...Kelly's never had a serious relationship, so this was a bit of a shock to us. But she *is* an adult, legally anyway." She glares at Kelly's dad for a minute, causing another low growl to slide out of Teddy. "And if you make her happy, and she wants to go with you, then we won't stop her. However, if you hurt my little girl, just know that we have twenty-five acres out behind the house and nobody would find the bodies." She glares at both of us for a minute before pulling Kelly away from Teddy and giving her a hug.

"We love you sweety, we just worry, ok." She kisses Kelly on top of the head. "And if you need anything, we're right here...and if anything happens, we'll take care of it, ok. Just remember, I'm too young to be a grandma, yeah?"

Kelly snorts at that and hugs her mom back before pulling back to meet her eyes. "Thank God, Mom. I don't plan on having kids for...ever. You know that. The guys and I already talked about it. None of us are ready to start a family yet, if at all."

Her mom kisses her forehead before stepping back. "Ok, just be safe. We love you."

Kelly's dad finally steps in, pulling her into a one-armed hug. "We love you Sprout, we better hear from you at least every couple days. Call us, otherwise I'm comin' over with Rufus." He glares over her head at both of us again. I look down at the big brown dog that's lying by the door. Its tail thumps against the floor when it meets my eyes, and it gives me a big doggy grin. Yeah, it looks about as fierce as Jake—though the way he acted earlier to keep Kelly safe, maybe I shouldn't discount him.

Kelly's mom claps her hands together. "So, are you all staying for dinner? I can make more spaghetti!" Her voice is bright and too chipper. Also, Teddy still looks too pale.

"If it's ok with Kelly, I think we'd like to just get her a couple of changes of clothes—and whatever she needs for a few days, and then head out. We're all still settling in and learning about each other, plus that'll give her a reason to come back this week. If that's ok with y'all?"

Kelly nods and her mom gives a hum of assent. Her dad looks like he wants to say something, but Tuck's voice yells from the other room again. "Ok, I'm just gonna grab a plate for myself and take it upstairs away from all the drama. Bye, Kelly!" Her dad mumbles something about a smartass, and stomps back through the door to what I assume is the kitchen. Her mom lets out a little puff of exasperation, and points towards the stairs.

"See, I'm outnumbered now...but you get to see how it feels soon enough." She chuckles, hugging Kelly again and taking off into the other room. Her voice carries back but I can't make out everything, only a few mumbles about men and impatience.

Teddy still looks wobbly, but insists we help Kelly. I walk behind him up the stairs in case he falls. She leads us to a room down the hall, and I don't know what I was expecting, but this wasn't it. The curtains are a heavy rainbow of colors with tiny star shapes sprinkled across the surface, there's a gauzy top layer that probably diffuses what little light comes in. But that's the only part of the room that I would consider even remotely girly.

She has bookcases lined up against one wall, and they are full to the point of overflowing. Comic books and manga are perched on every available surface, but other than that the room's surprisingly clean. There's nothing on the floor, the hamper is put away in the corner beside a rather lopsided look-ing wooden chest. There are a couple of shirts tossed across the bed that Kelly rushes over to hang up and put in the closet.

The bed itself is a simple affair, a twin-sized pallet bed with a navy duvet and two pillows. She drags Teddy over and pulls him down to sit on the side, making it look even smaller. Kelly places her hand on his head, checking his temperature and looking into his eyes. "Are you ok? You look kinda sick." Teddy just closes his eyes and leans into her hand that's pressed against his forehead.

"Flattery will get you everywhere, Pixie. Maybe just not at this exact moment." His arms come out, wrapping around her waist and pulling her close, pressing his forehead against her stomach. His eyelids seem too heavy for him to open.

Kelly looks to me and nods at Teddy and the only other door in the room—the closet she hung clothes up in earlier. I step over to it, it's tiny, with only one rack for hanging clothes...and hey, more books in stacks of milk crates. This is going to take at least a few trips in the truck for all her books.

My brain catalogs what she'll need and what can stay. Obviously, the bed and dresser can stay, I can build her any type of furniture she wants. For now, I do a quick scan until I see a duffel bag and toss it out to the bed beside Teddy. Kelly got him to stretch out, but the bed's too small for his frame so his feet hang over the end. There's no room for her to cuddle unless she lays on top of him. Not that he would mind.

Her hand's running over his hair, but when the duffel hits the bed, she meets my eyes again, we don't even need words. She bends down and kisses him on the forehead so I can take her place while she packs up some clothes. Kelly goes to her dresser and digs around for a bit before looking back over her shoulder at us. She pulls out a couple of handfuls of lacy sheer fabric and stuffs them in the bottom of her bag before adding plain cotton underwear and bras on top.

Teddy's face is turned towards her, and he lets out a low chuckle at her attempts at being inconspicuous, causing her cheeks to turn an adorable shade of pink. She hurries over to the closet grabbing out several shirts and dresses and shoving them on top of the underwear. After she adds a couple of pairs of jeans and shorts to the bag, she has some trouble zipping it closed.

Kneeling on top of the bag to push everything down, she looks back at us, lets out an exasperated huff of air, and comes over to pick up a charger and earbud case from the table. Shoving them on top of everything else she, tries again. Her adorable blush has gone almost atomic red by the time she gets it zipped, and I almost feel bad asking her if she needs any of her bath stuff. Her eyes get huge for a second, her tiny foot comes down with a stomp. "Oh....Sugarsnaps!"

She tries to march out of the room, but trips over the bag on her way. Thankfully, she regains her balance with the help of the doorframe and stomps down the hall. I hear her footsteps and muttering all the way there and back, when she returns with a bottle of shampoo, conditioner, and a toothbrush. She's blushing and looking at her feet when she comes in. "Sorry, the soap and toothpaste and stuff are mine and Tuck's, so I just grabbed my hair stuff and toothbrush. I hope we can go to the store soon so I can get a few things."

Like she even needs to ask.

Teddy and I will both give her anything she needs or wants.

"As long as it can wait until tomorrow, I think we need to get our omega home and tucked in. Maybe some chicken soup?" I look between the two of them, and they both nod. Kelly goes to try to unzip her bag, but I don't know how she expects to squeeze anything else in there. I help Teddy stand, then grab the duffel by the strap and toss it over my shoulder. "Can you just carry those out to the car, I got the bag?" I nod at the stuff she has in her hands, and she starts to protest before just nodding, and mouthing a silent 'Thank you' to me.

I head down the stairs first—again, just in case either of them fall. Teddy is close behind, his hand on my shoulder to keep himself steady. Kelly follows behind after closing her bedroom door. Her dad's standing in the entryway again when we come in. "Call me anytime you need me, Sprout. I'll come running. I love you." He gives her a big hug, squeezing her until she squeaks before he lets her go.

"Daddy, I'm still in town. And I don't even have all my clothes. It's not like you'll never see me again." She hugs him back and he ruffles her hair.

Glaring at Teddy and me again over her head, he tells us, "You boys take care of my little girl."

Teddy mumbles a low, "Yes sir," before shuffling towards the door. I'll call in an order from the diner for some chicken soup, and I'm sure I have soda crackers at home. Kelly kisses her dad on the cheek then follows Teddy outside, helping him get situated in my truck.

"I'm serious Sam, you better be careful with her." I can't even be mad at him, since I'd already tear down the world to keep her and Teddy safe.

"I'm not gonna tell you not to worry, Rob. But I can tell you that as long as Teddy and I are around, then we'll do everything in our power to make sure that Kelly stays safe and happy." He grumbles a bit but sticks his hand out for me to shake before turning around and heading back into the kitchen.

I get outside and Kelly's standing by the open passenger door of my truck. Teddy still looks ill, but not as bad. "Do you want me to order some soup from the diner or a burger...or...?" I trail off, hoping they'll tell me what they want. But Teddy just stares. Of course, he's never been to the diner, so he doesn't know what they have.

"I can pop by the store. If you wanna take Teddy home, I'll run in and grab some canned soup, or anything you might need. It'll give me a chance to pick up soap and toothpaste, so we don't have to leave tomorrow." Kelly smiles at me, and I pull out my wallet to hand her my debit card. She just stares at it for a minute before flicking her eyes back up to mine. "I do have a job, and money...just tell me what you need."

Together we make a short list of medicine and foods that might sit ok on a sick stomach, as well as stuff for hamburgers and foods that Kelly and I can take turns cooking, without her setting herself on fire. She leans into the truck, kissing Teddy quickly on the lips, and he whines a little when she pulls back.

"I know, Big Guy, but I'll be home soon too, ok. Just keep Sam entertained till I get there."

He chuckles softly, reaching out to run his fingers down the side of her jaw. "Miss you already, Pixie."

She closes the door after he pulls his hand back, and leans into me, pressing her face against my chest and breathing in deep. My arms come around her automatically, holding her close. I don't want to be separated, even for the trip home, but I let go when she pulls away.

"You both look like I kicked your puppy, I won't be that far behind you. And this way we can have the whole day tomorrow to get to know each other better, without having to deal with shopping or family stuff, yeah?" Teddy and I both nod, and I climb up into the cab of the truck with him. He leans over, pulling against the belt and pressing his face to my shoulder. He releases a deep shuddering sigh as we watch Kelly hop in her tiny car and take off towards town. We follow behind all the way to the store, and he waves out the window when she pulls into the parking lot.

Chapter 14

Teddy

Why does everything hurt?

It's too hot. Is nobody else feeling this?

What's up with spring in this place? Seriously, this is fucking miserable.

I just want to curl up in my nest and sleep...I need my blankets, and my pillows.

And my nest is back at the omega center...FUCK!

Why am I so fucking needy?

SHIT!!!

"Hey, um, Sam...we might have a little problem." Sam's head swings to me, concern written in every line of his body. "Yeah, um...I'm hoping it's just a spike...but this feels an awful lot like the start of a heat to me. I don't know if it's because my hormones are crazy from meeting my pack, or stress...or what. But you mentioned having a nest at the house, how much work would that take to finish?" The last bit comes out as a groan when my stomach cramps and I clamp my lips together to stop the whine that tries to escape.

A loud, "Well fuck!" erupts from the other side of the truck. That reaction's not a good sign. The whine I was holding back slips free at the upset alpha. His hand snaps over to cover mine, and his thumb traces along the back of my knuckles as his purr starts up. "No, no, it's ok. It'll be ok. We can figure this out." He tries to reassure me, but the hand holding mine is shaking as well.

"I...I can't have them pack up my stuff, I can't have anybody else in my nest, it would cause more problems than it solves...I can order some new nesting stuff. But it'll take a few days to get here. You have enough bedrooms in the house, maybe I can just borrow blankets from those? Just in case. I need a backup plan for now." I don't like the slight edge of panic in my voice.

We pull into the lot in front of Sam's house, and he turns to me, his hand coming up to cup my jaw. "If you're worried, we have a Nest-n-Stuff over in Springfield. We can order some stuff tonight and I can go pick it up tomorrow? Until then, you can have every scrap of fabric in this house if you need it, ok?" His purr ratchets higher as he unclips my seatbelt and pulls me across the bench towards himself. His lips come down on mine, stealing my thoughts and reassuring me that everything will be ok, I have my alpha here, my beta will be home soon. We can do this.

I sigh when he pulls back, breaking contact and staring into my eyes. "I've never been through an omega's heat before, but I've seen the aftereffects on Joseph's pack after Brice. It's...intense. But we'll take care of it. Maybe we can get Kelly some toys so she can be a stand-in alpha for you." My own purr starts up at the thought of Kelly with a strap-on knotted dildo, because: Yes, please!

I didn't think about it before, but that's hot as hell. Also, with only one alpha in the pack, Sam might need the help. But damn, the image is in my head now, and I have to deal with the erection from hell as well as this damned fever and nausea.

I just wanted snuggles!

Sam gets out of the truck and comes to open my door, offering his hand to help me down and chiding Jake not to jump up since I'm wobbly. He leads me back inside—followed by a bouncing Jake—and sits me on the couch, before depositing Kelly's bag at the bottom of the stairs. I want her to join us up in the master bedroom tonight, but neither of us wants to pressure her. Sam goes into the kitchen and brings me a glass of ice water and a can of soda, then sits close to me on the couch and pulls me against his side. His hand runs up and down my arm, fingers tracing the edge of one of my cuffs. The subject will come up eventually about why I don't take them off, but I don't want to deal with that now, my mind's scrambled enough as it is.

I'm still hard from what he said a little while ago, and I want to lean over and unzip his pants, to see if I can get him into the same state with my mouth. But my stomach gives a sharp cramp, and any thoughts I have of teasing the alpha fly out of my head. I don't get it. If this is a heat spike or pre-heat, why aren't I dragging Sam up the stairs to the bedroom and demanding he fuck me until I feel better?

Part of me wants to call my mom back and ask her for advice. I could call Candice, she's an omega, but it *is* her wedding night, so she might be busy. Shit. Another tiny frantic whine builds in my throat, my mind panicking that I don't know anyone here who might have any idea. What about Sarah? I know she's on break too, but maybe she knows. I don't have anybody else to call. I pull out my cell and scroll through my contacts until I find her number. It's not late, but I don't want to bother her. So, I just text.

Teddy:

Hey, Shorty, I have a pack/heat question for you, I might need help from your sisters. Can you message me when you get time?

Three little dots pop up almost immediately. Thank fuck.

Sarah

Sup, X-Thicc. Sis both right here. Whatcha need?

Teddy:

Great. Well, good news/bad news. I'm visiting my cousin, but I started feeling fucked up.

Teddy:

I have a fever and feel nauseous, and really uncomfortable. It almost feels like my heat is trying to start, but don't want to jump an alpha, I just want snuggles. I can't really ask Brice about it, since it started after I met his pack lead's brother…awkward family bullshit.

Sarah:

Freaky. Yeah, lemme ask my sisters if they have any experience with this kinda thing. They're here for dinner with their packs, so it might take a bit to get some answers. I'll get back soon.

I put away my phone, hopefully one of them will have some idea of what's going on. Sam pulls me into his arms, holding my body against his chest as he rumbles out a purr and all my muscles go limp. I feel like a pile of omega mush...and much better actually. Still hot, but not as ill. We sit like that on the couch for a bit longer until Jake jumps up and wags his way sideways to the door just before someone knocks. Sam grumbles a bit but goes to answer it, scowl already firmly in place.

Kelly steps through as soon as it's open, and he frowns. "You know, if you live here now, you don't have to knock."

She blushes and looks at the floor, mumbling out an apology. She's loaded down with bags, and Sam and I swoop in and take them all from her and head towards the kitchen. She steps back outside followed by Jake—tail still wagging—before returning with another haul of bags, and her bathroom stuff.

"Jeeze, Sugar, did you buy out the whole store?" Sam laughs as he takes the bags from her hands again and puts them on the kitchen counter.

She blushes harder this time and shuffles her feet. "No, but...we need to be ready, for...anything. And I just wanted to make sure."

I'm watching her and her adorable blush, so I don't realize anything's up until I hear a loud whistle from the dining area. "Just how many of these things you think we'll need, Kelly Girl?" My eyes pan over to Sam, and he's stacked seven small boxes on the table, I have to squint to make out what they are.

Condoms, different sizes and colors by the look.

Oh, and one says 'alpha' in big bold letters.

Guess we know who those are for.

Kelly's currently the color of a tomato, and staring intently at her feet, her fingers twisting together in front of her. "Well, even if I can talk to Doc on Monday, any birth control has a delay where you still have to use an alternative. And...well...what happened earlier. I...I want to do that again, with you. Both of you." Her eyes come up and flick between Sam and me before dropping back to the ground.

Well, at least this erection's good for something now.

"Mr. Wells was restocking at the store when I was trying to figure out what kind we might need...and I panicked and just grabbed a bunch. I don't even know." Her hands are over her face, and her voice is muffled. When I hear a chuckle from Sam.

"You can say that again, Sugar." He's holding another bag with even more small boxes in it. "Hey, some of these are flavored. I thought you liked Teddy's snickerdoodle."

Kelly looks like she's ready to melt through the floor if it would help her escape, so I step forward and wrap my arms around her. Pulling her still body against mine, I whisper to her, "I'd rather be prepared than have to stop midway. So, thank you, I'm sure we'll use them all...eventually. Besides, Sam and I were talking while you were gone, and I need to ask...What are your thoughts on pegging?"

Sam lets out a low growly chuckle as he continues to unpack groceries, but Kelly just looks up at me, her brows furrowed. "What's pegging?"

Sam's guffaw from the kitchen startles Jake enough that he scrambles up from where he was lying under the dining table, bonking his head in the process, and knocking over several of the small boxes that were stacked there.

Chapter 15

Kelly

I t took Teddy and Sam awhile to stop laughing long enough to explain to me what pegging was, and I'm sure I looked red as a tomato by the time they finished. I mean, I've heard of strap-ons, but it wasn't something I ever imagined doing. Of course, now the idea of doing that to Teddy is making me all hot and squirmy. Just picturing the big omega at my mercy.

Dang-it girl, get your head outta the gutter, you need to make sure he's feelin' better.

He looked sick when you left earlier, that was the whole reason you went to the store.

Until you got sidetracked by the big colorful display of condoms.

He is looking a bit better though, less pale.

All good points. But before I can let my brain deep dive into any of that a loud ringing draws my attention to the coffee table. Teddy jogs over to pick it up before it can go to voicemail. His eyebrows draw together as he slides his thumb across the answer button, and suddenly a very loud, very vibrant, very female voice starts yelling from the phone. "You filthy slut, you found a scent match! Holy Shit! Congratulations!"

The crease in Teddy's forehead deepens. "What? Sarah, what are you talking about? That's like a myth, right?"

But the voice, Sarah, just talks over him. "Your scent match! Oh, my fucking God! Shelly said a friend of hers had those same symptoms after she met some alphas at a center mixer. It was like insta-lust, but you know the rules, we have to do the slow courting thing. She got super sick the next day, kept thinking it was heat flashes and nausea."

Teddy nods at the phone, like she can see him. "Wait, Shelly's your sister, right? So, one of her friends from the center?"

Another loud female voice in the background cuts through. "Well, I wouldn't say we were friends exactly, she was kind of a bitch. But she was in the same dorm, and when you have to share a communal kitchen with people, you learn things."

The first voice screeches back, "Do you fuckin' mind, I am on the phone! Anyway, apparently you need security and comfort that you aren't getting from your alphas. Hey! Assholes. If you aren't purring for Teddy, I'll track you fuckers down and beat the shit out of you! You better purr for your fucking omega or you're gonna have to dig a size eight and a half wide outta your ass, you hear me?"

Sam rumbles in the background. "Sorry, it's nice to meet you. We kind of all fell asleep earlier. Don't worry, we'll take care of our boy. We just weren't sure what was wrong."

Loud shrieking from the other end, apparently this Sarah is excitable. "Oh my god, Teddy, was that your alpha...He sounds fuckin' hot! I told you before, I'll tell you again. Fuck Steve and Garret ok? You got a fuckin' scent match. I am so fucking jealous right now! Ok, Extra Thicc, I'm gonna let you go get some. Call me back soon, when you have time. I miss you, bye!"

The phone hangs up and Teddy just stands there staring at the screen like it holds the mysteries of the universe. I let him have a few moments to let his brain reset, before finally giving in to my desire to go hug him. He seems surprised at first, but then wraps me in his arms and pulls me tight against him. "Betas don't purr, do they?" he mumbles against my head.

"No, sorry, we're gonna need Sam for this one. But I can give you all the snuggles." He pulls away, chuckling lightly before we both turn to Sam who has finally finished putting away the groceries I bought, and is trying to stuff boxes of condoms back into the bags. He gives us each a kiss on the forehead as he takes the bags upstairs, probably to the master suite, before returning and going back towards the kitchen.

"Ok, Omega, let's get you fed and cleaned up and ready for snuggles. And lots of purring. Sound good?" Teddy relaxes against me, and I feel silly just standing here, so I wander over to ask if I can help him. He must hear me coming because before I have a chance to speak, he does.

"Nope, Sugar, you already went to the store and hauled everything inside. If you wanna ask Teddy what kinda soup he wants, you can, otherwise I'll make up some tomato with grilled cheese sandwiches. Sound good?"

Teddy walks up behind me, wrapping his arms around me. He moves silently for being so big. His chin rests on top of my head, and I feel his answer as much as hear it. "Sounds great, actually. You sure you don't need any help?"

Sam turns around and looks at both of us. "I'm not going to be able to get you two to go sit down and rest, am I?" He lets out a mildly annoyed sigh, and points to the cabinet two doors down from the stove where he's working. "Teddy, can you get down bowls and plates for soup? Silverware is straight down below. Kelly, please get me out whatever kind of cheese you can find in the fridge, and the bread and butter from the pantry."

He waves vaguely at a door on the other side of the fridge without looking. Teddy gives me a puzzled look but heads for the cabinet that Sam pointed him to, pulling out some nice looking stoneware dishes. I give Sam the side eye, even my parents' dishes don't match. Though I guess when you have kids that are super clumsy and break everything, that makes sense.

I head over to the pantry first—and holy green guacamole—it's bigger than my closet at home, and super organized. Little labels line each shelf, plastic bins are labeled for bread flour, all-purpose flour, sugar, and three different kinds of rice. I didn't even know there were three different kinds of rice. Wow.

I look all over for bread and finally see a wooden box that has 'Bread' carved into the front of it. Not sure how I missed that. I open it to grab out a loaf, but my brain goes scrambly when I see multiple packages, so I just grab the whole box. On the second shelf over there is a glass butter dish, so I scoop that up too before returning the stuff to the counter beside Sam.

I'm tempted to sniff the butter to make sure it hasn't gone bad...Whoever heard of keeping butter in the pantry? My parents have always kept it in the fridge. I guess we'll find out soon enough. I open the stainless steel door, and it isn't as well organized as the pantry, but that's hardly saying anything. I didn't notice earlier when I was getting stuff out to make lunch—the bread was already out on the counter then—but I just realized that everything actually has a proper place. Fruits and Vegetables are divided between the two crispers, and the place I snagged all the sandwich stuff from earlier actually has a label of Deli written on it. I didn't even notice because the fridge was so empty, that was just about the only thing I saw.

I grab out sliced American, Swiss, and provolone cheeses.

Why does one man need so much cheese?

There are a few blocks of different kinds in here too in another drawer marked "Dairy" but I just grab the pre-sliced stuff.

I mean, I get it, cheese is delicious...but still. Maybe he likes to make charcuterie?

That sounds fun, maybe he can teach me.

For cripe's sake Kelly, focus.

I must have been lost in various thoughts of cheese, because I nearly jump out of my skin when Teddy's big hand lands on my back. "Hey, Pixie, did we lose you to something horrifying growing in the back of that thing?"

I stand up, hearing a mildly affronted scoffing sound from Sam. "Yeah, I don't think so. There was just a lot to choose from, sorry." Teddy gives me a puzzled look but takes the packages I hand him and puts them on the counter beside the bread box.

We both look at Sam, who has pulled out a medium saucepan and a skillet and is squinting disdainfully at the side of the can of tomato soup before sighing again and popping it open to pour it into the pan. "So, what kind of grilled cheese do you two like?"

I stammer for a minute, trying to figure out if this is some sort of riddle. "Um...the kind with bread and melted cheese."

Teddy snorts at my answer and Sam just chuckles before he tries again. "Ok, what kind of bread do you want on your sandwich?" Are there options? I never really thought about it. I mean, you go to a sub shop, and you have a choice of whole wheat, Italian, or something herby. But I never put any thought into it.

"Do you have any seedless rye?" asks Teddy while I'm still contemplating the various types of carbs that I have yet to discover.

Sam shuffles through the box, "Nope, sorry. I have seeded rye, white, wheat, sourdough, and I may have some brioche left in here, if you want me to look." He pulls out a couple of slices and pulls the top off the butter dish to slather some on one side.

Teddy thinks for a moment. "Nah, just the sourdough for me. Thanks." Both their heads swivel to me and I panic.

"Um, yeah, sure. Sourdough...sounds great!" I try to smile but it feels too wide for my face.

What have I gotten myself into?

Maybe I should look up what sourdough is on my phone, so I'm not surprised with whatever I get.

Did I get out the wrong cheese?

Oh no.

Sam takes out four more slices of bread and spreads butter on them too. Then he looks at the cheese slices I got out. "Hey, Teddy, can you grab out the block of cheddar, and maybe some gouda. Just whatever else you think these need?"

I did get the wrong cheese.

Yes, I know that there are different kinds of cheese...but grilled cheese was always just American slices on whatever bread was in the fridge.

Are the guys cheese snobs or am I a rube?

Crud.

I wander back over to the dining room table and pull out a chair to watch my guys make sandwiches. Sam keeps adding stuff to the soup—he has a big spice rack, but I've never seen Mom add anything other than just pepper and maybe a little salt after tasting it. Teddy grates a couple of different big blocks of cheese and slices thin slivers off another one before putting them all back, along with all the unused cheese slices I got out earlier. I feel kinda silly and useless right now. Maybe I should go take a shower and get cleaned up while they finish.

Before I can plan my escape, Teddy comes over and sits down across from me. It's not a huge table, just a basic square one that has the center that pulls apart to make it bigger. We have one similar to it—but not as nice—at home, but we rarely use the fold out leaves. Sam comes over a minute later carrying a plate with a bowl of soup and a sandwich cut in half on it. It smells so good. I don't remember grilled cheese ever smelling this good. Maybe there *is* something to having fancy bread. My stomach makes a loud grumbling noise, and Teddy smiles at me, a low chuckle rumbling out of him.

Sam sets the plate down in front of me, running his hand down my back before going and getting one for Teddy. He puts it in front of him and leans in for a kiss before going back one last time for his own, and taking the chair on the side between Teddy and me. I feel something brush against my knee seconds before a cold, wet nose presses against the outside of my thigh. Looking down, I see Jake under the table, giving me puppy dog eyes. But he's not getting my sandwich. This thing smells so good, and it's hard for me to wait for the guys to start. No one seems to want to though, so after a few seconds of everyone looking at each other, I dive in. Holy guacamole, this is amazing. It's all crispy and golden and the cheese is melty and tangy. I want to try it dipped in my soup, but I think that might kill me at this point.

I finish off half of it before I even realize, and then look at Sam, embarrassed by my terrible table manners. Mom would be furious, but he's beaming at me, looking pleased with himself. He's only taken one bite out of his sandwich, but a quick glance at Teddy shows that I'm not the only one who left my manners at the door. He's finished half his sandwich too, but completely forewent the spoon option and just picked the bowl up to drink straight from it.

I'm relieved that they aren't having second thoughts about me because of my manners as I pick up my spoon and taste the soup. It doesn't taste the same as I'm used to, but it's still really good with all the spices that Sam added. If Sam cooks like this, it makes me wonder if everything I hear about alphas being no good around the house was wrong. I know Jacks does most of the cooking at Pack Asher's house. But I was under the impression that it was unusual for alphas, and cooking was mostly an omega or beta job. Hopefully, this is a regular thing for him because I wasn't lying earlier when I told him I could only make sandwiches and burgers.

I hope I didn't disappoint them with my sandwiches.

Teddy finishes his soup and uses the other half of his sandwich to mop up what's left in the bowl, and Sam gives a small purr of satisfaction. Now that I've gotten past my initial shock and hunger, I slow down and enjoy the food. Sam passes Teddy half of his sandwich and goes back to the stove to bring over more soup, which Teddy slurps down quickly. His color's looking much better, but his eyelids are drooping, and he looks like he could fall asleep at the table. He shakes his head a little before getting up to go rinse his dishes and put them in the washer while Sam and I polish off our food. Teddy manages to get the cheese and bread all put away before we have a chance to help, and Sam takes my plate and bowl with him and finishes cleaning the kitchen.

Teddy leans heavily against Sam and they have a quiet exchange, but I don't hear much of it. I don't want to listen in, but they aren't being secretive, just not overly loud, and my mind's all foggy now that I'm full of food. Teddy runs his hand down my hair as he passes behind me. "Gonna go get cleaned up, meet you upstairs for snuggles?" he asks before walking down the hallway to the first door on the right. Sam must have put his luggage in there earlier.

I sit there at the table, and Jake presses his cold wet nose to my leg again, looking betrayed that I didn't share with him. But he scrambles away when Sam's voice raises. "C'mere Jake, got some dinner ready for you too." He looks upset when he sees only kibble in his bowl, but goes to town on it anyway, little hard chunks scattering around as he crunches away. Sam washes his hands and comes up behind me.

"You want to get a shower too, Sugar? Before bed?" I nod and smile up at him, but the exhaustion has hit, and I feel like my head's stuffed with cotton. Sam offers me a hand up, and I cling a little even after I'm standing, feeling uncoordinated and half asleep already. "You gonna be ok in the shower, Kelly? You look a little wobbly there, girl." I nod a bit and start marching towards the bathroom before remembering all my stuff's out here. I spin around to get my shampoo and start to go down, only to face-plant against Sam, who rushes up behind me, arms outstretched to catch me.

"Do you need some help? You look pretty unsteady there." I shake my head, my eyes feeling like they're rattling side to side in my skull with the movement, but it switches to a nod as I start to tilt sideways just from the headshake. Sam picks me up, cradling me against his big body, and then grabs my new box of soap and the shampoo and conditioner I brought from home. He carries me up the stairs towards his room, and I melt against him. He feels so good, and I am just so tired.

We get back to the master bedroom, and he sets me down on the bed before taking off his shirt and jeans, standing there in nothing but his underwear. Then he goes to the bathroom to start the shower. He walks straight out to the closet and pulls out another T-shirt and a pair of shorts before he helps me stand and slide out of my shirt, shorts, and panties. He fumbles a bit with my bra clasp; I hear a low growl rumble out of him after a little while of his big fingers trying to manipulate the tiny hooks. He had such an easy time with them earlier, I don't know if it's a different angle, or maybe he's tired, too. Regardless, his growl soons changes to a snarl of triumph a second before my last bit of clothing falls to the floor..

Once I'm stripped, he picks me back up and carries me into the shower. Opening the glass door, he steps inside, testing the temperature of the spray against his forearm before he sets me down on my feet, and tilts my hair back under the spray. He's still wearing his underwear, but I can feel his hard length pressed against my stomach as he pulls me forward and lathers shampoo in my hair. He doesn't say anything about it, and I waver from side to side as he moves me where he needs me to go, rinsing the shampoo and then conditioning my hair. Soaping me up and scrubbing all the glitter off my arms and shoulders while my conditioner takes effect.

After I'm completely rinsed and cleaned, he turns off the water and holds my hands while I step out of the shower. He grabs a fluffy towel off the rack and blots my skin dry, more gently than I ever bother being with myself. I usually just wipe down quickly and wrap my hair up to keep the cold water from dripping down my back. He mutters a curse to himself before calling out the bedroom door. "Teddy, you up here? I'm drippin' all over the place here." Teddy comes in wearing a pair of Simpsons sleep pants and nothing else. The fog in my brain shifts enough that I want to lick him.

Well, we didn't have dessert, and he does taste like cookies.

I giggle at my own thoughts as my guys exchange a look over my head. Teddy takes my hands, drawing me back into the bedroom, still wrapped in a towel with my wet hair dangling down my back. I try to pull back towards Sam, but Teddy just leads me until he can sit on the side of the bed with me in front of him. "He didn't want to make you uncomfortable by being naked, Kelly. But now his briefs are soaked, and he didn't want to drip all over the rug. Let him get himself cleaned up, then he'll be in for snuggles, ok?" I nod limply, my head feeling like it's on a spring.

Why am I so tired after eating?

Is it just all the stress from today catching up?

"Do you want me to bring your luggage up so you can have your own pajamas, or will these work?" Teddy nods to the clothes that Sam brought out earlier and I don't want him to leave, so I just point at the men's clothes that are available.

He puts my hands on his shoulders and holds the shorts up so I can step into them before shimmying them up my legs and under my towel. We really can't do the shirt without me flashing him, not unless I want it soaked by my wet hair, so I whip the towel out from around me and bend over to twist it around my head before I can drip all over the place.

Unfortunately, when I try to straighten out, my body just laughs at the effort and I end up sprawled across Teddy's lap, his arms holding me tight. My nipples are hard from the burst of cooler air, and he groans when I press against him. His face drops close to mine and he nuzzles under my jaw. "I want you, Kelly, but I think we both need rest."

He's not wrong. I finally manage to stand up and he helps me get the shirt on over my towel wrapped hair. It falls mid-thigh, and I could probably sleep without the shorts, but I don't want to wake up horny and try to jump an alpha or omega in their sleep. So, I leave them on.

By the time Teddy has gotten my hair unwrapped and we fluff it out to dry, Sam comes out of the bathroom. Teddy picks me up and deposits me in the middle of the bed before climbing in behind me, snuggling up against my back with his arm draped over my waist. His rumbly purr vibrates through my whole body and makes me melt. I try to argue that he needs to be in the middle so Sam can purr for him.

Then Sam is cuddled up to my front, his arm draped over my waist too, holding Teddy's hip on the other side. His loud alpha purr starts up, and the whole bed shakes a little with it. My mind tries to protest that Teddy's the one who needs to snuggle, but I can't make my mouth work to get the words out. My eyes blink slowly, taking in the big alpha in front of me. I blink again, trying to wake up to get Teddy to trade me places, but my eyes won't open. I don't remember anything after that.

Chapter 16

Sam

I wake up to the sweetest beta pressed against my chest. One hand tucked under her chin, the other hand holding onto my chest hair. Which is slightly painful, and most likely what woke me up. She murmurs something in her sleep and yanks again.

Yeah, that will definitely open your eyes.

Shit.

Last night hit her hard. I think all the confrontation, grocery shopping, then a big dinner knocked her for a loop. If she isn't feeling better today, I'll take her and Teddy both to the doctor. I look over her shoulder, taking in my omega. He looks so much better this morning. He isn't as pale, and he's smiling in his sleep as he buries his face against Kelly's hair. I hear a small murmur as he pulls her closer against him, causing her to yank against my chest hair again. If this keeps up, I'm gonna have a bald patch there.

Stroking my fingers over her jaw, I make quiet susurrations—trying not to wake either of them up—but to get her to at least relax enough to let go so I can slip out. It's bright outside. I forgot to close the curtains, and I need to get up and let Jake out before he has an accident. Her fingers finally loosen enough for me to escape, and I slide out of the bed, not bothering to put on anything more than my shorts so I can take care of Jake as soon as possible.

I open the door and almost trip over the big lug. He's laying sprawled on his back in the hallway. His eyes pop open and he wags at me, his legs flailing in the air as he tries to roll over. "C'mon, bud, let's get you outside," I murmur quietly to him, patting my leg when he finally manages to get upright. He follows me downstairs, only looking back at the bedroom door and whining once. By the time we reach the back door, he's practically wiggling in circles around me.

I open the door and barely manage to get the screen unlocked before he pushes it open and bolts outside, running back behind the shop to take care of his own business. Leaving him to it, I wander towards the kitchen, headed for the coffeepot. I can get that running before I start on breakfast. It's a good thing Kelly picked up all the staples yesterday so I actually have stuff to cook this morning.

I don't usually bother for myself. It's easier to just fix something fast. But I need them to know I can take care of them. I grab out all the ingredients to make stuffed French toast and strawberries. I remember hearing Brice complain about not getting anything but decaf, and I don't have that. So, I also pull down my sampler box of tea and put the kettle on. According to Brice, omegas are supposed to avoid stimulants if at all possible due to hormone fluctuations. I like tea well enough, but sometimes I need my fucking caffeine fix.

I just finish mixing up the cream cheese for the French toast when I hear Jake scratching at the screen door. It's still cool enough to leave the back door open, and no one comes around that way anyway. I let him in and he scrambles to his food bowl, glaring at me when he beats me to it since I haven't filled it yet. "Sorry, buddy, I've been kinda busy." I pat him on the head and pour a big scoop of kibble into his dish. He's already scarfed most of it down by the time I finish washing my hands and get back to chopping.

The strawberries are sliced and cream is whipped when I make my way upstairs. Teddy's still holding tight to Kelly, and he's purring in his sleep. Part of me wants to wrap myself around both of them again and go back to bed. But after yesterday, my main priority is making him feel secure. I sit on the bed beside him, and he pulls her closer as his body rolls towards the dip in the mattress. Running my fingers over his forehead and through his hair, I'm glad to see his fever's completely gone. He nuzzles against my palm, but when his tongue comes out to lick my fingers and nip at my thumb, I know he's just faking sleep. Probably to keep snuggling our beta.

I lean down to give him a kiss and his mouth opens for me as soon as our lips touch. He lets out a low moaning whine, and I'm suddenly rock fucking hard in my sleep pants. Which do *nothing* to hide my erection. He chuckles quietly, murmuring against my lips. "Feel free to come back to bed, Sexy. I'm sure we can think of a good way to wake up Kelly that she would enjoy. Plus, open up a few of those boxes she got last night, try them out."

I can't stop my loud bark of laughter, and Kelly jolts straight up in bed, looking around groggily. Teddy glares at me as I pull back, but there's no real heat in it. "Sorry guys, breakfast is just about ready, and I didn't want your food to get cold."

He grumbles at me a bit, but swings his legs out of the bed beside me and sits there for a minute, getting his bearings. Kelly circles the bed, running her hands over his forehead and through his hair as well. "Are you feeling any better?"

He smolders up at her. "Well, I could be *more* better." He waggles his eyebrows and she smiles back.

"Nope, let's get you some food first. We can play later." He grumbles but lets her pull him off the bed and we all go downstairs.

There are still a few minutes left on the coffeepot, but the kettle's puffing out little bursts of steam and half whistles, so I turn off that burner. "So, who gets coffee, who gets tea…" I open the door to the fridge, doing a quick scan. "And who gets orange juice?" Kelly stands beside the sampler pack of teas reading the box while Teddy looks longingly at the coffee.

Must be a shared omega trait.

Not that I blame them, I can't imagine.

"Do you have any Constant Comment or Spiced Chai?" he asks me.

It takes me a minute to think because I don't drink tea that often. "Check the pantry, second set of shelves on the right, third shelf down, wooden box. If I have anything that's not in the sampler, it'll be there. I know I used to, but I can't remember when I drank it last." Teddy walks over to the pantry still casting longing gazes at the coffee, I hear a few grumbles, and I think he called me obsessive. Well, he's not wrong, but I like a tidy workspace. Lord knows what he'll think if he ever comes out to the shop. He leaves the pantry carrying a packet of orange and spice tea. Good flavor, naturally sweet, but I guess I must have been out of the others. I make a mental note to put them on my grocery list, along with a canister of decaf.

Kelly pulls the orange juice out of the fridge for herself, and I get a cup of tea steeping for Teddy while I start plating the first batch. I make them sit down and enjoy their food while it's still hot since I can only do a few pieces at a time and ideally you need the contrasting temperatures when serving this. It's just as well, since Teddy finishes everything off, and takes me up on the offer for a second slab and more strawberries. Jake's circling the table, waiting for someone to drop something, and I lead him outside with the promise of a slice of ham if he'll play outside while we eat. He hops around in circles, before taking off after a squirrel in the backyard.

Kelly's putting her plate and glass in the dishwasher when I return and declines my offer for more food as I finish cooking the last few slices and settle in next to Teddy. She comes back to the table with a cup of coffee and sits down beside me, running her foot over mine under the table and then smiling as she kicks me lightly. I guess this is happy-flirty Kelly. It's nice. Teddy finishes his breakfast and tea, then loads his own dishes in the washer before coming back to sit down too, still looking at her cup of coffee. I need to make getting decaf a priority.

Kelly takes a sip from her cup and he watches her, licking his lips. I'm about to insist he goes and gets some damned coffee before he gives me a nervous breakdown when she speaks up. "So, do we have any plans for today? I know yesterday we said today we were going to spend the day talking and getting to know each other. Did you have anything specific in mind?" I don't think she means anything by it, but Teddy bites his lip and wags his eyebrows at us both.

Fuck my life.

Not that I don't want to, I would love to spend the whole day in bed getting to know every inch of both of them. But for Kelly's peace of mind if nothing else, we need to talk so she knows this isn't just about sex. Kelly's giggling at the faces he makes at her, but they both sober up when I touch his hand. "I am completely onboard with that plan later, but I really do think we should spend some time together today, actually talking. Come on, I can show you the basement." I take my last bite of breakfast and put my plate in the sink. I'll come back and wash the breakfast dishes in a bit.

Chapter 17

Teddy

Sam wasn't lying when he said he had a man cave down here. Though judging by the look on Kelly's face it'll be a pack cave soon enough. She wanders over to the flat screen television that takes up a good chunk of one wall and starts perusing the video games there. There are a few retro systems, one that looks like it might be a raspberry pi setup, and then a couple of newer consoles. Everything is lined up on neat custom shelves with slots for the controllers and built-in battery chargers. There's a bar area in the back with a big theater style popcorn machine on it and the glass front shows a variety of candy. In front of the giant TV are six alpha sized recliners with super plush seating. I guess he was going for the full theater experience.

The other end of the basement has a pool table and a new looking arcade tower. Kelly's still looking through the video games, but when I look over, Sam's scratching the back of his head and staring at the floor. His eyes flick up to mine and he blushes. "I don't know, I always thought I would join Joseph's pack, and I drew up plans for a pack game room and entertainment stuff. I wanted to contribute something no one else could, you know? Something that would make them happy, or at least let them see me as more than just a tag-along. Once it became obvious that *that* wasn't going to happen, it seemed a shame to waste the time and effort I'd already put into it."

He's staring at the pool table now, and I look around the room, realizing he built most of this stuff. Not the chairs, probably, but the custom video game layout, the bar, and apparently the pool table. I wonder briefly about the arcade system.

"Wait, you mean you built a pool table?"

It's hardly the most impressive feature in here, but damn. He meets my eyes, his blush deepening. "Well, yeah. I mean. I like pool. I also drew up plans for a library, on that wall." He points to the bare wall behind me. "But even though I had the whole basement resealed, I'm still getting slugs in here sometimes."

Kelly gives a little shriek and trots back towards the stairs. We both stare at her while she bounces from foot to foot. "Yes, I like nature, I do *not* like slugs. They creep me out, ok? I stepped on one, one night, in the dark, trying to go to the bathroom. I didn't want to turn the hall light on and risk waking up Tuck. And it got stuck between my toes and was really hard to get off. I kind of panicked and woke my parents up with my screaming." Now she's the same red shade as Sam; they look like adorable bookends.

Sam turns halfway, so he can see us both as he speaks. "As I was saying, I'm still working on some sort of leak in this back corner. I keep a dehumidifier down here and it isn't really a problem, but I want to get it completely fixed before I bring anything else down. I could have converted the nest to hold all this stuff, but it seemed wrong, even though I never thought I'd have an omega." He looks sheepishly at me when he says the last bit.

"Oh, I know what we can do!" Kelly is hopping up and down on the stairs, still stealing glances at the ground like a wave of slugs is going to come barreling through the room and cover the stairs. She grins excitedly, eyes swinging between the two of us. "I know that you were worried about your heat starting. And it's not supposed to for a while. But why don't we take a trip over to Springfield? We'll have a long truck ride to talk, then you can pick some stuff out to order for the nest. Maybe we can grab lunch while we're out. Maybe go by the bookstore in the mall. Just make a day of it together?"

She looks hopeful when she mentions the bookstore and my mind flashes back to all the books stacked around her room when we were there yesterday. I was pretty out of it, but I remember there were a lot. She glances back to the stairs before hopping up one more step, causing a dark chuckle to rumble out of Sam. "Ok, Sugar. If Teddy feels up to it, we can take a trip to Nest-N-Stuff and go to the mall. Make sure that the two of you have anything else you need to be comfortable here." Kelly squeals and looks like she wants to hop off the stairs and wrap her arms around him, but then thinks better of it.

It doesn't take long for us to get ready for the day. Kelly and I dig through our respective clothes till I'm back in my standard black jeans, black T-shirt, black overshirt, and black sneakers. She's wearing another pair of cutoffs and a tiny shirt that has a black-and-white image of a bald guy in a cape on it. She slips on her dusty sneakers from yesterday after knocking them against each other on the porch. Jake must hear her because he comes barreling around the side of the house, knocking her into me and licking at her hands.

"Oh, you big booger. Now I need to go wash my hands before we leave, or I'm gonna smell like dog slobber all day. I love you slobber muffin Jake-y!" And now she's talking baby talk to the dog while rubbing his ears. "Are you gonna stay here and guard the house like a good boy? Are you?" She pats her thighs twice and Jake leans against her with a groan while she scratches his ears again. I think the dog's as smitten as me and Sam.

After a few minutes, she heads back inside to wash her hands and grab some water, and I follow Jake around the side of the house, just taking in the surroundings, since this is going to be my new home. Soon I hear the screen door on the front porch close and Sam calling my name. He's leaning against the driver's side door of the pickup while Kelly tries to climb in the passenger side. I walk up behind her and put my hand on her ass, squeezing a little as I give her a boost.

She giggles as she crawls across the cab and finds the center lap belt. Sam lets out a grumble about her not sitting in the back seat of the cab but doesn't make her move. I offer to trade, but I don't think being squished up against Sam would be the best option, plus my longer legs need more floor space.

Kelly just grins at me and shakes her head. "Nope, center seat gets to control the radio. Mine!" She starts flipping through stations as soon as the truck gets turned around. Sam and I both groan when she stops with something upbeat and poppy. She laughs again and keeps going. There aren't going to be a lot of stations out here, probably nothing like I normally listen to, and I vow to introduce my pack to proper music—the stuff I have on my phone—soon.

She stops again and starts singing along with a song that I think is by the band Dropkick Murphys. Sarah was playing them one day at the gym—it's kind of a punk rock with bagpipes song. Not my personal favorite, but not bad. Sam grumbles again so she turns to him. "Ok, Sam, what kind of music do you like?" He mumbles a few things off, but the only one I catch is Johnny Cash and there's no way in hell I'm doing that. I can do older metal like Nine Inch Nails, or some of the newer stuff like AleStorm and other Pirate Metal. I can even listen to punk and grunge. But I'm pretty sure my ears are going to start bleeding if we listen to country.

Kelly, true to her word, controls the radio for the whole trip. It seems to take about an hour to get to this nesting store they were talking about, and I pull up my banking app to check my balances when I see the sign for it on the highway. I have a lot of stuff already back at the center that we can plan a trip to go get soon, but for now I need a place where my inner omega feels safe and comfortable. I can at least grab some basics that'll go with what I already have, once I can pick the rest up.

Chapter 18

Teddy

We pull into the parking lot and get out, Sam and I flanking Kelly as she bounces around looking at everything. Sam grabs a cart as we walk inside and pass the bathroom section. I mostly need bedding at this point. I'm not opposed to new soft towels too—the ones in Sam's downstairs bathroom were like drying off with sandpaper—but right now I need bedding and nesting supplies.

We get approached by several salespeople, who all try to talk to Kelly and ask what she's looking for. After the fifth time of her trying to explain that it's my nest, I just tell her we want something soft in dark jewel tones or black, preferably in a Minky fabric or an Egyptian cotton. That way she doesn't have to keep trying to convince them that I'm the omega, and they stop walking off in a huff. I really don't like this fucking store.

We eventually find our way back to bedding, and there's a huge machine that claims it's for stuffing your own pillows. I admit my curiosity is piqued as I look around at their shell options. Unfortunately, while almost everything is a soft fabric, the colors are all pale pastels and variations on white. I really like the textures, but I can't handle a nest in pastels. I could buy a box of dye...but then I would have to take them home, unstuff them, dye them, and then re-stuff them, and that just seems like a lot of work. I stand there contemplating my options, and don't even notice that Kelly's gone until she returns with an employee.

I hear a whispered mumble of, "I hate this fucking machine." The pimply faced beta boy stares between Sam and me, and my rumbly growl slips out.

Before I can say that I don't want to use their machine, and ask if these colors are their only options, Kelly pipes in. "Sorry, the manager said that there was a kiosk near the machine that had more color and texture options that we could order with however much fill we want. But I can't seem to find it. Can you please help me?" The kid looks at Kelly like he's about to swallow his tongue, giving her a once-over and smoothing down his employee vest, his eyes lingering too long on her unmarked neck.

We need to take care of that asap.

"I'm sorry Miss Omega"—his voice cracks at the end like he's trying to make it sound deeper than it actually is—"it's just over here on this other side, if you want to see if there's anything you like. I'll be happy to get an order sent in and have it shipped wherever you want."

Kelly's eyes flip up to mine and I nod to her. But her mouth drops open when she gets around to the actual catalog. It's huge and filled with fabric swatches. She tries to pick it up to bring it over to me, but her arms tremble and strain with the effort. I scoop it up and put it back on the display stand so that I can look over her shoulder.

Wrapping my arms around her, I lean down to press my face against the side of hers as she flips through the book, stopping to read different fabric descriptions and so I can feel samples. We make it through the first few pages before we're interrupted by a burly beta security guard. "Sir, I'm going to have to ask you to step away from the omega or provide proof of pack."

Sam's low growl is a menace, making the security guard tense and reach for his belt. Kelly bursts out in almost hysterical sounding giggles and I just give up, pulling out my omega center ID and passing it over to the guard before turning back to Kelly. "Yeah, Kelly, step away from the omega unless you have proof of pack." She's a better sport about it than Sam, and gives me a big hug before going to stand by him while the guard stares fixedly at my ID, his eyes flicking rapidly between me and the small, laminated card.

Fuck my life.

After much longer than it should take, and some discussion on his phone, the guard gingerly passes me back my ID. "Sorry,

Mr. Darnell, we have store policy in place to protect unmarked omegas." I sigh again, continuing to flip through the sample book. At least I had time to pick out a few options while he was running my identification. Now that my inner omega is interested in buying nesting stuff, I know I'll obsess over it until I get something sorted out. I pull out my cell and take a few pictures of item numbers I want as well as make note about what fill percentage I want for each option.

Kelly disappeared again while I was perusing the options but pops up behind me like a fucking meerkat right as I close the catalog. Her cart's stuffed with sheets and blankets with the materials and colors I talked to her about earlier. "Hey, sorry, I figured we wanted to leave soon. So I grabbed what you mentioned earlier, but we can put back anything you don't like. I wasn't trying to take your choice away. I just didn't figure you'd want to be here after all the crap."

I pull her into a hug, murmuring thanks against the top of her hair and looking around for the beta who called security on me so I can place my order...and of course the little ass wipe disappeared.

Kelly kisses my cheek, and passes me the cart to go through and see what I might want to keep or leave at the customer service desk for re-shelving. She did a great job actually, almost everything here is stuff I would have chosen myself. I might have gone with a few different colors, more deep burgundy and less dark forest green, but she still did an amazing job, and I don't even know if those options were available. She even picked up mattress protectors and a flyer to order blackout blinds. I look around to tell her how impressed I am, but she's disappeared again. This time with my phone.

Sam's still with me but staring over the shelves towards the front of the store. "Yeah, she went to customer service to get your pillows ordered. You wanna go meet her so we can grab some lunch?"

Fuck, how does she keep her mind this organized? I can barely function with one thing at a time most days and she did all my shopping while I was feeling up a bunch of pillow samples?

I grab the handle of the cart—much to Sam's annoyance—and we quickly walk to the front to meet up with our beta. There are a couple of alphas standing over by the door that haven't taken their eyes off her since I spotted her across the shelves. They look like shifty fuckers in need of a beat-down after the trouble we've had here. I walk up to Kelly and wrap my arms around her, glaring at them both until they shuffle their feet and walk off.

Kelly cuts through my aggressive haze. "Hey, Teddy, I'm glad you're here. Your notes didn't say how many of each one of these you needed, and I was about to come ask." She turns back to me, wrapping her arms around my waist and nuzzling against my chest, causing my purr to start up involuntarily. I feel her hands on my ass when she slides my phone back into my pocket. "Sorry I stole it, I just wanted to make things easier for you."

"Miss Darnell, if you can just give us your shipping address and sign here, we can get all this finished up." The weaselly beta from earlier turns around, his jaw drops as his eyes flick between me and Sam.

Kelly's high, clear laugh is muffled against my chest. "Not Darnell...Actually Sam, I don't know what our pack name is...what *is* your last name?" The kid fidgets, shifting from one foot to the other as I step forward and fill out the number of each kind of pillow on the paperwork laying on the counter.

Sam takes Kelly's hand, his thumb rubbing across the back of her fingers. "My last name's McKinnley, but we don't need two Pack McKinnleys in town. So I'm open to suggestions. If Teddy wants to use his name, since he's not from around here, we can do that." I smile over at him, torn on the idea. The plan with Steven and Garret was always to take my last name for the pack. Their family is pretty well known, and we didn't want to automatically be lumped in with them.

Sensing my hesitation, Kelly reples, "Ok, so I guess it'll be Miss Parker then, at least for now." She hugs me again as I finish filling out paperwork and scan the QR code to do a quick search on different colors for the sheets and blankets she picked out. I add another few of those to the order in different dark shades, just for some variety.

Sam steps in, passing a smiling Kelly off to me as he fills out the shipping information. The beta rings up our purchases including what's in the basket and I see Sam visibly swallow. He's doing mental calculations in his head before I step forward and hand over my debit card.

"Now hold on, I'm supposed to buy the nesting materials for you. You're *my* omega." Sam actually looks upset that I'm paying for my own stuff. Kelly's smile drops at the pain in his voice and she looks between us.

I forget that pack dynamics are new to her. "Sam, I have my own money. I'll explain later, but for now, just let me do this. You're already feeding us and giving us a place to live. I need to help out, ok?"

Sam looks back and forth between the two of us, his ears are red. "But how am I supposed to prove that I can be a good alpha if I can't take care of you?"

Kelly and I move simultaneously, both of our arms wrapping around him. I growl at the beta behind the counter who's still staring at us, and he finishes ringing me up, quickly handing me the receipt, which I stuff in my pocket. Sam swallows again before turning sad eyes to me and then burying his face in Kelly's hair.

Pushing the cart with one hand, I lead them both out to the truck and fold down the tailgate. Shoving Sam to sit beside me, Kelly takes his other side and we both lean in against him, offering what comfort we can.

I don't want to talk about this—it always makes me feel gross—but I might as well get it out of the way. "As you guys know, everybody thought I was going to be an alpha, yes?" Sam nods but doesn't look at me. Kelly's watching us both, she looks like she's trying to figure out which one needs a hug more. My fingers trace along the edge of my leather cuffs—it's a nervous reaction, but I can't help it. Both their eyes seem drawn to the movement as I keep talking.

"Well, I've always been...big. When I turned eight, I had already known Steven and Garret for years. Everybody knew we were going to be a pack. Gramps...Er...My Pop's Pop...Murphy's dad said he wasn't going to let his family look like paupers in front of the Carson Pack." I pause so they can take that in. The Carson pack are rich, like stupid rich. My parents were well enough off, upper middle class to be sure, but not like that. I only met Vee and Garret because two of my dads work for theirs. We met when I was a toddler at some sort of social event that I was too young to even remember. After that we stuck together like glue.

I clear my throat. "Anyway, Gramps started an account for me. He put a few thousand in to start and added to it each month. Instead of birthdays or Christmas, I just got money put into it. He said it was so when I started a pack, I'd be set. We'd be able to use it to pay the fees to the omega center to meet a good omega or put a down payment on a place of our own. It was barely a drop in the bucket compared to what Vee and Garret would contribute, but it was something that would come from me and give me more standing in the pack."

I swallow again, nausea rolling through my stomach. "At least, that was the plan, until it turns out: Hey, your grandson's an omega. The old man hit the roof. He demanded the money back. But he had set the account up in my name, with Murphy as my guardian."

"Gramps couldn't do shit about it. They got into a huge fight. Murphy argued that all the interest it had accrued in eight years was mine, as well as any holiday gift money that had gone in. He offered to pay Gramps back for the initial investment, but the old man started to yell that he didn't have a grandson anymore since I wasn't an alpha. Mom hung up the phone on him before Murphy could say anything else. She told me she didn't want to hear him, but I think she didn't want me to feel like the reason Murphy couldn't talk to his family anymore."

Staring at the ground, I can't look at Kelly or Sam. I don't want them to see me cry. Alphas aren't supposed to cry.

Not that I'm an alpha anymore...or ever.

I sniff back the tears that try to escape. "So, yeah...I have a nice little nest egg that I use when I need extra stuff. The omega center covers all my school stuff, and the fees for housing and food are pretty much taken care of with grants. But I should take care of this. It's been growing for nearly twenty years, I might as well use it to help start my pack, right?" Two pairs of arms come around me, holding me close as Sam's loud rumbly purr feels like it's shaking the entire truck.

Kelly pipes up. "Ok, so...not your last name either then...is it the same as your gramps?" I nod dumbly at her. "Yeah, he can suck it. Not his name. Well, how about Carpenter...that's what Sam does, right? Go back to the old way of naming. We can be Pack Carpenter?" She leans over to Sam, giving an exaggerated wink and whispering loudly. "Just be glad you don't run a septic service."

His head drops to my shoulder as his body shakes, and I only hear the barest mumble. "Jesus fuck, Sugar, really. That was awful."

Kelly snuggles back against my side giggling loudly. She finally calms enough to take a deep breath and stand up. "Well, if you wanna be that way...come on Mr. Shitter and Mr. Shitter, let's get the truck loaded and go get some lunch."

Her laughter and the shock of hearing her use profanity for the first time knocks me out of any lingering sadness. Sam and I load up the back of the cab with blankets and pillows, tossing the sealed packets of sheets and sheet protectors in the bed of the truck. We can move them up to the cab too when we go in to get food.

Kelly stops me before I can help her back into the cab. Her arms come around my neck, and she stands on her toes to kiss me on the chin. "I'm sorry that so many people suck. But you know you're ours, right? Sam's and mine?" I nod at her somber tone. "Ok, well, as long as you know, you're stuck with us now, I'm not going anywhere, and I'm pretty sure you'd need to scrape him off like a barnacle if you wanted to get rid of him."

Sam's voice comes from the driver's seat, through the open door. "She's not wrong!" I pick Kelly up, my hands going under her butt to hold her close and kiss her the way I've wanted to since I woke up this morning. I want to tell her I love her, but I'm still worried about scaring her away since she's new to being in a pack. But I know it's true. These two are already so much a part of me that I need them like I need air. I can't lose them, no matter what.

part of me that I need them like I need air. I can't lose them, no matter what.

Chapter 19

Kelly

After everything else I don't feel like being around people, so we grab our burgers to go. I haven't been to a Red Rogers before, but Teddy and Sam both say they make great burgers. Honestly, it's kind of overwhelming when they each pick out toppings I've never imagined on a hamburger. I go with bacon and cheese, because why mess with perfection?

We each get a burger and steak fries with shakes. Sam gets something called campfire sauce, but I just want catsup. I can only have so many gastric adventures in one day. While we wait for our food, Teddy pulls up a map on his phone and finds a park three blocks over for us to sit outside and enjoy the nice weather.

Our little picnic's wonderful, and I'm glad that we get to have some fresh air after being in the stuffy store for so long.

My plan was for us to go to the bookstore next, but I kind of just want to get back to the house and stretch out for a long snuggle with Teddy. I don't mind customer service, I have to check into that persona for work in the mornings, and to a lesser extent for classes in the afternoons. But this is supposed to be my break, and while I don't mind helping Teddy and Sam shop for nesting stuff, I was about ready to go off at the people in the store for upsetting them both. I know Mom says you get more flies with honey than with vinegar, but sometimes I feel like I need to just pull out the flyswatter instead.

This burger's better than just about any takeout I've had. It can't beat homemade, but it's super good, and I steal a little bit of Sam's campfire sauce to try with my steak fries. That's good too, but I mostly enjoy the way he acts affronted. Teddy distracts him so I can steal the tiny takeout cup. True to form though, when I try to escape with my prize I trip over my own feet and go down.

I manage to spill all the campfire sauce, but my shirt now smells delicious. Teddy grabs my arm to help me up, but Sam doesn't seem to realize what's going on and tackles him from behind in retaliation for the distraction earlier.

Things finally settle down when Sam gets Teddy in a head-lock while I roll around in the grass laughing, covered in sauce and bits of grass. A woman with a baby carriage and two smaller kids in tow glares at our fun. Not sure what crawled up her butt and died. We weren't hurting anyone…except my shirt, which is smeared and stained with sauce. Now I really don't feel like going to the bookstore. We clean up our mess as best we can, and head back to the truck. Sam and Teddy take turns brushing me off and picking grass out of my hair.

Before I can climb my sticky self back up into the truck, Sam takes off his flannel overshirt. He hands it to Teddy then starts to reorganize the truck a bit in just his tank top, while Teddy leads me to the public bathroom to get cleaned up and changed. I use my now dirty shirt to wipe off as much of the sauce as I can before washing off in the tiny sink. They have the loud wall-mounted hand dryers that won't do any good to help with drying off, and no paper towels. So after I get my shirt damp, I turn it inside out to wipe the splatter of sauce out of my hair and off my glasses. I don't even know how it got there. Seriously, there wasn't that much in the cup that I stole. I guess I'm just talented that way.

When I'm as clean as I can get, Teddy bundles up my shirt and wraps me in Sam's flannel, rolling up the sleeves and tying it around my waist so it doesn't come down to my knees. It's well worn—frayed around the collar—but so soft, and it smells like him. His warm cedar and sawdust scent makes me feel cozy and I wonder if I can take a nap on the drive home. We get back to the truck, and Sam already has it on and the heater running. The temperature's dropped since we left the house this morning, and he *did* give me his flannel. But the warm air on top of his cuddly shirt and my full stomach makes me yawn and blink.

"Are we still going to the bookstore, Kelly, or are you all tuckered out?" He looks at me as Teddy gives me a boost into the truck and gets my lap belt secured before getting himself buckled in. I can't stop the yawn that makes my jaw crack and starts Teddy yawning too. Sam lets slip a small yawn of his own and a slight chuckle before we all manage to get under control.

"Sorry, Sam. I am full of food, covered in saucy goodness, and I need a nap. Can we, maybe, take a raincheck on the bookstore?" His hand runs over my still damp hair as he looks past me to Teddy, who just nods and wraps his arms around me, pulling me against him, and yawning again.

"Alrighty then, lemme make a quick pit-stop for some coffee, then we'll head home and look at getting the nest sorted out...and maybe a shower." He smiles at me, chuckling to himself as he wipes the hand that was in my hair on his jeans. I must have missed some of the sauce. Teddy's already breathing deep and easy. He fell asleep almost as soon as we started snuggling. I close my eyes and drift off listening to Sam flipping through radio stations.

Teddy

I wake up when my head bonks against the window. Kelly's cuddled up against my chest. Her head resting almost under my armpit, and I don't understand how either one of us slept like that. Sam's humming along quietly to something on the radio that I can't quite make out, just that it has a little twangy sound to it. The driver's window is open a couple of inches, and he has a paper coffee cup nestled between his thighs. I must make some sort of noise, because his eyes flick over to mine. "Hey, I thought I'd wake y'all up when we got home. Everything ok?" He reaches over and turns off the radio.

I stretch the arm that Kelly isn't wedged under. "Everything's fine. I just whacked my head on the window. Sorry I crashed so hard. I guess yesterday was kind of crazy and then the store...I think the big lunch just knocked me on my ass. Sorry." I feel kind of like shit making him drive home on his own. I need to be using this time getting to know my alpha better.

We pull into the dirt lot in front of the house and Jake's lying on the porch, his tail already going before we even stop the truck. As soon as the engine shuts off he jumps up and lopes over to the passenger door, standing on his hind legs and looking in. His eyes zero-in on Kelly and he starts licking the glass. Her eyes blink open now that the truck isn't moving, and she snorts a laugh when she sees him.

Sam gets out and pats his leg, calling Jake away from our window and towards the house. He unlocks the front door and swings it open before coming back to check on us, then starts hauling in our purchases. I haven't actually seen the nest yet, but I'm loath to admit how excited I am at the prospect. Kelly smiles up at me and slides out the door on Sam's side. I guess I'm not moving fast enough for her. As soon as she's outside, she hops up on the back tire and swings her leg over the side of the truck, almost losing her balance and falling over backwards. Sam runs back into the yard, arms outstretched like he can catch her from the front porch.

Thankfully, she manages to right herself and falls forward into the truck bed. Her head pops up, grinning at me a few seconds later, but Sam lifts her under the arms and sets her back on her feet in the dirt. She huffs at him for a second before Jake goes barreling around the front of the truck, tongue already out like he's going to lick the air all the way to Kelly. She squeals and giggles and takes off running towards the house. "I gotta get a shower before Jake tries to lick the sauce off me!" is all I hear as she disappears through the front door.

Sam leans over the side of the truck and grabs a few more packaged items we brought home that wouldn't fit in the back of the cab. He taps on the window as he passes me, still sitting in the truck, his eyebrows raised as if to ask if everything is ok. I nod, finally unclipping my seatbelt and sliding out of the truck. I grab Kelly's still damp shirt and a plastic wrapped blanket from the back before heading inside. Dropping the shirt in the hamper by the washing machine, I stop...I don't have any idea where the nest is other than somewhere on the first floor.

A few seconds later, Sam comes out of a room at the far end of the downstairs hallway, and I wave my bag of blanket at him. He smiles and waves me over. "Ok, now...the nest isn't done. Yet. We can fit it out however you want. But lemme show you what we're working with, so we can figure out what you might like. Make everything just the way you want it." He rubs the back of his neck, and his cheeks are flushed. I understood that it wasn't furnished, but just how bad can it be?

He throws open the door he's standing in front of, and I realize that was a terrible question to ask myself. Whatever I was thinking, this is worse. This is so much worse. My inner omega screams at the mess; the bare plywood floor is littered with dust and chunks of plaster. The walls are covered in plastic film, but you can see the pink insulation rolled into the cavities behind it. I can't even tell if there's any glass in the windows, or just more sheets of plastic. There has to be, right? Otherwise this room would be freezing. Fuck me.

Sam is staring intently at me, and I swallow hard, trying not to show just how uncomfortable this makes me. He reaches out for my shoulder and my body sinks against him, seeking comfort from the chaos around me. Omegas don't like chaos—it throws us for a loop; and seeing what's supposed to be my nest so completely gutted is freaking me out.

"Sorry, I didn't mean to spring all this on you. I didn't make it a priority when I was rebuilding because I didn't think I'd need it. But don't worry. I should be able to get the sheetrock back up, and the windows replaced in a week or so. The floor might take a bit longer, depending on what you want. But I don't have any special orders due this week, so I have some leeway on work stuff. I can get the rest of these batts of insulation put up tonight if you don't need me for anything. Then start on the drywall after I file the pack registration tomorrow."

He looks at me hopefully as he rattles off information about paint colors and carpet versus hardwood. My eyes keep flicking around the room, and I whine. I can't help it. My nest is supposed to be a safe space, and right now it barely exists.

I bolt from the room, Sam following close behind me. I look down, noticing that I'm still holding the blanket, and set it down at the foot of the stairs for now—until I can figure out where it needs to go. Sam comes up behind me and wraps his arms around my shoulders. He rumbles out a loud purr, and while my body melts against him, my mind is racing, spiraling into a panic. I still have a few weeks till my heat starts. This shouldn't be a problem. But my omega is going mental at the thought of not having a safe space for our heat. Sam's arms squeeze around me tighter, and he pulls me around with him when the bathroom door opens.

Kelly steps out in a billow of steam—she has a towel wrapped around her body and another around her hair. Her glasses are fogged up and she stumbles forward, her hand tracing along the wall as she tries to make it to the stairs. She gets about a foot away from where Sam's hugging me before she stops, her head tilted back. Staring up at us through her clouded glass. "Sorry, I was in a hurry to get clean. I forgot my clothes." Sam chuckles in my ear, and the sound sends a shiver up my spine, my earlier panic receding with need as my mind finally processes the hard body pressed against me. I tilt my head back, nuzzling against his jaw, and his arms tighten around me.

"Woah, Teddy, you ok? Your scent just went off like a bomb. Is everything alright?" Kelly. Dear, sweet, innocent Kelly has pressed against my front. She finally takes off her foggy glasses and is squinting up at my face, trying to make out my expression. I would think the problem was obvious as my hard dick is being ground into her flat little stomach when she stands on her toes, trying to see my face better. She blinks once...twice. Understanding dawns.

"Oh. Sorry. Sorry." She drops back on her heels, her face a bright pink as she slides her glasses back on and makes her way around us and up the stairs. "I'll just...um...clothes." She stumbles on the top step, her towel unwrapping. She manages to catch it and herself, clutching the cloth to her chest and straightening her body before scurrying into Sam's room. I guess she forgot that we were behind her, because holding it over her boobs didn't cover anything from down here.

Chapter 20

Sam

I can't believe I forgot about the nest.

Well, ok, I didn't forget. I just didn't see a point in worrying about it at the time without an omega. And now an omega lives here, and I need to haul ass and get it finished. But even now I'm torn. I need to get this done—I saw how panicked Teddy was—but I also need to spend time with my pack. We need to get to know each other.

In the interest of compromise, I help them pick out a movie downstairs and microwave some popcorn for them. Kelly's apparently a big fan of comedies, and Teddy suggested Monty Python and the Holy Grail. He says it's his friend Sarah's favorite movie, and he's sat through it dozens of times with her.

When I leave them to it, he's going on about swallows and coconuts. I love watching the two of them interact, but that room isn't going to finish itself.

It takes me longer to get ready than it does to actually finish unrolling and stapling in the big batts of insulation. I learned the hard way that I don't want to deal with fiberglass without long sleeves, safety glasses, and a mask. In fact, the more of my body I can cover, the better. That shit itches for days if it gets on you. Thankfully, I finish up and get the plastic sheeting back in place before the movie ends. At least, I think so. Teddy and Kelly are still downstairs.

After a thorough shower, I wander back downstairs to start dinner. I head to the basement to see what they might like to eat—and holy fucking shit. Well, it's a good thing the chairs down here are wide.

Kelly's in Teddy's lap, straddling his thighs, her hands gripping the top of the seat behind his head. She's bare from the waist down, and he has her shirt pushed up. His hands are cupping her pert little tits, his mouth covering most of one completely. Her head's thrown back as she rides him. They both have a light sheen of sweat, almost glowing under the low light. They look fucking amazing together, and I'm not sure if I want to join them or just watch.

My mind swims at the thought of what I could do to them, together or apart. How it'll feel to have Teddy helping me train her to take my knot. I know we have to go slow for that, but fuck. I bite my lip, trying to suppress a groan at the thoughts swirling through my head. Kelly's head snaps forward, her wide eyes blinking up at me. Her hips stutter for a moment, but relief washes through me when she doesn't try to cover up.

Teddy slowly releases her nipple, and his head turns to me. I can just see the smirk on his face as his hands slide down to her hips, helping her move against him. His own loud moan echoes hers, but her eyes stay on me, never losing contact as he slams her hips down. He seems to be getting close, his legs tense as he rises out of the seat to meet her on each downward stroke.

Kelly's shaking. She seems to be having trouble. It may be the chair or the position, but I would be strongly remiss if I didn't offer to lend a hand. As I get closer, she reaches for me, and I can't stop myself from claiming her lips. Teddy trails kisses across her chest as he grinds her hips down over his length. He's still fully dressed, but his jeans are pulled down enough to free his cock so she can ride him. I run my hand through his hair, over his shoulder, and down his chest, pivoting my wrist so I can rub circles around her clit. She's already so close, and it doesn't take much before she cries out, shuddering against him. His voice echoes hers as he pulls her down hard, his face buried in her neck.

I pull my hand back, adjusting my own erection to relieve some of the pressure. Kelly's eyes open, and she blinks at me while reaching for my zipper. Her eyes are huge behind her glasses as she looks up, holding my gaze when she pulls my hard cock free. "You don't have to do anything, Sugar, I just wanted to lend a—" My sentence cuts off in a garbled moan as she takes me in her mouth. Her eyes still locked on mine, her tongue rolls against the underside of my shaft, and I grab the chair Teddy's sitting in to keep my knees from unhinging. Bringing my free hand up to cup her cheek, I try to finish what I was saying earlier. "Fuck, Kelly, that's amazing. But you don't have to. I just wanted to make you feel good." She blinks up at me before lowering her eyes and bobbing up and down on my shaft.

She's still straddling Teddy, and I look over to meet his eyes. He has a huge grin on his face. One of his hands is cupping her breast while the other slides between their bodies, his thumb mimicking the small circles I was making around her clit earlier. She groans around me, and the hand not holding me upright moves to wrap in her hair. I'm already about to come, and that's pretty fucking embarrassing. I gently tug against her hair, trying to slow her down. She moans deep in her throat, the vibrations driving me closer to the edge. My hips twitch on their own, not sure if I need to pull away or thrust forward.

My hand tightens on the back of the chair, the leather creaking under my grip. Teddy moans again, his fingers moving faster. She inhales sharply, adding more suction, and I pull her hair again, trying to get her loose, or at least warn her that I'm about to lose this battle. Her eyes roll back up to me as she shudders—I can't hold back anymore. My hips thrust forward on their own, and an explosion goes off right at the base of my spine, small jolts of pleasure sparking over my whole body. She sputters and coughs as I unload down her throat. Teddy groans again, his hand moving to grip her hip, tight enough that her skin's dimpled in and gone white. Her eyes, when they meet mine, have tears in them, and any pleasure I feel flips over to guilt in a heartbeat. I drop my eyes, trying to back away.

"Shit, Sugar, I'm so sorry. I didn't mean to...I tried to pull away...I..." I don't even know how to apologize properly.

Oh, sorry I choked you when I came down your throat.

Yeah, that sounds great.

Fuck me.

Her hand strokes down my hip, and I look at her again, the least I can do is meet her eyes when I apologize. She's collapsed against Teddy now as he peppers her shoulders with tiny kisses. Somehow, the eyes that meet mine aren't angry. She grabs the edge of my pants and tugs me back towards her. "No sorrys," she sighs out. "We made each other feel good, right? Please don't be sorry for that." I don't know what else to say, what else I can give this sweet girl. So I bend forward and capture her lips with mine.

She meets me enthusiastically, and I can taste both Teddy and myself on her lips. I groan again, wondering briefly if she went down on him before I arrived. Still, I pull back before things can go any farther. "Come on, you two, let's get cleaned up so we can get dinner started."

Teddy holds himself, keeping the condom in place as Kelly slides off of his lap and stands on shaking legs. Pulling her shirt down, she stares at me sweetly. "I don't know if I'm hungry, I just had a couple of big sausages. I might just be ready for bed."

Teddy snorts laughter at her terrible joke, and even I can't stop my smirk since she managed to say that with a completely straight face. She passes me, still carrying her pants in one hand. Unfortunately, her saucy exit's ruined when she trips over her own feet walking up the stairs.

Chapter 21

Kelly

It's frustrating that even though I get a week off college for break, I still need to go into work this morning. And it got cold again! Teddy and Sam are gonna be busy. They need to file the pack paperwork, and I'll go down to the courthouse after work and sign off on it. Then Sam says he needs to work on the nest. I might ask if he wants me to see if Xan can help. I know he loves building stuff, and if time's an issue, I'm sure he'd do it. Unless he takes a bunch of time off for their honeymoon. I hadn't really thought about that.

But he and Gabe work for beer and pizza. Maybe with three guys working on it Teddy'll be able to stop stressing. He says he's not, but he's been tense since we got home yesterday. Then Sam immediately went to work on fixing it up, so it's pretty obvious what's going on. I need to call my OB-GYN and see about getting some new birth control this week. Especially since it usually takes a couple of weeks to be fully effective—at least the pills did. I'll need to ask.

While Teddy and I were good with using some of the ridiculous amount of condoms I bought, I want to make sure we don't have any accidents. Plus, I really want to feel him completely, both of them.

Not even sure where that came from.

Never been with a guy without one.

It just feels weird having something between us...and that doesn't make sense either.

I get dressed in my work jeans and a T-shirt. Gabe and Xan don't really care what I wear, but Mom taught me that I need to be at least a little professional for work. So I usually just wear a black button up with my jeans. Originally, I wanted to go with white, but after a couple days at the shop it dawned on me that white shirts in an auto shop were a terrible decision. Regardless, it's my off week from school, and I didn't pack my work clothes when I was grabbing stuff from my parents' house, so this will do for today.

I finish moving my few clothes into the unfinished bedroom downstairs. I sleep with Teddy and Sam in the master bedroom upstairs, and I'm sure that we wouldn't have a problem fitting all our clothes in his huge closet, but I just need a space of my own. Like the nest, my room still has plastic on the walls, and exposed insulation, but I just need a spot that can be mine for now, even if it's just a place to store my duffel bag. Plus, I like being downstairs for a change. I mostly get the downstairs bathroom all to myself since "my" bathroom is as unfinished as "my" bedroom. Bonus, no Tuck here to use up all the hot water.

Score!

The smell of bacon hits me as I leave the bedroom. Sam's an amazing cook—I can't believe he never bothered doing it for himself. I love my mom and her cooking, but Sam's food is a whole new adventure and I've never heard of a lot of it. But I love bacon, and no real surprises with that. I head into the kitchen and Teddy's already at the table cutting into an omelet...*weird looking omelet.* There's a big platter of bacon on the table, and a bowl full of cut up fruit chunks. Also, a carton of orange juice, the full pot of coffee on a trivet, and a jar of salsa.

Do these people have something against a simple breakfast?

A moment later Sam pops out of the archway from the kitchen carrying a plate with another omelet that he sets in front of the chair across from Teddy. "Behold, my take on a loaded Denver Omelet with diced ham, four kinds of cheese, bell peppers, onions, and tomatoes. Let me know if you prefer something else in it." He's looking at me hopefully and I try not to cringe at this abomination that sounds like eggs and salad toppings.

Sitting down at the table, I watch him bustle back to the kitchen—probably to finish his own "omelet"—and use the serving spoon to grab some orange and yellow chunks out of the sliced fruit. I don't recognize many of these. I know bananas—those aren't here. I know apples, oranges, and I even remember eating pear slices at school. I think I smell a pear. Maybe those are the white chunks I snagged. But fruit should be fairly safe from surprises. Totally on board with the idea of bacon, I add a few slices of that to my plate too.

Eyeing the "omelet" suspiciously, I won't lie, it smells good. But up until a few days ago, I didn't even think about there being four different kinds of cheese. And while everything he's made so far has been wonderful, for some reason the idea of him ruining a perfectly good, simple breakfast food has me taken aback. Still, I trust him, so I should try it at least. Preferably before he comes back so I don't make a fool of myself if I hate it. Law of averages, right? Not everything he makes is gonna be good.

I cut the corner off and stab it with my fork. Unfortunately, I'm too slow as he comes back into the room just as I'm about to take the plunge. He has a big smirk on his face as he sits at the spot between Teddy and I. "Oh, good. I was hoping I'd get back in time for you to taste it. Sugar, you need more vegetables in your diet. Don't think I haven't noticed that the only ones you seem interested in are the steak fries and that horrible canned tomato soup. I don't even know if that has a full serving of 'em in one bowl." He watches me as I nibble on the corner, not getting anything but egg flavor. I give up and pop it in my mouth.

Holy guacamole!

I haven't tried guacamole either, but now I kind of want to.

There are *so* many flavors. I thought it was gonna clash really bad, or at least be too many vegetables. But everything's so well balanced. I never had an omelet before that wasn't just egg, cheese, salt, and pepper. My parents didn't eat out much. We'd sometimes order a pizza or grab burgers at the diner, but I never thought anything about breakfast would be this different. Even omelets were a rare occurrence. Most mornings we just grabbed cold cereal, but sometimes on the weekends Mom would make a big breakfast of biscuits and gravy, or scrambled eggs and sausage. Heck, a few times she even made muffins, and those were great.

Teddy and Sam both watch me as I nearly inhale the rest of my omelet and the bacon I put on my plate. I can't eat all the fruit I picked out—the omelet was bigger than I expected—and I'm not even sorry about that. I lean back in my chair, wondering if I need to unbutton my jeans when the grandfather clock in Sam's living room strikes seven.

I have to leave in fifteen minutes, or I'm gonna be late to the shop. We don't open till eight, but I like to get there at seven thirty so that I can take care of any paperwork the guys left me from the day before. Plus, it's Monday, so I need to go over the weekly schedule and check out the inventory to see if I'll need to ask Gabe to order anything. He never even notices we're getting low on office supplies until the printer runs out of ink or throws up an out of paper error after they empty the last ream.

I stand up and take my plate to the kitchen, giving it a quick rinse and putting it in the dishwasher along with my silverware.

I pack up the various cheeses and veggies on the counter and put them back in their respective spots in the fridge. Sam and Teddy wander into the kitchen with their used plates and the coffeepot.

"Shoot, I forgot to grab a coffee. I don't think that's happened before," I muse to myself before rushing through the dining area and into the bathroom to brush my teeth and pull my hair up into a ponytail. I run back to my room to grab my socks and head towards the door, grabbing my keys and sliding my shoes on as I reach for the doorknob.

Before I can get outside, Teddy speed-walks out to me, carrying a to-go mug. "Two milk, three sugar, yes?" He hands me the mug and gives me a quick hug before turning around and walking towards the stairs.

Sam steps up next. "Be safe, Sugar. We'll get that paperwork filed this morning and then be home all day if you need us, ok?" He gives me a quick kiss on the forehead before adding, "Watch out for Jake, he's crazy this morning." He chuckles softly, opening the front door for me, where Jake's laying on his back in front of the screen door, his tongue hanging out and his tail wagging.

I hear a muttered, "Oh lord," before Sam walks off, and then the sound of the backdoor and a loud whistle. Jake flops over and then nearly trips on his own legs scrambling around the side of the house to get to the back door. I would have been happy to let him in the front, but I couldn't open the screen without hitting him with it. Big goofball.

He barrels into the room now, already licking the air before he even gets to me. "I'll see you after work too, slobber muffin." I barely manage to escape his wildly swinging tail without getting knocked over again, but at last I'm out the door and into the car. I see Jake's face pressed against the screen as I pull away and try to remind myself to pick him up a chewy treat when I go by the store later.

It's chilly on the way to work, overnights and mornings are still pretty cold, and my car takes forever to warm up enough for the heater to work. The drive is over quickly since my mind's preoccupied with everything that happened this weekend, and my stupid heater's just barely started putting out warm air.

I need to set an alarm to call my parents later to check in, so they don't worry. And I make a note of that next to the note in my phone to call my OB's office. Xan's already in when I pull up, which is strange—I didn't expect to see him so soon with the ceremony only two days ago. He has bay number one opened up, and Candice's old mustang pulled in and on lifts. I'm bundled up in a jean jacket I had in the car, and my teeth are nearly chattering when I get out. My breath comes out in steamy puffs as I stop to make sure everything's ok. He seems fine in just his usual coveralls. I'll need to ask Sam if alphas just run hotter than betas.

As I get closer, Xan answers before I have a chance to ask if anything's wrong. "Mornin' Kelly! Just getting Candice's car in for a quick checkup and old-school safety inspection this morning before anybody gets here. Jacks picked up car seats last week and is really excited to get them installed. I want to make sure everything's on the up-and-up before we start down that road. Plus I need to make sure all the rear seatbelts are secure." His eyes scan over me, taking in my light coat and tense shoulders. "Heater not workin'?"

I smile through my now chattering teeth. "It's great once it heats up, but it takes from Sam's all the way here to get that way."

He stares at me for a few extra seconds before his eyes flip over to my little car, then he holds his hand out. "Gimme the keys, I'll check the thermostat and give everything a once over after I finish with this one. There're only a few appointments this morning so it should be fine for me to stay in this bay till I finish up." I'd like to tell him not to worry about it or how much I appreciate the help. But I know he and Gabe would just shrug it off. I've been with them for a few years now, and they said it's too weird charging family. I appreciate it, since I need to go to the store today to get a few more groceries, as well as whatever copay I need to have for getting new birth control.

Pulling the keys back out of my pocket, I toss them to him—he manages to catch my poor throw in the air and smirks at me. "Now, get inside and get warmed up...and can you start the coffeemaker, please? That thing hates me." Smiling to my-self, I head inside to get the day started. I have no idea what kind of vendetta the coffee maker has with Xan, he's usually great with all sorts of electronics, but he can't seem to turn this antique on without red lights flashing an error code.

Regardless, I get a fresh pot started, then send a quick text off to Sam telling him about the car, asking if he needs me to pick anything up for dinner when I stop to grab groceries after work. The store's only a block and half down the road from the shop. Then I put my phone and bag in the locked cabinet in the breakroom and pull up the schedule to get work orders ready for the day.

Teddy

O f course, the pack registration office has a line this morning. Why wouldn't it? I mean, small town, I'm not hugely surprised. Fucking frustrated, yes, goes without saying. Surprised...no, not really.

Sam and I stand in line behind a group of five guys who look fresh out of high school. The space is too enclosed to pick out individual scents, but together they smell like some kind of minty fruit salad. At first, they posture and try to look tough. Then they spend the next fifteen minutes trying to look behind us and around us, probably looking for the source of the omega scent.

Surprise!

I wish Kelly was here, I could use a hug. I'm not trying to make people think she's my omega, I'll happily take on any role she wants me to. It's just that being close to her calms me down, I don't feel so self-conscious about being an omega when I'm with her.

One of the guys in front of us finally figures it out, and I want to put my fist through his leering grin. Sam pulls me tight to his side, his loud possessive growl alerting the rest of the assholes in front of us that something's up. Thankfully, the clerk takes that moment to open the door and call their group in. But I hear a whispered exchange as they go through the door, and the other four members stare until the hydraulic arm on the door finally pulls it closed.

Sam pulls me into a hug, and I take a deep breath of his cedar and sawdust smell, easing some of the tension in my shoulders. His purr starts up and I want to melt against him. This weekend was crazy, but I don't regret any of it. I just want to be able to hurry up and start our life together. Which means finishing the nest and going back to the omega center next week when they reopen from break to clear out my dorm room. Once Mom and Dads are back, I can head home and get the rest of my stuff from there. But I'm looking forward to introducing them to my mates. And if what Sarah said is true about being a scent match, I know Mom's going to be over the moon.

Not that I expect her to be happy about the no grandkids situation. But I never really thought I'd have kids anyway. I've never felt the way I do with Kelly. I never expected I would fall in love with a woman. It's true, I love Sarah like an older sister, but Kelly's the first time I've ever really been attracted to a woman. I always expected that when I formed a pack with Steve and Garret, that Garret would be the one to deal with the issue of having an heir with our omega for his fathers' company. It's kind of a moot point now. Regardless, Kelly doesn't want kids, now, if ever, which is fine with both me and Sam. We can cross that bridge when we come to it.

The five leering idiots finally come back out, and Sam holds my hand while we continue to wait in the lobby. The clerk finally comes out, takes one look at us and says, "Marriage licenses are down the hall, second door on the left. Next!" But we've already spent an hour here, and I know my patience has run out. Sam snarls and the woman doesn't even look taken aback. She sounds almost bored. "Sir, if you had read the directory at the front you would know this is pack registration. You must have at least three people to form a pack."

I decide to step in before Sam can get security called on us. "I'm sorry, ma'am, our beta couldn't get off work to come with us this morning. She's going to be by this afternoon to sign." I can't even pretend to look sheepish, but she gets it faster than the assholes that just left at least.

"Sorry sir, it's *very* Monday and I've already had a morning. Please come this way." At least she doesn't think we're purposefully wasting her time. Sam already downloaded all the paperwork last night, and we filled it out before we came in—other than paying the registration fees, we should be golden.

"Ok, Mr. Darnell and Mr. McKinnley?" Ruth, according to her nametag, looks between the two of us. She squints at Sam for a moment. "Are you Joseph's brother? He's such a nice young man." I bite back my laugh because Joseph is neither nice nor young, and I'd still like to bloody his fucking face after he upset my mates this weekend.

Sam just nods and mumbles a quiet, "Yes ma'am," as she continues to look over our paperwork.

"And your beta is one, Kelly Parker, yes? Age twenty-two?" Sam swallows hard and nods. "Ok, thank you. If I can just get some ID, please. Ms. Parker will need to come down and show hers as well as sign this for me. Then we'll get you all set. I assume, as the lead alpha, that this will be registered under McKinnley Pack?" Sam looks at me for a minute, and all I can do is shrug. It's his choice. As long as I can be with them, I don't care.

"Actually, ma'am. It's Pack Carpenter. We don't want to cause any confusion with my brother's pack." Sam's voice shakes slightly, like he expects harsh judgement at this statement.

The clerk gives a slow blink and looks between the two of us before her voice takes on a too cheerful tone. "Of course. Congratulations Mr. Carpenter and Mr. Carpenter. I'll get this filed as soon as I can. And you should receive your registration notice in the mail within five to ten business days after Ms. Parker comes in with her identification." She goes back to writing, effectively dismissing us.

Sam pulls me into a tight hug that we both need, and my body relaxes just from his scent. Kelly will be by this afternoon, and then we can get everything sorted out legally. Once we have the signed proof of registration, I'll officially be released from the omega center to be with my mates. I pull away from Sam and take his hand as we leave the building and head out. I'm hoping he can teach me how to do drywall so I can help him with the nest.

Kelly

Lunch time finally rolls around, and Xan still has my car up on the lift. I'm starting to get hangry, but I can give it a bit more time before I ask. I hate to be a bother when he's doing something nice for me. This morning's kept me pretty busy, but I was able to call the doctor to set up an appointment to talk about birth control on Friday. I also talked to Mom earlier, since Dad's at work today. She sounded fine, but she was worried. I can't completely blame her. Being with Sam and Teddy seemed pretty strange to me too, but it still feels right. I understand her trepidation, but don't know any better way to reassure her other than just time.

Finally, Sal walks into the office with a completed work order for an oil change. Things have slowed down, but I don't know how she or the new guy, Ray, normally work their lunches out. I'm usually headed to class before now.

I wave her over to tell her I need to walk down to the grocery store to pick up some stuff and grab a bite before I get grumpy, but the phone starts ringing. I heave an over-dramatic sigh, smiling to Sal to let her know I'm not actually upset. No one else is in the office with us, so I just hit the speaker button to pick up and try to smile despite my stomach grumbling. "Gabe's Garage, this is Kelly, how can I help you?"

An angry voice growls over the receiver. It sounds slightly tinny like they're on speaker too. "Yeah, sweetheart, you can get us a mechanic or somebody in charge to talk to. We're having some car trouble. Thanks." I pause for a beat unsure how to answer, when Sal's arm reaches past me and hits the end call button.

"Sorry Kelly, they can call back when they stop being an asshole." But now my eyes and nose are burning...and I don't know why. I think that jerk on the phone was just kind of the icing on the cake of my weekend. Before I know it, I'm leaking profusely. I hear a heartfelt, "Shit," from Sal just before her warm arms wrap around me and she pulls me in for a hug.

"Aww, Kelly, you know they were probably just having a bad day. You can't take fucks like that personally. You wanna go call

Sam and Teddy and have 'em bring you some food? You been here for at least five hours, and I haven't seen you eat anything. You gotta be hungry by now." She knew I left the reception with them this weekend, so I filled her in on everything else during a break earlier.

She's right about the food, of course, and that just makes me cry harder. Everything with Sam's family, my parents, and now this guy—I don't know why it hit me so hard, but I really need some fresh air to dry my eyes out. "Can you just...can you tell Xan I need to walk down to the store and get some lunch? I'll message my guys. But I need to know when my car's gonna be ready so I can go to the courthouse and finish up the pack registration."

Sal pulls me back in for another hug. "'Course, Kel. You can't take care of the rest of us if you don't take care of yourself. Go get something to eat." The phone starts ringing again as I grab my jacket, bag, and phone out of the office and take off down the street towards the diner. I just need a quick bite, shopping on an empty stomach is a bad idea. It's good that I always wear jeans and sneakers to work. It's only a couple blocks, but I'd hate to walk it in heels.

Chapter 23
Steve

Fuck this shit.

Fuck Grandpa, fuck Dad, and fuck Garret with all their building a family bullshit...just fuck everybody, I want Teddy.

Garret's in the front seat beside me, pouting as we drive towards the tiny town of Oak Flats. What the fuck kind of name is Oak Flats anyway, and why did Teddy's mom say he was staying here? He should have gone back to the fucking omega center so that I could court him properly. Not this bullshit where he thinks he found a fucking alpha in the middle of bumfuck nowhere. Where the fuck even are we, Louisiana...Mississippi...some shit out in the middle of fucking nowhere...not even sure if they have fucking Wi-Fi out here.

Garret groans beside me. He hasn't really stopped bitching since I told him I was coming after Teddy. Fuck, I'd rather he didn't bother to tag along, but he says he has to. Because if I'm going to get my ass handed to me by Teddy's new alpha, then he wants to be there as backup. I appreciate it, really, but fuck, you'd think he could stop complaining since he's the one that insisted on coming.

At least this time when he talks it's actual words instead of just muttered grumbles. "Find me some place to get some god-damned food soon, or else. I'm getting hungry over here." So his earlier bullshit wasn't hangry, just moody bitchiness. Fuck me, *all the nope*. I pull over—there isn't exactly a curb here, so I just hope for the best as we crunch onto the gravel on the side of the road. The GPS shows a diner in town, and a mom and pop type grocery store. Fingers crossed they have a deli or some shit. Not that I would admit it to him, but Garret's right, I kinda need a little nosh myself.

"Looks like another four miles into town, then we can hit the grocery, grab a few things for while we're here. Sound good?" The only reply I get is more unintelligible grumbling, so fuck it, I'll take that as a yes. I put the SUV back in drive and check my mirrors...It's no surprise at all that I see *no one* on this deserted stretch of highway. Why the fuck would he come out here any-way?

Just as my tires start to grip the asphalt again I hear a loud pop and a hiss. Garret's side of the SUV settles noticeably. That at least gets some reaction out of him, even if it is all profanity.

Never actually heard the term "horse biting bitch" but I guess after a solid three minute rant he was running out of material. I don't even bother getting out to check, just search on my phone again for garages in the area.

Of course, there's only one. Why not?

I hit dial, because we're gonna need a tow truck, regardless. We both know how to change a flat tire—in theory—but I'll just let the Alpha Automotive Association deal with it. I pay for the shit, might as well use it. It rings through the front a few times before a feminine voice picks up. "Gabe's Garage, this is Kelly, how can I help you?"

And fuck me, I wasn't quick enough to respond.

"Yeah, sweetheart, you can get us a mechanic or somebody in charge to talk to. We're having some car trouble. Thanks." Goddamned motherfucking Garret.

There's a beat of silence before the phone hangs up.

"This is the only fucking garage for forty goddamned miles, you shit. Let me talk!" I slap my brother in the back of the head. We have a silent battle of wills for a few minutes where he glares at me, but at least he keeps quiet while I hit redial. It rings twice this time before a different female voice answers. "Gabe's Garage, Sal speaking, what can I do for ya?"

"I am so sorry, first of all, my brother was an asshole when we called a minute ago. But regardless, my name's Steven, and we really do need help. We've had a flat about four miles outside of town, and need a tow truck, and at least one new tire."

Sal has a deep and kind of sultry chuckle that makes the hairs on the back of my neck rise as she answers, "Not a problem, man. I'll pass along your apology when Kelly gets back from lunch. Now, as for your problem, do you see any mile marker signs or anything where you are?"

"Honestly, it's all flat, with nothing but grass...we may have passed a barn a few miles back." Her laugh is lighter this time, like she's genuinely enjoying us being lost. Not that I blame her after Garret earlier. "My GPS just shows us four miles south of town."

"Ah, yeah, ok, so you passed Springfield about forty-five minutes ago? Yeah, I know where you are. Just gimme your call back number, vehicle make and model, along with the color. I'll see who I can send out there, shouldn't be more than fifteen minutes." She makes a few hums of confirmation as I rattle off my information, before I thank her for her help.

I feel like I should apologize again. "Thanks Sal, I really appreciate it. Oh, do you need my AAA information or can you just get it when we get there?"

"We can take care of that when you get to the office. Kelly handles all that stuff, and she should be back from lunch by the time we get you sorted out. See ya' in a few." She hangs up and at least Garret's stopped glaring at me. Unfortunately, that doesn't stop the lecture he starts in on again.

"What are we doing here, bro? I know you and Teddy were together. I get that you miss him, but he's an omega now, and omegas don't share. You know how Dad and Grandpa are about family. Dad wants grandkids man, we can't have Teddy if we want to have kids or a real family." I know all the excuses, but fuck, we've been to multiple omega centers trying to find a match, someone we can agree on, and it's just not happening. Teddy was more than just my friend. We knew we were going to be a pack; we knew we were going to be together.

I can find women attractive, in an aesthetic way. Just like I can find a piece of artwork or a song beautiful, but I've never met a woman, omega or beta, that I want a relationship with like I had with him. Hell, I've met very few men that I can see having a relationship with like we had. Teddy's special, he's mine, my teddy bear, and his designation coming in as an omega just confirmed it.

Not that we've seen each other since that happened. Our dad found out, flipped his shit, and forbade us from seeing him again. But fuck that miserable lonely old bastard. I need Teddy. Neither of us have much else to say as we sit here and wait for the tow truck.

Thankfully, it's only ten minutes, but it's a hell of a shock when a tall alpha female steps out and introduces herself as Sal. She smells kind of like shop grease and pine, and I'm not sure how much of it is her, and how much is her job. She asks how we're doing and makes general conversation with us as she gets the SUV hooked up, and Garret and I join her in the front of the tow truck while she takes us back to town. We tell her we'll be staying in town for a bit, but not the reason why. If she knows Teddy, we don't want him to find out we're here yet and avoid us. She tells us that the pack that owns the garage is out for their honeymoon, so they aren't readily available, but she and Kelly work together as temporary office managers until the Gabe of Gabe's Garage returns.

We pass the grocery store I was looking for just before we turn into the parking lot of the garage. I tell Sal that we're going to walk down to grab some food while they get the car pulled in. She pushes some papers into my hands to sign, and makes sure I hand over the keys, then waves us off so she can get back to work. I hand the papers to Garret—he's the paperwork guy. He glares at me, scribbles his name a few times, and hands them back to Sal.

We skip the front office and head straight towards the store. Garret pulls me down the sidewalk, his stomach rumbling is a loud background to the frustrated grumbles coming from his mouth.

It takes us less than two minutes to walk the block and a half to the store, and thank fuck for the heater in here. I didn't realize how cold it was until I started walking, but winter and I are not friends. The air inside is warm and a sweet smell tickles my nose in the most amazing way. From the way Garret groans beside me, I'm guessing he smells it too. I need to find the bakery in this place and get some of whatever the fuck that is.

Garret practically marches over me, headed down the main aisle—his head swinging from side to side, nose twitching as he searches for whatever's giving off that amazing scent. He stops suddenly, head turned to the right, and I plow into his back before I can catch myself. He's like a solid fucking wall right now and I just bounce off him, ready to give him hell for stopping so suddenly.

But when I look at his face, all I see is hunger. His pupils are blown, and his nostrils flare as he takes in the source of the scent. There's a woman down the aisle, omega if I had to guess from the scent, long brown hair pulled up in a ponytail, silver glasses perched on the end of her nose as she scrolls through her phone, adding things to her shopping cart. It feels like iron bands circle my chest, and I can't breathe.

Garret growls low and deep in his throat and I can relate. The scent coming off this girl smells like spicy cookie heaven, cinnamon and vanilla with a tiny hint of something floral. Who the fuck let an unbonded omega go to the store alone? I know this is a small town, but come on people, safety! Anybody could show up. Case in point as I reach for Garret's arm, trying to stop him as he marches towards the girl.

And she *is* a girl, probably a few years younger than us. At most I'd say she's in her early twenties. Where the hell is her guardian? I catch up with Garret halfway down the aisle and wrap my arms around his chest, trying to distract him long enough to come to his senses. "Dude, what the fuck! You can't go around accosting random omegas. Her alphas are probably in this fucking store. Do you want your ass kicked?" His growl ratchets up at my statement about her having possible alphas, and we finally draw enough attention to ourselves that she notices.

She takes us in, a quick up and down, and then lowers her head and scurries away as fast as she can push her cart. *Fucking hell.* Garret shakes me off and stalks after her. "She's ours. Can't you smell it?" Unfortunately, I can smell it. I know exactly what he means. Everything about this scent screams out that it's mine, and that's not gonna work for me. I came to this town to get Teddy and no delicious smelling grocery store omega is going to change that. But I don't want to fight with him right now, so I need to get this shit sorted out.

"Ok, I'll look for her. You go find us some food. You're acting a little nuts right now, man. You'll scare her off if you keep this shit up." His eyes squint at me, assessing if he can trust me in this, but eventually he just nods and walks towards the end of the aisle where she disappeared. He looks up, taking in the store map signs before nodding back at me and turning away from the direction of her escape. Hopefully, once we get some food in him, he'll be less feral, and with any luck, she'll be long gone.

Garret

I know Steve's gonna be pissed, but I can't walk away from this. I make sure he sees me turn down away from the omega that just rewrote my fucking world, and I go down two aisles before doubling back behind him. I glance down the aisle I left him on, and he's still there, staring intently at the ceiling. I don't know what exactly is going through his head, but I don't care right now. I know he loves Teddy. He's always loved Teddy, and I'm man enough to admit that there were times when I felt like the odd man out with my own twin.

Maybe I'm being petty, but I just want someone to want me, not my family name, not our family money, not because twins are a novelty...just me. I want to be enough for someone...just once. Teddy's great. He was almost as close to me as Steve—I would have been happy to be in a pack with him. But I've never been attracted to him the way Steve has, and I'm pretty sure the feeling's mutual. He's my friend, but I can't be in a pack with just the three of us.

I let Steve believe that I agree with Pops and Gramps, but the truth is, I don't really care if we never have kids. I don't hate children, I just never imagined my life with them. But while I don't want to lose my brother, I can't live the rest of my life feeling like a third wheel.

Hurrying through the store, I keep a watch out for the pretty omega. I can scent her, but I don't see her anywhere. Heading towards the front of the store, I hope I can catch her before she leaves. Even if I can just get her name, I can try to find out more. Maybe somebody at the garage knows her. It's a small town, everybody knows everybody else, right? I speed walk past the cash registers and see a light brown ponytail disappearing out the door—I run to catch up.

There she is, in the parking lot, just standing on the sidewalk, cart full of bags. I wonder if she needs a ride somewhere.

Shit, the SUV's at the shop. I bet I could carry all those bags to the shop for her, then offer her a ride once it's fixed. Will she think I'm a creep if I offer? Fuck, that sounds creepy even to me. Ok, play it cool.

Still, gotta give it a try. "Hi, um, Miss, do you need some help?" She turns towards me and draws back. She's bigger than most of the omegas I've met, but I'm still a good head and shoulders taller. I stop with several feet still between us. "Sorry, it's just really cold out here, and well, our SUV's down at the shop, but we can give you a ride once we get it fixed. That is, um, if you need one? I don't know how long it's gonna be, though, sorry."

Fucking hell, I sound like a babbling idiot.

And she's staring.

Great.

Her brows draw down, an angry look marring her pretty features. "Sorry, I'm waiting for my pack to come pick me up. And my name's Kelly, not sweetheart."

Steve's right.

I am such a fucking asshole.

Chapter 24

Kelly

I call Teddy after I eat a quick sandwich at the diner. I feel better just hearing his voice. I have to apologize a few times for making them worry, since they know I should have been home already. Still, they agree to come by and pick me up to take me to the clerk's office and then take any groceries I get back to the house. I don't know how much longer my car's going to be, but I don't want to miss the clerk today and then have to wait until tomorrow or later to finish filing our pack registration.

The store's pretty empty this time of day, and I can make it through the list that Sam sent fairly quickly. I don't recognize everything there, but that's why they make labels. I'm walking down the bread aisle since the list says bagels...but there are five different flavors. I message Sam and Teddy back to ask which ones they want while I grab a loaf of whole wheat bread off the shelf. I know Sam has his bread box with everything but the kitchen sink, but I feel kind of twitchy right now, and just need something familiar. Besides, if I get that and a jar of peanut butter I can take it back to the office for Xan, Ray, and Sal. Ok, probably not Xan, since Jacks usually packs him a lunch.

My phone vibrates with a group chat from Teddy and Sam. Teddy asks for both cinnamon and blueberry bagels, and Sam needs everything bagels. I look at the shelf and grab those, then toss in an onion bagel for myself, because I'm feeling adventurous. Marking bagels off the list, I hear a loud scuffle and hushed whispers. As I look towards the center aisle, there are two large guys that I don't recognize standing there.

Both of them big, both tall...probably alphas going by the size and the pheromones coming off of them. The one in front's a classic pretty boy with tanned skin, short blond hair and big blue eyes. His pupils go wide as he stares at me, nostrils flaring. The face peering over his shoulder is identical in structure, but the similarity ends there.

His eyes are a vivid emerald green, his hair longer, and bleached white, the roots a darker brown than his friend's blond. It seems to be pulled back into a short ponytail. Not as long as Teddy's, but past his shoulders. The whole look combined with his pale skin and how gaunt he is almost makes him appear skeletal. It's an unusual enough aesthetic that I would have remembered seeing him around town. His arms are wrapped tightly around the bronze god in front of him. And he has tattoos on both hands. Most of his body is blocked, but they look similar enough to be related.

Either way, I'm out. I grab my cart and hurry away, figuring Sam can come back to the store later for whatever I missed, but these two are creeping me out. Raised voices sound behind me as I make a beeline for the front of the store and the checkouts. It's not a lot more people, but it's something. Pulling up my phone again, I send a message to the chat asking how much longer they'll be. I don't mention the two guys. I don't want to worry either of them.

Billy, the cashier, gets me checked out in record time, and I take my cart and bolt out the front. Teddy said they were less than five minutes away. I'll just stay by the curb so Billy can see me from the register in case those creeps come back.

I wait for another couple of minutes, staring at my phone, willing a text or any sort of information to come in. But I know that wishing for my guys to be here won't make it happen. My eyes flick back and forth from where I can see the garage and farther down the street. I think I see Sam's truck coming up the road. Thank goodness. That skin crawling feeling is back and I was starting to wonder about the feasibility of taking this cart back to the shop and just returning it later.

A hesitant voice sounds behind me. "Hi, um, Miss, do you need some help?" I turn slowly, now that we're out in the open I can definitely smell that this guy's an alpha. He smells like what I imagine a thunderstorm over the ocean smells like...minus the fish poop. Kind of salty and fresh with that weird hit of ozone on the back of your tongue. But his voice. I know that voice. Why do I know that voice?

He stops with several paces between us, but I know that alphas can move fast, and it would only take him a second to close the distance. "Sorry, it's just really cold out here, and well, our SUV's down at the shop, but we can give you a ride once we get it fixed. That is, um, if you need one? I don't know how long it's gonna be, though, sorry."

Wait...the shop?

That's where I know his voice.

I can feel an angry scowl forming, and it's not a nice look, but I can't help it. "Sorry, I'm waiting for my pack to come get these so I can go back to work. And my name's Kelly, not sweetheart." He gapes at me like a fish for a minute, his ears taking on a hint of red. At least he's embarrassed by how he acted earlier. That's something.

His not-quite-look-a-like comes tumbling out the door at that moment. "God dammit, Garret. I thought I told you to find us some food. What the fuck, man?" I start backing away as waves of anger roll off him. He doesn't seem angry at me, but I don't want to get caught in the middle of a fight if one happens.

Then, wonder of wonders, I hear the slightly squeaky brakes of Sam's truck, and turn my head right as it pulls up next to the curb. Sam jumps out of the driver's seat, glaring hellfire and brimstone at the two alphas who have moved their argument entirely too close to me. Losing all my confidence, I practically throw myself into his arms. Once there, he picks me up and starts purring as he walks me towards where Teddy sits in the passenger seat. Of course everything comes to a screeching halt when the door opens and one of the two alphas behind me lets out a loud bark of surprise.

Teddy's eyes flick from mine over my shoulder to the two behind me, and his face crumples as he pulls me against him. His whole body shakes and any predisposition I had to act the damsel in distress goes right out the window. If I had a crowbar, I would be letting loose on these two for whatever they did to make Teddy upset.

I wrap my arms around him and pull his head down to my chest, whispering quiet words of comfort. He takes deep inhales against my collar and cries into my shirt. I barely notice Sam as he loads the groceries in the back of the truck and snarls angrily at the two strangers.

Even when he finally gets back in the driver's seat, he glares at them through the window. I turn my head enough to see them and the blond god is staring straight at me. They've switched positions though, and now he's the one holding his darker half back as he strains towards the truck, eyes fixed on the part of Teddy's big body that can be seen around mine. The blond's eyes flick back and forth between us as he pulls the other guy closer.

I don't know what they did to my omega, but I might need to kick someone's butt.

Sam

*S*hit! *Shit! Shit!*

Something's wrong, and I need to fix it. Teddy sounds devastated and neither of us can get an answer out of him about what's wrong. I pull into the parking lot at the garage so Kelly can run in and let them know she needs to leave. She was supposed to leave a while back anyway. I doubt anybody's going to be upset. She runs into the first bay and Xan smiles and waves. But all good humor drops from his features the longer she talks. I've pulled Teddy across the seat, but there isn't enough room here to pull him into my lap.

His hands are fidgeting with those leather bracelet things he wears, rubbing circles around the outside and up the inside of each arm. I haven't taken the time I should to ask about those. I haven't seen him take them off. Even last night in the shower he only took them off while he was getting clean and put them on again as soon as he was dried off. If it's a religious thing I should probably try to ask without upsetting him. Just, not right now.

Kelly gestures down the street towards the store and points at the truck where Teddy's curled against me. Xan's expression is thunderous as he glares between the road, us, and the front office. Even when his gaze stops on us, his ire seems to be directed towards the two guys who were following Kelly at the store. I'm not sure if they're gonna get their car back in one piece if he has any say in the matter.

Finally, Kelly stops talking. She's understandably upset, but Xan gestures towards the office and waves her off, before glaring back down the street. I'm half surprised those two assholes aren't trying to follow her, but better for them that they don't. She sticks her head in the front door and says something to Sal behind the desk who waves in return. Then Kelly is sliding back in the passenger side and pulling Teddy towards her.

His sobs have tapered off to a quiet sniffle. His reaction threw me for a loop. We've only been together for a few days, but that's enough to get a feel for him, and he doesn't seem like the crying type. I understand that he's under a lot of stress but this seems extreme from what I've gleaned of his personality so far. "Sorry, Xan said Candice's car took longer than expected, but he should be done with mine in about an hour. I can come back this afternoon or get it tomorrow. Whatever works best for you."

Kelly strokes Teddy's hair, making soft soothing noises against the top of his head where he's curled against her. "Do you think y'all can take me over to the courthouse real quick so I can sign that paperwork then come back and let me get my car?" Her eyes finally meet mine, and she looks as confused as I am about what's going on.

Teddy nods against her chest and makes a muffled sound that I take as an affirmative. Kelly squeezes him tightly. "Oh, Teddy, if we need to we can go straight home, afterward. I just didn't want y'all to have to bring me in at seven-thirty in the morning. But we can do whatever you need, ok?"

Teddy takes a deep shuddering breath and looks back and forth between the two of us. "No, I'm...I'm ok, that was just a surprise." The smile he turns to me is watery at best, he looks like he's going to cry again and a low growl rumbles through my chest. I put the shifter in drive and we pull out of the lot towards the city center where the old courthouse is. Thankfully we're heading away from the grocery, since I see those two fucks walking down the sidewalk.

It takes every ounce of my willpower not to turn around and knock them senseless for whatever the hell they did. But I don't want Teddy anymore upset, so I glare at them quietly in my rearview mirror as we pull away. My purr fills the truck. I need to comfort my omega and beta both, but I'm not sure what else I can do until we get home and I can hold them properly. Then get them both fed and cuddled up together so I can get more work done on the nest.

Chapter 25
Steve

I wasn't expecting that. Part of me is relieved that the girl we saw wasn't an omega, but that means that the situation with Teddy is an even bigger shit-show than originally anticipated. Seems like the scent that was screaming at my brother and me was his. With luck, this will at least get Garret to stop fighting over making Teddy our omega, though now I have to figure out how to get him to come back with us. There's no way in fucking hell that I'm leaving without him. Dad and his legacy bullshit can fuck all the way off.

I drag Garret back inside because right now he's just staring off after that damned truck. I don't know what the fuck that girl said to him, but by the way Teddy clung to her when he saw us, she's important to him—which means Garret upsetting her is just going to make this harder all the way around. And that big fucking alpha. Shit. I mean, he wasn't that much taller than us, but fucker looks like he lifts cows for fun. What the fuck. Maybe that's why Teddy likes him, he makes him feel like an omega. He could probably pick my boy up and princess carry him if he wanted to.

The kid behind the register—Billy according to his nametag—stands up straighter and glares at me as I walk back into the store. "We don't want any trouble around here. If you harass anybody else, I'll have to call the police."

His back is stiff as a board, but his eyes shift from side to side, and I can admire his conviction, even if I don't appreciate it. Time to do some damage control, I don't know how long we'll be in town, but I don't want to deal with cops. "Sorry, man. We thought we saw a friend of ours and wanted to say hi." It's a thin excuse and he doesn't look like he believes me. Fuck, I don't blame him, it was shit.

"Miss Kelly didn't look like she knew you"—his expression shifts—"but I'm sure if you ask down at the garage where she works, Gabe or Xan'll be happy to help you out." He's outright smirking now, and yeah, I think we better avoid those two at all costs. I wonder if the alpha in the truck was one of them.

Also shit...Kelly from the garage. No wonder she looked ready to bludgeon Garret to death. If it's the girl who answered the phone earlier, I don't blame her for wanting to slap him stupid. Of course, as smitten as he seems now, maybe this'll teach him not to be an asshole to people. Looking back to the still smirking Billy, "Hey, you guys got a deli or anything in here? We came in to find some lunch while our tire gets fixed."

He looks like he's actually thinking about it for a few seconds. "Sorry, Sir. We only have prepackaged deli stuff. The diner is a couple blocks down after you pass the garage. They're about the only place around here to get hot food, unless you want to head towards the interstate."

Figures.

"Thanks, man. I appreciate it." I drag Garret back outside into the chill. He hasn't said anything since Kelly and Teddy rode off with that alpha, with luck they'll be gone before we get back to the shop. I'd like to avoid these Xan and Gabe guys that the cashier mentioned too, if possible. I'm pretty sure that's more trouble than we can handle at the moment.

Garret

She's gone. I know now that it was probably Teddy we smelled. And, *yes*, that's a fucking shock. I need to check in with Steve and see if he's ok. But I can't, I can't seem to do anything. My mind is static right now. I mean, Teddy is...ok, he's sweet, and he's like family, but I don't like him that way. I don't like any guys that way. I can appreciate how a man looks and decide if he is attractive or not, but I really don't want anything to do with a dick that isn't mine.

And Kelly, fuck me. Did I already ruin it? I mean, obviously she has a pack...with Teddy, who's our omega.

Will they join us?

Can we join them?

There are three of them and only two of us.

How would that work?

Shit, what are the dads gonna say?

Do I really care?

Fuck!

I need to find out more. Spinning on my heel to march back into the store, I nearly run headlong into Steve, who's coming out the door at the same time. "No dice on the food situation unless you want pre-packed lunch meat or peanut butter. We need to head down to the diner about three blocks that way." He points down the street, and I see Kelly standing in front of the garage talking to someone inside. Maybe I can apologize. I mean, I should tell her I'm sorry and explain...I mean...Shit. It's no wonder she was so pissed.

It's ok, I can figure this out.

First, go catch the girl before she leaves

Second, apologize to the girl.

Third, a miracle happens.

Lastly, she forgives me, lets us court her and Teddy.

Then we join her pack.

Everybody's happy?

Shit, that's not gonna work.

Ok, fuck, think of something else. I need to ask Steve about this. He knows Teddy better. I mean, we both know him, but I've never kissed the guy, or…anything else they've done that I don't want to know about. That being said, other than apologizing, I think the best way to get Kelly to like me is to win over Teddy.

Ok, this is a plan, or at least the start of a plan.

Shit, like…eight percent of a plan?

My mind spins as Steve drags me down the street. The truck with Kelly in it pulls out and drives away, and I feel like someone stole all the air out of my lungs. I need her.

What the fuck?

She isn't even an omega.

My instincts are going fucking crazy right now, they don't care that she isn't an omega.

I'm in a daze as we make it to the diner and sit down. I stare out the window as Steve orders us each a burger and fries. You can't really go wrong that way. Even if a place has shit for food, burgers are straightforward. I don't mean gourmet shit, just plain meat, cheese, bun…maybe if you're feeling frisky, get some tomato and onions on there. Easy.

I watch the cars pass the window where we're sitting. The truck doesn't pass by again, so I don't think she's going back to the garage today. There goes my plan to catch her there to apologize, or at least talk. I can't stop thinking about her. Every time I try to think about something else, it circles back to her. Teddy? Yeah, apparently, they're together. The car at the shop? Oh yeah, no she works there. Home? I don't want to go home without her. And how's that for fucked-up since I don't know the first fucking thing about her. I mean...she's a beta for fuck's sake, I shouldn't be this obsessed.

Fuck!

Our food finally arrives and I stop looking out the window long enough to take in my surroundings. It's not a huge place, less than twenty tables to be sure. They have an old style counter with barstools, which make everything feel kitschy. Picking up my burger, I take a bite. Maybe it's because I was super hungry, or because my whole fucking worldview was recently turned upside down, but it's a damned good burger. Slightly crispy edges, toasted bun, the whole nine yards. There's a pile of toppings off to the side, and some very frozen tasting French fries, but the burger itself is solid.

We finish our food, neither of us really talking, or even making eye contact. Steve looks about as desolate as I feel, and I get it. Seeing Teddy today must have thrown him for a loop. Pain and frustration are coming off him in waves. I should have noticed it before, but I've been kind of preoccupied with my own world crumbling over a stranger.

Sorry, Bro, bit mentally preoccupied.

Fuck, I really am just an inconsiderate asshole.

Now that I have something in my stomach, self-reflection is more of a thing.

What the hell is wrong with me?

Seriously, first I bitch at the girl.

Though in my defense I didn't know who she was.

Then I follow her around the store and chase her outside.

Even if I hadn't been an asshole, that would be enough to freak anybody out.

Steve is the one staring out the window now, so I guess it's my turn to get him moving. Walking up to the register, I pay for our food and ask for a couple of to-go cups for our drinks. I get Steve up and he seems broken, empty as we walk back towards the shop where we can hopefully pick up our vehicle, and then see about finding a fucking hotel in this damned town. We need to regroup and make a plan. As much as I want to, I don't think I'll be able to get more information about Kelly from the shop where she works.

It's only a couple blocks back to the shop, but the temperature seems to be dropping fast and the wind has picked up. What the fuck is it with this town? If it fucking starts snowing, I'm done with this shit. Just put me on a goddamned plane back to fucking L.A. I don't fucking do the cold.

Lie!

I know, I can't leave. Steve won't abandon Teddy again, and I can't go without Kelly, even if she isn't an omega. I just fucking found her, and I don't care if it was Teddy that we were scenting on her, I need her. Holding Steve close, I lean forward in this stupid fucking wind as we trudge towards the garage. We don't have time for this shit. I need to find Teddy to snap Steve out of his freaky zombie state. Will that help me find Kelly? Ok, yes. But I'm trying to be at least someone altruistic, considering the shape that Steve is in. He seems to have shut down now that he has food, I don't know why the delayed reaction, but I got this. We count on each other…We used to count on Teddy too, until…

I don't want to fucking go there. I don't. I don't hate him, I mean, yeah, I feel kind of betrayed, but it wasn't his fault, he had no way of knowing he would be an omega, I just…I can't always be on the outside looking in. I can't always feel like the odd man out. It's exhausting. I was never opposed to sharing an omega with the two of them, they were my brother and best friend. A tiny voice in the back of my mind whispers that it might not be too late for that. I mean, not Steve, I love the guy but turns out he isn't into women. At all. If it was an omega heat situation, I think he would be fine. From what I've heard the pheromones mean you basically stay hard whether you want to or not.

Ugh, I don't want that for my brother either. Dad's gonna be pissed regardless. I'm not ruling Kelly out to have kids, if she wants, but she's not an omega, and that was an integral part of Dad and Grandpa's plan. Fucking legacy bullshit. Break up our fucking pack. We went to the fucking college they wanted, got the fucking degrees they wanted, looked for a fucking omega that we were never going to agree on because Steve only wants Teddy, and I want someone to want me for me.

The short distance back to the garage seems to take forever. Steve and the wind have slowed our pace considerably, and there's sleet coming down by the time we arrive. I open the door and shove Steve into the warm air. The bell overhead jingles loudly, but no one comes out. I expected Sal to be here since Kelly left, but there's no sign of her. We don't have any jackets, so I lead Steve over to a waiting area and wrap my arms around him, trying to help stop his chattering teeth.

It takes a while, but once I regain feeling in my fingers, I walk back over to the counter, staring out the window into the garage proper. I see our vehicle jacked up, and the flat front tire off on the ground beside it. Sal isn't working on it. A younger looking guy with white-blond hair in a ponytail is pulling down a tire off the wall, so hopefully that will be for ours. Sal seems to be having a heated discussion with a jacked looking beta. He has a small raggedy looking car up on lifts and I wonder briefly that it still runs at all; it looks more rust than metal at this point.

Then I chide myself because whoever owns the little rattletrap probably drives it more out of necessity than desire. In a town this size, you probably need a car just to get around. I don't imagine they would have a plethora of sidewalks once you get out of the main drag.

After a few more minutes Sal throws her hands up and marches back into the front office. She pulls up short when she sees me, and her friendly demeanor from earlier is gone. *Shit.* I can't say I blame her, but I am curious about what Kelly told her. Does she know about Teddy and Steve? Does she know that I followed her out of the store like a man obsessed?

Her eyes flick from me to my brother—still looking catatonic in a plastic chair—and back before she speaks. "Yeah, so...Xan wants to talk to you before we finish your car. You might have guessed but Kelly already left, so he'll need to run your paperwork for AAA."

I offer a smile and try not to show that I'm screaming inside because I want to have the pretty beta here again. Go back in time a few hours and not be such a complete and utter bastard. Before I can formulate a response, the beta Sal was arguing with earlier walks in. He's only a few inches taller than her, and I'm almost knocked over by the waves of dominance and anger that roll off of him as he glares at me.

Wait, the cashier at the store mentioned a Xan.

Oh...Fuck.

Yes, Kelly definitely told them what I did.

What we did?

Doesn't matter.

"This is Xan, one of the owners of the garage, and my boss. So, I'm just gonna go help finish up your tire so we can get you guys outta here before the weather gets any worse." Sal beats a hasty retreat back to the garage while Xan continues to glare at me.

"Listen, man, I don't know you, and I don't want to fuckin' know you. My original plan when Kelly stopped by earlier was to get your tire fixed and get you the fuck outta this town ASAP.

But it don't look like that's happening in this weather." His hard stare flips between me and my brother who still hasn't responded. "Kelly's worked here for years now. She's a good person, and she makes my job a hell of a lot easier than it used to be." He slams a handful of paperwork down on the desk. "Also, I don't know what you dipshits did to Teddy, but he made my omega smile, and she doesn't like people in general. So lemme give you a piece of advice. Stay the fuck away from Kelly's pack."

It finally registers that this man is an alpha. I've never seen one that was this short before, seriously, he can't be over six feet, if even that. I close my eyes and take a deep breath, trying to focus so I can stop thinking of him as an "alpha: now in fun-size". He looks like he might actually kill me if I make that comment.

If he could reach.

Shit…Garret, don't laugh.

Don't fucking do it.

A small snicker escapes my lips, and his response is immediate as a tire tool lands firmly on the top of the desk, his hand closed tightly around it. Fucking hell, I must be hysterical, because I feel like giggling again at his display of anger.

Pull it together man!

Do you want to be beaten to death in the middle of bumfuck nowhere with a goddamned tire iron because you couldn't stop laughing at the miniature alpha.

Shit!

What the actual hell is wrong with me?

His fist is still clenched around the hunk of metal, and his eyes squint as they glare over at me. Finally, his hand relaxes and he pulls the keyboard out on a sliding tray. Releasing a loud breath, he starts typing. "Fuck my life, I hate this part. Ok, I'm going to need your AAA card, payment information, and ID so I can get this shit done and get you the fuck out of here before our office manager comes back and I have to either stop her from beating you to death or help her hide bodies. Neither one sounds like a fun afternoon, and I just want to get home to my mates."

Kelly

The courthouse took longer than I expected, and I really want to just go home with Teddy and Sam, fix some hot cocoa, and snuggle. They both came inside with me, thankfully, otherwise they might have frozen. What happened to the weather? I knew it was cold, but snow...really? I want to stop and get my car before the weather gets worse. Also see if they want to open tomorrow depending on what happens tonight. The second one I can do over the phone, but if I'm already there, it's easier to just do it all at once.

Sam looks at me questioningly, and I turn to Teddy. "You gonna be ok to drop me back at work so I can get my car? I wanna get home for warm snuggles, but I also kinda wanna get it so it's not sitting out in the parking lot in case we get snowed in for a few days." I don't plan on getting snowed in, but this weather is nutters. Oh no! "Wait, no, we need to get home now, did you let Jake in before you came to get me?"

Sam smiles at me. "Don't worry about your slobbery admirer. He's inside, probably laying on the couch right now where it's toasty and warm while we're out here freezing our asses off. I can drop you off at the shop and then we'll wait to follow you home just in case this shit causes issues. Alright, Sugar?" Teddy nods beside me, he still hasn't really talked, but he doesn't look as bad as he did earlier. Sam spent the entire time that we waited in the courthouse purring for us, and while his loud rumble now sounds a little hoarse, he keeps going.

All the bay doors are closed when we get back to the garage, and I worry for a minute that they closed up and left before I could get back. I wouldn't really blame them. This weather is awful, and the roads are already starting to get slippery. Thankfully the lights are on inside, and as soon as the truck is parked, I jump out and sprint towards the front door. Unfortunately, I don't run well at the best of times, and the ice on the ground doesn't help. I only make it a few steps before my feet try to go in opposite directions and I start flailing, until big warm hands wrap around my waist and hold me steady.

Teddy looks down at me. He's still pale and his eyes are bloodshot, but at least he's smiling. Still, his rumbly voice doesn't do a darned thing for my wobbly knees. "I would say we need to stop meeting like this, Little Pixie, but I do enjoy you ending up in my arms." I feel like this snow should turn to steam before it reaches my skin as a full body blush rolls through me.

Sam comes up behind Teddy, supporting both of us as we make it to the door. I'm so busy watching my feet to keep from sliding again that I don't notice who all's inside until I'm trying to open the door without knocking us all over. The warm air rushes across us making my cheeks sting, and I hear Xan's voice. "Thank fuck you're back, Kelly, I can't get this stupid card to go through and I need to get these guys out of here before the weather gets any worse. Plus, I need to get home. Jacks is going crazy with worry, which is making Candice worried. I tried calling to tell him I was fine, but he suggested I just lock these two out of the shop with no car and come home."

I start to laugh, because, yeah, I can totally imagine Jacks doing that. But it turns into a croaky sound as my brain catches up to what else he said. My eyes snap up, taking in the aggressive blond alpha who followed me out of the store earlier. I really thought they'd be gone by now. Spinning around, I need to get Teddy back to the truck before he gets upset again and keep Sam from maiming these guys for whatever they did to upset our omega earlier.

I shouldn't be surprised when my feet slide again and I have to grab onto said omega to keep from falling on my butt, but as I look up into his face, he isn't looking at me. He's staring across the room at the alpha with the bleached out hair, his pupils yawn wide, and his arms wrap around me and pull me close as I try to steady myself against him. I crane my head back, trying to see more of the alpha, but he seems as engrossed in the stare off as Teddy, his body looks so tense that I can see it vibrating from across the room. Teddy's voice whispers over the top of my head, and I can barely hear the single word as his breath ghosts through my hair. "Mine."

Sam

What the fucking fuck? I wanted Teddy to stay in the truck, but I can't blame him for trying to keep Kelly safe. Then I was so focused on keeping my mates upright that I didn't notice everyone else in the room until Teddy froze up in my arms. Xan is still behind the counter, he's saying something, but I don't register what. My focus is solely for these two alphas that might threaten my pack.

The pretty boy by the counter is intensely focused on Kelly, but she doesn't even notice since she's looking up at Teddy. His eyes are locked with the bleached out skeleton, and a low possessive snarl rips from me without my permission. The urge to drag both of my packmates back to the truck and take them home is overwhelming. Teddy mumbles something against Kelly's hair, but I can't make it out. I do make out the needy whine that slips free next though. And I'm helpless to stop my body from moving to block these two new alphas from my pack.

Teddy peers around me before looking up and meeting my eyes. "I'm sorry, Sam, he's mine too." I choke for a second, we just got the pack registered today. It takes a moment for my mind to catch up and register that Teddy said 'too', so he isn't going to leave. But I'm not sure what that means for this new alpha also being his.

I turn my glare on this stranger, but all his focus is on Teddy, and it's obvious they knew each other before today. The look of longing in the stranger's eyes as he stares at my omega makes my chest feel like it's split open.

Kelly lets out a loud squeak and I hear feet rushing across the tile floor then she's pulled away from my side. The other alpha—fuck, all my attention was focused on my omega. My head snaps around as Teddy reaches for her. She's been pulled close to this stranger, and my mind spins, unsure if I should stay with Teddy or try to help Kelly. Xan has no such compunctions as he vaults over the counter, tire tool raised, and fury written across his features. "I warned you, asshole."

Everything stops when the stranger drops to his knees on the floor and wraps his arms around Kelly's waist. The top of his head is pressed against her stomach, and he just keeps mumbling over and over. "I'm sorry." I know Kelly told me what happened earlier, but this seems a bit over the top for being an asshole over the phone. Even for trying to track her through the store, it seems excessive.

Kelly looks confused too, but brings her hand over to touch his hair. She's looking down at him, and I would pay every fucking cent I have in the bank to know what she's thinking.

At the gentle contact his head tilts back, the look of utter devotion directed at her is something I've come to see a lot of lately from Teddy, and fuck, even when I catch sight of myself in the mirror. I can't even blame Jake for being so obsessed; she seems to draw us all like moths to a flame.

Kelly studies him for a moment as he nuzzles his face into the hand she put on his hair. He's finally stopped apologizing, but the raspy, "Please," that he whispers across her palm causes her to shudder and me to see red. It only gets worse when he buries his face against her stomach and inhales deeply, a shudder wracking his body.

Chapter 27

Steve

I found him.

Holy Fuck.

I saw him earlier for a moment, but he disappeared again, and I was starting to wonder if it was just my imagination—wishful thinking.

No, he's really here.

He's in the room.

His scent, spicy cinnamon and vanilla.

Every molecule of my being screams out that he's mine.

There does, unfortunately, seem to be a large growling problem. He's standing right in the way and keeping me from grabbing Teddy and pulling him out to the SUV so I can hold him again, touch him, taste him. Fuck, I've missed him so damned much. He doesn't look exactly the same. I mean, it's been years, fuck, almost ten years since I saw him.

He's taller, which is ironic since he's an omega. His hair got longer and my hands itch wanting to run through it. The piercings are definitely new, and my dick hardens as I briefly wonder what else he might have gotten pierced. He looks softer in some ways, thicker around the waist, but his broad shoulders and muscular arms say that under that omega padding is the alpha I fell in love with.

He stares at me, my longing reflected back in his eyes. At least until Garret decides to do something stupid again, striding across the room and grabbing the beta girl, throwing the two other alphas in the room into chaos. But we don't need her, we have our omega, he's right here. Maybe he thinks that Teddy wants her, so we need to bring her along too.

That's fine, whatever my teddy bear wants or needs, I can deal with that. As long as he's mine, I can deal with anything. Then Garret throws us for another loop, dropping to his knees in supplication, like he's found his life's purpose, his omega. But that can't be right—*we* found *our* omega, and it's Teddy. Maybe he wants her for Teddy? My love was holding on to her pretty tightly earlier. Maybe he thinks Teddy needs her, but my teddy bear just needs us. *Me.*

My gaze swings back to Teddy. He's not looking at me anymore, he's looking at them. His posture tense, arm extended. Shit, ok, well, we can do it that way. If he thinks he needs the beta girl for now, then we can keep her too. This other alpha might be a problem though. He's a big fucker.

While he's distracted, I move closer—I need to feel my omega, verify that he's really here. That this isn't all wishful thinking. The big alpha's focus is completely on Garret and the beta right now. Inching closer, trying to keep him from noticing me—I reach out, my finger trails down Teddy's arm. He's cold under my fingertips from the storm raging outside, and it feels like sparks going off under my skin where we touch.

Teddy's head snaps back towards me, his eyes meeting mine. He bites his lip, a whimpering sound I've never heard from him slips free. My alpha sits up and takes notice and I lock my muscles to keep from reaching for him and wrapping him in my arms.

Unfortunately, the other alpha also noticed, and he's glaring down at me. He doesn't try to move me, so he can glare all he wants. He can do whatever he feels he needs to do, as long as I can stay close to Teddy. Hell, if Teddy wants to stay here, I can do that. As long as we're together, I can do anything he needs me to.

Garret

She's here, and she's even more perfect now that I can touch her, scent her. I'm still catching hints of Teddy's spicy cookie scent, and a cedar that I'm assuming is the big growly one. She has a pack, but she isn't marked. Fuck, I don't think I'd care if she was. I just need her. That subtle hint of lilac changes my entire world. It's something that's wholly her.

My face is pressed against her stomach before I register the mini-alpha from behind the counter is standing over me with his fucking tire iron. I guess he did warn me, but I could die happy right here, that would be fine as long as she was the last thing I saw. Her hands running over my hair cause my purr to start automatically, and the rest of the world fades away as I breathe her in. Nothing else matters now that I've found her.

I don't know how long they let me stay like that. I know it isn't long, because the skin on her arms is still covered in goosebumps from the cold when they bring me back to reality. Xan is closer now, the tool hanging loose by his side. "Seriously, Kelly, I need to close up. If you can dislodge this guy and come get his AAA card sorted out, that would help. Fuck, I can give you the keys to lock up if it'll help, but Jacks and Candice need me home." He doesn't seem to care what I do, but when Kelly pulls away, I let her go. Hopefully we can talk properly after all this.

I don't deserve her.

Why would she bother talking to me?

Climbing to my feet, I watch as she circles behind the counter and starts clacking the keys on the keyboard, her eyes flicking between my driver's license, membership card, and the monitor. I watch closely as she chews lightly on her bottom lip, and I want to reach out and touch her, pull it free before she hurts herself. I zone out, watching her work. Barely noticing the heated discussion between her alpha, Teddy, and Steve. I should probably be more concerned with that, but I can't seem to find it in myself to care what they do.

It takes her less than four minutes to finish, but Xan is already pacing back and forth across the room, casting glares at me and Steve alternately. There's a loud decisive key click and the printer starts up. Xan grabs the paper off of it before she has a chance to and shoves the stack and a pen at me—so I have to read over to see where I need to sign. He circles the counter to stand behind her. "Ok, so...what the fuck was I doing wrong, because I should have had this finished and gone home twenty minutes ago?"

Kelly smiles at him gently and runs him through everything she did, he lets out a loud curse at one point. "Ok, so fuck me...I wasn't checking one box, and it kept kicking it back to...and it wasn't even his information it was ours. I'm sorry, Kelly Girl. I appreciate it, you know the more stressed you get the harder it is to even do easy shit, yeah?" Kelly gives him a pat on the shoulder, and I manage to bite back my growl at his familiarity and the fact that she touched him.

I tear my eyes away and look down at the paperwork to get it signed, handing it gently back to Kelly, while Xan goes over to the door and pulls it open, turning off the lights. "Kelly, I appreciate your help, let's just file that when we get back in. Everybody else, move your asses, we're closed!" He practically shoves Steve and me out the door, handing me my keys back when I cross the threshold. Kelly and her pack follow, and before I can blink, he's locked the door and set an alarm. He doesn't even wait for us to leave before he climbs into an extended cab pickup and takes off out of the parking lot.

The big alpha is trying to herd Teddy back to their truck, and while I don't want Kelly to be out in the cold any longer than she has to, I also don't want to leave her. My fingers are numb as I reach out, overwhelmed by the need to touch her, pull her against me, keep her warm and safe and protected. But I don't think she'd welcome it. She doesn't know anything about me other than that I was an asshole earlier. And I completely deserve her scorn. I just hope I can fix this, make it up to her. I settle with holding out my hand for her to take and walking her safely across the slippery parking lot. Steve is standing in the open door of the truck, looking longingly at Teddy and his alpha...I need to find out what the hell his name is.

I hear Teddy's voice despite the wind. "Um, where...where are you staying? Kelly said that the only hotel is out by the interstate." Steve turns to me, but honestly, I haven't even thought about it. He was in charge of this entire trip, so I just glare back. "Did you book a hotel? Did you even look for hotels, or were you all, 'Let's go get Teddy' and forget about human needs like food and shelter?" Am I being a smartass? Yes, undoubtedly. Do I care at this point? Not at all.

Kelly giggles next to me, and my whole body warms. *Snowstorm, what snowstorm?* I look up and now their alpha is looking between the four of us...and growling loudly. Kelly squeezes my hand again, and my brain shifts, I need to get her out of the cold. I shove Steve aside and lift her up onto the seat of the truck.

Stroking her hair back, I know I need to close the door, but I don't want this to be goodbye. It's too much to hope she shares my thoughts, but she does speak. "Maybe you should call them, make sure they have a room available, before we leave you out here in the cold?" She's biting her lip again, and I want to kiss it free from her tiny teeth.

Steve curses loudly behind me. "Sorry, the signal out here sucks." He wanders around the lot, waving his phone in front of his face trying to get reception. He finally stops near the door we just came out of and taps the screen a few times before putting the phone to his ear. He brightens after a few moments then speaks...then scowls. Then scowls harder, hanging up the phone and rubbing his hands down his face as he walks back to where I stand trying to block the wind from getting in the truck with Kelly.

"They don't have any rooms. The storm...there was a big wreck out on the interstate and several cars have come in since then, deciding not to risk it until things clear up. So they already have a waitlist for any openings that might become available."

He looks from me to Teddy again, and I hear Teddy whine, but it seems far away as I finally give in and gently close the door to keep Kelly warm.

I turn back to him. "Well, Bro, looks like you should have booked a spot in advance. Now we get to sleep in the SUV. Dibs on the middle seat!" But he isn't looking at me, he's staring into the idling truck, watching as Teddy talks heatedly to the other alpha. I tap Steve on the shoulder. "Hey, did you catch that guy's name, Teddy's alpha?" A low snarling growl rips free from him before he jolts and takes a deep breath of the freezing air.

My toes have gone numb.

How did I not notice before?

Shit.

"Sam, his name's Sam. He's the head of their pack."

With my realization that I am slowly standing out here freezing, I grab Steve's hand and drag him back over to the SUV. We need to make a new plan. Standing out there in the freezing winds and sleet isn't going to get us anything but hurt. I still have the keys, so I shove him in the passenger seat and then rush myself into the driver's, starting the ignition and then cranking the heat all the way up. It'll take a while to get warm now that I'm no longer in Kelly's orbit. I can feel the frost that's settled on my hair and skin. Neither of us even brought a coat. Fuck, I don't think I even own a coat. I own a few light jackets because it just doesn't get cold at home.

Steve's teeth clack loudly as we both stare at the truck idling several spaces over. There seems to be a heated discussion going on. "So, he's the head of their pack, how many more are there, did you find out?" Out of the corner of my eye, I see him shake his head, but I can't take my eyes off Kelly in the truck. I have no doubt that I'll be sitting here watching her for as long as they're in the parking lot. It feels like forever that they go back and forth before the alpha, Sam, drops his head to the steering wheel with a look of defeat.

He opens his door and strides across the lot towards us. He's sure footed despite the ice, and I envy his confidence. However, when he raps hard against my window, I don't want to roll it down. This guy is big, and I'm worried he's about to drag me out and beat the shit out of me in some sort of random show of possession. "Bro, look up where the nearest hospital is, you might need to drive," I whisper to Steve as I step back out of the SUV. We just got this fucking thing fixed, and I am in no mood to be dragged through a window if a beating *is* coming.

Sam looks at me hard. He also looks really pissed. "So...Teddy wants you to come stay with us until this storm blows over. He can't stand the idea of you two sleeping in the car in this weather. He says you three grew up together and despite everything, you're still his friends." He rubs his hand up and down the back of his head before cursing loudly. "Fuck! Feel free to say no."

I look over at Steve who looks confusedly back at me. "Sorry, Sam, I'd rather couch surf with strangers than sleep in my car in this weather." Sam glares at me again for a few seconds before he lets loose a loud sigh.

"Yeah, I was afraid of that. Shit. Ok, just follow Kelly in her little car. Me and Teddy will be right behind you in case you get separated." He turns abruptly and marches back to the truck, taking Kelly's hand and leading her to the little rust bucket Xan was working on earlier. He waits while she gets situated and the car starts before stomping back over to the truck and Teddy. Kelly fiddles with something on the dashboard, looking intense before a smile breaks across her face and her hair blows back. At least it seems like the heat works in that little deathtrap.

After watching her put on her seatbelt and make adjustments I glance over to Steve, but he's still watching the truck intently. Glancing that way, I can see why. Teddy and Sam have their foreheads pressed together, while Sam cards his fingers through Teddy's hair before pulling him in for a kiss. The tenderness seems a stark contrast for the surly alpha, but I can't really blame him for his shit attitude after having to invite two strangers into his home. Especially other alphas who seem obsessed with his pack.

Finally, Kelly pulls out of her parking spot. She stops where the road meets the lot and waits for us to pull up behind her. There's no other traffic and she pulls onto the road slowly, turning back towards the diner and our temporary residence until we get this chaos sorted out.

Chapter 28

Kelly

I hate driving in this weather, and my whole body is wound tight by the time I finally make it home.

Home, yeah, as strange as that sounds, it already feels like home. I'm glad that Sam has such a big parking area in front of his house since between his truck and that SUV, my little car wouldn't have any place to sit in a garage. I wait until Sam's truck pulls up before I get out and scurry to the door. I don't have a key yet, and Jake starts barking when I scramble up the steps, trying not to fall on the slippery surface. Garret, I remember his name from the driver's license I was looking at earlier, rushes to stand behind me, arms out like he's going to catch me if I start to fall.

Less than a minute later Sam appears with Teddy and the one Teddy said is named Steve. It took me a while to realize earlier that these two, Garret and Steve, are the two guys Teddy was supposed to form a pack with. I didn't catch it until I was looking at his license, and then the last name Carson rang some kind of bell. Then in the truck when Teddy said they grew up together, our conversation at Nest-n-Stuff came back. Any sympathy I had for them being out in the cold evaporated. But I don't think Sam can actually say no to Teddy, so here we all are.

Sam opens the door and Jake comes barreling out, running straight to me and knocking me into Garret's waiting arms. So, I guess I'm glad he was there to keep me from falling, even if he is a butthead. Jake sniffles around both our legs before whining a little and then running back around the house. Poor guy's been trapped inside for a while. Garret gently lets me go, and they all wait until I'm inside, followed by Teddy before they finally come in out of the cold.

Big alpha idiots.

Ok, not Sam.

But the other two, yeah.

That's probably not fair, but I don't care at this point.

I need to find out exactly what happened from Teddy.

Why he broke down earlier.

What it has to do with these two.

And if I need to stay mad at them.

It's hard to be mad when someone drops to their knees and looks at you like you're their own personal savior.

Sam's talking behind me and I catch the last few sentences. "Jake usually sleeps on the rug in the kitchen, but lately he's been crashed out in front of our bedroom door in the mornings. If you want to sleep on the couch, you'll have to deal with a cold wet nose. Otherwise, we have one spare bed in Teddy's room, you can share or fight over it. I don't care which. Now I need to go get dinner started for *my* omega and *my* beta."

Steve raises his hand. "So, it's just the three of you then?"

There's no way to miss the snarl that curls Sam's lip before he shakes himself and regains control. Taking a deep breath, he says, "Yes, it's just us three. If you want to help me feed them, come this way." He waves his hand towards the kitchen before marching off, Garret following close behind. I briefly wonder if I can ask him to make a hot soup again. This weather makes me want soup, but I don't want to impose.

Teddy and Steve are watching each other warily, but nobody's talking. Touching Teddy lightly on the shoulder makes him startle. "Sorry, but I need to go get changed out of these wet clothes. I just wanted to let you know."

Teddy looks at me, then down at himself. "Yeah, that's probably a good idea." He looks over at Steve. "Can you let them know we went to get cleaned up and dried off?" He turns away before Steve can give a reply and takes my hand, leading me down the hallway to the first door on the right. I haven't really been in here, but he closes the door as soon as we're inside, leaning heavily against it and wrapping his arms around me.

"Fuck, Pixie, I'm sorry. I panicked." I turn in his embrace, my hands coming up to his cheeks, pulling him down so I can pepper his face with kisses.

"Don't apologize, please. I saw what happened earlier. I'm sorry I couldn't make it better. I didn't know what was going on. Do you want me to sic Jake on 'em?"

He laughs against my lips, his arms squeezing me tighter before his whole body relaxes. "You really think the slobber monster has a mean bone in his body? Well, ok, maybe for you he does. Pretty sure that he's like the rest of us and would do anything to keep you safe and happy." He brings his head down to mine, pressing our foreheads together, and kissing the tip of my nose. His lips barely curl up at the corners. "I just realized your clothes are next door, aren't they?"

It's so nice to see him smile again. "Yeah, and I'm not sure which bathrooms work down here other than the main one, but I just kinda want to stay here with you for a couple minutes sharing your body heat. Is that ok?" His arms tighten again, and before I know it, he's picked me up completely and carries me over to the bed. It's nothing special, not when compared to Sam's big bed upstairs, but it still has a soft comforter and pillows.

Teddy perches me on his lap and reaches over to undo the laces on my sneakers before pulling them and my socks off. If Mom could see me leaving my wet shoes on in the house, I'd get the lecture of a lifetime.

Once my cold sneakers are off, Teddy stands me up, slowly unbuttoning my nice work jeans and sliding them down. He hums in irritation at the goosebumps running up and down my legs. Standing up, he toes his own black sneakers off and marches to the bathroom.

I hear the water come on and then he comes back, pulling his shirt off over his head. He blushes for a minute, holding it in front of him, trying to cover up his stomach. But here's the thing. Teddy is strong. He's not alpha strong, but from what we've talked about he still goes to the gym regularly with his friend Sarah. While he doesn't have a washboard stomach, he isn't fat either. He's a little padded but still so hot. I squirm a little as he finally drops his shirt to the floor and stalks across the room, his hands going under my shirt to slide it over my head before gathering me up and carrying me to the bathroom.

We both have too much on our minds to really be playful. But it's still comforting to have Teddy take care of me, stripping us both completely and then holding me as the hot water warms up my whole body. He washes and conditions my hair with his horse shampoo and then bends down so I can return the favor. I thought he was joking when he told me about it, but no, it's in these two huge bottles with horses on the packaging. Plus, it makes his hair super soft, and it doesn't hinder his own scent. He lets me borrow his soap while he rinses his hair out, and then takes it back and washes my back for me. By the time we finish, I'm just about ready to curl up and sleep for the rest of the day. But Sam's making dinner, so that would be mean.

Teddy dries me off by blotting the water off my skin gently, running a detangling brush through my hair and blotting it with a towel until it is mostly dry. He's making it hard not to drag him over to the bed and demand all the cuddles. Once I'm as dry as I can get, he pulls one of his T-shirts over my head, fluffing my hair out behind me. "Sorry, Pixie, I don't think my underwear will really fit you, but this should do until you can get to your own clothes. I'm gonna go see what I can help Sam with." He kisses me on the forehead before leaving and I scurry down the hallway to the room I claimed.

If it were just the three of us, I wouldn't even worry about it. It's only been a couple of days, but I already know that they're my family now, which means that I'm completely comfortable walking around without a bra on. But now these two new guys—Teddy knows them, and I don't want to embarrass him. I go over and pull out a sports bra and a pair of fleece pajama pants covered in snowflakes. It seems highly appropriate, and soon I'm completely warm and toasty, and hunting down my guys to see what I can do for them.

Stepping out of my room, I hear a low growl and grunting—I hurry down the hall towards the living room. Worrying that Jake got tired of having new people in his house and tried to take a chunk out of someone, I don't expect to see Teddy pinning Steve to the couch, hands fisted in his hair, plundering his mouth like some kind of pirate god. But that's what it is.

Is it hot in here?

Chapter 29

Sam

Jake prances around my feet, waiting to see if I drop any food off the counter. I heard him scratching at the back door when I came in to start dinner and immediately let him in. He ran a tight circle around the kitchen island and then slid under the table to roll around on his back. But he only took a couple of minutes to defrost and by the time Garret walked in, Jake was already in full on begging mode.

With two extra people, I'm going to need to extend the table for this...and hope I have a couple of extra chairs.

Maybe we should just eat in the living room.

I set Garret to pulling out ingredients for a potato and leek soup. It's hearty and should be easy to make enough for everybody, and it gives me an excuse to make a side salad. Kelly needs more leafy greens.

Just as I start to chop up the potatoes Steven walks in and tells us that Teddy and Kelly went to get cleaned up and into dry clothes. My mouth waters and my dick twitches in my pants imagining what they might be doing in the shower together. I cast a surly eye over my "houseguests" because if they weren't here, I could go join my pack.

Having delivered his message, Steven meanders back towards the living room, while Garret just stands there being useless. Is that a fair assessment? No. But I don't rightly give a shit after how my omega reacted to them earlier today. I would have been totally fine leaving them in their fucking car if it didn't upset Teddy.

That's a lie…I don't know what I would have done, but bringing them home was sure as hell not my first choice. Cutting the bottom end of the leeks, I open and clean them, before passing them off to Garret to dice for the soup. Then I put some bacon in the oven for toppings and finish cutting up potatoes. Putting everything in the Dutch oven, I leave Garret to stir it—on pain of no food—and go to check on my pack.

Walking into the living room, I immediately see why Teddy says he's a switch, as he's very aggressively kissing the whimpering alpha on the couch. The man has turned into a sodden puddle of need as he begs repeatedly for something, his whispered words nothing but a jumble of pleas as Teddy's hand fist his hair. Holding him in place to bite and suck down his throat, leaving red marks along his jaw and neck—there is a clear outline of teeth marks to be seen where the collar of his shirt is pulled aside.

A small moan draws my attention to the other side of the room—Kelly is staring intently at the two on the couch. Her front teeth are sunk into her bottom lip, and I want to go replace it with my own, pull her close and nibble on it. Her scent isn't as strong as Teddy's, but her arousal is clear in the air. I'm torn for a moment, wanting to mark them both, stake my claim on each of my pack members. But Teddy seems to be doing well enough on his own, so I stride across the room, scooping Kelly into my arms and carrying her back to Teddy's room. The room itself smells like a shower, and I can scent him on the shirt she's wearing. Fuck, I need to claim her now, need her to smell like me too. Double fuck, all the condoms are upstairs.

I was worried on Saturday; I didn't want to do anything to scare them away. But the way they reacted to my taking control was promising, more so after seeing Teddy on the couch earlier. He looks like he understands the need for control: aggression, pleasure with just the hint of pain to help it blossom. And that's what it is, a need. I need to take care of them in every way possible, my alpha won't let me be any other way. I hope they're willing to give up control, at least in this. Willing to let me take care of them.

I sit down on the bed, turning her to straddle my lap. Rubbing my jaw along hers, I start trailing kisses down the column of her neck. I wonder if she would be upset if I marked her neck like Teddy was doing to Steven on the couch. Scraping my teeth over the skin at the base of her throat, I'm rewarded with a low moan and her tiny body wriggling against me. I lick over the same place, but this time she giggles, her chin coming down to block my access. Ahh, she's ticklish. That could be fun for later, but not now. I need to use firmer pressure.

I trail kisses up her neck, causing more squirming and giggling. It's adorable, but not really what I'm going for right now. A quick nip on her earlobe makes her twitch in a different way and moan again. I'm starting to wonder if my little beta likes a little pain with her pleasure. Running my hands down her sides, I cup her ass and squeeze a little harder than would be comfortable. Her shocked gasp and roll of her hips against my stiff cock is a good sign and I bury my face in her shoulder, nipping and sucking on the tender skin there.

I need to mark her, need to make sure everyone who sees her knows she's taken. Even if that's only in the house. If I can't leave a permanent mark right now, I'm gonna do my damnedest to at least leave a few temporary ones. I bite down harder where her neck meets her shoulder and she shudders against me, a loud whimper slipping out, her hips grinding down on me. I grab her ass in a bruising grip, pulling her against me and thrusting against her heated core as her movements grow more frantic. Her hands come up to tangle in my hair, pulling and twisting against my scalp...and I am about to embarrass myself.

Holy Fuck.

Slow down Sam.

You do not want to have to walk back to your bedroom with a fucking come stain on your jeans.

Maybe I should just leave her wrapped around me and go upstairs that way...It should work just as well as marking her.

But it might embarrass her.

Another alpha would get the message though...still, I don't want to upset her.

Oh no, looks like there's only one thing to do.

Standing up, I turn around and lay her on the bed, legs draped over the side before I slide her snowflake sleep pants down her legs. Hmm, no panties. The logical part of my mind tells me it's because she had a shower and hasn't had time to finish getting ready for bed. The illogical alpha side says "Fuck it, open invitation!"

Guess which one I listen to?

Dropping to my knees I wrap her thighs over my shoulders, leaning in to swipe my tongue up her slit. She doesn't have a sweet taste like Teddy does, being a beta. It's more of a salty-tangy flavor with just a hint of her lilac scent, and it makes me growl low in the back of my throat. Her hips wiggle away as she giggles again.

Ok, so that's not gonna work.

How did Teddy do this on Saturday?

Wrapping my arms up over her thighs, I pull her back to my mouth. From this angle my thumbs can hold her open so I can taste her properly. I bring my face up to her core and the low growl rumbles out again, causing her to twitch and try to pull away. So, maybe the vibrations from that are what's causing the problem. Pulling her tight against me, I swipe my tongue hard over her clit and am finally rewarded with a low groan and her legs tightening around my head.

Gauging her response between hard licks to sucking to scraping my teeth over her, she soon has her hands fisted in my hair again, pulling me against her. She seems to like the sucking best, followed by light teeth. But while she's moaning and grinding against me, it isn't pushing her over the edge. Unwinding my arm, I drop her leg down to the outside of my shoulder, her whole body is shaking and I briefly wonder if my growl would still tickle at this stage. But I need to feel her come, so I'm not going to sabotage myself by experimenting right now.

Now that she's spread open for me, I lean forward again, thrusting my tongue inside of her. Her back bows off the bed, so I insert two fingers, and she is so fucking slick right now. There's still a tight squeeze, because she's so small in comparison, but her whole body shudders and I clench down on her thigh, my fingers leaving white indents on her soft skin. Her head thrashes from side to side as I pump my fingers inside her, and when I pull out to add a third, she lets out a needy whimper that almost makes me come in my fucking pants.

Using the hand that's already slick with her juices, I reach down to pop the button on my jeans and unzip enough to pull out my cock, hoping it'll relieve some of the pressure. I'm so fucking hard right now I could probably use it to hammer nails—I wanna hammer *her*. Taking a deep breath to center myself and keep from coming I get a flood of her scent, and it almost tips me over the edge.

So that wasn't a great idea on my part.

I groan as her lilac scent fills my lungs.

But fuck it all, there is no protection down here. Instead, I bring my fingers back up, I turn my head when I thrust them inside her, biting down on the inside of her thigh. Not hard enough to break the skin, but there will definitely be a bruise there. I almost lose my grip when her hips jackknife off the bed and she lets out a long keening cry. I secure my hold to keep her from flopping off the bed entirely, and yeah, that's probably gonna leave more bruises. Fuck, I hope she doesn't hate me after this. I love the idea of marking her, as long as I don't actually hurt her.

She finally settles down, and I scissor my fingers at her entrance, earning me another heated moan. If she's comfortable with it, I'd like to practice to see if she'll be able to enjoy being knotted one day. Just the idea freaks some betas out, but fuck, I can only hope she wants to try as much as I do. Pulling my fingers free, I give one last long lick from core to clit, gathering up her taste so I can keep her on my tongue as I stand up. Maybe if Teddy's done making out with Steve on the couch, I can go give him a taste.

Standing up, I'm still painfully hard. Kelly sits up and reaches for me, but I gently grab her hands. The little pout she gives me is adorable and I lean down to nip at her lips. "Soon, Sugar. I don't have condoms down here, and I want to be inside you when I come." She gives a full body shiver and pulls one hand free from my grip to reach out and stroke me. I'm already leaking pre-come like a fucking faucet and my pants are about to be a mess.

I grab her hand again and pull it away. She grins up at me in response, like the mischievous pixie that Teddy keeps calling her. "If you wanna be a brat, Sugar, I can treat you like one. But that means you're going over my knee later and I'm going to have to redden that pretty little ass before I fuck you tonight. Is that what you want?" It's impossible to miss the way her eyes get bigger and her breathing speeds up. Still holding her hands, I pull her forward so I can kiss her properly. I plunder her mouth, making sure she can taste herself on me before pulling back, I leave her breathless and reaching for me.

"Come on, I need to go finish dinner so I can feed everybody. Can you check on Teddy, see if he made a mess on the couch?" That playful smirk is back on her lips, but she slides her pajama pants back on, wiggling a little once they're in place.

"I still feel all slippery and squishy down there." She smirks up at me and I groan again. Fuck, this dinner better hurry the fuck up so I can carry her upstairs.

Chapter 30

Garret

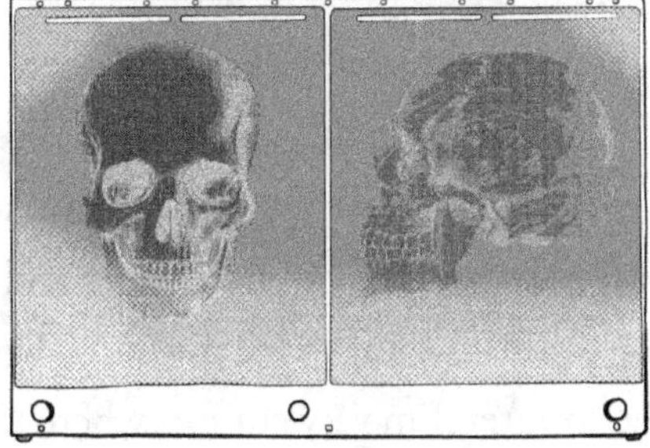

All I want to do is finish this damned soup. I don't even know what the hell I'm doing. I tried to go look for Sam earlier, but he disappeared and hasn't come back yet. When I went into the living room Teddy had Steve pinned to the couch, rocking against him and biting his neck and jaw. I could hear my brother moaning, and that was more than I needed.

All the nope.

I didn't need to see that.

I didn't need to hear my brother cry out, "Fuck, Bear, I missed you so much!"

I definitely didn't need to hear the grunting that followed.

Now I don't need to leave the kitchen again, I can just stay in here, stirring this fucking pot of overcooked soup until someone comes and tells me it's done. Yup, just me and the dog. I can't even remember his name. In my defense it's been a busy day, but at least he's not bad company, seeing as he's just lying on his back next to the pantry. Every time I look his way, his tail starts wagging and I hear the *thump, thump, thump* of it against the door.

Fuck me, I hope that's his tail and not my brother.

The solids in the soup have very nearly liquified with heat and my constant stirring, so I turn the heat to low to keep everything warm and rifle through the fridge for soda or something to drink. There are a few bottles of microbrews and a half dozen cans of soda. No one is coming to tell me no, so I grab a can and lean against the counter. I'm very curious where Kelly and Sam are, but mostly Kelly. But I *would* also like to know what the fuck else I need to do with this fucking soup. Once I finish the can and locate the recycling bin, the silence becomes obvious.

In truth, I don't want to look back in the living room. Are they still there? Did they move to Teddy's room? Are they still wearing clothes? Because I do *not* need to see that. And where the actual hell is Sam? This is his goddamned soup.

Fuck my life.

Fine, fine, whatever.

Creeping towards the living room, I move as silently as I can. Steve and Teddy are both still on the couch, but it almost looks like they're asleep. One of those assholes better know the proper way to clean the upholstery, I don't think Sam's gonna be real hospitable if his omega fucked my brother on the couch, or even just left stains from all the bump and grind. Taking a deep breath, I let out a sigh and pass through the room.

Kelly's light lilac scent is heavy in the hallway, and it draws me in. Is that where Sam is? The low murmur of voices draws me to the right, and I knock lightly on a door. Sam yanks it open glaring daggers at me. He smells like Kelly, a lot like Kelly. His face also looks like a glazed donut, so it's not hard to figure out what they've been up to. I don't mean to be petty, I really don't but shit. "Well, while everyone else was having fun, your soup liquidated."

I reach out and push the door open enough to see Kelly, and nod in greeting. "You can deal with it, I'm going out to get a fucking change of clothes so I can get some sleep. Maybe the goddamned hotel will have space in the morning." Spinning on my heel I march to the front door, and that big ass dog comes bouncing out of the kitchen to follow me outside. "Don't think you wanna go out there, buddy, it's cold as fuck." I reach down to rub his floppy ears with one hand before swinging the door open. He just looks between me and the open door before nope-ing out back to the kitchen.

The freezing air that blows inside causes my brother to jerk and sit up from his position half under Teddy. I take no small bit of satisfaction in his startled look before I walk out and close the door quietly behind me.

I can't believe I finally found my person, my fated one, and I went from being a third wheel with Steve and Teddy to a fifth wheel here.

I fucking hate my life sometimes.

Steve

Garret is super pissed, and I hate that for him. I hate that my brother is so upset, but he just doesn't understand. Teddy is mine, this missing piece of my soul. I didn't even realize it until I saw him again, scented his omega. I've loved Teddy for as long as I can remember. I don't even really remember anything before him, he's just always been a part of my life. It wasn't until we got older that I realized I loved him differently than I did anyone else. Everything just feels right with him. Now I have a good guess as to why.

Though considering how he teased me and treated me earlier, I wonder if fate fucked up our designations and I was the one who should have been an omega. Fuck, the way he held me down and plundered my mouth. I just wanted to melt against him, let him have all my control, let him do whatever he wanted as long as he stayed with me.

The sound of footsteps brings my head around. Sam and Kelly are coming out of the hallway, she turns to go up the stairs, while he goes into the kitchen, muttering darkly about soup. That, at least, explains some of Garret's attitude. He wanted the beta, Kelly, and he doesn't do guys. Well, tough shit, it's their house and her choice if she doesn't want him. Nothing against her, but she's a beta, they don't feel the same pull that alphas and omegas do anyway. Besides, whether she comes with us, or we stay here, it'll be because my teddy bear wants her and she wants him back. But who wouldn't want him? He's aggressive and dominant, and smells so fucking good it makes my dick hurt.

Rolling as best I can to let him get some rest, I slide out from under him on the couch, and he settles in. There's an embarrassing wet spot on my jeans but fuck it, I'm pretty sure they already walked through the room earlier when Teddy was hellbent on ravishing me. While I'm not exactly an exhibition-ist, I just can't find it in me to care. My omega got big while we were separated, not quite as tall as us, but he has broader shoulders. I roll him backwards into my vacated spot on the couch so he can be more comfortable. Once Garret gets back in, I'll go grab my bag so I can get changed. For now, there should be a bathroom around here somewhere that I can start getting cleaned up in.

I walk down the hallway that they came out of earlier when the scent hits me. Ok...so, yeah, that would explain it better. The scent of Kelly is nearly overwhelming. Sam's is here too, but mostly I'm getting a hard shot of lust and possession from it. Garret's scent is barely noticeable, and he smells upset—sad almost to the point of devastation.

Well...Fuck. I try a few doors, but there's no bathroom down this hall. Lots of rooms with plastic sheeting on the walls, and stacks of drywall and insulation scattered around. There has to be one downstairs, logic says that houses are built with a guest bathroom. Heading back towards the living room I let my eyes roam, front door, then doorway to dining room that leads to the kitchen, fireplace, other doorway to the kitchen and through that, a backdoor. Turning in the opposite direction, I see stairs and three more doors. Here's hoping.

The first door I try leads to a closet...The whole thing smells like Sam, and a quick scan doesn't seem like anything would fit Kelly. Teddy could wear his stuff, but nothing in here smells like him, and the random jumble of work boots on the floor are nothing he would wear, unless his fashion sense has changed drastically. It could have, but once again, the scent is wrong.

I close that door and try the next one. Bingo! It totally smells like Kelly in here. Well, she's just going to have to share, because I'm not sitting through dinner with come cooling in my damned jeans. It's my own fault, really, but I'd do it again in a heartbeat. That being said, it really is uncomfortable. So, I pop my fly and peel down the sticky mess, wiping as much as I can up with toilet paper. I don't see any washrags, and honestly it would be creepy to use someone else's stuff for this.

Having done the best I can with the resources available, I pull my jeans back up and try to situate myself as much as possible. My shirt doesn't come down far enough to completely hide the spot, but they all knew what was going on, or at least strongly suspected. Teddy was pumping out omega pheromones like a freight train, it would have been hard to miss. I leave the bathroom and Garret is back inside. He's standing over Teddy's sleeping form on the couch, shaking his head. He looks depressed, but my snarly possessive growl rips free anyway, snapping his head up to meet my eyes.

"Bathroom?" is his only reply, and I can just nod, feeling too off kilter to do more. He inclines his own head in reply and stalks past me through the open door. I can tell when Kelly's scent hits him by the groan that comes out. Fuck me, what a shitshow this is turning out to be. Stepping over to the couch, I run my fingers through Teddy's hair. It's gotten longer, but it's beautiful like this. The piercings are new too, obviously. It's been so many years.

Fuck, I just want to carry him into that bedroom I saw earlier and snuggle him all night long. But he might be hungry, so I need to make sure he's fed first. The alpha part of me that I mostly ignore is riding me hard to take care of him, and make sure he has everything he needs. Which is going to be difficult trapped in someone else's house in a snowstorm. But I'll do what I can.

Walking into the kitchen the scent of food hits hard, finally making its way past the omega pheromones I've been huffing.

Sam and Kelly stand at the counter. She must have come back down while I was getting cleaned up earlier. Sam is scowling down at a long pan full of bacon that looks like it's been cooked to within an inch of its life—like he can magically make it un-blacken through sheer force of will. Kelly has her hand up, rubbing small circles on his back as he mutters, "Could have at least taken the bacon out, I could smell it burning as soon as I walked in...Would have been impossible to miss."

The situation becomes more clear; they left Garret alone to cook dinner while they had fun. And then he found them afterwards. So, maybe his tantrum isn't as unwarranted as I thought. But still. "It's your own fault, you know." Two pairs of eyes swing towards me. "Garret can't cook to save his life, you're lucky he didn't burn your house down." We always keep at least two fire extinguishers in the kitchen at our apartment, just in case. The man is accident prone as well as scatterbrained in the kitchen. I don't care, I could live off takeout and frozen burritos—much to my family's disgust—but they should be aware of the danger.

Speak of the devil. Garret walks in, his hair's damp, and it looks like he took a fast shower and put on clean clothes. Sam scowls at him, but his only other reaction is to drop the pan of burned bacon on the countertop. Garret either doesn't give a shit, or wants to be an asshole, because he goes over, grabs a blackened slice and pops it in his mouth. "Oh, extra crunchy, awesome. This day sucked ass and swallowed, so I am gonna go crash. Other than the probably come stained couch." He looks pointedly at me. "Do you have someplace else I can sleep? You mentioned Teddy's room, but I don't want to put him out. Also I have no idea where it is."

Oh, yeah, he's still pissed. He grabs another slice of bacon and Sam glares harder at it, tracking the movement from the pan to Garret's mouth, his upper lip curling in a suppressed snarl as Garret continues talking. "Shit man, just give me some private space away from everyone having sex, and I'm golden. I don't even care if there's a bed, I can fucking sleep on the floor if it's not putting someone else out." Sam looks taken aback for a second, cool calculation in his eyes.

"There's one finished room upstairs that we've been sharing, then Teddy stores his stuff downstairs in the spare room. Kelly is keeping her stuff in the other downstairs bedroom, but it's not really fit to sleep in without windows, especially right now." He looks over at her, and she just nods, so he continues. "Fuck, ok, there's the couch, but Teddy's commandeered that for now. I have some theater chairs that recline in the basement if you want to try those."

Garret nods and looks around. To my great surprise Kelly steps forward, which earns my brother another glare from Sam. "Come on, I'll show you where it is, unless you'd rather sleep on the floor. I picked out the next most finished room to store my stuff. It doesn't have a bed and is probably super cold right now, but if you want the floor, you can have it." She takes Garret's hand, and he follows behind her like a lovestruck fool.

Shit.

Chapter 31

Kelly

It still embarrasses me thinking that Garret almost walked in on me and Sam earlier. Just a few minutes before, I was sprawled across the bed with no pants on. That would have been awkward. Leading him back into the living room, we pass the stairs and the bathroom to the door that leads down to the basement. It has one of those dual light switches, so I can turn it on at the head of the stairway or at the bottom, and I flick the switch before leading him down.

We reach the bottom, and the shock is clear on his face as he takes in Sam's man cave. I don't really think that it should be called a man cave—I totally want to hang out down here. Maybe once he gets the shelves put in for books, he'll let me store my manga here. I still need to get back to my parents' house and get the rest of my clothes and stuff, but there isn't a hurry. It would probably be a good idea for me to call them and check in again anyway with all the snow. They might get upset if I don't let them know I'm alive and not "dead in a ditch somewhere" from the storm.

When I open my fingers to let go of Garret's hand, he tightens his grip. *Ok, so we'll keep holding hands, that's fine.* I curl my fingers back around his and he relaxes slightly, but now he's the one leading me around the room. He takes in the video game setup, and then the bar off in the corner and pool table. Finally, going back to the chairs in front of the TV. I can't stop the blush that heats my cheeks thinking about what I did with Teddy in those chairs. Or that fact that I've been secreting away boxes of condoms around the house in handy places, at least until I get to my doctor's.

When I went upstairs earlier, after Sam licked me so hard I saw stars, I grabbed a couple boxes of them and stuffed them in Teddy's room in case the need arises again. Similarly, when I had to run upstairs during our movie this weekend, I grabbed some of the regular and alpha sizes and put them behind the bar. The guys'll probably think I'm nuts if they come across random boxes of condoms scattered around the house. But better to be safe than sorry, and I don't know when or if I'll be ready for kids in the future.

While I'm zoning out, Garret turns towards me. He steps in close, removing almost all space between our bodies. His hand that isn't holding mine comes up to cup my cheek. The movement too intimate for complete strangers, which we very nearly are. The look in his eyes is so sad as he stares at me.

"I need to apologize again. I know that nothing I say will make you not think of me as an asshole for how I behaved earlier. But I *am* sorry. I've been so stressed lately but that's not your fault. It's not even a good excuse. But still..." He trails off and I look up, wrapping my free hand around the one holding mine.

"Do you wanna talk about it? Why you're stressed? Is there anything I can do to help?" His body sways towards mine until I can feel his breath against my forehead. I hear him take a deep breath and his whole body shudders.

"No, Kelly, I appreciate it. You've done enough, and thanks for showing me where I can sleep." He tries to pull away, but I don't want him to. And when his eyes meet mine, I feel an overwhelming need to help him feel better. It's not quite the same feeling I have with Teddy and Sam of being home, but it's not completely different. Almost like he could be part of my home if I let him in.

Still holding his hand, I lead him over to the chairs and set him down in one, plopping myself down in the one beside him with my feet under me, and turning so I can face him. "Ok, open invitation didn't work, so now I'll demand. Garret, what's stressing you out? You'll feel better if you talk about it."

That at least earns me a small smile, but he sounds hesitant as he starts talking. "I didn't want to come on this trip." He stares intently at my face. "No, that's not...Ugh. That's not the whole thing, and it's just. Shit...let me start over from the beginning." He takes a deep breath, running his hands down his face like that'll help him line up his thoughts.

"I'm not sure how much Teddy told you, but we grew up together. We were inseparable since we were little—he's like my brother. But as we got older, it became apparent that he felt differently, at least he and Steve...um...they were still kids, but they didn't feel the same way about each other that I felt about them." He swallows hard and stares at me, willing me to understand the simple concept that his brother and Teddy fell in love.

I can't stop my small scowl. "Yes, I know. Teddy loves him. I got that part. Continue."

He lets out a sigh of relief. Maybe he's just embarrassed talking about it. "Ok, so, yeah. We went from a trio of best friends to a two-way love interest and the tag along twin. As you can imagine, it kinda sucked. So, when we got a call from Teddy saying his designation came in and he was an omega, Steve was thrilled. He said everything was great. We could still start a pack with just the three of us." He pauses the story, and his eyes meet mine, pleading with me to see the problem. Of course, being the odd man out is never fun. I get that.

Heck, even with Sam and Teddy, I feel that way sometimes because they're alpha and omega, and I'm just the clueless beta. They don't do it on purpose, but sometimes it's like they already have a connection I'm not part of. But we haven't been together for very long at all, so I hope it'll get better in time. That being said, if I'm understanding Garret correctly, this was going on for a while. Poor guy.

"Of course, Dad was mad. He told Teddy's parents in no uncertain terms that he would never be a part of our pack, and we needed a female omega to produce heirs." He sighs again, staring down into his lap. "Like having kids should be an entire fucking life goal. Jeez." His eyes flicked up to mine. "Sorry, if you want kids, that's cool. Great, even, for you. Not all of us want that. I'm not against it, but it's not my goal in life to produce children to take over my dads' company. I don't actually know what I want to do, but I know that isn't it." He sighs again.

This man is gonna hyperventilate if he doesn't stop it.

"Anyway, as you can imagine, Steve was inconsolable. We didn't even hear from Teddy again after he called to tell us he was an omega. Dad blocked his calls, he wouldn't let us see him. It was a mess. Moreover, as we got older, Dad started demanding we visit different omega centers and try to meet a female." I couldn't hide my wince at that. It's no wonder Teddy broke down crying earlier, or that he was so...enthusiastic on the couch.

"It's been almost nine years of us going to college, trying to meet someone, going to omega centers, trying to meet someone, Dad constantly harassing us to try to settle down...and meet someone. It's exhausting and repetitive and we were never going to meet anyone that we could agree on, anyway. It's been a huge waste of time." My confusion must show on my face because he smiles before he continues, "Steve's gay, Kelly. Like, Full six on the Kinsey scale. He says he can find women aesthetically attractive in a subjective way, but nothing about the female body appeals to him sexually. And, quite frankly, I don't like dick. I mean, I have one—it's nice enough if I do say so myself—but I don't want one from anyone else." I can feel the blush in my cheeks and ears.

Garret smiles at me again, reaching out to cup my jaw. "But you, Kelly, you are so fucking beautiful. I knew from the moment I saw you in the store that you were mine."

My eyes go wide, and I can only try to explain. "No, that's not...You, both of you, smelled Teddy on me—he smells like a snickerdoodle. Like an omega. I'm just..." I trail off, not sure how to explain any better than I did with Sam and Teddy that I'm a beta, and therefore can't be his.

His smile is soft. "But you, Sweetness, you smell like lilacs. You smell like mine." His hand slides behind my neck, fingers winding through my hair.

Gently, giving me plenty of time to resist, he pulls me forward into a kiss. My toes curl under me and I moan against his mouth, giving him the opening to slide his tongue along my lips and barely dip inside. His other hand comes up and wraps around my back, pulling me closer, over the arm of the chair and into his lap. I settle against him, and he's already hard underneath my butt. I wiggle around and he groans into me. His hand on my back tightens in my shirt while the other one comes down to grip my hip, grinding me against his erection.

It's too much, too fast as his hips thrust against me, and I pull away from his kiss, gasping for breath. He tries to follow me, leaning forward, but he looks startled, and stammers out another apology. "Shit, Kelly, I…I'm sorry. Again. I feel like I'm always saying that to you. It's no wonder you don't want to—" I silence him with my fingers against his lips. I just need a minute to think. These alphas and omega are really turning my world on its end.

"No, Garret, you didn't do anything wrong." I meet his eyes, and he looks worried. "You feel really good. Too good, in fact. I'm just…how do I say this? Betas aren't built like alphas and omegas. We don't see someone or scent someone and suddenly know." His gaze ping-pongs around the room, looking anywhere but at me. "No, listen." I take his face in my hands so he has to meet my eyes. "I didn't say I don't want you. It's all just really fast, ok? I just met Teddy and Sam this weekend and already…well…you know. I'm just having a bit of an attack of conscience because I thought I was gonna either be alone my whole life, or meet a nice beta guy." His sudden snarl doesn't even faze me after dealing with Sam and Teddy.

"The point is…" I rub my thumb between his eyebrows, smoothing out the scowl. "The point is, this is all new for me. So just please be patient while I get myself sorted out. We know where we each stand now, yeah? I know how you feel, but I need to sort out how I feel. Still, something about you does feel like mine too. Not as much as Teddy and Sam. Not yet. Give me some time? Please?"

He pulls me hard against his chest and murmurs against my hair. "Take all the time you need, Kelly. I'll be waiting until you get tired of me and tell me to get lost, or decide you want me." I can feel his small sad smile against the top of my head, but the only answer I have is to hug him back.

Chapter 32

Teddy

Waking up with your face pressed against a couch and humid dog breath panting in your ear is now one of my least favorite things. Sitting up, I try to dodge Jake's tongue as he takes a lick at my side of my head. Shit, where the hell did Vee go? I shouldn't have taken things so far earlier when he called me 'Bear', but it brought back so many memories and I kind of lost myself for a bit. Giving Jake a firm pat on the head, I try to stand up, only to get flogged by his excited tail. Fucking hell, this dog is always happy.

Finally managing to stand, I don't see anyone else in the living room, but there are voices coming from the kitchen. Leaning heavily against the wall, I feel kind of dizzy again, and hopefully, it's not that fucking omega insecurity bullshit from before. Sam purred, I felt better, fixed. There's no time to deal with my body's crazy omega hormones, not when I need to figure out what's going on with Vee.

He's standing by the stove with Sam when I stumble into the kitchen. They're both glaring at something in a pot on the burner.

Oh, shit, yeah, Sam was gonna make dinner.

What happened?

I must make some noise, because two sets of eyes turn to me. Then Sam is gathering me up against him, his arms tight around my back and his jaw and chin rubbing over the top of my head, scent marking me. Vee tries to step up to my back and Sam looses a low rattling growl.

Well, this shit's gotta stop now.

Sam reluctantly lets me go when I pull back, and I have to avoid Vee's reaching hands as well. Nope, we're not gonna go there. I circle around the kitchen island to put some space between me and the growly alphas, as well as give myself some time to think. Sam looks smug, and Vee looks like I slapped him—but I don't owe him shit, despite what happened on the couch earlier. He fucking abandoned me.

Looking around, I don't see Kelly...or Garret. And I want to snarl myself at the memory of him dropping to his knees and holding *my* pixie. "So, where's Kelly?" Sam's face falls and now Vee looks smug.

Well...fuck.

Before I can go hunt that asshole alpha down, Kelly comes back into the kitchen. She takes one look at all of us standing around, shrugs and leaves again. The sound of Jake's toe nails rattling across the floor follows shortly afterwards, and when I peer around the doorframe to see if she's ok, she's stretched out on the couch with her arm over her eyes. Jake is prancing in circles around the couch, his tail occasionally thumping against her when he passes the front. On his fourth circuit, she finally moves her arm to defend herself. "Seriously Jakey, I don't have enough going on without you beating me to death with your butt-club?"

Jake spins around mid-prance and starts licking the arm she was using to keep from getting hit. She starts giggling. "Ok. Ok! You're forgiven, you big slobber muffin. Oof!" She lets out a whoosh of air as he tries to climb on the couch with her. She scrambles to sit up before the big dog can land on her, and he flops down on the cushion where her head was, looking longingly at her before dropping his droopy face into her lap.

"Yeah, buddy. I could get used to the adoration too. Cripes, why is everything such a mess?" She rubs his ears as his big eyes stare lovingly up at her, his tail swinging back and forth into the arm of the couch. He takes up more space than she does. But despite her upbeat attitude and smile, she seems stressed or upset, and I'm not sure how to help.

When I pull back into the kitchen, Sam and Vee are still casting angry looks back and forth. I take in the no longer bubbling pot of soup, and the box of bread that Sam pulled out. Fuck it,

I'm hungry and emotionally exhausted. It looks like Kelly and I both need a hug and a snuggle. So, it's time to fix a couple of bowls, drag my beta upstairs for cuddles, and hope for the best.

Sam looks like he wants to protest when I start pulling down bowls. Thankfully, he gives up quickly. It does kind of surprise me that he has so many nice dishes. I mean, my parents do, but they're a fully formed pack. I have a feeling if I look hard enough, Sam actually has a china cabinet or some shit around here. Like despite what he told me earlier about thinking he would never have a pack, he renovated this house and outfitted it for one. He doesn't seem like an optimist, so I'm curious of his reasoning.

Regardless, I get down five of each of the big stoneware bowls and plates while Sam busies himself in that weird bread box of his again, pulling out a variety of different rolls and loaves. Fucking thing is like a Tardis, it must be bigger on the inside.

Vee is standing there not doing anything, so he can chip in too. "Hey, get in the fridge and grab some cheese to grate for this." He scurries over to follow my order, and it feels strange to be barking commands at an alpha. Not that I don't like it, but it makes a tiny part of me twinge a little. I still haven't figured out if it's a good part or a bad part.

Sam pulls out a grater and sets it on the cabinet with another bowl for cheese and goes back to sorting bread options. Despite the earlier tension, we seem to be moving around each other without any collisions or messes—it's kind of a relief. Not gonna say that I wasn't worried with how strained everything felt earlier. Especially if we're all stuck together for a few days until the weather clears up.

Vee emerges from the fridge carrying a big block of colby-jack cheese and a bundle of chives and starts rummaging through cabinets. A few seconds later Sam pulls open a drawer and puts down a cutting board in front of him and points to the knife block sitting near the back of the counter. He grumbles angrily at the bacon and pulls out his own board to chop it up. The whole process just feels seamless and soon Vee is helping me pull the table apart to insert the leaf while Sam gets more chairs.

They start setting out food on the server while I head back into the living room for Kelly and try to figure out where Garret went. She looks up at me as soon as I walk in, giving me a little half smile. *That's the look that says something's wrong.* There's no room on the couch without sitting on her or Jake, so I just give her my hand to help pull her up, much to his annoyance. "Dinner's ready, Pixie. Do you know where Garret's at?"

She shuffles a little from one foot to another and won't meet my eyes. Her gaze flicks to the basement for a moment before coming back to me, and I wrap my arms around her for a quick hug. It's over so much faster than I want. But I need to make sure she's fed before I carry her upstairs for snuggles and sleep. I'll just have to tide myself over with a little kiss on the forehead and sending her after food while I go try to locate one of my former best friends.

There aren't any sounds when I open the door to the renovated basement. There's some light coming from downstairs, but the overhead bulbs are off. I don't want to trip and kill myself falling down these damned things, but I also don't want to blind Garret if he's sitting in the dark. I may be pissed at him, but that's just a dick move. Using the flashlight on my phone, I make my way down the stairs where I find him passed out in the chair that I was in yesterday when Kelly rode me. A growly possessive part of me wonders if he figured that out or if it's just a coincidence, and I want to shake him awake to ask him. But that might upset Kelly, so instead I settle for poking him repeatedly in the shoulder. Progressively getting harder until he startles up and glares at me.

"What the fuck, Teddy? It's been a long...really fucked up day. I kinda just want to pass out away from everyone in hopes of being able to get a hotel tomorrow. I won't get in your way, I just...need some space." He looks up at me, and it feels like I'm being torn in two. The growly part that wants to keep Kelly just for me and Sam, and the other part that doesn't want my friend to hurt. He fucked up, repeatedly. Not just with me, but how he treated *her* earlier.

Logically, I know that it should be her choice on if she accepts his apology and allows him to court her...or whatever the fuck he plans on doing. Garret is obnoxiously old fashioned in some ways. He's an alpha, so he has all the instincts riding him hard, especially the way he acted around my beta earlier, but I know that their family has always been harder on him since he's older. By, like...less than two minutes, but who the fuck knows with a family like theirs.

Marc, their parents' pack lead, was always a massive douche canoe about how we would all find our omega and start a family to carry on *his* legacy. Vee decided long ago that that would be left up to me and Garret, preferably just Garret. He would be willing to share me with an omega, but he didn't want a female, he didn't want kids, he really just wanted it to be the three of us, well, two of us, but Garret's his twin, so they're pretty much a package deal. Even if I can't imagine being with him in the same way I'm with Vee. He's like that obnoxious stuffy brother that you pretend to just tolerate, but you really love his quirks—and you're just kind of waiting for someone to come along and turn his world upside down.

All of this runs through my mind while he stares up at me, exhaustion written plainly on his features. Fuck. "Sorry...um...Kelly wanted to know if you wanted to come get some dinner with the rest of us?" He looks at me for a slow blink.

"You wanna try that again? I fell asleep after she tucked me in, so she knew I wasn't planning on having dinner."

Shit, ok, plan B.

"Fine, asshole. I thought you might be hungry, even though you tried to ruin the soup. I came down here to invite you up to share dinner so we can all rest afterwards. And maybe, if you're nice, share one of the beds with the rest of us. The one upstairs is big enough for everybody." Shock passes over his features, so I hurry to clarify. "*To sleep only.* Sam built the damned thing, It's fucking huge. Kelly can barely crawl up on it as it is. But it's cold enough tonight if you or Vee want to cuddle for body heat, I don't think Sam would mind."

Sam will definitely mind. But before they were assholes, Garret was the closest thing I had to a sibling. If Sam wants to spank me later for speaking out of turn...well, I'd probably enjoy it. But he doesn't need to know that. Garret grunts as he tries to stand up. "Shit, my leg fell asleep. Gimme a few minutes. I'll meet you upstairs."

Pretty sure his difficulty standing up has more to do with thinking about Kelly in bed than his leg falling asleep. I smelled the pheromones when I came down. Hence the merciless jabbing for a wake-up call. But, as long as he respects her choice, it's all good.

I spin on my heel, waving back over my shoulder as I take the stairs two at a time. My stomach lets out an obnoxious gurgle, demanding I return and get some food so we can have cuddles. Now I just need to break the news to Sam and Kelly that we may have company for those snuggles. Fucking moment of weakness.

Chapter 33

Sam

Did I blow the soup issue out of proportion earlier? Yeah, ok, I'll admit I did. Was it mostly a reaction to an unknown alpha invading my space while my beta was in a vulnerable position? Probably. Am I going to apologize? I probably should, but no. I'm letting them stay at our home and feeding them. They're both alphas, they should understand how bitchy we can get. Though, if they've never had an omega maybe they don't get it. Still, it's not my fucking fault.

We all sit around the table together eating dinner, and I'll admit, it's nicer than I imagined it would be. Kelly and Teddy take the two ends, and I sit with my back towards the kitchen. Making Tweedle Dee and Tweedle Dum take the far side, kind of cramped in by the wall. I could have moved the table a bit to give them more room, but once again, I'm feeling a bit possessive and petty.

I was really looking forward to taking Kelly, and probably Teddy, upstairs after dinner to make damned sure they were covered in my scent. Now Teddy looks guilty as fuck and Kelly looks like she wants to take the spare room by herself. What a shitshow.

"Ok, so, let me get this straight. What, exactly, did Teddy say?" All three alphas turn our gazes on my omega, who squirms lower in his seat, knowing he's in trouble.

Steven is the first one to speak. "Well, um...sir."

Oh, hell no!

I hold up my hand, stopping before he can say anything else to piss me off.

"Sam, it's just Sam. How the fuck old do you think I am? Really?" Being called "Sir" seems to have triggered something. A really big part of me is frustrated, because the age gap already bothers me. Another, smaller, darker part of me would very much like Steven to call me Sir again, preferably with a lot fewer clothes on. Maybe while Teddy holds him for me.

What the ever loving fuck is wrong with me tonight?

Steven looks at me, a small shudder rippling through his body, and it seems I wasn't the only one with that train of thought. Teddy's eyes flick between the two of us and his smile looks positively predatory. Kelly—dear sweet, not as naive as she pretends to be, Kelly—continues on eating her soup, choosing to ignore the pheromones that flood the room while Garret lets out a choked wheeze.

He swallows thickly a couple of times, then his voice comes out in a cracked, "Sorry." He swallows again, and he speaks a little clearer. "Sorry again about the soup. I...I don't cook. I mean I try...I *attempt* to cook, I *am* willing to learn. Things just seem to burn or melt when I enter a kitchen...occasionally burst into flame. There was that grease fire at the apartment that was totally my fault, but the other time, I was following directions, they were just wrong and the marshmallows on the s'mores brownies caught fire under the broiler..."

He's looking a bit green now, and I guess I should be glad that overcooked vegetables are the least damage my kitchen suffered with him in here alone...for over a half hour...in an unfamiliar space.

Ok, yeah, I'm an ass.

"No, *I'm sorry*...shit, I didn't mean to just drop that on you and take off. You're a guest and that wasn't proper. I got a bit distracted, but that's no excuse for leavin' you to do all the work." Now Kelly's blushing and looking at me. "Not that it wasn't worth it, Sugar. But it wasn't right to leave him alone, either." Her gaze flicks between the two of us and she blushes harder. I'm not a hundred percent sure exactly what's going through that cute little head of hers, but it's probably something dirty. For all she acts sweet and innocent, I remember coming into the basement yesterday and seeing her riding Teddy, and then sucking me off.

Fuck, I really am a dirty old man.

I pick my bowl up, draining the rest of my soup, and then mopping it out with my roll—then push back from the table. "Now, if y'all will excuse me, I need to go get some work done on the nest before bed. I was gonna try to get the Sheetrock up today so I could get the putty set to dry. Hopefully get it sanded down tomorrow and ready to paint. Though I wanna get Teddy's opinion on texture first."

The whole table looks at me like I've grown a second head, and I realize talking about the steps taken in reconstructing a room probably doesn't make a lot of sense to anybody else. Now I feel like I just started rambling. Scooping up my bowl, I head into the kitchen to rinse it out and put it in the dishwasher. Living alone and subsisting on takeout, I rarely run the stupid thing, and it's an old habit to keep the food from getting stuck on before I can wash it. Though, it's not a bad idea to run it tonight with this weather. It'll help keep the pipes from freezing.

Kelly comes in before I manage to escape out the other door, and I take her bowl to rinse and put in the washer as well. She's shuffling from one foot to the other, looking like she needs to tell me something. "Hey, um...can I help with anything? I used to help Dad sometimes in his shop. It wasn't anything professional, or...you know, big. But I can hold nails, or you can teach me?" This last bit is said with a touch of hopefulness, and I can't help but soften at how sweet she is, how much she wants to be useful.

"Sure thing, Sugar. Let me go grab an extra pair of safety glasses for ya. Then I can show you how it's done, ok?" I'm a terrible example; I rarely wear the stupid things unless I'm using the saw. But I don't want to set a bad precedent when I'm teaching her. If she's gonna learn how to help, she is gonna be protected while doing it.

Opening the back door, I get hit with a face full of freezing wind and snow. Shit. The sound of mad scrambling is the only warning I get before Jake slams into me, nearly knocking me out the door in his bid to go play in the snow. He should be good for the few minutes it takes me to pop over to the shop for glasses.

Sure enough, less than five minutes later when I get to the back door he's dancing back and forth from side to side, glaring at me for letting him out in the first place. He noses me out of the way to get inside first, and the sound of his nails on the wood floor disappears into the living room before Kelly's loud shriek. "Gosh darn it Jake! Your nose is frozen, baby. Don't press it against me. Come on up here on the couch. Let's get you warmed up." That dog is living his best life right now and Kelly is gonna spoil the shit out of the big lug.

Taking off my boots again so I don't track snow through the house, I look in on the dining room where Teddy, Steve, and Garret are still eating. I'm not sure if they got more or are just going slow to not have to talk. Either way, it's the work of a moment to collect Kelly and escape any more awkwardness to the nest.

Neither of my tool belts will fit her narrow hips, and if she's going to be helping me, she'll need the carrying capacity. I buckle my favorite one on and turn around to find that she's extended the other to its longest setting and slung it over her shoulder like a bandolier. Screwdrivers and pliers hang at an angle from shoulder to hip, and she holds the drill up to her face with both hands, squinting at the side. She looks like she's trying to audition for the part in some sort of action film.

Kelly Carpenter, construction commando!

Fuck, today has been too damned long.

Still, my chest gives a happy little squeeze remembering she now shares my pack name.

"Sorry, this was right over where the shoulder goes, and it's too big for me." She's still squinting at the drill in her hands. "Jeez, Sam, how much does this thing weigh? It's like lugging around a suitcase full of bricks." Taking the drill from her with one hand, I take the battery pack off and set it on the workbench before handing the tool back.

She swings it around a few times in one hand. "Oh, yeah, no. That's so much easier. Thanks!" When she tries to slide it into a new sling on the belt it refuses to go in at that angle and makes a loud thunk sound when it hits the floor.

"Shoot, sorry, lemme get that!" She bends to pick it up, but apparently forgets to calculate the extra weight of the tool bandolier she's now sporting and starts to fall over. I manage to grab her shoulders and keep her upright, slipping the belt over her head so she can regain her balance. She smiles sheepishly as she takes it from me and puts it back on its hanger on the tool bench. She looks around the room, probably wondering what else she can hurt herself with, so I hand her a box of screws, a level, and a tape measure she should be able to clip on her jeans pocket. Her hands are now full, so hopefully she won't pick up anything else that might cause injury.

It's my own fault. I accepted her desire to help, forgetting how clumsy she is. How she fell and scraped her knees when we met, how she's almost fallen down the stairs three times already. Maybe I should knock down some walls and make the master bedroom downstairs, so she doesn't have to risk using them so much.

I'm getting ahead of myself.

Later, nest first.

Securing safety for the uncoordinated beta as soon as I'm done with this.

While this place suffered massive disrepair, at least the bones are still solid. None of the drywall for the first part needs to be adjusted, and the bottom of each section goes down fast with Kelly leaning against each piece to hold it in place and handing me screws to anchor them to the wall studs. Things get a bit trickier when I have to start trimming pieces to fit. The ten-foot ceilings in this place are great for being able to actually stretch...but repairing the walls means cutting down two foot sections, and I have to have Kelly hand up the parts while I stand on a stepladder. Still, the extra help is very much appreciated and goes faster with her assistance.

It takes less than two hours for us to finish putting up the drywall, despite a few almost disasters due to lack of coordination. But we're both safe and whole, and I'm a bit relieved when I can send her off to get cleaned up and ready for bed while I finish adding joint-compound to the newly constructed walls. We didn't make too much of a mess, but she'll feel better after a hot shower and getting the plaster dust out of her hair.

This part doesn't take as long—there's no measuring or hefting objects—it's just tedious. By the time I finish, my legs feel like they're about to give out, and I have to drag myself up the stairs. That is definitely another point for moving us downstairs. My back is aching and getting old fucking sucks. My bed is full of people right now, and it's hard to suppress my snarl when I remember that Teddy invited the two alphas to "preserve body heat". Fucking bullshit.

He's lying in the center with Steven wrapped around his back, and Kelly pressed to his front. Garret is on the other side of Kelly, his face buried in her hair, and they look so relaxed and peaceful that I want to kick these two alpha assholes out of my fucking house into the snow and let them freeze. As it is, I'll settle for moving Garret over after I get cleaned up. Let him keep my spot warm until I get washed up, and can snuggle my pack properly.

Chapter 34

Garret

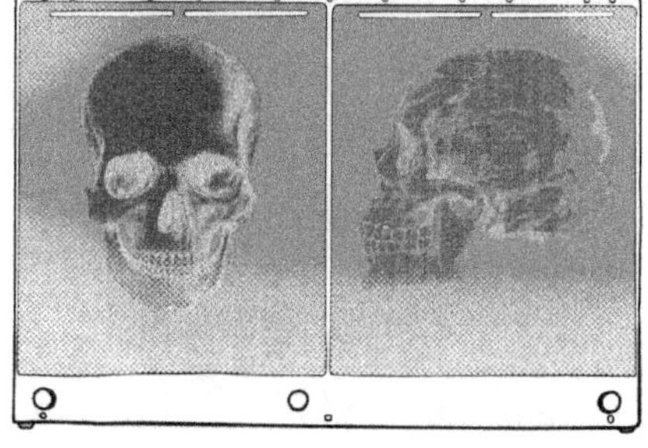

Loud ringing draws me out of a dream where Kelly and I embrace. Nothing overtly sexual, but holding her, caressing her hair, breathing in her lilac scent and just being warmed by her arms around me. The reality is sadly dissimilar. The ringing sounds again, and several mumbles are heard across the big bed before Sam finally rumbles out, "Shit!" There's a long beep where he accepts the call and fuck, someone better be dying. It's still dark outside. He doesn't say anything, but there's a voice on the other end.

Suddenly he's wide awake and sitting up. He jostles Kelly, who was sandwiched between him and Teddy. She sits up too, panic written across her features. What the hell is going on here? He listens intently for a minute before his voice comes out roughened with sleep. "Shit, what about Pack Garcia? Moen? Allen? Well, can't any of the police lend a hand? I know Miller would be...Shit. Ok, no....Yeah. No."

His hand comes up to rub down his face. "No, I'm sure Joseph told you not to call, but fuck him...Yeah. Yeah, no. I'll be there as soon as I can. Wait, is Pack Asher gonna be there? You know Leo's a vet, maybe some of his training...? No, I get it. Yeah, lemme just get my pants, I'll be there as soon as I can. Shit, if they're waiting on me just have 'em grab my gear, I'll meet 'em on site."

Another loud beep ends the phone call and then Sam's crawling over me trying to get out of the bed. Kelly's still sitting up, she looks adorable and sleep rumpled. I want to slide into the warm spot that Sam left and pull her against me, but something about the half a conversation I just heard pulls at my mind.

Sam has turned on the bathroom light so as not to disturb everyone else, and he rushes through putting on clothes. He's struggling with getting socks on when I manage to pry myself away from the bed. "What was that about, is there some sort of emergency?"

Sam's eyes flick up to me quickly, and then back down to what his hands are doing. "Yeah, fire, probably somebody's kerosene heater or something. Unfortunately, with the storm a lot of us can't get out. So, we're down our normal first responders and three of our usual fire fighters. Otherwise, there's no way my brother would have let them call me in. Fuckin' asshole."

I grab my pants from the pile on the floor and start scrambling to yank them on, but his big hand on my shoulder stops me. "No way, you're staying here. I don't need a tag-along. This is gonna get fucked, especially once everything's been put out and my family's involved."

I glare up at him, shimmying my legs to finish pulling up my jeans. "You're short EMTs? Are you just planning on pulling a medic out of your ass then? No, do you have someone else to call who might have medical training or is going to school for a medical degree? Yes? No? Oh, I'm sorry, I heard you say a veterinarian was going to be there. Well, that's just great!" He glares harder, but I just can't seem to stop pushing now.

"Best case scenario: we get there, you don't need my help, and I sit in the truck catching up on the Greeking Out podcast while you do your thing, then I can drive you home, or to the hospital as needed afterwards. Worse case, someone gets seriously injured, including you or one of the guys on your team, and no one's there to help." He starts to interrupt me, but I keep going. "Yes, I'm sure you've all had basic first aid training. But just in case. Wouldn't it be better to have an extra set of somewhat knowledgeable hands on deck?"

He looks like he's about to tell me no, but if he really cares about these people, I know he'll relent. I get my pants fastened and yank my dirty socks and shoes back on. The shirt I was sleeping in will be fine for this. Though I do wish I'd brought a heavier coat.

Kelly's sitting up in the bed watching us both. And she reaches for Sam. A small pang goes through my chest, but I know I haven't earned that yet. He gives her a quick hug and a kiss on the head before he tells her, "Love you, Sugar, stay here, be safe. Call me if anything happens." Then he bolts from the room and I hear his boots pounding down the stairs. Briefly meeting Kelly's eyes, I wish I had something I could say, something profound. But I got nothing.

Instead, she speaks. "Keep him safe, please." I nod as I turn to leave the room, and I barely catch her quietly whispered words. "Please be safe too, I need you both to come back in one piece." If only there were more time I would pull her into my arms, promise her anything. Of course I'll keep Sam safe. Of course I'll make sure he gets home to her. But all I have time for is to turn, meet her eyes, and nod in acknowledgement before I'm following Sam down the stairs.

He throws me a heavy coat out of the closet in the living room, and I'm trying to get the zipper done in my still half asleep state when Steve clears his throat from the top of the stairs.

"Sorry, I was trying not to wake you all up. Sam got a call from the fire department. I'm going along to help in case they need an extra hand and could use someone with a medical background. Go back to bed and snuggle Teddy so he can give Kelly cuddles."

His lip curls up in annoyance, but then he yawns so hard that I can hear his jaw crack from all the way down here.

Waving his arm at me, he turns and heads back towards the bedroom—I hear the door click closed again. Turning back, I see Sam standing by the door with his hand on the nob. "Shit, I've never left anyone alone in my house before, this is weird. He gonna be ok?" He nods back towards the top of the stairs where Steve disappeared, and I hope so. I know he wants Teddy, I know he doesn't want Kelly, but I'm pretty fucking sure that Teddy would choose her at this point. We have a lot of shit to make up for, but that's a future me problem. Current me needs to get the hell going before something burns down waiting for us.

"Teddy'll keep him in line, one way or the other. Let's go." Sam smirks at me, and I actually didn't mean for that to come out sounding sexual in any way. But after what happened on the couch earlier it's easy to see why it might come off as such. Letting out a heavy sigh, I open the door, getting smacked in the face with icy wind and snowflakes for my trouble.

I fucking hate the cold. This is why I live in Los Angeles. We might get a mild chill on occasion, but nothing like this crazy shit. Pulling the coat up around my ears, I plod down the steps and head for Sam's truck, waiting on his slow old ass to unlock it. It takes less than thirty seconds, but I'm already glaring at him and shuffling from foot to foot when he arrives. He raises his eyebrows at me and opens his door.

Does no one in this godforsaken podunk lock their fucking cars?!

I feel like an idiot.

A frozen idiot.

Well, you know what they say about assuming things.

He smirks at me again as he turns the ignition—the switches are already flipped over to heat, but of course the damned thing has to warm up to be of any use. Sam's chuckling at my frozen expense as we creep down his driveway. It's still dark and the fat flakes falling from the sky are swirling around and obscuring the road. He seems more cautious than anything, which I can understand. We won't do anyone any good if we crash before we get there.

"So, we're headed to the station first. If we miss the truck then no worries, we can meet 'em there. The fire's outside of town and the station's on the way. It's too much to hope you have any experience with this, isn't it?" Sam glances my way quickly while he's talking, but his focus is almost entirely on the road and the winter storm we're stuck in.

"Experience being a firefighter? No, none at all. I just started my medical residency a few months ago. The hospital I'm working with said I'll be taking a turn through the ER to get the full experience, but I haven't done it yet. Sorry." He gives a curt nod at my reply, and then says something unexpected.

"Listen, I'm...I'm sorry about earlier. I mean, this whole day has been a shitshow with trying to register the pack, and then you and your brother showing up. My whole family situation is a trainwreck, and my brother is in charge, so it's gonna be even more fucked up on location. I didn't exactly want to drag you into all this drama. But if you *are* gonna be stickin' around, you'll find out sooner or later."

He continues on, giving me a quick rundown on the weekend they had. How he's been packless until he met Teddy and Kelly, and his brother is upset about that. I think he's leaving some stuff out, because not all of this makes sense. He tells me briefly about the drama with Teddy's parents and how happy they are for him. I cringe inwardly, because his mom is gonna be super pissed when she finds out that Steve and I are back in the picture.

She loved us growing up and was always excited to hear about our future pack plans. But after Teddy presented as an omega and Dad refused to let us even speak to him...Let's just say she's not my brother's biggest fan and has had more than a few choice words to say about him when speaking to my mom. Not that I don't agree. Jessica has always doted on Teddy, and she was always kind and supportive to us. Even with his and Steve's relationship, she was never anything but positive about the situation.

Sam also tells me about Kelly's family—all betas—their reticence to approve of her joining a pack as the only female. I have a feeling that's going to come back and bite me in the ass if we do stay. Not that my inner alpha thinks there's any chance of that not happening. As far as he's concerned Kelly is ours, and we're not going anywhere. That being said, it's entirely her decision if she wants me, she and Teddy already have a pack with Sam, so I guess it's his choice too if he can accept us into it.

Rubbing my hands down my face, I sigh and let his words wash over me as we finally turn out onto the paved road and into town. The trip to their home earlier only took half the time, but it wasn't dark, or this slippery yet. There is so much shit to unpack here, but the one preeminent part is what I focus on. "So, if he brings it up, are you going to tell him you're expanding the pack with two new alphas?"

Sam jerks as if I electrocuted him with my question and his glare swings my way.

"I'm gonna take that as a no then. I thought he might bring it up since I'm showing up with you, and we may or may not be sticking around. Depending on what you three want?" The last bit is phrased as more of a question than I intend it to be, but he eventually nods in reply.

"If he's dumb enough to bring it up in the middle of all this, then I'll tell him we're considering it. Does that work?" His eyes meet mine for a second as we pull into the fire station, and I know he's expecting a reply.

"Well, if he asks me, can I just tell him it's none of his fucking business?" He grunts out a chuckle, and puts the truck into park, nodding at me before we both get out to face the unknown and the fucking freezing ass wind.

Chapter 35

Sam

The firetruck's still in the bay. The towns barely big enough to afford one, but under normal circumstances that's all we need. The doors are rolled up and people scramble around inside trying to get organized. Gabe takes in Garret and me and waves us over. "You know, this isn't a bring-your-kid-to-work-day kinda thing, right?" Gabe doesn't have much room to talk since he's my age and expecting twins.

"Har de har har, smartass. This is Garret. Garret, this is Gabe, lead alpha of Pack Asher, and all around hilarious mother-fucker." I nod back to Garret before returning my attention to the man in front of me. "Is Leo here? I thought he could give Garret a rundown on what to expect." Gabe's eyebrows go up.

"Garret's a medic, he's in town visiting family and friends and staying at my place. When I got the call, he offered to help." There, not exactly a lie.

Gabe nods and waves his arm, and a few moments later the giant alpha appears behind him so he can make introductions. "Sam brought help if you need it, this here's...um...Garret?" He looks from me to the alpha standing beside me, and I see Garret nod from the corner of my eye. "Leo, this is Garret, he has medic training and came along in case you need help since we're shorthanded." Leo reaches out and shakes Garret's hand, and they start to talk quietly while he leads him over to the lockers.

Gabe grabs my attention again as I'm heading towards the lockers myself, but I stall out. "Joseph's gonna flip his shit when he sees you, you know that right?"

I sigh and shrug, because what else can I do? "You'd rather be shorthanded?"

He shakes his head, but the smile he gives me doesn't reach his eyes. "Not at all, I just wanted to warn you. After what happened this weekend, I figured you'd be expecting shit on that front." His upper lip curls in a snarl, and I'm glad that he's not blaming Joseph's outburst at the ceremony on me.

Fuck, yeah, that all started at his bonding ceremony, didn't it? These last few days have just been crazy. "Yeah, sorry about that. I didn't mean to cause a scene at your pack's big day. I really—"

He cuts me off. "Sam, man, you saved Jacks. Pulled his unconscious ass out of a fire, when I was barely fucking coherent. We're good, no apology needed."

I'm trying to scramble into my boots as his head swings from me to Garret. "Also, congratulations on finding your pack. How's that goin'?"

I just manage to wedge my foot down into my boot as another truck pulls into the parking lot. At last, we can get this show on the road, but I answer Gabe anyway as we climb on board. "Well, it's fucking complicated, that's for damned sure." He just chuckles and shakes his head as Joseph climbs out of his own truck. His glare stays fixed on me the entire run across the lot until he's climbing into the driver's seat of the firetruck, and we pull out into the frozen night.

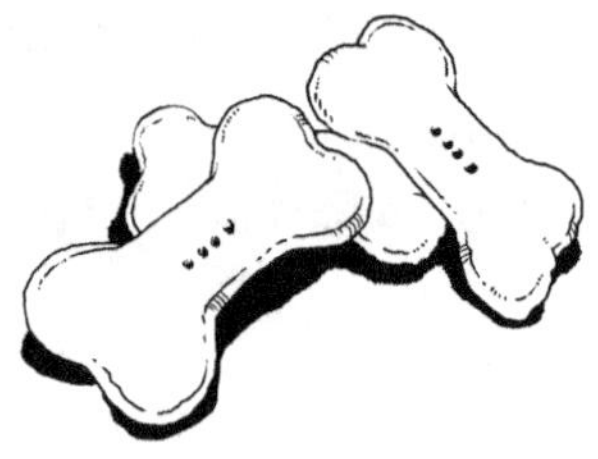

The wind plays merry hell with the truck, and we slide several times before we arrive on scene. Gabe is on one side of me and Garret's on the other. He's still in deep discussion with Leo, and I'm glad he has someone to talk to so I can think for a few minutes. Only three of Pack Asher and a few lone alphas were able to make it out, and I'm starting to appreciate Garret's willingness to volunteer.

Not that I'm letting him get anywhere near the actual fire, but it'll be good to have an extra set of hands to help out.

Things are always crazy in these situations. Maybe if he and Steve stick around they can join up, get trained properly and be more helpful. But that's a thought for another time. Though, the way Xan was glaring earlier, these two are gonna need to do more damage control for how they treated Kelly.

We—surprisingly—manage not to hit anyone or take out any street signs on the drive over. A couple of cop cars are already there—they were probably closer to the scene when the call came, and didn't have to wait for a team to assemble to get here. I look at my watch and it's already been over thirty minutes since I got the call in the first place. That's a nightmare in and of itself, but this weather wasn't helping anybody.

Once we're stopped, we all pile out and get to work. Joseph takes Leo over to talk to the people standing on the sidewalk. For lack of a better option, Garret follows along like a baby duck, his head following the conversation even though he doesn't join it. According to Gabe, Jacks stayed home with Candice in case anything happens with the storm or her pregnancy. And according to Xan, because he demands that at least one of them gives their omega a proper honeymoon, and he refused to leave.

Gabe and Xan locate the nearest hydrant. We have it on the map, but it's buried under a snow drift. Xan gets to work uncovering it while Gabe unrolls the hose. Everyone rushes around, but I'm standing like a statue—half waiting for information about people inside, half waiting for my big brother to throw more disappointment my way.

Garret wanders back to where I'm standing sheltered from the wind by the side of the truck. "No one seems to be letting you know, but the people on the sidewalk over there said this is their house, and the whole family is out. Their kids and cat are sitting in the car across the street out of the storm, but everyone's safe."

I appreciate him coming to tell me, and I wave him back towards the truck to get warm. When my eyes scan back over the sidewalk, Joseph's glaring at me. I knew he was gonna be an asshole, but I came anyway when they needed me. Fuck, it felt so good being at home cuddled with Kelly and Teddy.

Instead, I'm standing out here, freezing my ass off and about to deal with drama bullshit. There's really no way to mentally brace yourself for this kinda thing. There's no way to know what he's going to try to throw in my face this time. If he's still pissed about Teddy and Kelly, the age difference, the fact that I brought Garret...Fuck me, he's probably pissed that I even showed up right now.

If all he wants to do is throw my pack back in my face, he can fuck all the way off.

Shit, maybe he wants to fire me?

Can they fire you if you volunteer?

Pretty sure they can.

But this isn't a huge area, and on nights like tonight when we're already short staffed...

I guess it doesn't matter, it just means more time to work on the house and spend with my pack.

Now I kinda want to just quit so I'll have the extra time for them.

Nah, they'd want me to help if I could.

Joseph stomps across the street to where I'm standing by the truck, waves of dominance and anger rolling off of him.

Oh, great, it's to be another public shaming.

Goody.

Fucking crawled out of a warm bed for this shit.

"What the fuck do you think you're doing here? You've got a lot of fucking nerve showing your face around here after the shit you pulled!" Gabe perks up when the shouting starts, and while my main focus is on my brother—who is losing his shit right now—I'm not so far gone that I don't pay attention to my surroundings.

Before I can even try to stop the vitriol spewing out of Joseph, Gabe is there, and he looks pissed. He grabs Joseph by the arm, pulling him away from my face, and I barely register that the shouting has also brought Garret back out of the truck. "Are you fucking kidding me right now, Joe? Seriously. Starting this shit at my fucking bonding ceremony wasn't enough, now you gotta start it on a fuckin' job? We were called out here to help people, which you have done jack-all to accomplish. Thank fuck Leo, Xan, and Paul are actually trying to put out the fucking fire right now...and Paul's not even on our team, he came with the fucking cops!"

Gabe's waving his arm at the house that's still spitting and sputtering flames as two of his pack mates and Officer Paul work the hose. I feel like an asshole for not going over there to help, but with no one but Garret clueing me into the situation, I didn't want to risk getting in the way and making things worse. "Get your head out of your ass and get your shit together, man." Gabe reaches for my jacket. "Come on Sam, we need an extra set of hands over here." I don't actually care where he's dragging me right now, I'm just glad to get away from Joseph's bullshit.

Chapter 36

Garret

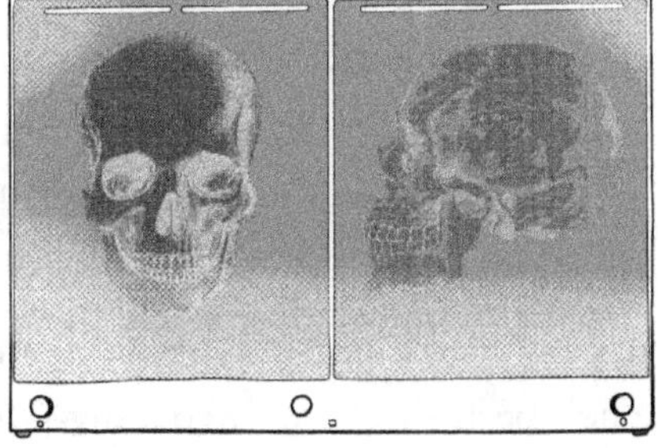

I t's not my finest moment being hunkered down in a firetruck in a snowstorm while other people do all the work. But I'm pretty sure I'd be useless right now out there. I haven't been trained to do any of the stuff these guys have, and when they're already shorthanded, adding in my bumbling inexperience might make the situation worse. I came to help if there was a medical necessity, but thankfully all the people and pets in the house are safe, if not happy.

There didn't seem to be much of a fire when we arrived, more than the owners could have put out, but all the snow seems to have kept the blaze down, which is pretty fucking miraculous. Leo pulled me with him to check the people out, but the woman said that their son got them up, he was overheated and when he woke up, he saw lights dancing on the ceiling. It was already too big to put out, so she and her husband each grabbed one of their kids and ran out of the house. Luckily her phone was charging by the bed so she was able to call 911.

The husband walked down to their neighbor's house to borrow some blankets for the kids, but the older couple just drove down and everyone piled in the back of their car to keep warm until we arrived—including the cat who apparently came running out of the front door shortly after he left. Leo looked it over, and while it's a cranky bastard—understandably—it seems mostly fine.

Xan must not have told Leo about what happened earlier today, because he's been surprisingly friendly—as opposed to the death glares I've been getting from the mini-alpha. I should probably stop calling him that, even in my head—I'm pretty sure he'd savage my kneecaps if I accidentally said it out loud. Honestly, it's so fucking weird to have someone as big as Leo and him in the same pack. The other one, Gabe, is almost as tall as Leo, but it doesn't look out of place on him since he looks like he could tear my head off without much effort.

Now there's a lot of yelling coming from the side of the truck. I think it's Joseph, Sam's brother that Leo tried to introduce me to earlier. He's glared in my direction a few times but hasn't deigned to actually speak to me. Which is fine—honestly the guy looks like an asshole. He also looks vaguely familiar.

Then I hear another voice, I think this one's Gabe, he didn't say much, but his voice almost sounds like he gargles gravel on the regular. Fuck, but I sound like a judgmental asshole in my own head tonight. That being said, this day was a fucking rollercoaster from hell, so I'm gonna give myself a pass, just this once.

Something slams into the side of the truck—not hard enough to rock it, but it's still a pretty loud bang—and I pop my head out the door to see that yeah, it's Sam's brother, the douche. Apparently, he just hit the truck. I don't know what the clang was, and if he wants to have a tantrum at his age, that's up to him. Unfortunately for everyone, my opening the door draws his attention. His hard glare turns to me, but he doesn't have anything on the angry stare of the mini-alpha I dealt with earlier—he doesn't have anything to hold over me.

"What the fuck are you looking at, you little shit?" His low growl is menacing, but I don't have the time or inclination to deal with anybody else's bullshit, so I just ignore him and shut the door. Alphas don't generally like that, and the next moment he rips the door open. His face is an ugly mottled red as he reaches in, grabbing at the jacket that Sam let me borrow and trying to drag me out of the truck. All I wanted to do was stay out of any more fucking drama...and now this.

Before he can pull me more than a couple of inches, we're both yanked out. He flies backwards across the road, and I get unceremoniously dropped to the pavement. Fun-size is beside the open door of the truck, along with a man in a blue police officer uniform. "I know he's kind of a punk, but I get dibs on kicking his ass first for how he treated Kelly today, get in line, shit-head."

Ahh, shit.

I didn't want to get arrested tonight.

Wait, what did I do?

I mean, I was an asshole earlier today—but right now, what did I do?

Is it illegal to pretend to be a firefighter?

I mean, strippers do it.

Then Sam's there with Gabe, who looks mad enough to have steam coming out of his ears. Sam picks me up off the ground, checking me over, and hissing at the scrapes across the palms of my hands from where I hit the ground. His reaction is confusing at best, more so when he moves me over to sit me down on a running board of the truck.

He stalks over to where his brother is laying on the ground looking dazed, and before anyone can react, he grabs the guy's jacket, pulls him off the ground and knocks the everloving shit out of him.

Everyone reacts. Gabe and Xan go to restrain Sam, Leo picks Joseph up off the ground. The tall alpha's mouth is set in a tight line as he looks over the asshole with the now busted lip. I have no idea what the hell I landed in the middle of, as I sit here in the dark, freezing my ass off, watching this fucking circus. Thankfully the fire is finally out, but these poor people don't need all this shit in their goddamned front yard while they're trying to deal with everything else.

Looking over at the family in question, they seem less bothered than the situation calls for. Maybe random street brawling is common in this area, but they look like they'd be set if they just had a blanket and a bucket of popcorn. What a fucking shitshow. I walk over to where Sam's sandwiched between Xan and Gabe, there's quiet talking between the three and Sam's knuckles look a bit worse for wear. I open my mouth to ask what happened. "Hey, um...if you have a first aid kit around here, I can patch your knuckles up, that's gotta sting like crazy in this cold."

I am an idiot.

Fucking certifiable.

Why did I just offer to do that?

All three of them are now staring at me, their faces ranging from disbelief to laughter. Xan is the first to react, doubling over in a fit of giggles. At least he finds the situation amusing. Gabe grumbles something low and growly, the only part I manage to catch is, "missing our fucking honeymoon for this shit," before he stomps over to where Leo and the police officer are talking to Joseph. I should probably learn more about the guy who wants to beat the shit out of me for unknown reasons.

I've had plenty of guys that want to beat the shit out of me before, but there's usually some sort of antecedent...I've never even met this asshole before tonight, at least not that I can remember. Finally, Xan straightens up, wiping a tear from his eye and grinning like a lunatic. "Shit, Sam, looks like you better take junior here home, it's after his bedtime. Let's go see if Paul can give you two a ride back to the station while we finish up here, yeah? Oh, and tell Kelly we're not open tomorrow, nobody in their right mind is gonna be out in this shit." He walks away, still laughing quietly, while I try to figure out how to apologize for whatever I did to piss people off today.

"Listen, Sam, I don't know what I did. Seriously, I was just sitting in the truck, trying to stay out of everybody's way since I wasn't needed. There was yelling and banging and when I stuck my head out the door your brother started yelling at me. I don't know who pissed in his cornflakes this morning, but—no offense—the man's got issues."

Sam lets out a loud bark of laughter. "Yeah. Yeah, he does kid. Listen, you didn't do shit. Like I was saying in the truck on the way over, he's pissed off that I formed a pack with Teddy and Kelly. Teddy's his omega's baby cousin, and well...I'm not exactly a spring chicken. Apparently, it's embarrassing to him, and you showing up with me put you in his crosshairs."

My thoughts go red at the thought of someone disrespecting Kelly. I totally did it earlier, but we've already established that I'm an asshole, and I'm trying to apologize. Would it make me a stalker if I said I was just going to keep apologizing until she accepts it. Yeah, that probably sounds more than a little creepy.

Also, it's a bit more information that he gave me on the drive, especially about Teddy being related to his brother's omega. Maybe that's why Joseph looks so damned familiar. Maybe I met him with Teddy when we were younger.

Sam seems to be waiting for an answer—possibly some judgment on his pack's relationship—he looks like he's braced, ready for me to be disgusted by him, but I'm going to have to disappoint him. Shit, I love Kelly, and my brother loves Teddy, it's not like I don't understand his reasoning. As for being old... "Wait, how old are you, Sam? I would have pegged you for mid-thirties, maybe late thirties going by the gray." Now I'm just being an ass on purpose to get him out of his head. He looks good—if I was into men, I could see the appeal of the rugged lumberjack vibe he has going on.

He lets out a low chuckle. "Let's go see if Xan sorted a ride for us, and get back to our beta and omega?" I almost trip over my own feet at what he just said, calling them ours instead of his. We aren't a pack, but maybe since Joseph lumped us in together, he feels like we need to present some sort of united front. I don't understand it, but I'll take the amiable Sam over the pissed off angry Sam any day of the week.

Chapter 37

Kelly

A loudly whispered argument wakes me up. Teddy's voice sounds angry, and the other one is whining enough to make me want to kick him off the bed and snuggle back up to the warm. But there isn't any warm. My head pops out from under the blankets, and I stare blearily around the slowly lightning room. Teddy's standing in the open bathroom door. His arms gesture angrily as he whisper-shouts at someone on the other side. No one else is visible, and I slide out of my pocket of coziness and pad in the opposite direction, towards the door to the hallway.

There's no telling what those two are arguing about. But an irate Teddy is better than a crying Teddy, and if he's dealing with Steve then the guy deserves to get some anger thrown his way. Jake's laying outside the door, and I almost trip over him in my attempt to sneak out. He hops up clumsily and presses his whole body into my legs, his big brown eyes looking up at me longingly. Before I've had a chance to give him any sort of ear scratches, his head cocks and he bolts down the stairs, his tail doing its best impression of a helicopter.

The front door opens just before we reach it, and Sam and Garret trudge in looking disheveled. Garret's almost knocked over in Jake's need to get outside. Both men have snowflakes in their hair, and *not* a light dusting. How did they get that much just coming from the truck? I catch the door before Garret can close it and look outside. There are huge white flakes still coming down, and the front porch has mostly disappeared under a drift. Two trenches are made though leading from the truck, which is already collecting a new layer.

Shivering, I close the door and turn to see if there is any way I can help. "Would you like me to fix you some coffee or tea? Something to help you warm up?"

They've both taken off their coats, and Sam is hanging them up in the closet by the door to the basement. He looks thoughtful for a moment. "Actually, hot tea sounds good. Let me go let Jake in the back, then I'll get cleaned up and start breakfast. Sound good?" The man offers to cook for me and take care of me and wants to know if that's ok? Of course that's ok!

I'm still gonna get the tea pot started while he's getting cleaned up though. Maybe I'll make pancakes if he takes long enough...and has buttermilk. You can make pancakes without it, but why would you want to?

It still feels like intruding when I go through Sam's pantry looking for ingredients. Pretty sure I'm officially moving in, but it's so well organized and I feel like I'm rifling through some sort of pretty show house that no one actually lives in because it's too clean.

Of course, the problem with making pancakes is everybody likes them differently. Mom makes hers super fluffy, which is good, but I can't eat more than four 'cause they're so big. Dad makes his really flat, but they have an amazing tangy flavor that he says comes from adding yogurt. The ones I've gotten a few times at the diner are pretty standard, not great, but not bad. They have a tiny hint of vanilla, but I think they use a mix, so that's off the table. Sam doesn't seem like the kinda guy who keeps pancake mix in his house. He said he doesn't like to cook for himself, plus it seems to be against his fancy cooking to keep something "ready to make".

Maybe I should call Dad and ask for his recipe.

Nah, he's either getting ready for work, or sleeping in with the snow.

I could look one up on my phone.

Those are always a crapshoot.

Grandma made the best pancakes, better than Dad, even.

I wonder if I can get her recipe from him sometime.

My mind runs in circles as I gather ingredients—flour, sugar, vanilla, baking powder, eggs, buttermilk. I strongly debate on the yogurt I picked up a few days ago. It's vanilla flavored so it would probably be fine, but I don't want to screw this up. Now, where does he keep his mixing bowls? I open all the lower cabinets where a normal person would keep those, but nope. Standing up, I try the ones over the stove.

Dang tall alphas and storing stuff in tall cabinets.

He probably doesn't even own a footstool.

I could climb the counter, they look sturdy.

Turning around I hop up on the counter, butt first. I'm wearing my sleep pants, but I'll still clean it before I start cooking. Getting turned around and up on my knees is harder than I remember from doing this as a kid. Of course, my pajamas are fleecy, so they want to slide around on the stupid shiny rock countertops, and I have to grab the door handles to keep from doing the splits up here.

Sorry, Sam, can you make another trip out in the snow this morning? I fell and broke my butt trying to make pancakes.

Yeah, I'm sure that'll go over well.

Finally victorious, I grab the mixing bowls out of the stupidly high cabinet and try to turn around, only to have big hands go around my waist holding me in place. Great, one of the tall alphas in question. The hands find the spot where my shirt is riding up from having my arms up, but they're so cold and rough against my bare stomach I let out a tiny shriek and almost fall backwards off the stupid counter. "Um, Kelly, what are you doing up there?"

"You wanna help me down, Garret? I'm not stuck, but I get the feelin' Sam's not gonna be super happy about me climbing on his counters. That bein' said, he shouldn't put his mixing bowls in really tall cabinets." The hands gently lift me off the counter and set me on the floor, and I smile up at the alpha I'm so conflicted for. We just met yesterday, and yeah, he was a complete jerk on the phone—but after talking to him, I kind of understand why. His life's been hijacked, and he's stressed. We all have bad days.

The question is, would he have apologized if he didn't think I was his? Would he still be a jerk, or is he actually a nice guy who was just having a rough time? Something about him draws me in, and it's not just how he was yesterday in person.

His scent makes me think of the ocean and thunderstorms, which is funny since I've never actually seen an ocean. Maybe it's because Teddy said they're from Los Angeles? Part of me wants to snuggle into him—which is less weird than it was the first time with Teddy and Sam—but also more frustrating since he was so mean. My brain's telling me to kick him to the curb for how they treated Teddy, and how he was on the phone...but mostly Teddy. I know he explained somewhat yesterday, but we really all need to sit down and talk.

Sam's not gonna like this, and I want him to be happy. My body decided that Teddy and Sam are mine, and my brain gave up and went along with it. They feel safe and like home. Now these guys...my body says that Garret's mine—not Steve—but until I know it'll work out for Sam and Teddy, nothing else is happening.

He hasn't stepped out of my space yet, even though I'm firmly on the floor now. I can't really step back either with the counter right behind me. I raise my hands up, and he smiles for a brief moment, it's beautiful. I almost feel bad for putting them on his chest and gently pushing him back out of my space. He goes easily enough, but I think he's disappointed I wasn't trying to hug him.

Sorry, we're not there yet.

Maybe soon?

I want to hug you and snuggle you, but I don't want to upset anyone.

I just need to keep the peace.

That last thought makes me cringe. I do like everyone to get along, but it was never a huge thing growing up. My family had arguments, everybody does, but never anything I really needed to act as peacekeeper for. Maybe it's just a beta thing, trying to keep everyone happy and relaxed. Alphas are generally considered the most volatile designation, but that's a fallacy. I've met alphas who are overwhelmingly aggressive, but I've also met betas that are nuts. I used to work with one of those—that was a shock.

Then there are alphas like Sal or Jacks or Leo, who are sweet and gentle, but will absolutely destroy someone if they threaten their people. That's supposed to be more of an omega trait. Then again, omegas are supposed to be tender and cuddly. Of the few I know, that only really seems to fit Brice. Teddy has been caring and gentle with me, but he looks like he could happily shred someone. And Candice is the farthest person I know from snuggly, at least outside her pack...plus that whole fork incident.

My hands are still resting on Garret's chest, and he moves to cover them with his own. Thankfully they're starting to warm up. He lifts my left hand from his chest and brings it to his face, nuzzling his jaw against my palm. It's not exactly a scent marking, he just looks like he needs comfort. Looking at where my hand is cradled in his bigger one, I finally see why they were so rough earlier. Dried blood and road rash are stark against the meaty part of his palm. It looks like he hit the pavement.

My eyes flick up to his face, no issues there, it doesn't look like someone knocked him onto the road. Maybe he fell, the sidewalks were probably pretty slippery out there, but I ask anyway, just to be sure. "What in the world happened to your hands? I know it doesn't get super cold where y'all come from, but you gotta be careful in the snow, it can get dangerous."

"Um, yeah...about that. I kinda met Sam's brother. Well, I mean. I'd heard of him before since he's mated to Teddy's cousin. But I didn't connect the dots, and since Sam said your pack's name was Carpenter it just didn't register. Regardless, he seemed really upset with me since I showed up with Sam, and ended up dragging me out of the truck." He looks down at his hand that isn't holding mine. "And I guess I got kinda scraped up. Sorry I didn't realize how bad it was. I mean, I knew it stung, but I thought it was just the cold. I'll...I'll go get cleaned up. Sorry if I bled on you."

Crud, pancakes can wait.

Trying to be as gentle as possible, I take the hand that's holding mine and lead him to the main bathroom down here, the one I usually use. "Come on, I think I saw some bandages in this one, and if not...we'll figure it out." He follows me along, staring at my hand holding his. His expression's almost vacant like he's lost in some sort of daydream. I don't want to accidentally hurt him, but he needs to pay attention before he walks into a door frame.

Too late.

Well, ok, technically it's my elbow that smacks into the doorframe, but it makes me jerk my hand out of his to grab my funny bone. He lunges to try to follow my hand and manages to kick the door frame. There's a sharp intake of breath and a pained groan as he comes out of the daze he was in. But then he grabs for the elbow I'm cradling against my stomach, carefully lifting it up and inspecting it while he stands on one foot. He's rubbing his injured toe up and down the back of his opposite leg.

We probably look like an uncoordinated mess right now. His big scraped palms run lightly over my arm, and he winces and gives me a quick, "Sorry," when I let out a pained giggle. Ticklish and uncoordinated is not a good look. I always hurt myself and then start laughing when someone tries to help.

Like, no, I really do appreciate your concern, but I can't stop the giggles.

Pulling my arm from his grasp, I meet his eyes. "Sorry, I'm super ticklish when I hurt myself. Um...how's your foot?" He lets out a loud hiss of breath and we both look down at his toes curling and uncurling.

The look he gives me is half smile half gritted teeth. "Well, it hurts like a bitch, but nothing seems broken. I'll live. What about you, hit your funny bone?" He nods to my elbow which I've gone back to rubbing.

"Yeah, sorry. But for now, let's get you cleaned and bandaged up. Do you need something for your toes or are they good?"

This at least earns me a small smile. "Nah, no way to bandage up blunt force trauma on the foot, I'll live."

This bathroom doesn't have a medicine cabinet, just the cupboard under the sink. Squatting down to look, I almost fall over backwards, my hand reaching out to grab the wall behind me before I land on the tile floor. I hear another sharp gasp at the same moment it dawns on me that I have a handful of denim.

Dreading what I might see, I twist around on the balls of my feet and let my eyes wander over to Garret. He's staring intently down at me, and specifically at my hand, which has a death grip on the knee of his jeans, holding myself up with them—pulling them down enough that a trail of sunny blond hair is now clearly visible between the top of his jeans and the bottom of his shirt. It's right at eye level

My gaze flicks back up to meet Garrets and he bites his bottom lip, heat filling his eyes. I need to get out of this situation.

Trying to pull myself up, I only manage to unbalance further and fall face first towards his leg.

The universe has a sense of humor, I just don't find it very funny right now.

Giving in and letting myself hit the floor has to be better than face-planting against his groin. Unfortunately, I forgot about my knees being banged up a few days ago at the ceremony, so when they hit the tile, I let out a tiny little squeal of pain.

These pajamas provide no cushioning between my already abused flesh and the stone beneath me. Scrambling back to my butt to save my knees, I'm scooped off the floor completely. This is the second time in less than a week that I find myself with bleeding knees, being held against a wide warm chest. But this one's vibrating.

Chapter 38

Garret

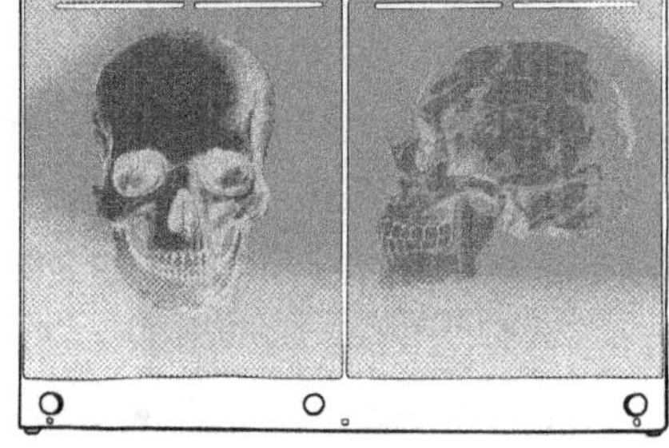

I don't even try to stop the purr that rumbles from my chest as I finally get to hold Kelly close. Picking her up when she cried out was completely involuntary. We're both lucky I manage not to brain myself on the counter or the towel bar while standing up. It would completely ruin any attempts at heroics.

She's not struggling against me, but I also don't want to risk making her uncomfortable. I let myself enjoy holding her for a moment longer before placing her gently on the countertop beside the sink. There isn't a lot of room to maneuver, and there's more than a little fumbling trying to find a place to sit her down so she can't fall off the side. Just having her trying to help makes me realize that this girl is insanely accident prone, and I breathe a sigh of relief that I caught her in the kitchen earlier before she could fall and do herself some real harm.

Bracing my back against the wall, I kneel down and roll up the legs of her fluffy blue snowflake pants. The fleecy fabric is incredibly soft, and I briefly wonder if she likes the snow, or if the pattern was just convenient. My mind isn't distracted for long, as a small patch of purple blooms on the fabric at the bend of her knee. When the skin there finally comes into view, it's easy to see where it was recently damaged. It doesn't look deep, but there is definitely blood trickling down her calf now. Shit.

Pulling open the cabinet door beside her legs I see, yes, one box of adhesive strips, no peroxide or cotton balls. When I turn the box over several tiny round bandages fall out. Why did he leave the whole box under here with just these? The box says it's assorted but there's nothing else here. My head thumps against the cabinet in defeat, but I can't linger. Kelly needs help getting cleaned up and patched, and I know I can do that.

Trying to pull her pants legs over the injury proves another problem, as she hisses in pain despite how gently I attempt to lower the material back over her. Finally she pushes me backwards, holding onto my arm so she can stand, and shimmy out of her pants. She holds the cloth away from her knees while she pushes each one down to avoid the tender skin. I'm not happy she's hurt, but at least the tears in her eyes are keeping my erection at bay when she stands up wearing just a tank top and panties.

Her tiny little growl of frustration is a bit of a surprise as she kicks her pants to the side and starts limping out the door, but that gives me an excuse to pick her up again to carry her upstairs. I head towards their bedroom on the second floor, and I believe that they have another functioning water closet there. I've barely settled her in my arms, my purr starting automatically again, when Sam comes down the stairs. He's followed by the surly looking pair of Teddy and Steve, and Jake, the big red dog.

Teddy growls—actually growls—at me when he sees me carrying Kelly with no pants on. Sam watches both of us as Teddy stomps over and snarls in my face, "What the fuck did you do? Why is she bleeding? And where the fuck are her pants?" He's jabbing me in the chest with his index finger, reaching across Kelly to poke me repeatedly, and I'm mildly amused when Kelly smacks at his hand as it passes in front of her.

"Come on guys, my legs hurt, and I just wanna get patched up…and I still need to fix Garret's hands where they got scraped. You know I hurt myself this weekend. Well, I fell over in the bathroom and made it worse. Then my pants got stuck on 'em. So, I took the stupid thing off to keep from hurtin' myself anymore, or staining 'em." She lifts herself up and looks over Teddy's shoulder. "Sam, where do you keep your first aid kit? There aren't any Band-aids that'll work in there." She points back towards the bathroom we just exited.

Sam's looks between us for a moment before he shakes his head and sighs. "The main one is out in the shop, but I don't need anybody else gettin' hurt trying to go get it in this weather.

Come on, I have a few things upstairs that should work." He turns around and marches back upstairs just as the kettle in the kitchen starts to whistle, causing Jake to let out a loud baying howl and rub his face against my leg. I think he wants to lick Kelly, but the way he keeps sniffing the air around her, maybe he can tell that she's hurt.

Teddy lets out a long string of mumbled curse words before stomping towards the kitchen, presumably to turn off the stove while I follow Sam upstairs.

Sam

First I get to come home to my omega arguing with another alpha in my bedroom, now my beta is dripping blood up the stairs. Life certainly has gotten more interesting since last week.

What's that old curse, "May you live in interesting times?" Sounds about right.

Garret follows me into our bedroom, skirting around the big rug I have by the bed. He may be an asshole, but he seems to be a considerate asshole.

Jake follows us upstairs, whining and circling Garret and Kelly, my dog seems to be as obsessed with her as the rest of us, except Steve. I'm pretty sure that if we left the door open at night, Jake would squeeze us all out of the bed except for Kelly, and then lay on her. But waking up with a face full of dog breath once was enough for me. He has a big squishy bed in the living room, another one at the end of the upstairs hall, one behind the dining table, and a cedar stuffed dog-house in the shop. Just in case he wants to hang out while I work. But for some reason, the last three nights, ever since Kelly started staying here, he falls asleep outside my door, like a big hairy tripping hazard.

The linen closet off the bathroom has way too much space, more than what I need for towels and fresh sheets. So, I keep backup first aid supplies in here: tweezers, adhesive strips, antibiotic cream, insect bite spray, you name it, and it's probably stuffed in a box in here, if I can find it.

Garret sits her down on the countertop between the sinks. She jerks up and lets out a tiny scream before relaxing back, looking embarrassed. "Sorry, cold on my butt." Garret grumbles but looks relieved that he didn't accidentally hurt her. Meanwhile, I pull out the crate that I think I put Band-aids in. They're not something I need regularly. If I get cut badly enough to need a band-aid and I'm out in the shop, I usually use superglue or duct-tape. Anything worse than that needs to go to the hospital.

Looking over at the medical student in my bathroom, he'd probably be horrified by that admission. Unfortunately, working with wood means I end up with a lot of splinters and cuts, even with the gloves on. When you've got a rush order to get out, you fix what you need to as fast as you can to get back to it. Thankfully, I've gotten pretty established, so there's less people I need to try to impress to earn repeat business. Most of my regulars know the quality I put out, it's why they're regulars.

The box of assorted bandages is at the bottom of the crate I'm looking through, and I pull it free with a triumphant smile and an, "A-hah!"

Now they're both looking at me. Garret looks annoyed as he glares at me and then looks pointedly at Kelly's bleeding knees. Apparently, my triumph isn't amusing. So, we can mark him down as considerate with a huge stick up his ass.

Good to know.

Kelly, at least, is smiling at me. Shit, she is the sweetest girl I ever met. I watch her as she looks back over at Garret, running her hand down his arm, and intertwining their fingers. Trying to soothe his irritation. Still, he takes the crate from my hands and roots around until he finds gauze pads, tape, and some ointment. He gently wipes away the blood and dabs on the antibiotic before patching her up with a combination of gauze pads, medical tape, and adhesive strips.

I'll concede that if he makes her happy, we can keep him. My lip curls up in an involuntary snarl at the thought of sharing my pack with anyone else. But whatever they need, they can have, as long as they'll still have me. Watching Garret as he stares longingly at Kelly, there is one quick thought that makes me smile. Now she has two alphas to keep her safe and protected, and to help her if she wants to try to take a knot.

My cock stirs at the thought of that, and I need to stop now before I make a damned fool of myself.

Time for a change of subject!

"So, breakfast? Anybody have any requests?" I might sound a tad too chipper considering how little sleep I'm running on and the situation at hand.

Kelly blushes, that sweet pink covering her cheeks before she stammers out, "Sorry, I started getting stuff out for pancakes. I wanted to surprise you...and I got sidetracked." She gestures towards her legs, and then at Garret's hands.

I completely forgot he got yanked out of the truck earlier. I don't even realize I'm doing it until I'm dabbing ointment on his scraped up palms, putting the gauze pads on, and taping them down. My work looks shoddy in comparison to what he did for her knees. Fuck it, I'm used to only patching up myself. He'll live regardless.

He looks up at me, his face a bit flushed and embarrassed. "Look, Sam...I, um. I appreciate the help. And, don't get me wrong, you're very attractive. You've got that whole silver fox thing going for you. But. Uh...I'm here for Kelly. I don't like guys...like...*like* guys."

I must be getting slow in my old age, because it takes about thirty seconds, and Kelly giggling beside me on the counter before I realize what he's trying to tell me, and I snort laughter—which is not attractive. I slap him none too gently on the arm, not enough to hurt but he needs to understand a few things. "Not a problem, man. I think you're kind of an asshole anyway. But if Kelly likes you and wants you, that's up to her. Everything that happens is up to her. You get me? And *if* she wants you, that makes you pack. It's on me to make sure the pack's taken care of."

He nods dumbly, rubbing his arm with the back of his bandaged hand. I didn't hit him that hard. That's ok, if she wants him to stick around, I'm sure he'll find his place. Plus, if I still have a spot at the fire station, I think he might make a good addition.

I offer Kelly my hand to hop down off the counter and usher her into the bedroom. "Well, now that the awkward bullshit's out of the way, let's go make some pancakes. Unless you need pants first?"

Chapter 39

Steve

These pancakes are going to be as chewy as a damned rubber boot. I should probably start over and mix with less aggression but shit. Teddy loves pancakes, and I figured I could take over from Kelly since she wasn't here, maybe do something to help me get back in his good graces. Now my frustration's just led to a mess and bullshit pancakes. I could fix these for everyone else and then make Teddy his own...but I would need to serve him last. Shit.

If he'd only accept my apology, or at least let me apologize properly. I don't even know. It started because when I woke up, I was the big spoon...unfortunately it was in a trio, and when I tried to tug my omega away from Kelly, he got defensive. I can't even put all the blame on him. I know he's hurt. But I need to find a way to fix this.

He won't even entertain the idea of coming back with us. He says he won't leave his pack—but there's no bite, so he could. If he really wanted to. I can't believe I'm being thrown over for a beta, and a girl at that. If this is a family thing, where he wants kids, I'm probably screwed. Maybe we can find a female alpha for our pack who he'd go for. Then Sam could keep Kelly, and Teddy could come with us. Heck, maybe Garret would even hit it off with said lady alpha. He's pretty flexible.

Not that I've ever seen him with anybody, but maybe he's just not interested. Is it messed up that I don't know if my brother is asexual or just picky? It doesn't matter, Teddy is so obviously ours that he can't even argue about it, I know he felt it too. I saw him chasing Kelly through the damned store after Teddy's scent. He thinks she's the one he wants, but he must be confused, she's not even an omega.

Teddy left me alone when I started cooking, I don't know where he went. Giving up on the batter, I check the fridge for any sort of berries or anything I can top these with that might make them salvageable. This isn't helping my frustration.

Footsteps sound behind me. Thank goodness Teddy's back. I can try to fix this. "So, what do you like on your pancakes? I don't see any strawberries, are you still good with just maple syrup and way too much butter?"

Instead of a reply, I hear Sam's deep growling voice. "What the hell happened in here?"

Ok, so on top of my aggressive mixing, I may have also made a bit of a mess with my measuring, but I was going to clean it up. Still, that's not Teddy. Straightening up, I turn to face the alpha that owns the kitchen where my life is currently falling apart. He really is attractive, and I can see why Teddy's drawn to him, he has that commanding presence going on. Oh look, he brought the beta too.

Yeah, no.

Still, Garret follows her through the door, and she accepts his hand when he winds his fingers through hers. Maybe it won't be so hard to keep her away from my bear. I reach up, rubbing the spot over my heart. When I turned eighteen I got a small tattoo of a teddy bear there. Garret knows about it, and he probably understands, but nobody else has seen me shirtless in years. It isn't as obvious now with all the coverups, but it was my first. Of course, Dad freaked out. I doubt I'd have to have gotten any of the rest of my ink if he hadn't seen that one.

Sam glares down at the mixing bowl like it's personally affronted him. He picks the spoon out of it and I watch the batter fall in a thick, smooth sheet from it. That doesn't look quite right, I thought this was supposed to be kind of lumpy, but not too lumpy. Shit.

"Yo, man, what recipe did you use for this?" Sam asks, still staring down at the bowl.

This is embarrassing to admit. "I...uh...I didn't? I mean, I used to watch the dads' chef make breakfast, so I just tried to do what they did."

Shit, ok, that sounds a lot worse when I say it out loud.

Teddy will be so disappointed if I make these for him.

Sam sighs, rubbing the end of his nose. "Ok, well, I don't want to just pitch it, cause it's a waste of food, so we can try making up a few after we get everybody fed. For now, hand me out a clean mixing bowl, they should be over the stove. Kelly, can you please go find Teddy? I want to make sure he gets food. We don't want him getting sick again."

Teddy was sick?

Shit!

Kelly leaves, dragging Garret along behind her like an obedient dog, and Jake, the actual dog, follows along happily wagging his tail. Sam grumbles to himself. He's pulling out an old book from under the cabinet when I turn around with the clean bowl he asked for. He starts flipping pages, and this thing looks like it's older than he is. There are notes scribbled in the margins, and some recipes have things crossed out and replacements carefully penciled in. My fingers itch with the desire to look through it myself, it's probably some sort of family heirloom though.

I always wanted to learn how to cook, but Dad said it wasn't something alphas should do. Of course I expect he'll lose his shit when he hears about Teddy being our scent match, so maybe giving him something less drastic to be pissy about will be a good start. I hand the bowl off to Sam, staring over his shoulder as he finally finds the section he wants. Homestyle Buttermilk

Pancakes according to the title. There are so many pencil and pen marks on this page, the original recipe is nearly illegible.

Sam starts opening drawers and pulling out measuring cups and spoons, and in no time he has a lumpy batter sitting in a bowl on the counter next to my monstrosity. "Ok, gonna let that rest and rise for a few minutes while I get out a griddle. You wanna stand back there, Steve?"

Shuffling sideways, my eyes are still drawn to the book as he moves around behind where I was standing, pulling out an electric griddle and putting up ingredients. He lets it preheat while he pulls out six plates, a butter dish, and a small pot of maple syrup from the fridge. At least he doesn't use the imitation maple flavored whatever the-fuck-that-is. That's all they kept at college in the Dining Hall, and it was horrible compared to the real thing. Garret never seemed to notice the difference and it often makes me wonder if my brother's taste buds work at all.

Finally, the griddle's hot, and he grabs a new stick of butter out of the fridge and runs it across the surface before adding a ladle full of batter for each pancake. This part I remember, the smell of the frying flatbread and the singed butter drags up old memories of sleepovers when we were kids. Waking up with Teddy and Garret, stampeding into the kitchen to climb up at the bar and watch Cook make breakfast. If Dad wasn't up yet, she would try to make shapes for us. They never looked quite like what she said they were, but young me thought it was the most amazing thing that someone could pour a pancake in the shape of a smiley face.

I'm drawn back to the present to see Sam start turning them on the griddle. He doesn't flip them in the air like Cook used to, but the memory still brings a smile to my face, and pokes little holes in the defenses I've raised towards this big growly alpha that stole my omega. Shit, I can't even blame Sam. The fault lies squarely with our old man, and us...me. I should have said something sooner. Shit.

Chapter 40

Teddy

Sam has a lot of game systems down here for one person. Considering how busy he sounds, it doesn't seem like he'd have much time to play. I open a drawer in his console storage and, sure enough, it's filled with game cases–over half of them, including the newest Legend of Link, are all still in the sealed packaging. Of course, I want to take it out and play now that I've seen it. I haven't really had much time to myself to relax with school and everything.

Would it be wrong to open his games and get things set up if he isn't here?

Maybe after I'm properly marked.

Until then, I still feel kind of like a guest, even with the paper-work.

Of course, now with Vee and Garret here...
Can I give Vee up again if Kelly's a sticking point for him?
She accepted me, all of me, even without a history.
Shit.
I wish I had my guitar here.
Jessie.
She always helps me relax.
Makes my brain zone out.

My fingers twitch like they're running over her strings. A quick riff playing across my mind to distract me. I sometimes make up songs, but usually just do covers. It takes too much out of me, letting my mind drift to stop and write down notes and words.

A mishmash of footfalls draws my attention to the stairs. The light ones are obviously Kelly, the heavy might be Sam or Garret, no way would Steve be hanging out with her. And then the scrambling claws on the wood announcing Kelly's ever-present shadow, Jake. His legs are so long and gangly, I'm not sure how he makes it down the stairs without tumbling and taking them both down with him.

They find me sitting on the floor with a stack of games scattered around me, and Kelly immediately crawls into my lap and starts shuffling through the cases. It astounds me how comfortable she's become with Sam and me over the last few days, especially considering how reluctant she was to start with. I know we haven't officially bonded, but it just feels so right having her close to me—there's no way I'm giving this up, even for Vee.

She zeroes in on the same game I was contemplating earlier, a huge grin splitting her face. "Hey, do you think Sam would mind...?" She trails off, bouncing excitedly, and looking hopeful. My cock stirs as her ass wiggles around on it, and she doesn't even notice how hard I'm getting having her pressing against me.

Make a guy feel inadequate over a video game, why don't you? I kid.

Mostly.

Unfortunately, Garret can be kind of a killjoy. He clears his throat, bringing both our attention around to him. He reaches down to offer his hand to Kelly to help pull her out of my lap. "We were sent to find you to tell you breakfast is ready. Kelly was getting stuff out to make pancakes, but I sidetracked her. So Steve tried to make some. However, I believe that Sam is the one that actually succeeded in doing so."

Oh, I love pancakes.

Steve knows that.

I wonder if this is supposed to be some sort of reconciliation from him being a douche earlier.

Once Kelly's up, she offers her hand to help me up. I don't want to risk pulling her back down though. I love this girl, but she's *the* most uncoordinated individual I've ever met.

Garret heaves a put-upon sigh and offers his hand as well, which I have no problem taking, and need more than a little restraint to keep from yanking him down onto the floor with me. He's still on my shitlist too.

Kelly leads the way up the stairs, followed closely by Garret and me, vying for who gets to walk directly behind her and watch her ass sway from side to side. We both lose when Jake shoves us out of the way, almost knocking us both down so he can press his cold wet nose against the back of her knees, causing her to squeal and stumble.

Garret's there before I have a chance to react, scooping her into his arms and out of Jake's reach. He makes it to the top of the stairs in three long strides and sets her down, safe on the flat surface. He must have noticed that she's uncoordinated too.

Jake prances in front of us, leading us all into the dining room, and Kelly grabs the table, pulling it away from the wall so Vee and Garret won't be so wedged in this time. She stares back and forth between Garret and me, holding her finger up to her lips in the universal sign for quiet. Her smile makes my chest ache. It's so sweet, and it seems like Garret feels it too.

She turns and walks into the kitchen, and I hear her ask Sam if he needs any help. Vee's voice answers back something snarky, but Sam's growl is loud and clear in reply, followed by, "I appreciate it, Sugar. But you go relax. He made this mess, he can clean it up. Breakfast'll be ready soon. Oh, can you please ask Teddy what kind of tea he wants this morning?"

There's the sound of someone snorting, and then a smack. Finally followed by Vee's voice in a whiney, "Sorry, Kelly." So, I guess Sam got tired of his shitty attitude towards our beta too. Good to hear it.

Kelly's lips blow across the top of her cup of coffee as I stare longingly at it. Fuck, I miss coffee. They mostly had decaf at the omega center—we'd sometimes get to go out in groups to the mall where they have a Starbees—and fuck me but I would give just about anything for a fucking double shot espresso right now.

She smiles sweetly at me, blowing another cool breath across the steaming surface. Then she starts giggling. "Sorry, Teddy, I couldn't help myself." She giggles again, putting the cup on the table. "This is yours if you want it, I picked up decaf at the store yesterday. It's instant, 'cause I'm pretty sure everybody here needs their caffeine fix. I wanted to tease you with it...but I can't if you keep looking at my drink that way."

"Looking at it what way?" Ok, yeah. I'm still staring at the mug, the little curl of steam coming off the top.

"Like you wanna make slow, passionate love to my coffee. Whisper sweet nothings into its bitter black deliciousness."

She's back to giggling again as she runs her fingers over the rim of the cup.

Well, shit. She's probably not wrong. I can't see my face, but I'm sure there's some longing there.

Fuck.

"Just give me the fuckin' cup, Pixie. Especially if you want me to do any of that to you later." Her giggles cut off with an abrupt choking sound and three growls start up around the table.

Gods save me from possessive alphas.

Ok, well, Sam's doesn't sound possessive exactly, at least not in an angry way.

Kelly smiles at me and slides the cup to Sam, who passes it on to me, along with a sugar bowl and bottle of heavy cream. "Sorry Teddy, I forgot to tell you when I was unpacking groceries yesterday." It's ok, I can forgive him, more so after I finally get to drink this. I add two sugars and a splash of cream and moan when the flavor finally hits my tongue. Shit, I sound like I'm doing something naughty with this coffee.

Oh, well, fuck it. I missed this.

Sam gets up and goes to the kitchen, returning with a platter full of pancakes. Vee already brought out plates and butter and syrup, then a few jars of jams and jellies. He leaves those beside my spot, so I move the whole lot to the server so everyone can have access. I don't want to bogart the strawberry preserves...I don't even like strawberry preserves on my pancakes, so who knows what's up with that. I thought for sure he'd remember that I only like butter and maple syrup. My whiny inner omega pouts a little that he forgot. Shit, it's been long enough, I shouldn't be surprised.

Still the look on his face is kind of smug when he sees me set all the extras away from myself, and he throws Sam a snarky look.

Nope.

Not my circus, not my monkeys.

Just going to eat these fucking pancakes.

Eat these pancakes and *not deal with crazy alpha bullshit.*

Nope. Sam put four of them on my plate, two look delicious, tall and fluffy, and they smell so damned good my mouth waters. The other two look more like half cooked dumplings. They're pale and look gummy. I glance around the table, and no one else has these horrors on their plate. When I meet Sam's eyes, he just nods and focuses back on his own plate. Vee watches the exchange blatantly, not even trying to be sneaky now.

I feel bad wasting good syrup on the abomination pancakes staring back at me from my plate. Better to get those out of the way first and use the others as a palate cleanser. Pouring a healthy dose of maple goodness over the top I try to cut into one, and it's like trying to saw through a flip-flop with a butter-knife. You know you'll make it eventually, but it's probably not worth the effort. Finally, I just give in and stab the entire damn thing, I can tear it apart with my teeth easier than this.

Raising it to my mouth I take a bite and it feels raw and doughy on the inside as hard as old boot leather on the outside. But the taste. Dear gods. It tastes like straight baking soda. That overly bitter slightly-soapy sweetness that makes my gag reflex react just from the flavor. What the ever-loving hell did Sam just feed me.

My eyes water as I spit the bite I managed to tear off into a napkin and head for the kitchen to throw it away and get water. It takes two glasses to finally get the flavor out of my mouth, and I lean over the sink praying to the cooking gods that it's not going to make a repeat performance.

When my eyes finally stop watering, I walk back into the dining room, giving Sam the hard glare he so justly deserves. Instead of responding to me, or even acknowledging my return he gives Vee a hard look. "And that, little boy, is why we use a recipe. I don't care if you pull the fucking thing off the internet. Don't go throwing random ingredients you find into a bowl and call it cooking. Maybe after a few years of experience with it, you'll have enough of an idea of what works to try that. But for now, stay the fuck outta my damned kitchen." Sam shoves another bit of fluffy pancake into his mouth, chewing purposefully.

Vee's devastated gaze turns to me, he looks like he's about to cry as he pushes away from the table and mopes to the kitchen with his still mostly full plate. Sam meets my hard glare now but doesn't let me start talking. "Your boy there wanted to make you pancakes. Don't worry, I checked what he put in; flour, water, baking soda, and some vanilla. Thankfully, he left out the eggs...but also the sugar. He was also only making them for you, so there wasn't too much batter. Still, if he's plannin' on sticking around, you might want to work on his attitude. If he's gonna be part of this pack, it's the whole pack. He doesn't get to exclude people he doesn't like."

Sam shoves a last bit of pancake into his mouth and stands up before I can reply. I don't want to defend Vee. Not exactly. That was awful, but he looked so upset. Still, I'm both shocked by Sam's offer to let him stay and understand his point of view about all of us working together. Garret and Kelly are the only ones left with me at the table, and Kelly gives me an encouraging smile while Garret continues to stare longingly at her. Seriously, it's actually kind of creepy now.

When I just sit there staring, she grows impatient and gestures with her fork in kind of a 'go on' motion. I realize her other hand is being held captive by Garret. Heaving a heavy sigh I stand up, the good pancakes have already soaked up all the syrup on my plate, and gotten cold, but I'm tempted to sit here and eat the damned things anyway.

Shit.

Taking my plate with me, I walk into the kitchen. Sam stands at the sink rinsing off his plate while Vee is by the stove, his shoulders slumped and looking defeated. I'm torn between wanting to go to him—he's mine, he's been mine since we were kids—and thinking he deserves to feel like shit after everything he put me through.

I don't get a chance to anyway before Sam turns and wraps him in a hug, tucking Vee's head under his chin. "I'm not tryin' to be an asshole here, Kid. I just need you to learn that your actions have consequences. Embarrassin' yourself at breakfast is a small consequence in the grand scheme of things. What you did to Teddy, rejecting him. That's gonna have some big fuckin' consequences. You gonna man up and accept 'em? Try to make it right? No more of this half-assed bullshit?"

As I watch, Vee nuzzles into Sam's neck, his shoulders relaxing by increments against the larger man. I must make some noise, because Sam turns his head to look at me. He shakes it once and I think he's trying to let Vee have some semblance of privacy. Turning as silently as I can, I walk back to the dining room, put my plate down on the table, and head to my room to get a shower and try to figure out the weird swirl of conflicting emotions in my chest.

Chapter 41

Sam

Why do I feel like I'm adopting puppies? Two of them; one who skitters across the floor pissing everywhere, that nips and growls every time I try to get close. And the other who just wants to lick everyone, trying desperately to get attention. Fuck my life.

Steve helps me finish loading the dishwasher and cleaning up the mess from breakfast, dutifully collecting all the condiments he took out to try to prove that he knows Teddy better and storing them away in the fridge and pantry. The kid seems like he wants to apologize and try to get back in Teddy's good graces. But he's acting more like a teenager with a first crush than a grown alpha, and I briefly wonder again about their upbringing and what kinda family they had that would deny them a life with an omega they were already involved with. Ok, Steve was involved with, Garret vehemently denies any attraction to men and has become obsessed with Kelly. Once again, as long as that's what she wants, and she's happy, that's all I care about.

Once everything is cleaned and put away, we retire to the living room. Kelly is already on the couch, sandwiched between Garret and Jake, but she looks up at me excitedly. "How can I help with the nest today? Are we gonna get more work done? When can we paint it? Oh, I can help Teddy pick out paint colors! Do you think he'd be ok with that?" Her questions are rapid fire, and I smile at how excited she is over making a nest for our omega.

Garret and Steve are staring back and forth between the two of us, and soon Garret pipes up. "What's she talking about Sam?" It's strange that they've been here less than twenty-four hours and I'm already contemplating their joining the pack, but shit. The pack's only been together for four days, so what the hell?

I look around, realizing I'm going to either need to build or buy some new furniture. The single couch and coffee table were fine when it was just me and Jake. Even with Teddy and Kelly it would have been doable. But with three alphas, a giant omega, a beta, and an overgrown lap-dog, we need more places to sit.

Maybe I could bring up the chairs from the basement.
No, what if they wanna watch a movie?
Shit. It's ok.

I take a seat on the stairs and Steve sits by my feet...weird. "Anybody seen Teddy, in case he wants to be in on this conversation too?"

The door opens down the hall and Teddy walks in. His hair is damp, and he smells like soap. "Sorry Sam, just needed a few minutes."

I drag him over to me and pull him in for a hug before he can object. He looks around the room for a minute, then goes over and stares at Jake until the dog relents and hops down onto the floor, surrendering his seat next to Kelly. Teddy sits down, and she leans into him, offering her own hug.

Another downside to being pack alpha, I guess, I get to do the talking. "Been here less than a day and already kicked off my own couch. Damn boy, you *do* move fast." My attempts at cutting the tension meet with massive failure as Garret pales slightly and stands up, shuffling away from the couch. Kelly looks exasperated for a moment, like she wants to say something, but then gives up and snuggles harder into Teddy.

"Christ, kid, I was tryin' to lighten the mood, sit y'er ass down." I wonder briefly again at these two's upbringing as Garret shuffles back to the couch, not meeting my eyes.

"As you boys may or may not know, I met Kelly and Teddy this last weekend at a bonding ceremony..." Garret's already heard part of this story, but I don't know how new it'll be to Steve. Relating the first few days with my pack, up to and including meeting them yesterday, takes longer than anticipated, and by the time I'm done, Kelly has curled up into Teddy's lap, both of them snoring lightly. Jake took her spot on the couch and is leaning against them both, leaving Garret out in the cold again.

Taking in the twins—Garret stopped me to clarify their relationship when I got to the part about them running into Kelly at the store yesterday—I suggest we take a break before we hear their side of things. And I want Teddy to be awake for this. If Steve's gonna try to get himself out of trouble, he needs to be able to come forward and explain to Teddy exactly what happened, and why it took him so long to come back for him.

Besides, I need to get back to work on the nest and, once I smooth out the joint compound, talk to Teddy about wall texture and paint. And windows, have to get the damned windows in before I can paint in this cold.

Stepping into the nest, I can understand why Teddy was so upset. The room doesn't look like much now, but once I'm finished, it'll be exactly what he wants. I pull out a bucket of drywall mud and start skimming the room. The sooner I can finish this place, the happier and more relaxed my omega will be. Plus, I can't deny that Kelly's excitement earlier was adorable. I feel like such a shit for not already having had this done before he came into my life. But there was no way to know.

Hours have passed before I finally leave the room. My back aches, my shoulders are stiff, and I think my arms want to fall off from spreading mud around the room all day. Big fucking room—nests usually are—but I'm getting too old for this shit.

Looking over at the grandfather clock, it's clear I missed lunch, and should have already started on dinner. What the hell are they up to that they let me disappear for this long? I wander through the downstairs, but nobody seems to be here. Opening the front door, all three automobiles seem to be in the same spots. Jake doesn't come running when the door opens either, which is strange.

I trudge upstairs. Maybe they're all in bed, without me. But no, the bed and bedrooms are all empty as well. Starting to feel concerned, I plod back down the stairs, gripping tightly to the railing because my legs feel like they're about to unhinge, both from exhaustion and worry. I nearly fall and crash to the bottom when I hear a loud screech coming from the basement. Kelly's voice raises high enough to carry to the living room. "No, stop. Don't you dare!"

Scrambling down the steps, it takes my brain a few seconds to comprehend what I'm seeing. They've reconfigured the chairs into a semicircle around the television, and they each have a game controller. A go-kart game is split into four sections on the television, and as I watch a blue turtle shell explodes across the screen, taking out the blonde princess on a pink motorcycle.

Kelly throws a look past Teddy like she wants to string Steve up by his ankles and beat him to death.

I settle back onto the stairs, grabbing my chest. It feels like I just ran five miles and my ribs are way too tight, like I can't get enough air. Kelly finally gets her character back on track, and comes in fourth place, still ahead of every guy in the room. When the tiles flip up on the screen, showing that she's been winning every race before this. She stands up to glare at Steve again and finally notices me collapsed on the steps.

She scrambles over the back of the chair, landing in an unladylike heap on the floor before popping back up like a deranged Jack-in-the-box. Her smile is huge as she runs over to me. "Sam, Sam! Sorry, we opened some of your games, but did you see! I won, I kicked all their butts!" She is bouncing around in circles and Jake finally makes it over from in front of the chairs too, where I can only guess he's been asleep. Together they hop around in a circle, her waving her game controller and laughing hysterically, and him barking and wagging his tail so hard that I'm surprised he doesn't take off like a damned helicopter.

Garret and Teddy are both turned around in their chairs watching intently. Steve looks between our omega and Kelly as she continues to dance victoriously around the room.

Fuck, she's adorable. When her mad flailing brings her close to me again, I half stand, wrapping my hands around her tiny waist and pulling her against me as I collapse back against the stairs. She lets out a loud, giggling squeal as I nuzzle into her neck and nibble up to her ear. The last few days have been stressful, hell, the last week has been stressful as fuck, but I need this. I need to feel and taste her again, both of them if they'll let me. I'm already failing because I didn't even feed them properly today.

Shit, I don't even know if Teddy ever got breakfast. I am such a shit alpha. First no nest, now no food. I don't deserve these two, but I want them. Everything passes through my mind in a flash as Kelly wiggles against me, finally settling down and curling tight into my lap. Ugh, I haven't even cleaned up yet. I'm sure my clothes are filthy. Still, she hangs on when I try to set her down, burrowing her face into my neck, and nipping at me with her teeth.

"Sam, I didn't get to play with you last night. You teased me yesterday, but then everything went crazy...I need you." Her tiny puff of breath against my ear warms my chest till it feels like it might burst. Unfortunately, it makes my cock feel like it's going to burst too, and I can't stop the groan that bubbles free.

"Kelly, Sugar...I gotta get cleaned up, Honey. You don't want me touching you with rough, mud-coated hands, right?" I expect her to say no, to hop off my lap and give me some space to go take a shower and change. Instead, she wiggles until she's straddling my lap, and grinds hard against me.

My head falls back as the breath rushes out of my lungs in a choked gasp. "Sugar, you're playing with fire here," is all I get out before her hands pull my face to hers.

"Please, Sam."

With a muffled moan against her lips, I lift us both off the steps and start up the stairs. My already abused back is screaming at me even though she barely weighs anything.

Not stopping on the first floor, I head from one set of stairs to the next, and straight for our bedroom. My hands are already rough with callouses. I can't imagine touching her soft skin with anything worse than that, anything that might hurt her. But this way I can get cleaned up and make her feel good at the same time. If the hot water in the shower helps to loosen up my damned back, even better.

Stopping at the bedside to grab one of the alpha size boxes of condoms, I carry her into the bathroom, turning the hot water on all the way. The last time I cleaned her up in here, she was pretty loopy, so I don't know if she noticed everything. Since I outfitted this room for a pack bedroom, the shower is a huge walk-in number with glass doors and four shower heads, plus one removable one. I plan on using that on her as soon as I get myself cleaned up.

Putting my hands under her ass, I lift her up and away enough that I can set her on the ground. She pouts in response, and I feel like turning her around and bending her over the sink to spank her ass for it. I'm pretty sure she'd enjoy that, but I never want to make her uncomfortable. We'll have to talk soon in regard to my need for control, and how secure she feels in giving it up. For now, I satisfy myself with watching her face as I peel myself out of my jeans and shirt. It's a hell of an ego boost to see such a pretty thing go breathless and needy when you get undressed.

She scrambles out of her own fleece pants and shirt and I let loose a growl when I see the bandages covering her legs that Garret put on earlier. Shit, I can't take her into the shower without those getting wet and needing redone. Fuck my life! "Hey, Teddy, you up here?" I call out the bathroom door and our omega comes scrambling in, looking slightly out of breath.

I point at Kelly. "Can you please keep the lovely beta entertained while I get cleaned up? I don't want her knees to get any more hurt." Teddy stares, eyes locked on my hard shaft, and I have to snap my fingers a couple of times to get his attention and ask again. He finally nods dumbly and leads a petulant Kelly out of the bathroom as I climb under the hot water. I allow myself a few seconds to soak in the heat on my sore muscles before scrubbing everything as quickly as possible so I can get back to my pack before another alpha or two tries to step in.

Chapter 42
Steve

I can admit when I'm wrong. Not well, I'll bitch a lot in the process, but I can eventually do it. Walking in to see my omega pinning the waif-like beta girl to the bed with his bigger body is *not* one of those times. So much so that when I start growling and snarling my brother has to drag me from the room.

Ok, I admit, we weren't invited anyway...but Teddy followed Sam and Kelly, and I followed Teddy...and for lack of anything else to do—I assume—Garret followed me. Now it's a whole train of clusterfuck.

My omega is covering the tiny wiggly beta, kissing her like he kissed me yesterday, grinding his hips against her, and as much as I hate it, I'm also now hard as fuck watching. Not because of her, I guess she's pretty enough. But my bear is a work of art, all thick strength, long black hair falling over them both like a curtain as he plunders her mouth. Her tiny desperate cries causing the dominant part of him I love so much to come to the front.

Now I'm not sure if Garret's holding me back, or I'm holding him. We're both snarling messes nearly frenzied with the need to get to our mates. He can fucking have her, get her away from Teddy...but I don't want to risk either of them getting hurt if Teddy doesn't want to give her up either. Shit. Maybe when Sam gets out of the shower, he'll take back over with her and then I can distract my omega away? Though, that leaves Garret, and I'm pretty sure Sam could kick his ass if it came to it.

Of course, maybe Sam and I could share Teddy and then Garret could play with the beta. There's no time to discuss this right now with him, though. He doesn't look in the most sane frame of mine as he watches Kelly writhe around on the bed. The snarl ripping from his chest sounds almost feral, and I wonder if I should slap him. Isn't that what you do with hysterical people?

This seems like that sort of situation, so I bring my arm back, just about to knock the shit out of my own brother in an attempt to bring him back to his senses when the bathroom door opens again. Steam billows out, followed by the scent of fresh cut cedar and a very damp, very muscular, very *naked* Sam steps out.

Is it hot in here?

It feels like it's getting hotter in here.

Holy shit, but I can definitely see why Teddy was attracted to this man.

He's tall, dominant, and smells like fucking heaven.

Plus, he looks like a marble statue that someone glued a merkin on.

And a god-damned chest wig.

They should have a better name for that.

Chest-toupe? Chest-erkin? Pec-weave?

Shit, I'm getting sidetracked.

Plus, I think I have a crush on my omega's alpha.

Fuck.

The high whine that comes from my throat startles me, and brings the big alpha to a stop. Looking between me and his packmates on the bed. I've never made a noise like that before, no idea how it even happened. He stares at me, a deep rattling purr building in his chest as he stalks forward. His voice is a low rumble as he closes in, his nose tracing along my neck when he leans down. "Are you jealous, little boy? You know you need to behave if you want to play with our omega." He circles behind me and his hand comes up, circling my throat and holding me in place as he turns us to face to the bed.

"Teddy's been a good boy, doing exactly as I asked. Entertaining my sweet beta while I got cleaned up." His teeth graze along my neck, making me weak in the knees. "I know you don't want to join that. But you need Teddy's permission to do anything else, don't you? And we can't very well leave poor sweet Kelly all alone, can we?"

He places a soft kiss on the edge of my jaw and my responding whimper finally draws Teddy's attention. His head snaps up, watching as Sam continues to tease me. "Now, are you going to be a good boy for me? Do you trust me enough to give up control and let me take care of you? Do you trust Teddy enough to know he'll give you what you need, even if you don't always understand it?"

We have Teddy's full attention now, Kelly's too. She's scooted up to the head of the bed and is watching us with half-lidded eyes. Her breath comes in a series of pants, and I can admit that she's beautiful like this, all rumpled, her lips swollen from my omega's kisses. I'm still not aroused by her, but I can see some of why Teddy wants her.

It makes me hate her a little more, since I can't ever have him the same way. She doesn't have to deal with the pressures of being an alpha. She can love who she wants to, and no one cares. There's no legacy to live up to, no family counting on her to carry on their alpha heritage. And as far as I know, no twin dragging her around making her meet potential mates that she'll never want.

I turn my ire towards Garret. He's standing in the doorway, his focus almost solely on Kelly, the soft little beta who stole my omega. The one who can give him everything he wants—claim him in front of her relatives, a family of his own if he ever wants them, someone who accepts him for what he is without listening to their asshole father and trying to be something she's not.

Garret looks towards me as if sensing my thoughts, his head tilted, as if asking if I'm ok. I'm not. Not really, but I nod anyway. I try to blame this on him, but I know it has nothing to do with him, and everything to do with our dads and grandpa. He never wanted Teddy, not like me. I know that he felt left out more than once, but at the time, I was too young and stupid to worry about it. I nod again, pointing my chin towards Kelly, so he knows I'm fine with that.

I know he wants her like I want Teddy. I've seen the look on his face, the same one I wear when I look at my bear, the longing so deep that every other feeling in the world fades out, and you're left with nothing but an empty hole where your heart used to be. Just waiting to see if the person you need more than air could possibly need you back, even just a little. I know the look. I know the feeling.

Moreover, I know what it's like when the one you need so desperately needs you back and everything feels so fucking right you can hardly believe that you ever got so lucky. I also know what it feels like to lose that person, and I pray for Garret's sake that he never has to deal with that soul-crushing sensation.

My brother looks past my shoulder—I feel Sam nod towards the bed then Garret's ensuing mad scramble up onto the mattress. He crawls towards Kelly, prostrating himself before her like he would give anything for her to just look at him the way she looks at Teddy and Sam. She looks from him to Sam and I feel that same nod against my hair right before she reaches for Garret, bringing him in for a slow kiss.

My brother's eyes close, his face a mask of rapture at being able to kiss the silly little girl in front of him. But what do I know? I'm even more fucked up. Dad would probably rather we claim a female beta than a male omega, at least then we could 'carry on the family legacy'. But all I want, all I've ever wanted, was him, my bear.

Another loud whimper slips out as I watch Kelly roll my brother so she's straddling his hips while he sits propped against the headboard. I'm feeling petty and jealous as his low groan rolls over me. It looks like she lost her pants and shirt at some point, but she's still in a pair of panties. Her hips twist and roll over my brother, dragging another throaty groan from him.

Teddy steps in front of me, sandwiching me between his chest and his alpha's. "Can you do it, Vee? Can you give up control? Let us take care of you?" He kisses my throat, his teeth scraping over the area opposite to where Sam's jaw's still pressed against me. "It's your choice. We just want to take care of you. Anything you're uncomfortable with, just say the word, and it stops. Anything you need, tell us. Yes?"

But I never have control. I'm never in charge of my own life. I've never been able to just do or have what I want, and I want this. I mean, I've always wanted Teddy, but him wanting me back after so long apart feels too good to be true. Can I have this? Is it too much to ask? Can I trust that he won't hurt me after I hurt him so badly? That's really the gist of it all. Can I trust these two with the few pieces of me that are still mine?

I want to. I want Teddy to touch me and hold me. The thought of being able to finally let go and let someone—even someone who's nearly a stranger—take care of me, to let me shut off my mind and all the worries and choices...It's amazing. My voice is a barely whispered croak, "Yes."

Before I have even a second to worry this was the wrong decision, Teddy's kissing me, his strong hands wrapped around my jaw, tilting my face where he wants me to go as he bites and sucks on my lips.

Sam's low growl vibrates through my back as his arms circle us both, and I can practically feel my bones melt under his dominance. My hands reach up on their own, stroking along Sam's arm, running up Teddy's chest. I need to touch him and be touched.

Please, Bear, don't hurt me.

You don't have any reason to be kind, but please.

Please forgive me for abandoning you.

Chapter 43

Garret

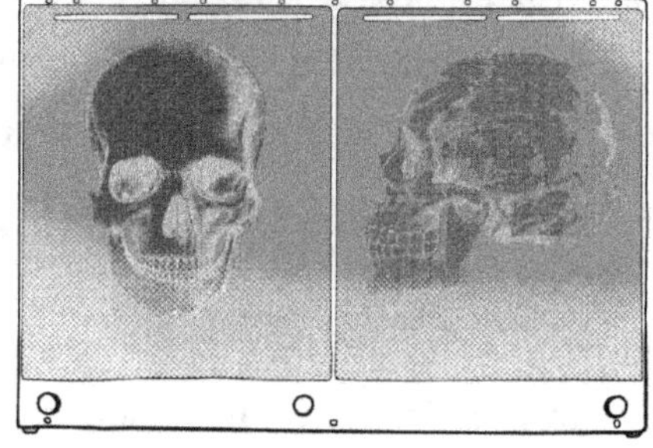

She's ok with this. I'm touching her, tasting her, and she doesn't mind. She's not pushing me away. I didn't mean to growl or get possessive. When I saw her with Teddy earlier, it felt like someone was ripping out my heart. I knew she'd been with Sam yesterday but he's her pack alpha. And realistically I know she's been with Teddy, he's her omega, but he was my friend first. A small illogical part of my brain keeps throwing out that he already has my brother, he can't take her away from me too.

That's insanity.

He's not trying to take her from me.

She's not even mine until she says she is.

Please, please let her agree to be mine.

I don't even care that she looked to Sam for confirmation earlier, checking in with the big alpha that it was ok for her to kiss me. I'll happily be whatever she needs or wants me to be. As long as she'll let me be hers. I need her more than I need my next breath.

Her warm hands slide under my shirt and up my chest; it feels like sparks are going off beneath my skin. She's still straddling my lap and grinding against me as her palms come up and cup my face, pulling me in for a kiss. She's so fucking perfect, with her smiles and her bright eyes. Her lips are soft against mine, and I close my eyes, reticent to stop looking at her, but needing to focus on the sensation. Nothing's been made official, and I don't know if I'll ever get to touch her like this again, so I need to be able to remember this for the rest of my life.

She's so warm against me, and I trace my hands from her hips up to brush my thumbs across her ribs before circling behind her and pulling her tiny frame towards mine. She's so much smaller than me. Taller than most omegas, but not as plush. She's still all gentle curves pressed against my harder frame, and I pull away slightly to yank my shirt over my head. Needing to feel that softness against my skin, I touch her with my calloused fingertips. Doing my residency at the hospital for these months has roughened the flesh of my hands, and I internally curse myself for not using lotion more to keep myself soft for her. I never want to hurt her again.

Her nipples feel like hard little pebbles rubbing against my chest as I bury my face in her neck and take in as much of her scent as possible. There's still the undercurrent of Teddy's cookie and Sam's fresh cut cedar, but her own trace of lilac is life, and I pull her tighter to me, huffing against her shoulder, trying to breathe her in.

Her nails scrape down my back and she wiggles against me, giggling.

Shit, I forgot how ticklish she is.

Taking the chance, I bite down none too gently where her neck meets her shoulder and I'm rewarded with a dark, shuddering moan, her hips twitching against mine. Her scent gets stronger and, *fuck me*, but I need to taste her. I roll us so that she's laying across the top of the bed and I'm on top, trailing tickling kisses with nipping bites down her collarbones. I stop for a moment to take one tight peak into my mouth. Laving my tongue over her hot skin before she starts wiggling again, I bite lightly, drawing another whimpering groan from her lips.

My teeth scrape over her flat stomach, and my mind flashes a brief image of a lazy morning snuggled in bed, intimate in another way, vulnerable as I see just how much I can tickle her before she gets angry at me. I want those; slow mornings, late coffee mornings, mornings where we just cuddle together and talk. She can tell me about growing up here, her family, what it's like being a beta...or anything she feels like, really. I just like the sound of her voice, her laughter. I'm momentarily tempted to blow a raspberry on her stomach just to hear her shriek and giggle like I know she would.

But I don't know if those mornings will ever get to happen, so I need to taste her while I can. Sear her into my memory in case Sam makes us leave or our father pulls us away again. I finally understand what happened to Steve, how my fun-loving, happy-go-lucky twin turned into a morose asshole, a shadow of his former self.

Kelly's hand in my hair brings me back to the moment. My gaze following the planes of her body up to meet her eyes. She silently asks if I'm ok, her long fingers gently brushing through my hair and down my jaw. I turn my head and stop dead at the sight of Teddy pressed between Sam and my brother. Kelly lets out a sharp gasp and my eyes are drawn back to her face as she's suddenly mesmerized by the trio at the end of the bed.

If this is my only time with her, I better make it count. I slide farther along the mattress, nipping against her hip-bone to draw her attention back to me before I finally make it to her mound. This close to her core, her scent's stronger, and my mouth waters for a taste. I've been told that omegas taste like their scent. Which means it's probably good they smell like dessert, but I've never experienced that. Until Kelly, I'd never really been kissed. I didn't see a point in getting attached to someone I was marginally physically attracted to if there was no way to keep them.

Taking a deep breath, my head fills with her subtle lilac scent, and something musky and slightly sweet. Keeping my eyes fixed on hers, I trace my tongue up her slit, soft and swollen with arousal. Slippery enough that my second pass slips inside, tracing over the more delicate skin. Her flavor bursts across my taste buds, and my eyes slip closed, savoring a taste I could happily wake up to for the rest of my life.

Wedging my shoulders under her thighs, I fall upon her, needing to lick up every last drop. I barely register her low guttural moan or her hands yanking at my hair. I don't even know if I'm doing this right. I just know I need to taste more of her. Using my fingers to bring more of her flavor out, I pump inside her, lapping up everything I can, her cries loud in my ears as I nip and suck against her tender places. Her body shakes and jack-knifes around me, almost dislodging me from my feast. I open my eyes to meet hers—they're glassy, and her skin's flushed. Her chest rises and falls rapidly with her panting breath, and she looks between me and the trio on the other end of the bed.

Turning my head, I'm momentarily stunned seeing my brother pulled tight against Teddy's chest. His back arched forward as the big omega grips his hair tightly, pulling his head back and rutting into him. Sam stands beside him, hand wrapping behind Steve's neck, voice soft and almost gentle. "That's it, my sweet boy. Let it out. You're safe. Shhhh. It's ok."

Sam closes his hand over Teddy's wrist, squeezing just tight enough that he has to let my brother's hair go, and Steve drops forward, his head flopping against Sam's chest, and I hear a muffled sob. The bigger alpha strokes his hair and holds him as he continues to make quiet, comforting noises.

I feel like I'm intruding, like I shouldn't be seeing this private moment. Especially not involving my brother. I crawl up Kelly's prone form. Still wanting to hold her, to touch her, to feel her against me. But my own arousal's gone from witnessing my brother breaking down between the love of his life and a big alpha that doesn't look like he has a nurturing bone in his body. I need to have her in my arms. My mind's a muddled haze, and I can't tell if this pack's the best possible outcome for us, or the worst.

Chapter 44

Sam

I think we're all a little emotionally wiped out after that, but I still need to feed my pack. Even if they aren't all my pack, or not officially my pack...however the fuck this works out. Teddy and Kelly are mine for as long as they'll have me. Steve and Garret...if they want to stay, I won't stop them.

Shit, I could probably use a hand around here. Kelly works part time, but I'm not sure I can support five adults with just the shop. What was it Kelly said? "We'll jump off that bridge when we come to it." I don't think that's how the saying's supposed to go, but the girl is a lot crazier than I originally realized. In a good way, but she's definitely gonna keep this old man on his toes.

Teddy comes out of the bathroom leading a limp looking Steve in a long sleeve shirt and sweats. I wonder briefly at the full coverage clothes, but the kid looks like he's about ready to fall over and sleep for a month. Not that he's actually a kid, he's a couple years older than Teddy, but still only twenty-seven to my thirty-four.

Fuck, how do I keep collecting these youngsters. Kelly's laying limp and satiated at the top of the bed with Garret wrapped around her like a blanket. His face is buried in her hair and despite the fact that he didn't seem to get off, he looks peaceful.

Though I can't forget how he looked earlier perched between my beta's thighs eating her like a fucking Thanksgiving dinner, and later the look of deep introspection when he saw his brother break. But Steve needed to, he's been so high-strung since he got here, pulled back and forth, jealous of Kelly, wanting to apologize but not knowing how to talk to Teddy. All they seem to do is sit in silence. He seemed like he was about to snap when I walked out of the shower earlier. He needed to let go, and I'm hoping now that he has, things can move forward.

There seems to be a whole lot of shit going on with these two. I've heard part of it, but not the whole story. Maybe I can get more information outta them before this damned snow finally clears off. Until then, I'm gonna take care of what I can...maybe use them as free labor to get the nest done faster. Smiling to myself, I pull a clean shirt over my head and head downstairs, leaving my pack and their paramours to get cleaned up and settled down while I try to figure out what to feed everyone.

I let Jake out the back door and he tears off through the snow—at least that finally stopped coming down—and sort through the fridge for easy but hearty food to feed everyone. It looks like there's a sandwich on a plate in here. I don't realize how hungry I am until it's in front of me. But I don't want to eat someone else's food. It's my job to take care of my pack, not take away from them.

It's harder to not think about eating when you're trying to decide on what to cook. Beans and rice would be good but take too long. Any sort of Tex-Mex would be hearty, but I don't know what's thawed out that would work for it. Maybe something with pasta, that's usually quick and easy. I still need to make Teddy and Kelly a proper tomato soup, but I don't have the patience for it right now, maybe tomorrow. Plus, we just did soup last night. I don't want them to think I'm a one-trick pony. Leaning forward, I drop my head to the counter. Fuck, I am fucking sore and tired right now.

The sound of scraping on the back door draws my attention, and I stand up too fast to go let Jake in. The world pitches and spins for a few seconds while I hold a death grip on the counter. Fucking hell. Once I can take a step without feeling like I'm on the tilt-a-whirl, I go open the back door and almost get plowed over by Jake. He rushes in, casting me dirty looks for taking so long to open the door. *Shit.*

Voices sound in the living room, and he bolts that way, almost knocking me over in the process. My head swims again, and I'm forced to lean against the island to keep from kissing the floor. I hear a stern, "No. Down. We don't jump up," from Kelly, and Jake slinks back into the room a moment later, looking dejected. He's so damned spoiled, and it's been less than a week.

She arrives a moment later and I'm still gripping the counter, trying to stay upright. "Shit, Sam, are you alright?" Garret's voice breaks through the buzz in my ears and I manage to lift my head as the world swims in front of me. He and Kelly each grab one of my arms and half lead/half drag me back into the living room, helping me drop to the couch. Kelly sits beside me, a worried look on her face. Her cool hands run over my forehead and cheeks.

"What happened? Are you ok? Do we need to take you to the hospital?" My sweet girl sounds worried, but it's not her place to worry.

I shake my head, making everything spin around me before I swallow and manage to speak. "No. No, thank you, Sugar. I just...I get low blood sugar sometimes. I completely forgot to eat since breakfast, and it just seems to have all caught up with me at once. Thank fuck it wasn't on the stairs earlier." I chuckle at my own joke, but she just looks horrified.

"Sorry, Sugar. Don't worry, it happens. I'll be fine. I just need to get something in my stomach real quick, then get started on dinner."

Her brows are still drawn into a worried scowl, but Garret's the one who speaks. "Shit, man, sorry. Kelly made you a sandwich earlier, but you never came out of the room when she knocked. Let me go grab it out of the fridge for you, if that's ok?" I nod numbly, unable to focus properly.

Garret leaves the couch and Kelly's hands are back on my forehead. "Are you sure that's all it is, Sam? I know you've been under a lot of stress lately. You can tell me if something's bothering you, you know that, right? We're supposed to take care of each other now." I smile as best I can.

She doesn't understand that I'm supposed to take care of my pack. It's my job, and something I need to do so they know I'm worthy. I don't want to contradict her, but I'm glad when Garret comes back with that sandwich and a soda, so I have a reason not to answer.

Teddy comes down the stairs, Steve holding his hand. They both look over at me and make a beeline for the kitchen. I don't know if I look as bad as I still feel, but gimme a few minutes to get my head on straight, and I'll be right as rain. Thankfully, the room's stops spinning by the time I finish my sandwich and soda.

Finally steady on my feet, I make my way into the kitchen. Teddy and Steve are standing side by side at the stove, each stirring a pot. Teddy steps away and goes rifling through cabinets, finally pulling out my colander and putting it in the sink before noticing me. "Go take a seat, Sam. We got this." A small growl bubbles free at being dismissed by my omega, but I clench my teeth tight to cut it off and step into the room.

"What the hell are you two doin'? I was gonna fix dinner." They both turn to look at me.

Steve ducks his head quickly, going back to stirring whatever he has on the stove, but Teddy steps up, his arms going around my chest. "We know, but you already take care of us...just...just let us do something for you, ok?" He squeezes me tight before stepping away to take the pot he was at earlier off the stove and pour a batch of elbow macaroni into the colander at the sink.

Steve turns towards me, a small smile making his face brighter than I've seen it before. "Besides, Bear's making me use a recipe, so we don't have a repeat of the pancakes. Plus, I don't think we can fuck mac-and-cheese up too badly. It just said I have to melt the cheese on low heat and keep stirring, so...that's my job. Teddy's doing the rest, and he actually took cooking classes at the omega center." Then he goes back to stirring with a look of intense concentration. Which I will begrudgingly admit, is kinda cute.

Kelly

They do a good job of teaching omegas how to cook at the center. I can never get my mac-and-cheese this creamy.

Even when it has a good flavor, the texture's off-putting, it's always kind of gritty. Teddy gets smug when we finish off the whole batch they made. Steve just sits there blushing and having goo-goo eyes at both Teddy and Sam.

I'm not jealous—not like I thought I would be if someone was flirting with my boyfriend...er...boyfriends? I'm not sure if it's because I know that packs usually have more alphas, or if I just feel secure in their affection for me. Or maybe Steve's not a threat because he already feels like pack. My brain hurts if I think about this too hard.

Since Teddy and Steve cooked, Garret helps me rinse and load the dishwasher while they distract Sam. He's been doing all the cooking, cleaning, and working on the nest while we played games earlier, so it's only fair for us to trade out and let him get off his feet for a while. He grumbles a bit at us when he sees it's done, but he also says thank you, so that's good.

Teddy sits on the couch between Sam and Steve and Garret pulls me into his lap while he sits on the hearth of the cold fireplace. It's freezing over here, and I wiggle against him, trying to collect his warmth. Sam notices and comes over, shooing us back to the couch to sit beside Teddy. Garret just lifts me up and carries me over, sitting me back in his lap once we're there.

Sam heads towards the back door, returning a moment later with a metal box like Dad keeps gun cartridges in. It's tall and skinny with a funky collapsible handle on top. He opens it up in front of the fireplace and pulls out bits of fluff and sawdust and some small sticks, building a tiny log cabin in the fireplace before setting it on fire. Once that has a nice little blaze going on, he takes his box back and brings a couple of split logs in, situating them around the tiny fire, and scattering some more kindling around to help it catch.

Soon we have a warm fire going, and Jake stretches out in front of it with a loud doggy groan. Sam comes back to the couch and looks us all over. "As soon as this damned weather clears, we're going shopping for a few more chairs, got it...now, move over." He wedges Garret out of the way, pulling me across his and Teddy's laps and purring until I go limp. Garret grumbles a little but shuffles halfway onto the arm of the couch, enough that Sam can settle in, and I'm the only one not having my butt squished right now. HA!

Pays to be a beta.

Oh yeah!

The fact that I'm half of any of their size probably helps.

Teddy rubs my feet while I burrow into Sam's chest, and I think I fall in and out of sleep. They talk about the nest, colors Teddy might want to paint it, flooring. Sam insists on real wood or cork to keep everything easy to clean. It just feels so good to be surrounded by these guys. Even Steve doesn't look as much like he hates me right now, so I'm gonna call that a win.

Coming fully awake, someone's carrying me. I bury my face against a hard chest and my lungs fill with cookie scented good-ness. Teddy. My sweet omega is carrying me down stairs, I don't think we've moved much before I woke up, so probably to the basement. I hear a few grunts and groans and open my eyes to see Sam, Garret, and Steve moving the chairs around so we can all see the big TV.

Sam settles himself into the chair in the center, reaching out and pulling me from Teddy's arms so that our omega can go join Steve and Garret in arguing over what movie to start up. My eyes start to slide shut. I don't even know what time it is, but I don't think it's super late. The last few days have just been stressful for everybody.

I'm shocked out of my almost doze by a loudly ringing phone. The first thing through my head is surprise that someone gets reception in the basement. The second is that neither of the twins or Teddy have moved since it started. They're all staring at Garret's phone in his hand. It must go to voicemail because it stops ringing after five times, and they all seem to finally take a breath. None of them has a chance to break the tension though, as it starts up again.

Grunting, Sam sets me down in the chair beside him, walks over, plucks the phone from Garret's unmoving palm, and slides the button to answer it. He doesn't even put it on speaker, and I can hear a loud voice on the other end. Steve and Garret are now staring at the floor as the voice continues to rage, even though no one has said anything on our end. Teddy looks like he's about to cry. Sam takes the three of them in, then hangs up the phone, cutting off the person who's clearly on some sort of tirade.

Garret meets his eyes first. He swallows a few times before he speaks. "That's our dad's ringtone...the one who wouldn't let us see Teddy. I think he might have finally realized we left." The phone lets out the loud blaring ring again, and Sam slides his finger across the red decline button. He looks at it for a few minutes before handing it back to Garret just as it starts to ring again.

"Turn this damned thing off and sit down. It's time we all had a talk."

Chapter 45

Teddy

We shuffle the chairs back around so we can talk without leaning over each other, and settle in. Garret and Steve exchange glances, but neither of them seems to know where to start. Finally, Sam lets out an annoyed groan, "Ok...let me try this. We're dealing with my family drama for my starting a pack with people younger than me. Kelly's family is scared shitless that a pack is going to take advantage of their sweet, naive daughter." He pauses to look around at us, and Kelly starts snickering.

"Yeah. Let's see. Teddy's family was under the impression that I kidnapped him from a mating ceremony his cousin took him to. Between my relatives and his, somebody called the cops and tried to accuse me of kidnapping Kelly...the omega. This week was nuts before you two showed up. So, let's make this easy. Teddy can start, then you two take over and you can try to explain why you abandoned him, and what the hell you've been doing since then. Sound good?"

Vee and Garret both look shell-shocked, but I'd be lying if I said I wasn't curious, so I start us out, rushing through the parts my pack has already heard, wanting to hear the alphas' excuses for myself.

I'm four when I meet Steven and Garret for the first time. We're at a work picnic for two of my dads—Murph and Noah—who work for their dads' company. Their grandpa started the Alpha Entertainment Company. Apparently, it was long enough ago that there weren't many TV stations and no streaming services. But Murph's in marketing and Noah works on the more technical side of things in broadcasting. They started working there early and are now high enough in the company that we have to go to stupid company functions, even though the dads don't want to spend what little free time they get with their co-workers.

They drop me off at the daycare center for the picnic. I don't have brothers or sisters, so I've always been good at playing alone.

Give me some blocks or some crayons, and I can chill for hours. That's probably not normal for four-year-olds, but it never bothered me—maybe I'm a freak. Not that my parents neglect me, but even with four attentive adults, kids can get lonely without other kids. I just didn't realize it until two wrestling six-year-olds tumble through the block city I'm building and destroy it.

They apologize, saying their dad's gonna be mad for making me cry, and help me rebuild everything. After that, I'm not lonely anymore. We spend the rest of the day playing together. My legs are shorter than theirs, but they never leave me behind. Even after the picnic we have playdates at their house.

As we get older, I sometimes get to have sleepovers there. They don't treat me as less even though my dads work for theirs, and whenever we're together, it just feels right. We spend more time together, every weekend we hang out at either my house or theirs. Mostly mine since their dad, Marc, is always super busy. We go to different schools. Obviously, their dad insists that they go to the private academy that's supposed to help develop strong leaders... you know the type.

Whereas I'm a public school kid. Already bigger than most by the third grade, I don't have to deal with bullies or anything, but I don't have a lot of friends at my school either.

When I'm in seventh grade and they're in ninth, Garret finally convinces their dad to let them take a year at my school. He reasons with the old man that it will be easier for them to get more real world experience in a public school dealing with a variety of different personality types, as well as possibly meet omegas. Even now their grandpa's riding them about their legacy and having to start a pack and a family. I don't know if the rest of their dads feel the same way, but neither Steve nor Garret ever argue against it, and that's enough.

Their designation comes in later that year. I'm not sure if it's a twin thing or just an alpha thing, but within weeks of each other they've both presented, and before long they're both noticeably taller than I am. Before that we were usually mistaken as the same age due to my size, but now there's no question to most people that I'm just a tag-along. But the twins never make me feel that way. Whenever anyone invites them out—the new rich kids in school—they refuse unless I'm invited along too.

My relationship with Steve starts to change. He's still one of my best friends, but it's more than that. I still care about them both, but it's different with him. I catch myself trying to always sit next to him at lunch or be closer to him on the weekends when we hang out. He always shares my beanbag when we play video games together. Just small things to be near each other.

Then, one night I'm at their place, we're all sprawled across their bedroom and Steve and I are arguing over what movie to put in. I want to watch The Lost Boys, but he's in more of a sci-fi mood. Sometimes we can compromise, but there are only so many times you can watch the Aliens franchise before you need a break. Garret gets up to go ask Cook to make us some movie snacks before she can leave for the evening.

Vee's holding the movie case over my head, just out of reach, and I tackle him to get it. Soon we're rolling around on the floor and he has me pinned down. We're both breathing heavy and then he kisses me. Everything else is kind of a blur. Garret comes back, calls us both weirdos and tells us not to be freaky when he's in the room. Then he shoves Event Horizon in the movie player, takes his bowl of popcorn and flops across his bed—effectively closing the matter with another compromise movie and leaving us to snuggle together on the floor while he plays games on his phone and ignores us.

He's always the odd man out with wanting to watch comedies, something I don't come to appreciate until I meet Sarah later at the omega center and her obsession with Monty Python.

When I'm fifteen, my own growth spurt hits, and everybody thinks that I'm about to present...but nothing happens. Vee and I are still very much in the hand holding and cuddling stage—we never get out of that, really. Don't get me wrong, the desire's there, but we want to wait until my designation comes in, and we're both fully matured, but it feels like my life's stalling out.

I still have two years left of high school, and they're set to graduate in a few months when my designation finally hits. Mom finds me one Tuesday morning when I don't come down for breakfast. I'm curled up in bed, my stomach aching worse than I've ever felt, and I can't even make it out of bed because my legs won't stop shaking, despite being overheated.

It might sound like I'm being an overdramatic teenager, but I'm very worried I'm going to die. I thought it might be food poisoning, or something that's going to kill me. It isn't until Mom walks in and I see the look on her face...I know it's worse. So much worse than food poisoning.

Murph comes next, trying to find out what's with all the crazy omega perfume filling the hallway. All he manages to say is, "Shit!" before he rounds up the other dads and leaves me alone with Mom to keep from stressing out the new omega with overprotective growly alphas. Mom gets me a heating pad and sits with me, rocking my too-big body back and forth and singing to me like she did when I was a kid until some of the fever starts to taper off.

I call the guys that night to tell them what happened, knowing this would change some of our plans, but that we could still be a pack. I could finally be with Vee how we both wanted. He sounds so excited on the phone, asking if he can bring me anything. He offers to have Cook make up some chicken soup for me...which is crazy since I'm presenting as an omega, not coming down with the flu, but I still appreciate it.

Garret doesn't say much, but Vee talks to me late into the evening. His voice easing some of the pain and giving me a sense of peace after the rough day I'd had. Mom says that's normal for omegas. Being in contact with their alpha helps soothe them, and it'll help even more when I can be around him physically, not just over the phone.

I don't make it back to school for a full week. Newly awakened omegas perfume...a lot. But Mom helps me where she can, with going to the store to pick up new slick wicking boxer briefs, and some baggier clothes so they won't pinch. At least until I can make the trip on my own. That's a story for another day but imagine my dads all surrounding me at the department store. Growling and snarling at anybody who gets close to the too-tall, string-bean omega who's puffing out perfume like a fucking Abercrombie & Fitch store in the mall.

I try to call Vee back every night during the week that I'm out, but it just keeps going to voicemail. I don't think anything of it until I get back to school, and they're gone. Rumors around school say that their dad wanted them to graduate from that fancy private school, so he had them both transferred back to finish out the year. Leaving the newly presented omega without his alphas—all alone.

Without anyone there to protect me, I can't legally stay in a public school. I'm not old enough to drop out and try for my GED so I need to transfer to the omega academy to finish out. Mom's devastated, since the closest one's a couple hours from the house and I'll have to live on campus. I'd planned on moving in with the guys when I turn eighteen anyway, but this is too early, and I'm alone.

Within a few months of my presenting, I'm completely moved into to the omega center that I'll spend the next decade at. Sarah sort of adopts me shortly after I arrive. I'm certainly not the youngest omega there, but I am the only male omega in our dorm. Kimberly, our dormitory supervisor, assigns her as my guide for the first week until I'm used to everything. And she just kind of sticks around after that.

Three years my senior, Sarah's already been here awhile. She's crazy but fun, and soon becomes my best friend, planning out elaborate revenge fantasies on the alphas who abandoned me, and taking me to the gym to work out some of my aggression and frustration.

I finally fill out, but not exactly in the way I had hoped. Omegas tend to have extra padding, so while I put on a lot of muscle, I never can get the really chiseled body. I look more like an alpha than anyone else, though, and Sarah and I often go together to the mandatory social events. Two outcasts together, she doesn't see the point of having a pack other than for heats and I don't want anyone but Vee...and no one wants us.

Chapter 46

Garret

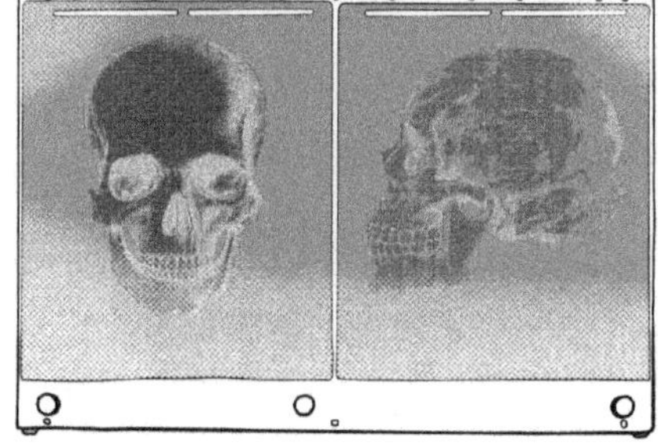

My angel glares at me from where she's curled protective-ly around Teddy. I can understand. Shit, I don't much like us right now either. Still, even knowing what happened on our end, we still come off sounding like assholes. Knowing it wasn't our choice doesn't make me feel any better. Remember-ing what happened to Steve...No. Teddy has a right to know that he didn't...that *we* didn't abandon him, not by choice.

Sam turns a cold stare my way, his eyes flicking between me and my brother. Any warmth he had towards us from before is gone, like it never existed. I don't expect that I can fix this. The situation was shit all around, but I need to at least explain.

Dad...Marc, had already been riding Steve's ass about Teddy. From the first time he figured out that they were more than just friends, he was pissed. He said it wasn't right for two alphas to have that kind of relationship, not unless there was an omega in the middle.

The irony of that statement and what I saw earlier isn't lost on me.

Grandpa, and Dad by extension, were ok with us being in a pack with Teddy, but the assumption was always that it would be the three of us with a female omega to carry on their legacy. I'd also learned early on that it would be me doing the carrying for our bloodline since—barring medical intervention—there was no way Steve was going to be inseminating anybody.

*S*teve *hangs up the phone. He's usually upbeat, but I'd never seen him this excited. I wish I could share his happiness, but I'm locked up tight. Teddy's an omega, he's pack...and I'll never find anyone who wants me for me. Shit.*

Still, my two favorite people in the world are meant to be to-gether and that's great...for them.

I can deal with this.

I mean, I haven't really had a girlfriend before.

So I can handle not having one now...or a mate.

Maybe I should just find another pack, somewhere I can be myself.

No, Dad would never let that happen.

It's not really his choice.

But I don't have friends, I have my brother...and Teddy.

That's always been enough.

I can deal with this.

I tell myself that for the rest of the evening, even as I will myself to fall asleep later.

The next morning Steve stumbles into our room, waking me up and yelling to know if I've seen his phone. I should probably look at separating our spaces soon. It was fine before, but the more involved he and Teddy get, the more privacy they'll need.

Of course, we'll be moving into our own place in a few months, so I could try to wait it out...but probably better to just take the plunge now and move into my own room. I don't want to have to be around a lot of omega perfume that's gonna drive my alpha nuts without any real release.

Steve's tearing up his side of the room. All his bedding's on the floor as he shuffles through it. He dumps out the drawer to his bedside table, feeling around inside of the cabinet to see if it fell in there, somehow. I don't know why he's so frantic, but I can practically feel his panic, so I crawl out of bed to help him look. "Ok, dude, calm down. Where did you last see it? Do you remember? Did you have it this morning at all? Did you plug it in after you talked to Teddy last night?" I don't mean to sound patronizing, but the angry snarl he turns on me says he takes it that way.

"No, I haven't seen it this morning. I plugged it in, right fucking here, where I always do, last night before bed. Remember? I was looking through nest Pinterest boards and trying to come up with some courting gift ideas. I started to doze off, so I plugged it in like always. It wasn't there when I woke up. I've checked the bathroom, kitchen, and living room. It's just gone." He brushes his hair out of his face, his eyes swinging frantically around the room.

"Alright, just...lemme grab mine and call you, then we can track it down. Sound good?"

He nods, shoulders relaxing. "Yeah, yeah. Sorry, I just feel panicky right now. After talking to Bear last night...I just. I don't know. I need to check-in on him, make sure he's ok." I nod, not really understanding why, but it's important to him, so I'll help.

Only, I can't find my phone either. I'll admit, I'm a little anal about making sure it's plugged in on my nightstand before I go to sleep. The cord's still visible where it was charging, but it's not there now. Shit. "Hey...um...Steve. There might be a problem." His body freezes staring where he's been scanning the floor, like it might magically appear out of thin air.

"My phone's gone too."

Steve tenses beside me, and I can practically hear the tendons in his neck creak as he turns to look at me. "What did you say?"

His behavior's starting to freak me out now. "My phone, it's gone too. I know I plugged it in last night."

He tears out of the room before I can even get a shirt on, but I hear him yelling from all the way down in Marc's office. It feels like a pit opens up under me as I hear Dad's angry snarl in reply and I rush downstairs to try to find out why my life has suddenly gone off the rails.

Steve's screaming at Marc over his desk. Both our phones are laying screen-down on the surface, beside our father's laptop, but it's what he's saying that freezes my mind. "I've already set up the transfer. Your mother can go get anything from the school that you need, but you will not be returning to that...cesspit. You will not be seeing that omega again. You will be returning to Bridge Academy, you will be finishing out your senior year, and you will start visiting omega centers to look for a proper mate."

His fist comes down with a loud crack on top of Steve's phone, breaking the plastic case. The resounding crunch is a death knell to any files or information that hasn't been backed up recently. "I've already spoken with the boy's parents and informed them, in no uncertain terms, that you will not be forming a pack with him, and you need a female omega. We are done here."

Steve glares over our father's desk, finally seizing the laptop and flinging it against the wall where it ends its life in a crackle of sparks and bits of shattered plastic. There's no warning as Dad stands up, his fist flying out and knocking Steve across the room. He lands in a heap on the floor beside the dead electronics. I rush to his side, my hands run over his head, feeling for anything wet, anything out of place. His cheek's already starting to swell and I spin on our father, ready to defend the only family I want to claim right now.

"I refuse to let you two throw away all my hard work over some boy. Get him out of here, and when he wakes up tell him if he refuses to go back to Bridge Academy then he can spend his last four months of high school overseas getting some real world training. Neither of you are to see that...omega again. Do I make myself clear?"

I turn back to my brother, checking him over as best as I'm able to with our father practically snarling down my neck. Sure, I wanted to go into medicine, but this wasn't how I planned to start. Hefting Steve against my side, I help him stumble out of the office. I have to practically drag him back upstairs to get him to our room. Snagging the first aid kit out of our bathroom, I manage to patch up his hand that got cut on some of the broken plastic when he hit the wall. Other than a few minor scrapes and his swelling jaw, he seems fine. But he's not saying anything.

We do what Dad asks, going back to Bridge to get our diplomas. In the fall, we start college. Dad knows I always planned to go into medicine, which was a fine profession

according to him. Steve finally agrees to go for a business degree. I believe he's under some misguided hope that if he just listens to what Dad says and follows his orders, maybe it'll earn him some flexibility regarding Teddy.

But my brother's not the same. His light's dimmed so much that it's barely there at all. He's gone from happy-go-lucky to a brooding, morose ghost who just follows me around campus. He doesn't even look angry, just...gone. It gets worse as we settle in. Dad starts demanding we visit omega centers to meet prospective mates.

Steve readily agrees, knowing he won't meet anyone else, and trailing along like my silent specter as I meet fawning young women who are overjoyed to be introduced to the younger generation of Pack Carson. I briefly hope that we can meet a male omega that will draw my brother's attention. But even the few we do run into don't bring out any response.

We studiously avoid the center closest to our home, traveling far out of state to meet and interact with some lovely young women who might cause a reaction in either of our alphas. But to no avail. While there are a fair share who seem more interested in our name or finances, we do meet some genuinely sweet people on our forays.

Which is all the more disheartening when I don't feel any real spark towards them. Their scents are amazing, they're all attractive, but like beautiful greenhouse roses, they don't feel quite real. None of them excites any real passion in either of us. Our father grows ever more agitated at what he considers our refusal to find an omega and settle down.

This pattern continues. Steve no longer feels like the twin I once knew. I know he's still in there, but the easy laughter is years gone. The friend I grew up with now a stranger in our shared home. He rarely eats, he doesn't sleep more than a few hours a night. He goes to school because he still believes if he just follows orders, eventually our father will relent. I don't have the heart to tell him that's never going to happen.

I graduate with my degree that I don't really want anymore. But maybe helping other people will, in some way, redeem me for not being able to help my brother. I start my residency and life goes on. Steve should be finishing his own college this spring. Getting the damned degree that Father demanded, it's going to be a hell of a shock to the old man that no one wants to hire his son who's now a canvas of tattoos and piercings.

There are only so many things you can hide in a three-piece suit. I don't care how expensive the cut is. The bleached hair and nose ring don't exactly blend in at the business college either. But what do I know? I'm just a different kind of ghost.

Chapter 47

Steve

G arret stops speaking, his deep shuddering breath the only outward sign that what he just said had any real effect on him. Hearing his retelling of our father's abuse in an emotionless, almost offhand sort of way is jarring. Like listening to someone talk about the weather. Nothing of note, just the facts.

Has he always been that way? Disinterested. Was there ever a time we tried to fight back? For the life of me, I can't remember one. It's just how things were. Not that anyone outside our family knew or saw. Can't have the world know about Pack Carson's dirty little secrets.

The father who never wanted children but "did his duty" and had them anyway. The disappointment he's always shown towards said children. The dutiful son that follows wherever he's led but takes no initiative, or the other son who loves another man and refuses to carry on the "family legacy". What a sight we must make.

*J*ust two more months. two months till I graduate and get away from this fucking school. Away from all the pretenders and the bullshit and suits. No...if I have to keep up this facade for Dad to let me have Teddy, that's ok. I can play professional, at least for a while. He'll have to see my dedication then. If he wants an heir so bad then we can look for a surrogate. Shit, we can get three or four as long as it doesn't involve my dick being inserted into anyone except Bear.

Fuck, I miss him so fucking much. I wish I could see him. Garret's kept us away from any omega centers that he may be staying in, but I know he doesn't have a pack yet. Ok, I don't know know, but he just can't. He has to be waiting. He has to know I'll come back for him as soon as I can. I just have to get through this.

Mom calls on Saturday night. My voice is hoarse from disuse, but she still talks to Teddy's mom, so I at least want to stay on her good side, even if the rest of them can fuck off. She asks if I'm sick, because my voice is so scratchy. I tell her it's just allergies, there's a lot of pollen around campus. Not that we live on campus, but I still have to go every day. She talks about how work's going with Dad and Grandpa. I wish they would both drop dead, but once again, I don't tell her that.

Then she drops the bomb. Teddy's mother called. She's on vacation, but she had to share the news. They just talked to Teddy, and she was so excited that her baby finally found his pack. My world implodes...empty, nothing. I miss everything else she says and eventually Garret takes the phone from my lifeless fingers. Mom must not have noticed that I died, because she's still chattering away, asking when we'll settle down and make her a grandma.

I want to take the phone from Garret and fling it across the room, deny the conversation. If I didn't hear it, it didn't happen. Instead, I force my voice out. "Mom, yeah. No, I wanna send him some flowers to congratulate him. Do you know where he's at?"

I'm not sure how she could believe that I would be happy that he was gone, that he found someone else, but she does. "Oh...hold on, Jessica told me. It's this little town...in Nebraska...or some-thing...maybe it's New Mexico or...North Carolina. I think it starts with an N. Hold on, maybe I wrote it down." My fingers squeeze the phone so hard I expect the screen to break. Garret peels it out of my hand and takes over as she rambles on, papers shuf-fling in the background. I can barely make out her voice as she tells about how he was visiting his cousin at a bonding ceremony in this tiny little town, and there was his alpha. Doesn't it sound romantic...blah blah fucking blah.

His cousin already had a bonding ceremony a long damned time ago. Does he have another cousin? Is it the same one? Maybe there was some sort of recommitment ceremony or something. Shit! That one lived in...fuck...what was the name of that place? It was basically a wide spot in the road...Flat Planes? Pine Springs? Timber Falls?

Fuck me, brain, why don't you work!

"Oak Flats, Mississippi, I think she said. Yes, that sounds right. I knew I wrote it down. I swear, I would lose my head if it wasn't attached." Mom giggles into the phone like she's said something hilarious and rattles off an address to go with the town. My teeth grind with the need to leave now that I have a destination. Leaving my phone with Garret, I turn and head to my room, quickly throwing together a suitcase and a bag of toiletries. I don't know how long it'll take to find him, but I can't let this go.

Garret isn't quiet when he follows me into my room. He's still talking to Mom, but trying to be polite when he tells her he's busy. He thinks he's about to be busy keeping me at home, but that's not going to happen. I brush past him right as he manages to hang up the phone. My bag hangs over one shoulder, and I grab the keys to my SUV from the wall by the garage. Plucking the phone out of his grip, I pull up the map app and see I'm looking forward to at least a twenty-seven hour drive.

He stares over my shoulder before jumping between me and the garage door. "Fucking hell man, seriously? This is what it takes to breathe life back into your crusty ass? Fine. whatever. Gimme five minutes to pack." I try to push past him. I don't have five minutes to spare. My omega's out there with someone else.

He grabs his own keys off the hook and then plucks mine from my fingers. Fuckwad. "Five fucking minutes, asshole. You can wait that long before you turn our whole goddamned life upside down. Besides, I don't want you driving goddamned twenty plus hours alone. You'll fall asleep and die. I see enough of that shit at work." He doesn't. He hasn't taken a stint in the ER yet for his residency, but I get his reasoning, even if I don't like it.

It's a full ten minutes later before we're actually on the road, and he insists that we stop for coffee before we leave Los Angeles.

Hang on Bear, I'm coming.

Chapter 48

Sam

*W*hat a fucking clusterfuck.

Seriously, how does this shit find me?

Not that I would trade Teddy or Kelly to avoid it...but shit.

There's a couple of rich boys sitting in my basement looking at my pack with near obsession levels of need. Also, at least one of their daddies is an asshole and that dickhead better stay the fuck away from Oak Flats, 'cause if I ever see him, shit's gonna get ugly.

I don't want to deal with this.

Fuck...welcome to being pack lead.

Kelly's huddled in Teddy's lap. Our omega's not crying, but he doesn't look far from it either. He holds her close, her head tucked against his chest as he looks at the brothers. "You...I...I'm so confused right now. Vee, how could you ever believe your dad was actually going to let us be together after that shit? He was an asshole when we were growing up, and he's still an asshole now. He was never going to let us...but you. You didn't say anything. You could have found me at the omega center, you could have told me what was going on instead of just letting me believe you didn't want me anymore!" Kelly burrows harder against him, her arms sliding between him and the back of the chair as she tries to hold him tighter.

Garret's voice is muffled, his face buried in his palms. "That was your plan? Seriously? That was it? I mean, I assumed it was, but I always just kind of hoped you had something better going on in that brain of yours. Jesus fuck, dude. Graduate and he'll let you have Teddy? That was the whole fucking plan?" He groans into his own hands. I know the feeling.

My voice raises above the muttering in the room, "Alright, kids...KIDS! Everybody chill the fuck out." All eyes turn to me.

"So, you two—" I turn towards the idiot twins, leaning forward and giving them my full attention. "What's your old man gonna do now? You gave up Teddy, went to college...almost got your degree. What's he holding over you that's kept you away for so long?" The two exchange a look like I must be the biggest idiot on God's green earth.

Garret speaks first. "Well, he's our dad..." I make a go-on motion with my hands. "And...um...money." His head drops back into his hands. "God we're idiots, aren't we?"

Steve finally pops up. "That's not exactly right. I mean, it's partly right, but not...shit. How do I explain?" I let him chew on his lip for a few minutes before I try again.

"So, basically, daddy's rich, and you don't know what to do with yourselves without money." They both look like I slapped them, and yeah, verbally anyway. "Steve, you were willing to give Teddy up for money. Is that what I'm hearing?" His confusion flashes to outrage.

"Of course not. I just...It's not that simple. I thought I could take time, take care of what needed to get done and then...then he'd have to let me...shit. No, Teddy was always the end goal. I just...got lost on how to get there."

The omega in question huffs behind my back and I hear a mumbled, "No shit, Sherlock," from Kelly. I bite the inside of my cheek to keep from smiling at the tiny beta and her rare use of profanity. I'm glad she's as protective of our omega as I am, and it's adorable.

Garret and Steve are bickering back and forth like a couple of hens while my brain works. Finally, I turn to Teddy. "I may not be great at saying it, but you know I love you, right?"

His breath catches, and he nods. Kelly smiles at both of us. "You too, pretty girl, you can't get away." She blushes that adorable pink that I enjoy so much. "Teddy, you've already made it...painfully clear that you want this little punk. That still true?" He looks at Steve, who's finally shut up and is watching us all carefully. Teddy nods, barely noticeable, but it's there.

"And the other one?" This directed at Kelly.

"Sorry, Sam, but he feels almost as much like home as you and Teddy. If that's ok with you. I don't want to make anybody uncomfortable." She presses back against Teddy who starts purring, kicking off Garret's purr in response.

Standing up from my chair, I turn a glare back to the twins. "Well, you boys need to deal with your daddies. Whatever the hell their issues are. Especially this...Marc, was it? They're not your problem anymore if you're here, you get me?" They both nod numbly in response as I point to the phone sitting in the cup holder of Steve's chair. "Pick up your fucking phone, take the goddamned call when it happens. Explain to him that you're done. If you can't even do that, then you don't deserve to have Teddy anyway."

My gaze swings to his brother. "You...back up your brother. If you think Daddy Dearest is gonna be pissy about a male omega, I can guaran-fucking-tee that he's not gonna be happy with you mating a beta. And I can't imagine that either one of you won't catch a load of shit for not being lead alpha. But fuck it, my house, my rules. Deal with it."

Turning to my pack, I say, "Teddy, remind me to call the fuckin' courthouse tomorrow, see if we can change our paper-work to add two more members. If we need to refile everything or if we can make adjustments since they probably haven't sent it in yet with this weather. I'll see what I can figure out later and fill everything out again, just in case."

Finally, I turn and hold my hand out to Kelly. "Come on, Sugar. I didn't get any sort of release earlier. I am tense as shit, and I wanna make you feel so good. That work for you?" She smiles at me and she takes my hand, letting me pull her up and against my chest. "So, it's probably not something you've thought about before, Kelly Girl, but would you be interested in training how to take a knot?"

Her sweet blush brightens her cheeks and she looks over at Teddy for a second before turning back to me. He answers instead of her. "Sorry, Sam, we already started on that a few days ago while you were working on the nest. Kelly asked if it was possible, and I was helping her out."

My look of confusion must be apparent by the sound of Kelly's giggling. "Teddy's not hiding a surprise knot. I can explain later, Alpha. You wanna take me upstairs and I can show you?"

Well, damn, I don't know what I did in a past life to get this lucky, but fuck me.

Wrapping my arms around Kelly, I lift her up and make short work of the stairs to get back to our bedroom. It's not my greatest moment leaving Teddy behind, but those boys need to sort their shit. This way they get the privacy to talk and I get to taste a sweet little beta.

Chapter 49

Kelly

Aww, Sam ruined his own surprise. Of course we were playing the long game. It's not like this stretching thing wasn't going to take a while to do. It's not exactly uncomfortable, and I imagine it'll feel really good once I have more experience. But trying it without the practice seems like it would hurt way too much to even be a possibility. Still, I do wanna try, not specifically for Sam, or now Garret, but because I think it could feel really good for me.

It's kinda like those ladies who get piercings on their nether regions. I'm not brave enough to do that. I don't like the idea of a needle down there, but I've heard it feels really good once it heals. I'm a total chicken, though. But this I can do, it's just a little stretch for now, and building up over time as I get used to it.

Of course, he brought it up, and now it's almost like he's trying to talk me out of it. My legs are wrapped around his hips as he carries me up the stairs. He's not lean like Steve and Garret, though Garret definitely has more muscles than his brother. He's not as thick around the middle as Teddy, but he's built like a marble sculpture. It's kind of intimidating, especially when he gets so intense.

"Kelly...Sweetheart. You don't have to do anything you're uncomfortable with. You know that, right? I mean, I'm flattered that you want to try, but I don't want you to get hurt in the process. So you have to tell me if I do anything that hurts, or you want me to stop. Tell me right away, ok?" Pulling myself tight against his chest I bite lightly against his neck, causing a full body rumble to go through him, and I can't stop the little squeak that pops out when it vibrates his solid length against my clit where we're pressed together. That's a heck of a shock, but also feels really good, and I melt against him.

"Sugar, if you don't stop that right now, we aren't gonna make it to the bedroom." His big hand comes down with a loud smack on my butt, and I start to bite at him again before realizing we may be in a bit of a standoff here. I really enjoy his hands on me. That dull ache in my backside from his swat a second ago makes me all tingly, and I want to taste him again. But he's right.

I haven't actually been with Sam yet. Teddy a few times, but Sam's sort of uncharted territory for me. I've seen him, I've tasted him. I was there when Teddy took his knot on our first day. That was what made me ask Teddy if it was possible for a beta to do it. We did some research, and the internet says yes. They even had several helpful sites and sold sets of toys to help you build up to an average alpha knot. When we went to Nest-N-Stuff and I wandered off, I picked up a starter kit to try out, and Teddy helped me with it later during our movie time.

Teddy's sweet and offered me a couple of his toys that he brought with him, he said they aren't the vibrating kind, so they're easier to disinfect, but he didn't want to bring anything that would make any noise while he was staying with Brice. At the same time, omegas have really high libidos, and he didn't want to turn into a "needy bitch" with no way to get any real relief.

He's so cute.

I can't believe I'm considering sharing sex toys with a guy.

Heck, that I bought a whole starter kit with different sized knotted dildos.

This is so weird.

"Sugar, what's going on in that head of yours? You went from wiggly to totally still. You zoning out on me? Do I need to do something to bring your mind back to the present?" We're finally in the bedroom alone, and Sam brings his big hand down on my butt-cheek again. It has the desired effect at least, and he now has my full attention. "Ah, there you are my sweet girl. I was tryin' to make sure you were ok with this. I don't want you to be uncomfortable, and we haven't exactly been together without Teddy."

Sam's adorable too.

In a completely different way.

He always checks in to make sure everybody's good.

I love how he wants to take care of me and everyone else.

It seems too soon to think of the L word with him, but there we are.

Pivoting my hips, I pull myself up against him and nip at his neck again, making his arms tighten around me and that low rumbly growl spill out. "You lookin' to get marked there, Sugar? I was plannin' on waitin' till Teddy's heat to bond you both, but if you need it now, I'm happy to oblige." My neck tingles at the thought, and I feel a whole body shiver run through me at the mental image of Sam and Teddy marking me. It's not something I ever even considered before. Betas don't mark their spouses, not usually. I got a hickey once, but I don't think that really counts.

"Fuck, Kelly Girl, I need to taste you now. Is that ok?" Sam doesn't wait for my answer, laying me flat on the bed and peeling my sleep shorts and panties off in one smooth motion. He pauses then and stares at me. His eyes are intense and it goes on long enough that I start to squirm in embarrassment. Finally he kneels on the floor, looking up at my face.

"Sorry, Sugar. I'm just tryin' to figure out how I got so lucky. You never seemed to notice me before Teddy came along, and I keep expecting you to come to your senses." He rubs a big hand down his face, and the rasp of his skin against his short beard is loud in the otherwise silent room. Rolling up isn't as easy as they make it look on TV, and I grunt more than once, trying to get to a good position to meet his eyes. I have ab-envy for my alpha. I'm not sure how he never realized I was attracted to him. I just never thought the feeling was mutual, because alphas are supposed to be with omegas, not skinny beta girls who still live with their parents.

"Sam, come on." Grabbing his hand, I pull him up to sit beside me on the bed. I feel a little silly sitting here in a T-shirt and nothing else. Especially with Sam being fully dressed in those jeans that look almost painted on. Seriously, his butt's a work of art in those things. I pat the bed next to me, trying to put us on more even ground...or it would if he wasn't so tall.

"Sam, I'm not sure how you missed me blushing every time you brought your car in, or the fact that I had to conveniently talk to Gabe or Xan whenever you stepped into the shop. I've always thought you were good-looking. But I never figured you'd be interested in me since I'm a beta. Always just figured it was a crush on the handsome older guy that would never go anywhere 'cause I was too young and not an omega. You never showed any interest, and I don't blame you for not wanting to come off as a creep, but I've always been attracted to you, even when I didn't think it was proper."

Sam looks at me intently, eyes searching my face for the truth behind what I just admitted. Without warning, he wraps his arms around me and pulls me across his lap, rubbing his jaw all over my hair, his cedar and sawdust scent growing stronger the longer he does it. It's gonna take me a while to get used to living with alphas, as I realize he's scent marking me.

"So, you're saying all this time, if I woulda just told you what a pretty little thing I thought you were, you woulda let me take you out to dinner? Well, I feel like a dumbass."

He spins me around so I'm straddling him and cups my face in his big palms pulling my lips to his and devouring my tiny squeak of surprise. When he pulls away, his voice is a low growl. "Fuck, I've already wasted too much time, just thinking you wouldn't want me because I'm too old." I want to argue that he's not that much older than me, but I don't have a chance to before his arms tighten around me, crushing me to him, and claiming my mouth again in a searing kiss that leaves me breathless and aching.

"Please, Sam. I need you." The words are barely out of my mouth when he curses loudly, standing up with me still wrapped around him, and heading towards the bathroom to grab one of the boxes of condoms.

"Sorry, Sugar. I'm not sure how long I'm gonna last, but I'll take care of you one way or another. I just need you too much to go slow right now. I've put this off for too long already." I'm wrapped around him like a spider monkey, hanging on to his neck and hips, so when he moves his hands to undo the button on his pants, I hardly budge.

The loose fabric on his waistband rubs against me, causing me to shiver at the cold feel of a metal button against my sensitive bits as he strides back to the bed. Nope, nobody's going down there to pierce any of my parts, not gonna happen. He unwinds my arms and legs from around him and gently lowers me to the bed before kicking off his pants and peeling his shirt over his head. I struggle out of my own T-shirt, not looking nearly as graceful as he does, and see him opening one of the packets.

It takes me a second once it's on to realize why these are labeled for alphas. They have the usual reservoir on the tip, but also a looser area close to the base where the latex flares out and gets baggy. I guess that's for a knot. Makes sense, even if it looks silly right now. Sam sees my goofy grin as I stare at his groin, and his eyebrow goes up in a silent question. "Sorry, I've never seen an alpha condom before...that's just weird."

He nods after a moment. "Yeah, Sugar. But if that wasn't there, it would break as soon as my knot swells. Wouldn't do much good in that case, would it?"

Shaking my head, I pay more attention to what the condom covers this time. Sam's a little bigger than Teddy, probably about average for an alpha. Nothing that won't fit, but I might be walking bowlegged for a few days after this. My mouth suddenly feels dry, and I lick my lips, causing another deep growl to rumble through the room.

My eyes flick up to meet Sam's and the heat I see there makes me squirm. My core feels all hot and needy like I'm gonna combust if he just stands there looking at me for much longer. My arms reach up towards him—it's not a conscious decision.

Then he's on me. His arms wrapping around my back and waist, pulling me tight against his hard torso as his body covers mine.

His lips crash into mine, his purr a soft rumble against my skin. He moves fast, but he's not aggressive and dominating like Teddy. The pressure varies, from soft, almost butterfly kisses to more desperate nipping of teeth and stealing my breath. His hands run over my body, sending a cascade of sparks under my skin as the rougher texture on his palms traces down my sides and around to cup my butt, pulling me into his hard length as he grinds down. I gasp out a ragged moan as I feel him. He didn't look this big, but a flutter of worry dances through my head as his lips leave mine, leaving firm kisses and the hot trail of his tongue down my throat. At least it's not tickling this time.

My hands tangle in his hair when he stops at my nipples. I need him to keep going. I need to feel him, but he seems content to lave my skin, biting lightly at me. Between his hot mouth and the cooler air in here, the stupid things feel like they could cut glass. I don't even try to stop my whimper as his hands circle down and his calloused fingers traced over my slit.

Not being an omega, I don't make slick, but I can feel how wet I already am just from his kisses. I want to feel him inside me. My first time, at prom, it was uncomfortable, but then Teddy made me feel so good with the knotting practice toy and himself. There's a building desperation, a need to feel Sam inside me. His big body pressed against me. His fingers delve deeper, gathering up the moisture there and rubbing it over my clit.

"Kelly, can I taste you? Get you nice and wet? I need to make sure you come first, because I don't think I can last once I'm inside you." Nodding dumbly, I'm not sure I can form words right now, but the smile that lights up his face is worth it. His kisses continue down my torso, making me squirm when he gets to my stomach. I don't know why I'm so ticklish there. But when he dips lower and runs his tongue up my center, any giggles I have come to an abrupt halt, and my whole body shudders.

His beard's scratchy on my inner thighs, and the difference in texture between his soft lips and prickly whiskers makes me shudder again. But then his tongue comes out and swipes all the way up, I nearly levitate off the bed. My hand comes down, tangling in his hair, and I'm torn between wanting to pull him up and have him inside me, or holding him down until I explode. It almost tickles, but it also feels so good, especially when he uses his big hands and pushes two fingers inside me. His lips wrap around my clit and his teeth graze across that sensitive little spot, making my hips twitch.

"That's it, Kelly Girl, just let go." His warm breath over my skin makes me shudder. I *want* to let go. His fingers curl inside me, looking for that one spot that I've only really read about. At first I'm embarrassed, needing to excuse myself to use the bathroom...but then all my muscles clench down as I feel like

I'm thrown headfirst into my release. My body twisting and thrashing involuntarily. My eyes squeeze tight, and bursts of light seem to go off in my brain. By the time my muscles stop twitching, I feel boneless, and it takes a lot of effort to open my fingers where they were clenched in his hair.

Sam smiles up at me from between my legs. His face is shiny with my juices and while I'm still limp from what he just did, it's also embarrassing. I've never come like that before. Like all my muscles contracted at once and then turned into jelly. He wipes his face off with the back of his hand and crawls up my body, one big arm wrapping around my waist to carry me higher on the bed.

Chapter 50

*G*onna have to teach this girl not to yank so hard, or I'm gonna go bald before I'm forty.

I mean, the last time she nearly pulled my hair out, she was asleep, and it was my chest-hair, but shit.

Rubbing my sternum absently, I stare down at my pretty beta. She looks up at me with the sexiest fucking bedroom eyes I've ever seen. She also looks languid and relaxed, like she could fall asleep at any moment, so I lean down and kiss her before I miss my chance...again.

Her breath comes out in a throaty moan as she wraps her arms around my neck, pulling me tighter to her body. So, not as likely to fall asleep as I initially thought. That's good. Her hands come up and tangle in my hair again, thankfully not tugging so much as holding my head. She nips and sucks at my lips.

Fuck me.

My hands slide down to circle around her hips, pulling back enough to get a good look at her. I've wanted her for so long now, I need to remember this, how she looks, tastes, feels. Fuck, I need to shut my mind off before I lose it right now. I mean, yeah, that happens when you get older, but shit.

She curls up and bites me on the neck again, and it takes all my willpower not to pin her down and sink my own teeth into her sweet little neck. But I should wait—wait until Teddy's with us...and maybe the twins. I don't know how that's gonna work out. For my pack's sake, I hope that they can pull their heads out of their asses.

Why am I thinking of them right now...or their asses? Ok, well, Steve, yeah, he wouldn't mind. But now's not the time when I have a sweet, willing, beautiful beta writhing under me and begging me to make us both feel good. "Sam, please. I...I need you." Her hips twist and writhe under mine, grinding against me. I want to bend her in half like a god damned pretzel and fuck her until she screams my name. I also can't risk hurting her, so at least for the time being, I need to go slow.

Leaning forward, I scrape my teeth down her neck. Enjoying the way it makes her whole body shudder and a little whimpering moan slip out. I pull her up the bed with me, rolling us so she's straddling my lap. This way she can control how deep and fast we go, at least to start. Grabbing her hips, I drag her over my shaft, rolling my hips against her. She's still so slick from before.

Catching her eyes, I need to know that she's really ok with this. When all I see is desire, I lift her up so she's centered over my cock. Fuck, I wish we didn't have to use the damned rubber for this. I need to feel her with nothing between us. Pushing my hips up while pulling her down, her hands come up to grip my shoulders. The air fills with her groan as she slowly sinks down on me, taking me all the way to my knot.

When I'm fully seated inside her heat, I take a moment for both of us. She's only really had sex with Teddy since we've known her, not that our omega's small. But she seems a bit shell-shocked, and this'll give her a minute to get used to my size. Plus, she so damned tight that if she moves now I'm going to go off like a fucking rocket—even with the latex dulling the wet clutch of her core. That would just be embarrassing.

Her fingers flex, digging into my skin, and after a bit, her eyes flutter open to meet mine. "Sam..." My name is barely a whisper, but I take that as an invitation and roll my hips slowly, just a tiny bit of friction, teasing her against my knot.

I'm rewarded with another tiny moan, and her hips twitching in my grasp. "You ready for me, sweet girl?" Her head nods down, but that'll have to do for an answer. I pull back and thrust up harder. Her fingers clench against me, and her hips raise up against my hands, slower and softer than what I was going for. But she's in charge...for now.

She sets a slow pace, rolling her pelvis all the way down till I feel my knot swelling against her entrance, brushing her clit on each downstroke. Soon she picks up the pace, and I already feel like I'm about to blow. My hands dig deeper into her hips, my fingers splayed across her ass, and pull her hard against me.

As she drops down, her eyes pinch and her brows furrow just a little. I can feel her stretch around my already swollen knot. I'm ecstatic that she wants to try one day, but this isn't that day, and I don't want to ruin our time together by letting her hurt herself to make me feel good. It takes all of my willpower not to thrust up into her, but she's just learning now. So I pull back and grit my teeth, trying to keep that little bit of distance we both need.

Her fingers tighten, nails cutting into my flesh, and her body seizes up, clamping down on my cock, strangling me, so I can barely move. My fingers leave white indents on her skin as I lose the battle with myself and my release hits, forcing a choked cry from my throat. She collapses against me, her head lolling against my chest.

A purr rumbles to life inside me, and my arms slide up to circle her narrow shoulders, pulling her close. Soon I'll get her cleaned up and tucked in so she can rest, but for now it's amazing to just hold her, relishing this moment of intimacy.

I don't mind sharing her with the rest of our pack, but there will be times when I'll want to spend time together, just the two of us. The way I imagined it before we met Teddy. What I used to picture when I would see her at the shop. My mind would throw out images of the two of us, curled up on the couch watching TV, or her in the backyard playing fetch with Jake, or maybe helping me in the kitchen to make breakfast on the weekends. Now the house is filled with both her and Teddy's scents, and while it warms my heart more than I could have imagined, a piece of me wants it to be just the two of us sometimes. Of course, I also want to be able to have time alone with Teddy.

I'm alpha enough to admit I was half in love with Kelly before we ever really talked. Her sweet smile and sunny demeanor, her subtle scent of lilacs, that adorable blush she always has going on. The first time I met her at the shop, I could barely get the words out that I needed an oil change on my damned truck.

Normally I'd just do it myself, but I'd cut my fucking hand open with a god-damned chisel, and it was just easier to take it in. I was lost as soon as I saw her, and just started bringing the damned truck in for everything it needed. Pretty sure Xan suspected the reason why, but I doubt Gabe ever clued in. He avoids the office like the fucking plague.

A soft snore breaks me out of my thoughts. Kelly's head's still nestled against my chest, and one hand has come up, gripping my chest hair again. I don't want to risk waking her up, but now I have to figure out how to get her settled and taken care of without losing another chunk of fur. Shit.

<h1 style="text-align:center">Chapter 51</h1>

Teddy

Vee, Garret, and I all sit there like idiots, staring at each other. I have no idea what to say. Ok, I have *lots* of ideas on what to say, but I don't think any of them would be kind. They gave reasons, even if they didn't make a lot of sense. I can only assume that Vee panicked or his dad scrambled his brains. That motherfucker. If I ever get my hands on that son-of-a-bitch, I'll wring his fucking neck for what he did to them.

Ok, so clearly, I still feel protective of the Carson twins, even if they are idiots.

My fingers itch with the need to release some of this fucking energy. I wish again that I had Jessie here. She always helps me feel better. Flexing my fists, I let my fingers run down imaginary strings again, playing the music in my head until my mind starts to relax. It's not as good as the real thing, but I'm pretty fucking limited in relaxation techniques right now.

Maybe I should spend my time more constructively and see about emailing the school to tell them I need to pick up my stuff...but I think I need the pack registration paperwork for that, or one of my parents' permission. Shit. That won't be a problem, except that they aren't home. Fuck my life.

Raising my head, my eyes catch Garret and Vee. Garret's still staring at the steps where Sam left with Kelly. His obsession borders on creepy with what almost seems like mania he has for Kelly. I'm a little surprised that Sam is so readily agreeing to letting them stay. Still...pretty sure I could take Garret in a fight if he tries to do something he shouldn't. Sam and I together, no problem.

Vee, on the other hand...shit.

He stares at me with the same fascination that his brother currently has for the fucking stairs. I know Sam left us down here to talk. He didn't explicitly say it, but I know he wants us to work our shit out. I'm just not sure how.

My fingers start sketching out the notes to Famous Last Words by My Chemical Romance. Thank fuck for MP3s, 'cause I would have worn out a fucking CD of that song after he left. Yeah, I know what the entire fucking album is about, but I wasn't in a good place at the time. Mom was terrified of what I might do to myself. It was...bad.

Seriously, I think changing all my clothes to black, taking up guitar, and getting my face pierced was probably a relief to her since it gave me an outlet separate from the depression and ugly things that seemed to be stuck in my head. Wondering why he didn't want me anymore.

Trying to shake myself out of my thoughts, I don't want to dwell on how fucked up I was back then. I didn't mention it earlier because...well...it freaks everyone out. Plus I don't want to give Sam any more reason to hate Vee, just because I made a stupid decision. Hell, I don't want Vee to know because he would worry.

But Mom was there. After...everything...she got me in to see a really helpful therapist at the center. Dr. Dana specializes in omega problems, including a lot of the anxiety and depression that are so common for us. She's the one who suggested that Mom get me Jessie and a bunch of books on learning to play guitar. She was right, of course. It was easier for me to express myself and my erratic fucking emotions more physically. Plus, learning how to play was a much needed distraction to my batshit crazy hormones.

Dr. Dana also helped me see that even if Vee didn't want me, it didn't mean no one would. I mean, let's be honest, nobody did for a long, long time because of my size and even at the omega center, I was more of a novelty. In truth, I got along well with a lot of the other omegas more than visiting alphas. Omegas saw me as less competition than the alphas did. Which is ironic on every fucking level.

I met Sarah right after I arrived at the center. Once I finished healing up, she took me to the gym to work off some of my stress. We both liked lifting, and it was a good way to burn off excess energy. Her sisters had already met their packs, so she didn't really have anyone else there either. We became workout buddies, and it helped to burn off even more of the excess energy I had going on. She helped a lot with explaining some of the freaky ass changes my body was going through, including how much harder I now had to work to build muscles. I feel a small pang of regret that I'm going to be leaving her there alone.

Vee opens his mouth, closes it, and drops his head in his hands. He takes a deep breath, before looking at me again. "Bear, listen...I—" *His* phone starts ringing this time, and he turns a bit green before he slides the button to answer it. I can hear Marc's voice from here, even without the speaker on. "What the fuck are you two doing? Did you actually fucking hang up on me earlier, you little shits!"

Ah yes, Marc Carson, head of the Carson pack and dear old dad to the guys who were once my best friends. What a fuck-stick. Steve opens his mouth, but he can't seem to make words. After a few seconds his father starts back up again. "Don't give me any shit, Steven. Your mother told me that she talked to you about that fucking omega, and now your GPS shows you in the middle of Mississippi. Really, fucking Mississippi? I wasn't born yesterday, you little come-stain. Get your ass back in the fucking car and go home, and take your brother with you. God knows he doesn't have an original fucking thought in his head. He'll follow you wherever the hell you lead."

Garret's breath comes in a series of harsh pants as he looks at the phone. Vee's still staring at the fucking thing, gaping like a fish as his father continues to spew vitriol at the brothers. I know Sam told them to take care of it, but I'm not sure if they can right now. Their old man's always been a verbally abusive piece of shit. I'm not sure if either of them is mentally capable of breaking out of it right now.

Fuck, I wish Sam was down here. Not so he can fight my battles for me, or for them, but as moral support. Marc's yelling hasn't slowed down. If anything, he's getting louder the longer neither of them speak. "You little son of a bitch! Don't just sit there gawking at the phone like the moron that I know you are. Answer me, goddamnit!" Vee's hand shakes as he reaches towards it. I don't know if he's going to hang up, hit speaker, or actually lift the damned thing to his ear and get yelled at up close and personal. But I'm done with this shit.

Vee meets my eyes as I reach for the phone. His mouth finally snaps closed and he picks it up, pressing the speaker key and holding it between himself and his brother. Garret reaches out a shaking hand and grabs Vee's wrist. They both swallow a few times before either of them is able to speak. Vee makes it first. "Dad, Dad...DAD! Jesus, shut up and listen." The line goes suddenly silent and if I didn't see the green button still glowing on the screen, I would think the call was disconnected.

The twins both jump at the voice that screams through the phone. "What the fuck did you just say to me, you little piss-ant? I dare you to fucking repeat that."

Vee swallows again. "I said, shut up and listen, Dad. Shit, we can't get a fucking word in edge-wise."

Garret chokes and starts coughing. There's no way to tell if it's shock or he inhaled spit, but he suddenly sounds like a three pack a day kinda guy as his voice croaks, "We're not coming home, Dad," is all he manages before he starts coughing again.

Marc isn't one to sit silently—ever—and before either of them can say anything else, his rant starts up again. "You know what'll happen if you stay? Your apartment, car, credit cards, school, even this fucking phone. I'll cut off funding for everything. You won't have a pot to piss in when I'm through with you. Omegas are a dime a dozen. Is he really worth losing everything you've worked for the last ten years over?"

Vee looks at me, his eyes bright with unshed tears. "Yeah, Dad, he is. He *is* worth it, he was *always* worth it, and I should have done this then. Everything's pointless without Bear. I don't care about school, where we live, nothing's as important as him. Just seeing him again after all this time, I finally feel like I can breathe again."

Marc's snarl cuts him off. "Oh, what a load of sentimental bullshit. I should have known better than to try to convince you, you little faggot. Garret! Garret, you were never involved in this stupidity. Get your ass back to Los Angeles now or you lose any chance of support to find your own omega. You'll lose your residency, and you won't be getting another one, that's for damned sure. All that time spent on college, wasted. Is that what you want? All so your brother can go off and play house with some nobody little boy."

Vee stares at his brother now. Garret has turned an unpleasant grayish green, but he manages to choke out a reply. "I'm not coming home either, Dad. I met somebody here...Her name's Kelly, she's mine."

Marc huffs out a sigh, his voice still angry, but less of a screech. "Why didn't you fucking start with that shit? So, you found your omega. Ok, well...that's something then. We can work with that. I'll need to get her information run though? We can't have just anyone join the Carson pack. Omegas are only after one thing, and we need to make sure she's worth the trouble of being brought into the family. You'll need to send me her full name and omega center ID number so I can get started on a background check before you do anything stupid like try to bond the little bitch."

Garret's back snaps straight and all his color comes back at once, quickly moving to an angry red flush. "Yeah...that's not gonna happen. Kelly's mine. She's a beta, and she's mine if she'll have me."

Now the choked noises are coming from the other end of the phone. "Christ on a crutch, are you two fucking serious right now? I forbid you two to start a pack with a male omega and a goddamned beta. You will pack your shit, you will get into the fucking car, you will start back to Los Angeles tonight. Or you won't have a car when you get up in the morning. Am I clear? I will have that fucking thing towed and you can walk back to L.A. when you finally pull your heads out of your asses."

Garret actually snorts laughter, meeting his brother's eyes. "You wanna tell him, or just let him deal with that pint-sized terror on his own? Good luck getting a tow truck out here, Dad."

Vee finally chimes in. "Even if we were inclined to agree, we're stuck, in a snowstorm, at our new pack leader's house. We aren't going anywhere for at least a few more days."

Marc's roar of anger echoes through the room. "Are you actually fucking telling me you are in the middle of bumfuck Mississippi, and you've packed up with some random alpha, a beta, and that fucking omega? I'm on my way. You two pieces of shit better keep your fucking mouths closed. Because if anybody has a fucking bonding mark when I get there, I will sue their fucking asses and have their pack permanently dissolved, do you understand me?" The call disconnects. I guess Marc had to have the last word.

Garret's back to that odd greenish gray, scrambling out of his seat and making a break for the stairs while holding his mouth. Vee's just gone pale, but sweat is beaded on his forehead and upper lip. "Shit...Bear. What...What did I do? He's coming here. He can't come here!" his voice rises in near hysteria. I pull him out of his seat and into my lap. Shit, it's a good thing Sam bought sturdy furniture. My purr kicks up, and he snuggles against me. He's only a couple of inches taller, but he barely seems to weigh anything. I wonder again at what they left out of their story from earlier.

<u>*Acknowledgements:*</u>

Huge thanks to My Tallest/ Husband/ Father-of-my-spawn/ Most-Supportive-Man-I've-Ever-Met. Without you to encourage me and help me make time, I don't think the first book would have happened, let alone the rest of my madness spilling out of my mind.

This story wouldn't have made it this far without the amazing support of my Alpha and Beta readers: Alice, Amanda, Debora, Jennifer, Catherine, Susan, Michelle, Jessica, Nicole, and Crystalizelle. You all are amazing, and I can't thank you enough for all the support and encouragement you give me.

More thanks to the wonderful people in the writing community, especially the OV writing groups. Specifically Vera Valentine who is an amazing woman and human seagull (her words) for compiling lots of author resources and sharing them to make life so much easier on everyone else.

Shultz, the mutt we had growing up which was supposed to be part German Shepherd and part Australian Shepherd and who was high-school-me's best friend and cuddle buddy. He bit my brother-in-law more than once for being a bully. I still miss you fluff-muffin.

Afterword:

Thoughts so far? Who do we hate the most? Joseph? Marc? Me for asking you to read this? All joking aside, I hope you enjoyed the first part of Building a Pack is Ruff. The next book is a bit of a bumpy ride. If you haven't gone and read The Purrfect Pack yet, I would suggest you do so now, Pack Asher has an even bigger role to play in this next story.

In other news, I finally got my website up...sort of www.ga ladrealsimmons.com go check it out and be sure to sign up for my newsletter so I can send you bonus content and stuff. I am working on that!

Super original, I know. Until then, thanks for hanging out, and I hope you enjoyed the story, and I hope you come back for part 2.

Galadreal Simmons was born at a very early age. She doesn't remember much of it, as she was tiny and squishy. Regardless, after 45 years...she's still short and squishy.

She was named after an elf proving that nerd genes run in her family. It is spelled differently, because try teaching a five year old how to spell something that long. When she was of an adult age, she had it legally changed to include the misspelling.

She lives in a not overly remote location in the southern United States with her husband, two small creatures that share her genetic material, and a cat named Nyx.

She enjoys reading, avoiding human interaction, and feeding crows in the hopes that they will form a crow army and do her bidding. So far, that hasn't worked out, but she continues to do it anyway—because they might be hungry.

<u>*Books by Galadreal:*</u>

<u>The Pack Pets Omegaverse</u>
The Purrfect Pack
Building a Pack is Ruff: Part 1
Building a Pack is Ruff: Part 2